SHOULD GRACE FAIL

A TWIN CITIES MYSTERY

PRISCILLA PATON

coffeetownpress
Kenmore, WA

coffeetownpress

A Coffeetown Press book published by Epicenter Press

Epicenter Press
6524 NE 181st St.
Suite 2
Kenmore, WA 98028

For more information go to:
www.Camelpress.com
www.Coffeetownpress.com
www.Epicenterpress.com
www.priscillapaton.com

Cover design by Scott Book
Author photo by Brett Dorrian

Should Grace Fail
Copyright © 2020 by Priscilla Paton

ISBN: 978-1-60381-768-4 (Trade Paper)
ISBN: 978-1-60381-761-5 (eBook)

Produced in the United States of America

In Memory of My Loving Parents, Philip and Marian Paton

ACKNOWLEDGEMENTS

MANY PEOPLE AIDED ME in the writing of *Should Grace Fail*. I wish to heartily thank those who provided me with information and encouragement: Lynn Anderson, Doug Beussman, Chad Christiansen, Jill Ewald, Katie Fick, Eric Knutson, Michelle Kubitz, Carl Lehmann, Katie Crosby Lehmann, Kent McWilliams, Leslie Moore, Annette Nierobisz, Carlo Veltri, Megan Voronyak and the staff at The Link nonprofit, and the staff at St. Paul's Vieux Carré. I could not continue writing without the generous and patient support of Jennifer McCord, Catherine Treadgold, and everyone at Epicenter-Coffeetown-Camel Press, the Twin Cities Sisters-in-Crime Chapter, and Mystery Writers of the Midwest.

On locations, some place names are real, others are invented, and all are used imaginatively. I could not improve on the Wilde Café or Betty Danger's.

As always, I am grateful for the grace of family. Their existence is my center. Thanks to David, James and Ishanaa, Liz and Seth, and the little ones, Aadyaa and Amiyaa.

'Twas grace that taught my heart to fear.
—*John Newton*

We are all in the gutter, but some of us are looking at the stars.
—*Oscar Wilde*

CHAPTER 1

THEY LIE WHEN THEY SAY THERE'S A CLEAN DEATH. To the living, a death may seem clean—quick, painless, without visible trauma. Yet body and soul are rent. There is a rupture, a shattering, a breakdown, an invasion of the organic. The path to death is septic, and nothing can purify the foul intent of murder.

Detective Erik Jansson of the Greater Metro Investigative Unit feared mutual contamination. He struggled into a plastic Tyvek coverall before checking the dumpster behind the convenience store. As he uncrinkled the shower-type cap, the wind whipped it away—his dark hair would have to remain exposed. The rest of the protective gear was handed over by a St. Paul uniformed officer, a woman who was petite next to Erik's 6'2" and about ten years younger. She couldn't have been more than twenty-two or three. Blonde wisps escaping her bun highlighted her girlishness, and she looked up at him, expectant. Erik, smart and good-looking, inspired expectations. In general, he met those expectations, but often at a cost to himself and by means no one could predict.

The woman officer repeated her request. She wanted assurance that the body in the dumpster was most sincerely dead. While Erik's coverall might not protect him from crud unknown, it blocked the gusts of a Monday morning in June. Six a.m. and the fifty-five-degree temperature proved that Minnesota did not play by the rules of any season.

The young officer reported that she and her partner responded to the 911 call a half hour earlier as the sun was rising. She recorded the scene with her body cam as she laid out a path with caution tape. Then her partner, a large man, hoisted her, a small woman, up onto the dumpster where she nearly did "a dive roll over the body." She retreated and called for assistance. When Erik arrived, she introduced herself as Dahlberg and her older partner as

"Rockers"—a story in that name that Erik couldn't take the time to suss out. Rockers returned street-side to shoo away vehicles and direct the arriving CSI team. The gas-station convenience store, one of a chain named *Celebrate!* for no discernible reason, had closed on schedule at 11 p.m. the night before and was due to open. The building and gas pumps stretched out on a corner lot a few blocks off Payne Avenue, not far from Lake Phalen Park where Erik had run the trails a few weeks earlier—he'd run the trails around every Twin Cities lake. St. Paul's eastside neighborhoods had much to recommend them: diversity, funky music venues, working-class stability, and old-fashioned residential streets with reasonably priced housing. Home values stayed low because of the crime rate, with drugs on the street and stolen cars moving to chop shops. This *Celebrate!* fell somewhere between blight and progress, half derelict and half remodeled, hence the huge green dumpster unit. The area around the dumpster appeared crudely swept, as if someone had swished a jacket back and forth across the gritty pavement.

Officer Dahlberg uttered a "Careful, sir" when Erik pulled himself up and hovered, hands and feet on the tape that marked the touchable dumpster edge. He could see over the palings that separated the commercial lot from residences, and the empty house behind the store showed fire damage. Erik, despite his athleticism, had difficulty keeping his balance. The booties over his shoes had little traction, and a misstep would pitch him onto the prone corpse.

The first look is the worst, and Erik was jolted by déjà vu.

He closed his eyes, smelled rancid cooking grease, and found relief in the fact that the body was an adult male, not a child or woman, a bias justified by the poor track record of men perpetrating and perpetuating violence. He opened his eyes and in a flash had a dizzying vision that the male corpse could be his, or his father's, or someday his son's.

Observe clinically. The head rested on a broken slat with the neck unnaturally twisted to expose the left rim of the face. Something about the head seemed familiar, probably the hue, that dead gray that replaces a Caucasian flush. The skin matched the gray buzz-cut hair, suggesting a man in his fifties. He was dressed in jeans, a polo shirt, and sneakers. No jacket, despite last night's chill. No obvious wounds, only dark splatter on the garbage bags. The man could have overdosed, and his "friends" got rid of the inconvenient corpse. This did not explain the blood spatter. Erik stretched to check for a pulse that he knew wasn't there. The man had wiry brows like Erik's father. Then Erik saw frothy droplets on those brows, maybe goo or spittle. Had someone *spat* on the man?

Dumped, the man had been dumped. Take a life for next to nothing, for an insult, for drugs, for access to a woman discarded in a week. It shouldn't happen that way—it did. Why? Erik in his restlessness twisted in his plastic cocoon, his foot slipped down, and fearing he'd slide under the dead, he wrenched himself back to the rim.

"Are you all right, sir?" Dahlberg asked.

"I see your hat." Erik pointed at her uniform cap in the corner where it had landed during her near somersault. Next to it, a condom wrapper and one sock—how did every garbage receptacle have that combo? "It'll have to stay for now." The foot that slipped had smears of brownish gunk. He looked away to Dahlberg, who was tucking a strand of hair behind her pretty ear. Erik shouldn't be noticing the appeal of a fellow officer, especially one who spoke as if he were the senior inspector in a costume drama. The wind ballooned his Tyvek and appeared to lift him up.

"Sir, maybe you should come down," Dahlberg fretted. "It's a tricky one, you might get hurt, sir."

Erik vaulted down by a pile of vomit at the dumpster corner. He considered asking Dahlberg if this was her first dead body, decided against it, but she noticed what he saw. "The employee did that, the one who found the body. He arrived at five to set up for opening, took out the garbage, and found the corpse. I sent him inside to wait because he said he might 'gross-out' again." She paused, holding a fist to her mouth as if battling a gag reflex. "Was that the right thing to do, sir?"

"Yes, good job." An uneasiness gripped Erik, and Dahlberg gagged. He smiled and redirected her attention. "Did you see the flowers by the fence, the dandelions? You got to give them credit for being sunny survivors." Sunny like her hair, which he didn't say out loud. She smiled back and handed him a small packet from the gear bag.

"That looks like . . ." Erik stopped. It looked like a condom packet. Dahlberg must have read his mind because she blushed. Women found Erik attractive, and then it hit them that his mind traveled down strange paths, as in his realization that he was *dressed* like a condom. "Ah, a cleansing wipe," he recovered. "Here's the CSI team."

A young man, the convenience-store employee, schlumped along the yellow-tape path before a CSI member could stop him. He didn't look old enough to sell the ice-cold beer the store advertised, though he probably imbibed it. Hygiene was not a priority. His "stay weird" t-shirt had a ripped hem and his cargo pants hung off his hips. His hair was matted, and Erik involuntarily ran a hand through his own and regretted it when he recalled the hand had been dumpster diving. He took off the gloves, used the inadequate wipe, then offered that hand: "Detective Erik Jansson, Greater Metro Investigative Unit, G-Met." He didn't explain that G-Met was dubbed the bastard offspring of the Bureau of Criminal Apprehension, the BCA. Whereas BCA had a statewide purview and elevated reputation, G-Met had the Twin Cities surround and was confused with the transit police.

"Oh, hey, yeah, Nick." Nick dragged a hand from a pocket to damply shake Erik's. "Uh, sorry about that." He squinched his nose at the stink of vomit.

"That's quite a shock to see what you saw after a breakfast of Super-Gulpy and chocolate-glazed doughnuts."

"Wow!" Nick dropped his jaw. "Wow, you're good. All that out of looking at puke!" Erik had simply surmised what a youth of Nick's ilk would eat at a convenience store. "I climbed in because I had, uh, dropped restroom keys in a bag, had to get 'em back. 'Course I could tell the guy's dead right away 'cause he's lying there creepy. I know about pulse from that zombie series where they gotta figure out who's living dead or who's dead dead. For survival, you know, of the species. Like once I got the keys out of the bag, I didn't touch nothing."

Nick searching the dumpster. Total contamination. As Dahlberg escorted Nick back to the store to be swabbed for DNA, Erik wondered if the teen could aspire to a position better than a convenience-store clerk. Nick paused to dig wax from his ear. Maybe not. Then again, who was Erik to judge another's worth or aspirations? He aspired every morning to . . . well, first he aspired to a run, followed a pulsing shower and dark roast coffee. Then he aspired to, hard to say, rise to a higher level in the human condition? He shivered. The unease returned, that déjà-vu feeling.

A man hopped out of the CSI van and barked orders: lead examiner Foster in his usual snakebite boots. Foster and Erik got along as two people who understood their charge and didn't fuss over rough edges. That arrangement was facilitated by the fact that the CSI lead showed up only once per case. Foster pulled a plastic smock over his head, put a hand on the van's hood, and hopped on one foot and then the other as he yanked large covers over the embossed boots. After instructing team members to inch forward from the van, he followed the path Dahlberg and Erik had taken.

"Jansson!" Foster boomed out. "Remember when you take off your prophylactic to stuff it back in its bag. I'll need it. The tech from the Medical Examiner's office is running late. Had to be scrounged up after the on-call dude called in with food poisoning picked up at an M.E. awards banquet. You'd think if anyone could detect spoilage, it'd be those guys." Foster rolled back his shoulders in a show of superiority and strode up. "This is a DNA madhouse. For the record, we in forensics are not insane. We'll only process the body and what's in closest contact. So who's the stiff in the can? Your foot's gunked. Did you taint the scene? Where's your partner? Don't see her around and she's not easy to hide. That Amazon, what's her name?"

"Deb Metzger." Erik and Deb had worked one case together on a trial basis, and the partnership stuck like chewed gum to a chair. It was not Foster's job to rag on Deb; by rights, it was a partner's. Erik employed adjectives in her defense: "She has a significant role in a major task force meeting"—i.e., she was attending. "It's you tech people who do the heavy lifting at the scene." This included lifting the body when the time came, at which point a driver's license might be retrieved. In the case he and Deb worked together, the body had been moved and identification removed, causing deadly delays in the investigation.

The potential for delay in this case didn't explain Erik's mental queasiness. The spittle on the man's brow? The prospect of working with Deb, who had the delicacy of a bulldog? The presence of the blonde officer and the physical attraction that divorced Erik felt for her? Felt despite his conflicted longing for his ex-wife. Odd that the Eastside patrol officers called G-Met directly rather than going through St. Paul Homicide.

No, there was something about that body Erik could not shake, a premonition that this was personal not just to the victim, but to Erik himself. A premonition that despite serving the greater good, his ultimate fate could be mean and lowly, his existence soon forgotten. He had to act against that.

CHAPTER 2

WHEN DETECTIVE DEB METZGER SAW THE URINALS, she realized her mistake. She'd ducked into a lobby restroom of the downtown Minneapolis hotel, the *LeClerc*, to muster the courage of her cause and relieve a bladder made nervous by the anticipation of public speaking. Instead a child at the sink gasped and turned the faucet so hard it extinguished the fire-breathing dragon on his t-shirt. He sputtered and let fly a word preschoolers shouldn't know, followed by "Grandpa!" A senior citizen turned from the hand dryer and screeched. A stall door banged open and a man with severe belt overhang squeezed out to bellow, "What's the *matter* with you?" People like this, not to mention ex-girlfriend-type people, groused that Deb had a chip on her shoulder the size of a concrete block. How would they even know that if they hadn't tried to charge her first?

"I have a right." Deb flashed the G-Met badge pinned inside her jacket lapel, and in doing so almost yanked her shirt open for a different kind of flash. Then she realized her error. The Frenchy italicized hotel signage resembled pretentious wedding invitations with the letters *M* and *W* hyper-curled beyond recognition. Deb was not classified as an *M*, particularly not as an *M* with foppish flourishes. But she was born to stand her ground, even if the ground was wrong. She pulled herself up to her height of 6'2"—in stacked heels—and said in her deepest voice, more butch than she intended, that she was in pursuit of a person who'd skipped out on a bill. She backed toward the exit and into a man whose smooth cheeks and horn-rimmed glasses made him look like a benign professor. "*Excuse you*," he laughed and put calming hands on her shoulders to pivot Deb in the right direction.

She did not belong in this place of pretension, a retreat for the preening rich. She poked her head into a recessed area where she wished she could flop down in comfort—the bar, closed at this morning hour. Etched on the bar's antiqued mirror was *Les Voyageurs*, a tribute to the nineteenth French-Canadian traders whose back-breaking quests in canoes were the opposite of what people were meant to experience at a *LeClerc*. Unlike the rest of the hotel, the Northwoods décor in the bar was ironic: wallpaper with walleyes and teepees and bears, oh my. Past the bar, Deb found the "appropriate" restroom, which had scrollwork décor even Frenchier than the men's room. The sconce lighting tinted her short blonde tips green. She adjusted her taupe trousers—same hue as the wall—and took five index cards from the pocket of her jacket. One card for each minute of her allotted time. She bucked herself up in this bastion of sniffy snobs. So what if she hailed from Mason City, Iowa? That meant she was grounded, because Iowa has lots of ground. She could handle the *LeClerc*.

Deb knew enough French to wonder if "the LeClerc" translated to "the the clerk." The musings in her head were drowned out by the rumblings in her stomach. She had managed only a bite of a charred English muffin to hold her until the 8:00 breakfast meeting. It was now 7:42, and she would be introducing the keynote speaker at 8:10. Twenty-eight minutes and counting. She was on a task force for the prevention of crimes against women and children and about to address a group of "stakeholders" in the human-trafficking issue. As a member of the G-Met Investigative Unit, she had to be a generalist: not every case would involve domestic and trafficking crimes, though god knows there were tons of those. In addition—an addition that could trip her up—Deb had a role in educating the public on these issues. In this case, she had to hang with representatives in the "hospitality industry," council members from the area, possibly the mayor of St. Paul, a judge, executives of nonprofits, a Native Communities representative, and community supporters who had money to spare.

Originally, Deb's role this morning was to silently represent G-Met at this First Annual 2019 Task Force Breakfast and nod in agreement while Task Force Chair Lola Scheers made the introduction. In the past, Lola worked undercover and dressed as a fetching prostitute, the Madam of Greater Metro. When baiting johns was replaced by rescuing trafficking victims, Lola changed her wardrobe and wrangled the task force into shape. It required wrangling because, shared mission aside, "stakeholders" did not agree on strategic priorities, budgeting, or who sits where at the table. Deb believed speaking her mind would be enough. Apparently, that was simplistic, and Lola had to seduce people into cooperation.

But accidents happen. That's what Lola said in her 6:00 a.m. call. The call had sucked Deb out of a dream cycle where she'd found the perfect—skip perfect—a *plausible* love interest for herself. Lola had to repeat that her husband had wrecked a knee when he tripped on broken pavement during his dawn run. Not that anyone would think bedroom antics caused the injury, Lola murmured in her lush voice. With her husband awaiting surgery, would Deb be so wonderful as to make the opening statement about the task force's purpose?

Seeing no escape, Deb said yes. That was before she realized she had no coffee in the apartment—damn self-checkout aisle where it's easy to leave things behind. A morning without coffee was a no-brainer, as in, without caffeine she was operating with no brain. She took a *wake-up-you-idiot* shower and called the G-Met office at 6:30 to clear her intro with Chief Ibeling. You couldn't just *speak* as a representative of a group; you had to receive *permission* and be *cleared*—further reasons Deb never coveted the role.

Chief Ibeling, a gruff early bird, answered on the first ring. She started with, "There's something . . .?" and he growled about her officemate Erik Jansson being with *somebody*. This threw her. It was totally out of character for Ibeling to gossip, totally a stunner that Erik had dropped the torch he carried for his ex-wife and found somebody new. Then it clicked that Ibeling meant Erik was with a *body*. Deb shook clear her un-caffeinated brain and reported Lola Scheers's request that she substitute at the LeClerc event.

After a leaden pause, Ibeling, also known as "Almost Allwise," stated a question: you know about the hotel family, don't you. Yes, she said, having seen the family's LeClerc Hotels here and there. He grunted assent, followed by a series of negatives: don't read verbatim from note cards; don't intone a memorized speech; don't sit down immediately to gobble from the breakfast plate. Then he dryly threw out, "And Metzger, don't be nervous."

Zero hour was closing in. Deb left her restroom base camp to notice a sign newly placed on an easel. "*L'Étoile du Nord,*" it read, "The Premier Hospitality Loyalty Program." The poster depicted art-deco people cavorting at a Mediterranean resort. In Deb's translation, "loyalty" meant, spend cabillions at LeClercs and you earn a measly free night in a dump. Was it legal for the hotel to coopt the Minnesota motto, *L'Étoile du Nord* or The North Star? And didn't a motto need verbs to inspire, like *Live Free or Die*?

Die. Erik, if he knew what was good for him, would call about that "somebody" and demand her presence, not that she liked him being demanding. He rarely made verbal demands; he silently invaded her mental space. Deb and Erik had been thrown together previously and it stuck like toilet paper to a shoe. Or Erik could call to plead that he was trapped in a well and she, like the hero-dog Lassie, could rescue him. If she felt like it. Lassie always felt like it, not that Deb was hooked on that old TV show, her mother's childhood favorite. Her uncle would whistle its melancholy theme, a tune that suggested little birds flying away forever, to make her mom sob in a Pavlovian response.

Nothing like the threat of public speaking to make Deb's mind wander the universe. Lassie's mind never wandered. Beyond the loyalty sign, Deb noticed others directing people to the event. At a table, a greeter asked her name and handed over a badge with Deb's title and name in italics. Only, the *zger* part dropped off so the emphasis was on *DetMet*, which sounded like mouse poison.

The greeter explained that two key personages had not yet arrived. One would be Nancy LeClerc, the seventy-year-old matriarch of the family-owned hotel business. Nancy LeClerc had been one of the first in the travel and tourism industry to sign "The Code." "The Code" pledged to protect adults and children from commercialized wage slavery and sexual exploitation, and LeClerc Hoteliers had taken the lead in spreading the news of The Code to the media.

The second, the designated speaker, worked in the gutter on behalf of The Code. Former policeman Dan Routh had become expert at pulling young people out of trafficking or away from life on the streets as addicts.

Deb was asking about coffee when she heard an "ahem" behind her. "Hello, I'm Arne Davis," a short man said. "I'm that unenviable thing called a middle manager. Anyhoo, we're so glad you could come, Ms. DeMetz?"

"It's my title, Detective Metzger, Deb Metzger, Detective Deb."

"Wait . . . you're the hooker, right?" Arne perked up.

"Um, I'm standing in for Lola Sheers."

Arne sagged. "Oh, she's the hooker. The oldest profession, still with us."

"Lola's a fake hooker, an ex-fake. Where's coffee?" Deb asked but Arne transferred his attentions to new arrivals.

As Deb passed elderly supporters seated along the wall, a woman stood to greet her. She reminded Deb that they had met on a "horrible" case involving an adolescent girl. Then she asked after Deb's partner, "that knife-blade of a young man, Detective Jansson." Erik wasn't even here, yet he was upstaging her. Then the woman laughed. "What a faux pas! I've worn the same shoes as you, Detective. Don't you love the comfort?" Her shoes were the size of a cocktail bun and Deb's were giant peasant loafs.

Before Deb could do more than nod, the sane man from the bathroom materialized and held out a creamy coffee. "Detective Metzger, this is for you. I'm Geoff LeClerc, Nancy's nephew." He pushed his horn rims up his nose. "She calls me 'Nephew' though I'm technically a second cousin but more like a son, since she raised me. She's arrived and would like to speak with you. Would you come with me?"

Aunt and nephew sounded easier to remember than the rest of the family web. "What's this about, Mr. LeClerc?"

"It's Geoff, and I'm not sure. I dropped by to see that the event gets off the ground. You investigate crimes against women and children, right?"

"Also homicide."

"We won't mention homicide in front of Aunt Nan." He smiled like they shared an in-joke and directed her to an anteroom, where a woman with a firm profile scowled out the window. Her silver hair was swept back in a regal wave and she wore a Chanel-style suit. Deb edited her observation—a real Chanel, complete with loads of pearls and the aura of the famous perfume. The middle-manager Arne stood slightly behind the woman.

Geoff pulled Deb forward. "Aunt Nan, this is Detective Deb Metzger, from the Greater Metro Investigative Unit. She's standing in today because—"

"Yes, yes, I know. Thank you, Geoffrey." Nancy LeClerc extended a veined hand tipped with lurid nails. "Detective Metzger, I must ask a favor. Dan Routh is supposed to give the main talk today about our anti-trafficking endeavor, especially given the Neanderthal sporting event that's coming to town."

"We don't need to editorialize," Geoff said, and Deb wondered which sporting event out of multitudes. "Aunt Nan, you remember I have to leave."

"Yes, I remember. I have no problems with my memory."

"Then I'll be on my way." Geoff gave Deb a thumbs-up on his way out, but his worried look did not boost her confidence.

Nancy resumed, "May I say, Detective Metzger, that we in the hospitality sector welcome events that promote our community. Consequently, we want to do all we can to ensure that these Neanderthals and their inebriated fans can't take advantage of our hotels to service their lust. Now Arne wants to scold me. Yes, I'm aware how the upstanding men and women of sports wish to protect . . .. Oh, fill in the spin on your own, Detective."

"Deb, you can call me Deb."

"I'm not about to be 'Nancy' to you, Detective Metzger. I'd be inclined if you could step in for Mr. Routh. He was to meet with me earlier, but reaching him is like raising the dead. My able assistant Jude hasn't been able to contact him by any means known to modern technology." A personal assistant stepped forward, stocky and seductive. How had Deb not noticed her? Jude was a name that could go several ways. In this case it belonged to a woman in her thirties, about Deb's age, who dressed office-punk. A fitted black skirt snugged in her waist, black ankle boots set off shapely calves, black hair hung in a sleek bob, and a gray-striped silk blouse added polish. She winked at Deb.

Nancy scowled. "I wouldn't think that a person like you, Detective, one who deals with murderers, could be so nervous." From behind her boss, Jude smiled wryly at Deb, her head tilted sardonically.

Arne, oblivious to Nancy's mood, offered encouragement. "You know how people when they're nervous imagine the audience naked? You could think of them as murderers. Nice murderers."

Nancy turned on him. "Really, Arne, naked Minnesota nice murderers? Detective, make the presentation about thirty minutes long followed by fifteen minutes for questions."

"Yes, but—"

"Surely, a person in your position is expected to make presentations . . ." Nancy paused before biting out, "*Detective* Metzger."

Deb glanced at Jude, who stared, unsardonically, at the floor. She then choked on her answer, which was fortunate because the answer in her head stank: *Presentations suck. And you're not the boss of me, lady. Ibeling's the boss of me.* If Ibeling wanted Deb to step up, he should telepath that command. What came out was, "Umm."

Nancy lifted her chin. "If you are indeed an investigator, you must have experiences you can expound upon."

"Ending a sentence with a preposition, Aunt Nan?" Geoffrey and his grin returned. "Give the poor woman a break. She's not used to speaking *off* the cuff. More used to putting *on* the cuff."

Dumb blinks everywhere.

"Oh, it's a pun," Deb burst out. "Because I handcuff—"

"Deb," Geoff cut in, "Aunt Nan is right. You have experiences the rest of us can't imagine. Of course, you should be allowed time to gather your thoughts. Aunt Nan, your guests can enjoy their coffee for a while longer. You should mingle."

Nancy frowned—the contours of her face indicated this expression was frequent. After a sigh, she left with Arne at her heels. Jude, her coy demeanor recovered, waved a hand toward the door of an unmarked restroom. Geoff mouthed, "I have to leave," and did so.

Deb stepped into the restroom, pink and too pretty to puke in. She looked at her phone. No message yet from Erik to save her from public speaking. She could push him down a well. She ripped her notecards and sprinkled them into a filigree wastebasket.

CHAPTER 3

E RIK STRETCHED AN ARM across his chest to relieve tension. He was watching the CSI team turn the *Celebrate!* lot into a game board with cordons and numbered markers. A fatal game had already been played and lost by the man in the dumpster, and this was an attempt to start over with new rules. The murder might be readily solved through surveillance and traffic videos, which Erik had requested over his phone. No need then to involve his G-Met partner Deb—strong vinegar looking for a pickle, she said of herself. The wind abated, the morning warmed, and Erik dared hope for a prompt resolution of the case. That hope did not stop him from feeling like a poached egg in his Tyvek suit.

A ladder leaned against the dumpster, and inside, Foster and a woman tech from the medical examiner's unit bagged the corpse's hands. Foster mumbled that it felt familiar. The tech asked Foster if he worked many dumpsters, but she cut short Foster's answering quips by asking Erik to climb the ladder for another look-see. She added that the man died about midnight and there was no wallet bulge in his pants.

"We may have a John Doe moved from the primary crime scene," Erik mused. The tech counted to three, and she and Foster made the flip.

The bloody corpse stared Erik in the face.

"I'm wrong." Erik almost backed off the ladder.

"Out with it, Jansson," said Foster.

The viscous smell made Erik want to retch and he talked hard through it. "I know him. Ex-policeman, Dan Routh with the St. Paul force. He retired early or was pushed out. Became a vigilante, rescuing addicts and trafficked kids. I never met him in person." To some on the cities' forces, ex-cop Dan Routh was a hero, an alcoholic who turned his life around. Others swore that during his heavy drinking phase Routh destroyed another officer's career. Or saved the force from a corrupt officer, a situation too familiar to Erik, who had suffered his own run-ins with problem colleagues. Enough people in blue reviled Routh that when he was slated to address the 2018 police academy graduation last December, there were nasty protests.

Foster interrupted Erik's thoughts with "I knew I recognized him." The M.E. tech reached beneath the body, and when she pulled up her gloved hand it was covered in gore. Foster whistled in surprise.

"You all right there?" Erik asked.

Foster grimaced. "The buck stops here. This is the crime scene. Dan Routh wasn't moved. Ton of blood underneath him. Stabbed right here in the dumpster."

Erik stepped to the ground. This was more than the tired cliché that no good deed goes unpunished. This was the ultimate punishment for good deeds. Here lay a man killed because he did what people like Erik did—took risks to save others. Then a voice, voices, Foster, the woman, were making light of the situation to stave off despair, saying that the detectives waltzed in and took the credit when the techs did all the work. Foster and the tech said that this time Erik was welcome to it. He could bear all the credit (blame, more likely). Too many hot-button issues: a dead peace officer (you're never fully an "ex" to the force); victimized teens and women; addiction; police corruption; protests. No investigator in his right mind would gladly take on such a case.

Erik had his phone in hand when he heard movement, checked over his shoulder, and saw pretty Officer Dahlberg exit the store and halt. Her words came back to him. *Careful, it's a tricky one, you might get hurt, sir.*

IT WENT LIKE A DREAM. Once Deb began, she knew what to say: how law enforcement, hospitality groups, medical providers, nonprofits, and public transport could unite to stop trafficking. She pointed out that the people trafficked and the traffickers themselves usually came from a background of poverty and abuse. She adapted a line from national experts that you can sell a drug once, but you can sell a person over and over again. Girls, boys, women, men—all could be trafficking victims. Deb talked of how Native American youth were vulnerable in this region because the assumption was that not enough people would care about them. LGBTQ kids bullied or tossed to the streets were victimized. Deb added that traffickers patrolled places that served young people with disabilities or disorders. Then she took questions, one concerning how she faced each day. Answer: coffee, exercise, and a fantasy series in which men wore kilts and women wore bodices. She deferred a question about interdiction training for hotel employees to Nancy LeClerc, who in turn deferred it to Arne Davis. Shortly before 10:00, Arne thanked everyone for coming and people started to depart. The personal assistant Jude touched Deb on the arm to escort her back to Nancy LeClerc.

"Deb!" Nancy took Deb's hands in hers. "You believe in what you do, excellent. I'd like to speak with you for another fifteen minutes, arrange workshops with our employees, get both you and Dan Routh in a room."

A buzz from Deb's blazer pocket interrupted them. "Thank you. I have to get this. Excuse me a sec." She returned to the anteroom, where she shut herself in the unmarked restroom. The pink soothed. Erik's number. He could've waited until she was back at G-Met instead of breaking in on her moment of glory.

"*What*?" Deb answered.

Erik sounded distant. "Morning. Are you where you want to be in life?"

"Huh?" Deb fingered cushy towels embroidered with either an entwined *LC* or bent spectacles. "What's with the philosophy? Where are *you*?"

"Heading to the morgue."

"Dead or alive?"

"This could be the end."

"Which end?"

"The wrong end. Disgrace, dismissal, despair."

"Whoa, melodrama's not your style. What *are* you trying to tell me?" Silence. She balled up the softest towel ever. "Are we on speaking terms? If so, speak."

Erik's answer was muffled. "You need to be with me on this case. It's not one to do alone."

"Why not? You'd be the department *wunderkind*, if it weren't for you-know-who. And you like to be alone, Loner."

"L-O-A-N-E-R, we all are at G-Met and we've been over this. Besides, you're profiling me."

"My profile looks good in this mirror I'm standing next to, and can't this wait? Whoever's dead will still be dead in another half hour."

"Dan Routh has been murdered."

"Huh? No. Gosh. Helluva excuse for not showing up."

Erik's turn to be blunt. "What?"

"We were supposed to team-tag as speakers."

"That's 'tag-team.' Routh was an ex-officer, loved and hated by other officers."

"You've experience being loved and hated by your associates in blue."

"Not an area where I care to add expertise."

"Look, I have to make my excuses to Nancy LeClerc, *La Dame des Hôtels*. Morgue or office?"

"Office. Be quick. Wait. If Routh was supposed to be at your event, the organizers may have had the last contact with him. Question them before everyone's on guard. Say something like you're concerned he had an accident. The office is tracking down next of kin, discretion advised."

Deb clicked off the call before he could order her around anymore and returned to the main room. The way Nancy twisted her pearls suggested their new first-name basis was endangered. Deb's phone buzzed again. She lifted it in signal to Dame Nancy and pivoted back to the unmarked restroom.

"LeClerc, a familiar name," Erik said as she shut the door.

"'Course it's familiar. On hotels, right in front of your face." Erik exasperated her, and the pink wall began to resemble a dissected membrane.

"Google 'LeClerc.' There was a suicide or killing a long time ago." He ended the call.

Deb searched her phone.

A *Minneapolis Star* article from fifty-eight years back announced the murder of Julia LeClerc by her husband. Julia had been having an affair. Her husband John shot her in the heart and injured her lover, who survived. John killed himself in prison, leaving behind their daughter, twelve-year-old Nancy, to cope with loss and scandal.

Nothing to do with the current situation. No telling how Adult Nancy might feel about the scrutiny of investigations, and no telling how she might react when it came out that her would-be guest had been murdered.

A knock on the door—Nancy's voice. "Deb, we need to get you and Dan Routh together. You could reach out with your police contacts. You haven't died in there, have you?"

Deb sort of wished she had.

CHAPTER 4

J UST WHEN DAN WAS DOING GREAT, he got himself killed. Distracted by that thought, Gordy Omdahl hit the pothole with a *thunk*. Ellie's paws skittered across the van's seat onto Gordy's lap, and tears flooded his eyes. The streets in St. Paul's North End received so-so maintenance, and Gordy swore this darn pothole had been reincarnated five times since snowmelt. By a sunny Monday afternoon in June, they should have that thing fixed good. He wasn't paying attention to the road—he of all people, with his auto-repair shops.

Gordy had gone to Dan Routh's house because it couldn't be that the man found in a dumpster was really his friend. Gordy phoned Dan last night to check in like always—no answer. He called after the News at Noon—no answer. Gordy texted, which he knew how to do—no answer. Probably Dan was dead drunk and sleeping it off. Gordy didn't mean "dead" that way, though it wasn't that long ago that Dan would drink himself stupid. With his spare key, Gordy could drop by and sober Dan up and it'd all be copacetic. He'd remembered the spare key. What he hadn't done was think through the whole thing. He had arrived at Dan's place a mile to the east and assumed that kids had wrapped the little house with sticky tape. Except it was police tape. A big man took his name, and ghostly people in white prowled, as they should do the way Dan died. Gordy had meant to pay back life for its kindnesses to him by guiding, protecting Dan. Instead, Gordy had failed at his mission.

He cleared his throat as he pulled into his driveway. Ellie's terrier head popped into view, and her snuffles steamed up his glasses. He shut off the van and held Ellie snug against his green-gray plaid shirt—green gray in his vision anyway. Gordy didn't see red. He depended on the kindness of salesclerks to coordinate his wardrobe and saw the world pretty much as dogs saw it, which was all right by him. The brown and gray bristles on Gordy's scalp matched Ellie's streaks, though her hair plumed while his grew sparser by the day, revealing the scar above his left temple. What could you expect on the far side of fifty? If only he could expect his knees to work without complaint. The left one protested with a bolt of pain as his foot hit the pavement.

Ellie yapped as she squirmed over Gordy's shoulder toward the street. The yapping set off Rainbow in her crate behind the garage door, and she joined in with the barking. A car door shut, and Gordy saw a man and woman next to a Ford Taurus. They looked real healthy, tall, with waists. Ellie yapped her lungs out as the man held up a badge and the woman held a thing he couldn't see.

"Mr. Omdahl? I'm Detective Deb Metzger. This is my partner, Detective Erik Jansson." She stepped forward with her hand out. "May I give your dog a treat?"

Gordy hupped an affirmative, and Ellie stopped her yapping pronto, tilting her straight-up ear toward the woman. She snapped up the treat, and Gordy set her down. Ellie pawed at the man's pant leg. When Gordy stooped to pull her away, his heart jumped into his throat. That set his head spinning so that he fell back and sat on the grass. Ellie licked his face, and the detectives helped him up.

"It's my brain," he said solemnly. "Don't worry, I'm training it. I listen to those Great Concepts lectures on the computer. You folks probably got 'em in college." Those talks sure went down rabbit holes, and Gordy missed a lot. He did understand that evil was active and that anybody could be a free agent to do good. Being an agent meant you had *agency*—you could help. Being free meant you shouldn't expect to be paid for doing what you should've done all along. Thinking made Gordy dizzy again, and too late he saw Ellie at the flower bed. "Ellie, not on the alyssum!" Ellie watered the flowers in her own way.

The man said, "It looks like your peonies will have beautiful blooms soon, Mr. Omdahl. Gordy had bought this rambler with its double corner lot for the flower beds. He enlarged them to make what the neighbors called a bloomin' crazy quilt because he put clashing colors together unawares. The, house though, could use interior work. In his dreams, a beautiful fixer-upper lady, a single lady who looked like the gal he was sweet on, Tamra, would show up with a plan, and she—

"Are you all right, Mr. Omdahl?" the man asked.

"Oh, sure, thanks, um—"

"Erik Jansson, Erik. And Metzger. You can call her Detective Deb. The crew told us you stopped by Dan Routh's house. We're sorry about your friend."

Gordy chewed his lip to keep from crying.

"He had a note on his kitchen corkboard that you were his emergency contact." The man had a steadying voice. "We can come back, Mr. Omdahl."

Gordy worked his lip a bit to speak. "I'm, um, his sober buddy. Call me Gordy. You didn't really find him in a dumpster, did you?" That Erik's face told him it was so. "Dan didn't deserve that. I bet he climbed in the dumpster because somebody called for help. He'd jump to help anybody. He's a good guy. You should know that, a really good guy."

Before Gordy's eyes became leakier, Rainbow distracted him with a reminder howl. "I gotta let Rainbow outta the garage if I can unstick the door. It goes off track and then I have to go through the house to lift it." The man went with him and they worked it open. Gordy warned him, "Rainbow, she has ta wind herself up and wind herself down." He unlatched the crate, and a collie mix dashed out to race around the flower beds three times clockwise, reversed direction, and sped around another three times, then flopped abruptly at Gordy's feet, panting. She noticed the strangers and this time the man held a treat. Rainbow took his treat with a crunch. Ellie left her spot on the sweet alyssum to yap at Rainbow for receiving attention.

"They're rescues," Gordy said to the detectives who, like the dogs, waited for an order to move. "We can all go"—inside was messy—"on the porch. Gosh, I feel responsible about Dan, ya know?"

The detectives looked at each other like they didn't know. There was something going on between the two, and it wasn't sex. Gordy sat them in the porch chairs and went into the kitchen for water. The dogs clattered after him to slurp from their bowls. Dan couldn't have been drinking enough to land in a brawl, *please, please, please.* Gordy rubbed his eyes with a dish towel and ran water into glasses. He returned to the porch, where the detectives had left him the rocking chair in the middle.

What's-his-name, the man, thanked him for the drink. "Why do you say you're responsible, Mr. Omdahl, Gordy?"

Gordy tapped his fingers against the sweating glass. "I've been Dan's AA sponsor for about ten years. That's how we met, at Alcoholics Anonymous. I've been sober for sixteen years, and Dan was just starting his new life then. We hit it off, I told him he could call anytime, and a couple of times he did, in a crisis." He had dragged Dan out of bars. The first time he'd done that, drunk Dan tried to slug him. That shocked Gordy, and it must've been because of the violence Dan saw as a policeman. "Dan was divorced by then, hadn't married the second wife yet. I mean, she divorced him too, a few years later, but it was better than his first marriage. The daughter and the stepdaughter, there's issues." He stopped rocking.

"Gordy?" the man asked.

"Oh, I drift, Detective—"

"Erik. Erik and Deb."

Nice Erik and Big Deb, right. "I'll tell you, Erik, I had a miracle happen to me, and I always hoped Dan would have a miracle. The first daughter, Brenda, the mother convinced her Dan was bad, planted what they call false memories about Dan beating them both. Dan would never do that."

"False memories are a tricky concept." Big Deb made a face that reminded Gordy of a marmot, not that she wasn't a good-looking woman. She reminded him of something else, he couldn't think what. She was talking serious, "Abusers can lie that their victims have false memories. They deny the reality of what people have experienced, a form of gaslighting."

Gordy considered, "I like gas lighting better than fluorescent, gas being old-fashioned and warm-like. Now those LEDs beat everything for efficiency. That first wife of Dan's, she's had a hard time of it with other marriages, what you call a shrew." He figured out what the scary woman detective reminded him of—not so much a marmot as a Wonder-Woman type, without the bra suit and patriotic panties.

The Erik man cleared his throat at his partner and mumbled that he'd met this Brenda and saw Gordy's point. She kept at it. "Are you saying the wife was . . . difficult?"

"That's it, I ran into her at a grocery store couple years back, and I asked if she wanted me to pass anything along to Dan. She spit a gob at me, said 'share that.' That first daughter, Brenda, broke Dan's heart, wouldn't have a thing to do with him. He admitted neglecting her when he was drinking, and that's bad. The second daughter, stepdaughter, I forget her name, they got along but she's grown. That's why he helps, helped those kids, the addicts and the slaved ones, you know. He missed his own girls, making amends. Come to think of it, people at the Resource might know what he was up to. They help kids and women who've got trouble? You know them? 'Course you do."

Big Deb nodded. "As his friend, Gordy, did he tell you what he was up to yesterday, Sunday? Did Dan worry about anybody in particular or mention names?"

Names, so many names. Gordy experienced a tremor. "Oh, ask about names and my brain goes out of whack. You didn't hit that pothole, did you?"

"I thought an asteroid had hit the street," Nice Erik said.

"An asteroid? Like killed the dinosaurs? That's a good one!" These detectives would be all right about Dan. "It's screwed up out there. Dan went for the addicts who wanted out, all kinds. He helped boys caught up in gangs or dealing and wanting out. One kid had a father who'd kill 'em if he didn't deal for him." Gordy ran out of steam and then remembered something. It couldn't be important.

"Gordy," Erik said, "Dan's F-150 pickup was parked at his house, and a van is also registered to him. We haven't come across it yet. Do you know what he usually drove?"

"His Caravan's at one of my garages. I loaned him a Chevy Express. Paneled sides, so's the kids' enemies can't see them when he transported them to a safe house. Wait, was it a carjacking? He's dead for *that*?" Gordy stood, and the blood rushed from his head. He grasped the rocker, which rocked, and when he lost his balance, the man gripped him. He muttered he had to feed the dogs and stumbled inside, followed by the detectives bringing their water glasses. He opened the cupboard and the dogs crowded him. He poured way too much food into the dishes and had to pull them away and start over. They were good dogs and let him take the food away.

"I can't have 'em getting sick." Gordy's hands shook as he set down the adjusted amount for the dogs. He wished he hadn't remembered that upsetting thing from last week. "I apologize, Detectives. I'm kind of rattled. It's . . . Dorothy's in for observation tonight, stomach trouble." There he was, before he heard the news of Dan, daydreaming about Tamra dressed as a fixer-upper lady. He should've been thinking about Dorothy. "I can't tell you what Dorothy's done for me. One look at her sweet face, and it's sunshine all day."

That nice Erik leaned in, and the woman, Big Deb, wasn't hostile at all but sad for him. She said, "We hope everything will be fine, Gordy. Did Dorothy ever hang out with you and Dan?"

"A few getting-to-know you missions to the convenience stores and parks where the addict kids hang out. Not when it was real dangerous, when pimps or dealers might be around. Only when Dan was asking what they needed and all. Having a strong female along helps." The woman nodded agreement. Rainbow's slurping filled up the space, and then she pushed her bowl so it clattered on the tile floor. Gordy scratched his scar. "Something Dorothy ate didn't sit good with her. Dead squirrel, most likely."

Big Deb gawked. Nice Erik opened his mouth and the words didn't come. Gordy was glad he wasn't the only one with that problem. Erik spoke slowly. "Is Dorothy one of your rescues?"

"I know, can you believe it? How could anybody kick her to the street where she had to lick up French fries by a dumpster? That's too much grease for her. Wait, you didn't think Dorothy was a person, did you?" He slapped his knee. "Pah . . . what a piece of cake! You thought Dorothy . . .." He slapped his knee again and teared up laughing, Ellie yipped, and Rainbow ran in circles. "I apologize, Detectives. Tamra's my friend, but we're not what ya call an item. I got hopes, though. You gotta see a picture of Dorothy. She's gorgeous." He pulled up a picture on his phone.

"Wow," from Big Deb. "Wow."

"She's beautiful," Nice Erik added. "I've never seen a Newfoundland colored like that. She is a Newfie, right? I mean that big black head and the rest of her white."

"She's a rare two-toner, like you mix polar bear with Labrador retriever and throw in extra sugar. She shows up and people calm right down."

"I see." Big Deb hesitated, "How much does she weigh?"

"Never ask a woman's weight, ha ha. She's one hundred thirty pounds, could lose ten. She ate roadkill or something, and that's why she's in for observation." He choked back a sob and made his face tight. He had to keep something back, too much on his mind.

Yet Erik read it. "Gordy, it's tragic what happened to Dan, and you have Dorothy to worry about. Talk to us when you're ready. Is there someone we can call for you?"

"My boys're working." Gordy picked up Ellie and sniffled into her neck.

Judging by the signals they were giving each other, the detectives seemed confused. Big Deb did the marmot face and Erik started up again, softly. "When a person you care for dies, it stirs up all kinds of memories, things that don't matter, things that aren't the whole man."

Gordy sobbed. "Dan was a good man. Impulsive as all get-out. That had to help him when he was police, acting fast? Jumpin' right in?"

Big Deb sucked in air, like she knew. "He's not the only one like that."

"I'd get fussed up over him. Last week he went to a bar to find a kid and ran into his old partner from the force, Jack, uh, Jack—"

"Don't worry about a name right now," Erik said.

"They got into a fight. Not physical, I'm sure, pretty sure. But it riled Dan and he dropped by after, saying, 'He took me wrong. He didn't get it.' People get inta fights and there's nothing to it, right?" Gordy ran out of air.

"That's most often the case." Erik stood and took out a card, Deb did the same, and they put the cards on the counter. "It looks like your dogs are ready for a walk. We'll show ourselves out. We're committed to doing right by your friend, Gordy."

For a young fella, that Nice Erik had heartbreak in him.

"We'll keep looking for your van," Big Deb said. "And give our best to Dorothy."

"Yup." Gordy bent over to leash the dogs as they left. It took a minute for Rainbow to sit still and his tears dropped onto her collar.

After the detectives drove off, Gordy walked the dogs in the opposite direction. He had forgotten about that messy fight—Meshbesser, that was the partner's name! Another thing bothered his head. Gordy patted his pocket, poop bags in place. Oh, he forgot to ask about retrieving a funeral suit. There was another thing about Dan. When Dorothy came home, he'd think better. It would come back to him. Most likely.

Gordy should take the dogs home before the neighbors saw him sobbing. Ellie found a place to do her business. Dan had told him he had business at a hotel. Hotels have names. Was it a girl's name?

CHAPTER 5

THE G-MET PARKING LOT SPREAD ITS CRACKS over Minneapolis, while the structure, a has-been from the 1970s, squatted over St. Paul. Or the G-Met property straddle went the other way around. Deb couldn't remember, and since the approach angled in from side streets, she was disoriented as she parked the G-Met Taurus. Not as disoriented as she had been at her previous job in Cedar Falls, Iowa, where the captain called her "transgerrymandered" and repeatedly asked if it hurt to have "that" cut off. "You're the dick, and I never had one," she wanted to snipe back. His putdowns worsened about the time Deb broke up with the girlfriend who could have been The One. Until said girlfriend huffed that not only did Deb have a concrete block on her shoulder, but that as a six-footer, she had in height what she lacked in depth. Deb didn't need depth; the depths were all rock and shadow. The end result: with professional and personal compatibility splintering, Deb landed in the G-Met job.

That meant being with pretty-boy Erik Jansson. If Erik had depths (people acted like he did), they were rocks and shadows impenetrable to her. He had ignored her as she drove them from Gordy Omdahl's back to G-Met. Admittedly, he'd been dictating notes into his phone, and upon arrival alerted her that they had been summoned ASAP to Chief Ibeling's office.

Their chief, "Almost Allwise" Ibeling, was ex-military. It was rumored that his wife, a professional caterer, had also been in the military, but you'd never hear about it since she was black ops. You certainly couldn't ask grizzled Ibeling, not a sharer, and he glowered per usual as Deb and Erik shuffled in like scrappy middle-schoolers. The HVAC vent blew a raspberry as Ibeling explained, "The Dan Routh killing. Nothing can be deferred with this case. Not that I expect you to have solved it in less than twelve hours. However, that would have been the optimum outcome."

Deb sat on a ladderback chair and figured that a public agency with more clout had absconded with the padded office furniture. Ibeling, not tall but that didn't matter, remained standing behind his desk. "Dan Routh was a fellow officer. He was controversial. We all are, at some point, if we do our jobs. This is about you doing your jobs. We must demonstrate that we in law enforcement can take care of ourselves so we can take care of others." The HVAC hiccupped, and Ibeling scratched his skull. "Enough with this friendly chitchat. Jansson, your update."

Erik poised on the edge of his hard seat. "Paul in our Cyber Unit is compiling security and traffic-cam footage in the area of the convenience store. The store's cameras were aimed away from the dumpster toward the entry and the pumps. Dan Routh's phone records have been requested, and Paul will check for a digital trail of Routh's whereabouts. I left a team going through Routh's house in St. Paul—a small place, the processing shouldn't take long. Before that, Routh's adult daughter, Brenda Hilbert, was informed of his death. The St. Paul police chaplain went with me to her place of work, the business office of a trucking firm, and he did the talking."

"You have Brenda's alibi?" Ibeling scowled at Deb.

"I couldn't catch up. I mean, I was unable to join them because of Nancy, I mean Ms. LeClerc, asking—"

"Jansson, daughter's alibi."

"We don't have it yet, sir." Erik's chair moaned. "Ms. Hilbert screamed at us to leave. The chaplain dodged a stapler she threw, and we left her alone with her . . . grief. She's a bit of a Valkyrie."

Ibeling tilted his head to the ceiling. "And what are you doing about this 'Valkyrie'?"

"Oh, that's it!" Deb burst out. "Oh, sorry. I just remembered, ride of the whatevers, Valkyries, it's a screaming piece of music."

Ibeling raised a paw-like hand as if to swipe it across her face, but Erik intervened. "A patrol is watching Brenda Hilbert's movements. Deb will talk to her when she's calmed down."

"I will?"

"Metzger, you had contact with Dan Routh before the task-force breakfast at the LeClerc," Ibeling stated.

"Uh, no, sir. I wasn't part of the program until the last sec, so, like, no need. I was just supposed to sit in the audience like a good girl." Ibeling's porcupine eyebrows bristled. "Well, be there to be supportive. I, like, didn't have the contact info."

"*Like*. Metzger, if I want adolescent speak, I'll teach a confirmation class. Jansson, take the lead and compile information about Dan Routh's time on the force, a checkered career to say the least. There will be rumors that he deserved this because of his so-called bad-cop days. Lord knows, nobody deserves a dumpster death." Ibeling pulled on an eyebrow quill. "If you're lucky, surveillance evidence will lead to a killer within the day. Don't count on luck. It may be necessary that you interview Routh's old colleagues."

Another moan came from Erik's chair.

Ibeling's growl lessened. "Putting fellow officers in the hot seat stirs resentments. You're seasoned there." Deb assumed her chief was referring to Erik reporting a past partner's sexist behavior, a matter that remained an open sore. "Fortunately, Jansson, you're not hung up on being liked. That's why people like you. But Jansson, no revenge fantasies." Ibeling crossed his arms. "Metzger."

She sat at attention. The HVAC belched.

"Apparently you're not hung up on being liked either. Read the reprimand from your last case, and remember, you're still under probation as a new hire. Work the angle at the Resource, the organization where Dan took the at-risk kids. Find out what Routh shared with those people. Get after it, both of you."

Erik stood to leave. Deb put her hand on the chair top to rise, and it cracked under her weight, catching Ibeling's attention. "Metzger, do get hung up on certain people liking you, Nancy LeClerc for one." How could Almost Allwise know already about their exchanges? "Acquire soft skills, ASAP. Keep in touch with Nancy."

"You know her?" Deb burst out.

Ibeling's growl had teeth. "Nancy was my babysitter. Out."

Erik drew Deb away before she could put her size-eleven foot in her size-ten mouth. Ibeling's humor was dry to the point of desiccation. Did that mean he was joking about Nancy being his babysitter back in the day? As for getting along with Rich Bitch LeClerc, Deb shook her head. *Soft skills, my ass.*

IT COSTS MONEY TO DIE, AND IT REQUIRES PROCEDURE.

Eight o'clock that Monday evening, Erik's temples throbbed against his fingertips. He poised on the edge of a mortuary waiting-room chair, and between throbs, noted that the carpet beneath his feet was a dismal yellow. Bruised banana—like the fruit that had been his lunch and dinner. He closed his eyes. The quest for justice had given way to public relations demands. After he and Deb left Ibeling, Brenda Hilbert called the chief to insist on seeing her father's body immediately. If not, she'd rant to the press about how her right to grieve was being denied. Ibeling relented, not so much for fear of publicity but out of respect for a policeman's daughter. The autopsy, though not the testing of samples, had been accomplished in hours, and the body transported from the M.E.'s antiseptic bastion to this private mortuary.

"Is that your stomach growling, or mine?" Deb asked from across the room. He'd almost forgotten she was there. "I'm ready for a serious drink.

My mouth's like the Mojave Desert from public speaking. I know, respect for the dead and all that." Deb stared at a praying-hands statuette on the table between them. "Like these things are supposed to be comforting, but this one, the hands cut off like that, it's ghoulish."

The statuette pointed at Erik. "Now I can't look at this thing without imagining a terrible swift sword." He moved the statuette to a side table across the room and commenced pacing.

Deb checked her phone. "So, she should be arriving soon. Hilbert— Brenda took her husband's name and kept it after their divorce. No Routh for her. She's had two DUIs, parking tickets, otherwise clean."

Erik paced. What was Routh doing in a dumpster? Was he chasing a pimp or addict? Going after a strung-out kid who panicked and stabbed his rescuer? Who spit on him?

"Partner," Deb startled him, "you're driving me crazy. Be a good doggie and sit."

He sat, fingers to temples again, counting the pulse.

It wasn't enough to silence Deb. "You know, you could talk, partner. Like what did Ibeling mean about your revenge fantasy?"

Erik was saved from answering when a woman in a somber dress slipped in, the mortuary director. "Detectives, I'd like to move you to our 'meat locker' when Ms. Hilbert arrives. I warn you, this is *not* our usual procedure. The deceased has been cleaned and draped, the chest wounds and autopsy stitches covered, but the facial abrasions are obvious. I do hope she brings a suit for him." She escorted them to a clinical room, where they were left alone with the corpse, covered up to the neck. Deb, not Catholic, crossed herself. Erik stood with his hands folded.

For once he broke the silence. "Did anything come of your task-force breakfast with the LeClerc group?"

"Don't know yet. I hate that PR namby-pamby."

"But if it prevents scenes like this . . .."

"Point taken. Here I thought I'd chosen an action career. Uh, the door."

The director showed in Brenda Hilbert, who took two steps into the room and stopped. She was dressed young in snug jeans and a lacy t-shirt but looked older than the age in the DMV system, twenty-seven. Her hair hung to mid-back, and a dye line above her ears separated the scalp's brown hue from jaundiced tangles. She snuffled and rearranged her patchwork bag on her shoulder. Erik was about to introduce Deb when Brenda demanded, "Show me."

The detectives stepped aside.

"You bastard!" Brenda charged and flung her bag at the corpse, partly dragging the drape to the floor. Erik tackled her before she could make contact again, and Deb rushed to pull up the drape. "Bastard!" Brenda screamed, and she and Erik spun around until she dropped her bag, which sent a Tylenol bottle rolling to a corner. She shook herself free of Erik, who had been manhandling her chivalrously, but manhandling was manhandling. He bent to retrieve items from the floor while Deb positioned herself with a broad stance between the woman and her father.

"Ms. Hilbert . . ." Deb started.

"I had to see for myself," Brenda spat at her. "My life . . . people push their way in, they wreck it, they disappear, they show up to wreck it again. Had to make sure he was gone, gone-gone." She bent to pick up her bag and caught Deb's eye. "What, were you going to say something, *Madam* Detective? Let me guess, people can still get to you after they're dead? They can't feel a damn thing so there's no point in kicking 'em in the balls, but you, you gotta live with the damage."

"If you could just . . . ." Deb caught Erik's warning glance.

"I see you two passing notes, 'This gal's crazy.' 'Swhat happens when you're abused."

"You've suffered, Ms. Hilbert," Erik said.

"Cut out that 'Ms. Hilbert' crap. Was Mrs. Hilbert, it didn't take. If you have to talk, I'm Brenda. What, why're you acting all polite, Mr. Detective?"

"Nothing, say what you want."

"Anything I say will be used against me? Is that what you mean? I didn't kill dear old Dad. Could've should've killed him years ago, the fucking bastard." She choked on curses.

"You're . . ." Deb's tongue tied itself. Erik mouthed the word "right," and she continued, "You're right, Brenda. A death like this, it unsettles everything. You're going to feel the way you feel."

"Yeah, what else would I feel besides 'what I feel.' " Brenda spoke to her father's feet.

"I'm sorry for it all," Deb said. "We can listen to what you have to say later, in a better place. You know it's our job to—"

Brenda whipped around. " 'Course it's your job, dickheads. I was a cop's kid. It's like having no father, it's all the job, and how Daddy had to recuperate by drinking himself into a damn fit. Shouting filth at Mom, and her cussing back." She viciously rubbed her cheek. "Now that's a sweet scene for you, Mom slapping Daddy so he'd stop calling her a poor excuse for a woman, me sent to a bedroom the size of a soup can, hungry, to do 'homework.' Wipe that pity off your faces." She moved in on Erik. "You're a cutie. Have you already burned through your starter marriage?" Erik flushed, and Brenda swiveled to Deb. "Have you even been able to get a relationship started?"

"Brenda . . ." Erik said.

"Let's do *ex*-Mrs. Hilbert. Who thought it was a good idea to perfume the dead? Stinks in here."

Brenda tossed her bag over her shoulder and stormed out.

A sickly heat oozed over Erik, and Deb was turning green around the gills. He rushed the two of them back to reception. Brenda was nowhere, and the director stood by the outside door. She released a professional sigh. "Grief is a monster, Detectives. Ms. Hilbert isn't ready to hear this today, but if her father died while actively serving the community, we offer a discount. Your families should know that too, not that I wish to upset you. I have brochures." She smiled, her voice perfectly modulated to convey both practicality and rue.

Erik rushed to the glass door and said, disgusted, "She can't go far." He dangled Brenda's keys.

Deb could strangle him. "*Urghh,* why didn't you say?"

The director intervened by extending mortuary brochures. "There's a coffee shop just outside. Our customers go there to consider their options."

"I'll wait in the car." Erik tossed Brenda's keys to Deb, shoved the door, and was gone.

DEB, DISGUSTED THAT ERIK WAS DISGUSTED, ran past the coffee shop to the Irish bar, where, as she suspected, Brenda sat in dark-paneled gloom. Foam dribbled down a mug onto the table.

"Ms. Hilbert, your keys." Deb steadied her breath and set them down.

Brenda sucked foam from the mug.

"Look," Deb placed her hands on a chair back as a compromise between looming over Brenda and cozying up to her, "I kinda get it. With my dad, me and my brother can't decide if he's depressed or a jerk. Right now, the vote's for a jerk who's depressed." Brenda sniffed, which Deb took as a question. "Oh, my dad's still kicking it in Iowa. When my brother was done being a high-school football star, Dad was only half with the family. He faked interest in my 'girl' sports, bragged to his buds when I won shot-put trophies. I went off to Iowa State and he divorced my mom. It crushed her, until she started having the time of her life."

"This is the time of my life. It's a suck-fest." Brenda swigged her ale. "Bleh, sour."

Deb could go for buddy time after all, order a Sprite and a beer and drink only one. Given her mood, it would be a waste of a Sprite. Brenda took another sour swig. "You're still here. Your dad didn't kick you out, you being butch and all? Was he a cop, jerk-cop dad?"

Deb sat up straighter. "He accepted it the way you accept a bum knee. He managed farm-equipment dealerships. Look."

"You want an alibi—that's what cop fuckers always want. I don't have one. Home. Alone. With the cat. What kind of proof is that?" Brenda choked down the ale.

Deb fought against her urgency and sat like she could relax. At hearing noises toward the front of the bar, she glanced over her shoulder. "Umm, there's a gal with one of those Celtic harps."

"Oh, hell no."

Deb had to say something fast. "Brenda, could Alexa be your alibi?"

"Who the fuck's Alexa?"

"One of those digital internet machines, kind of a bot servant that spies on you. I mean, did you do anything last night on a device with an IPO or location services? Were you logged into a home network?"

"I streamed *Father of the Bride* in bed with Routee."

Routee must be the cat. "That log-on would place you." Deb didn't believe Brenda could have killed her father. Too many unresolved issues.

"I gotta beat it before that goof-ball angel decides to play." Brenda instantly contradicted herself. She unstuck her mug from the table and nodded to the server to bring another. "Look, the stepdaughter from Dan's—my dad's— second marriage might know what's up. He was *nice* to her. Then there's the guy who was supposed to keep him sober. Because he pestered me about Dad, he's in my contacts. Here, Gordy Omdahl." She showed Deb the number.

"I appreciate it." If only Deb could find out something new. She was about to ask a direct question—did your dad beat you—and felt a mental jab at recalling Ibeling's order to develop soft skills. "You know, if you ever want to talk about your past, there's people, not just therapists, people who want to understand domestic stuff to work on prevention."

"You want to know if my dad beat me. Brenda threw her arm out and whapped the approaching server, who slopped the fresh mug and about- faced to fetch another. "Don't the fuck need nosy sympathy. He swatted me, sure. For a drunk—and sober, if I can remember him sober—he moved fast. Like he always had a startle response. Like he always came at me quick." She flinched. "Blurry, if he made contact."

Like father, like daughter. Brenda, charging the corpse, Brenda frightening the server. If Dan moved that quick, he might scare anyone, an innocent kid, into attacking him.

The server returned to mop up the spill under the mug and set down another, "On the house." Brenda could've offered it to Deb. She didn't. "Digital alibi, huh. I'm guessing, Detective, that your home life ain't any funner than mine. Fantasy romance with the pizza-delivery dude, your case a butch dudette. Take a fuckin' hint and leave."

By the bar, the self-assigned angel sang up in the ozone layer, but Deb wasn't feeling it. No high notes for her.

CHAPTER 6

TUESDAY MORNING, TWENTY-SIX HOURS AFTER discovering the body, Erik had to solve that murder and placate a child. The first part of the equation was the easier.

He paced his office while his five-year-old son huddled at the desk, drawing on printer paper. The boy's curly hair, a lighter shade than Erik's, had not been combed. It had taken fatherly pleading to move Ben from the apartment, and Erik hadn't had time to fight over the hair, let alone suit himself up. He was still in the casual clothes he put on first thing. Ben had shoved away breakfast and whined that his stomach ached too much to go to day camp. He could be upset that his mother had left him to attend a legal conference with her "boyfriend," that base duplicitous bastard mentor—Erik's descriptors, not Ben's. This meant a Day with Daddy that had to be abbreviated to twenty minutes. Erik checked his cell while pacing. Forensics continued to comb over the dumpster contents: fingerprints of suspicious local characters had been pulled from discarded Super Gulpy cups, and those characters turned out to have alibis and no connection to Routh. Patrol officers had not found witnesses. Deb had roughed out a report on a late-night Skype interview she'd done with Routh's twenty-three-year-old stepdaughter from marriage two, who lived in Phoenix. As a teenager she developed an affectionate relationship with Routh, though he remained anxious about hugging her. The marriage broke up because of her mother's worsening arthritis pain and Routh's binges. "He was kind to me," she said at the end. "It hurts to lose him." She would come to St. Paul in a few days to make funeral arrangements, and if necessary, they could follow up then.

In an hour, Erik and Deb had an interview scheduled with the director of the Resource. When Routh convinced a girl or boy to leave the streets, his liaison at the Resource would reach out to a shelter or the police. Erik needed a ploy to move Ben along. He stopped behind the boy and wondered if the scribbles showed talent.

"What are you drawing, Ben?"

"A sad pony."

Erik wanted to cry over Ben's downturned lip and bark at him to cut the act.

Then a thud, the door kicked open, and there his partner stood. In her right hand she held a travel mug like a weapon, in her other, a paper bag. The aroma wafted out. Deb Metzger could sprout a space-alien head at that point and Ben wouldn't notice because the aroma was of hot, cakey doughnuts.

"I guess I'm sharing," she said.

"Sharing is nice." Ben transformed from sad pony to hungry puppy.

"Good morning, Deb." Erik modeled politeness. "Ben, what about your tummy ache?" Ben had already stuffed a glazed treat from Deb into his mouth. Erik switched to, "What do you say, Ben?"

It came out garbled, "It's nice Detective Deb has food."

"And thank you." Erik started to wave away a doughnut but on second whiff, took one. His partner's expression suggested she hadn't thought he'd really take it. Since it was sticky, he crammed as much of it into his mouth as he could.

Deb gave Erik a what-gives look. "We do have a plan of action?"

Erik pointed to his full mouth and Ben said, "I can stay."

Erik swallowed and the sugar kicked in. "Thanks to Detective Deb, you've had breakfast and can go to camp."

"But my tummy ache might come back." He raised big blue eyes to Deb as possible intervener. Deb put a doughnut bite in her mouth to avoid answering. Ben mumbled, "It sucks."

Ben's grandmothers had forbidden that phrase, which gave Erik leverage. "All right, Son, that's enough, we're leaving." He turned to Deb, "I'll catch up with you." The case was urgent, tragic, requiring all their energies. As Erik closed the door behind him, Deb slouched at her desk, peering into a greasy, empty bag. *You can't solve a murder on an empty stomach.*

YOU CAN'T THINK THROUGH EVERYTHING ABOUT YOUR CHOSEN LIFE. The drama, for instance. For Deb as detective, walking into a situation meant walking into raw emotions. The emotions could be hers, when as a teenager she discovered a neighbor shot to death by her husband, or as an adult finding a man bleeding over a rent-to-own sofa, or a rich woman who waited two days before calling about the bruises around her neck.

It should have been no effing surprise that there was a scene at the

Resource.

At reception, a woman with white hair held high by a sparkly clip terrified the receptionist and pounded the desk so hard that the RESPECT sign on the wall jumped. The smell of cigarettes clung to her, and her large breasts strained against her tank top.

"*She here and you not telling me?*" She pounded again. Her slouchy bag slid off her shoulder and she hitched it back up. "My granddaughter, did he bring her here?"

A woman in her late thirties came through a secure entry behind the receptionist and announced herself. "I'm Sharon Nordin, Resource Director. We'll do all we can to help."

The grandmother remained belligerent. "What's that on your face?"

A port-wine stain mapped out Sharon's right cheekbone. Deb, who had seen Sharon at task-force meetings, admired that she made the splotch part of her style, today wearing a coordinating lavender blouse. "A permanent mark. Again, I'm Sharon Nordin. May I have your name and your granddaughter's name?"

"It's Luna Johnson. She ain't been home since Sunday morning. She's nineteen soon, told me she wanted to come here for job training, that kind of stuff. Ya'd remember how she looks. Witchy eyes with dark rings to 'em. She can spook people, only I don't know she's scary enough to keep bad men away. I'm her gammy. I wouldn't be hurtin' her. Are you hiding her from me?" She reached fast for her bag and Deb grabbed that arm.

"I'm Detective Deb Metzger. What's in the bag?"

"Let go, my phone!" The woman snorted. "I called ya when she didn't come home Sunday night and you stupid police say she's gotta be missin' longer before there's interest. You know, it were an ex-cop feeding her a line about trying to *help* her, said he worked here."

"Did your granddaughter . . ." Deb started.

"Luna. See, here she is." A phone photo showed a punk girl with coal-black hair and stunning eyes. At least she wasn't blonde. Traffickers exported blondes out of Minnesota to states where they were rare.

"Did Luna tell you the man's name, the one who wanted to bring her here, to the Resource?" Deb asked.

"He got to her?" She dug her nails into Deb's arm, and Sharon hit a button on the receptionist's phone. Deb didn't detach the arm because that would free the woman to reach for anything buried in her bag, like a gun. The woman wailed, "*What's happening?*"

"Are you all right, ma'am?" Erik had slipped in, must've delivered his son wherever. His somber face was at odds with his carefree outfit of chinos and yellow shirt. He put his hand gently over the woman's grip and she released it.

"Would you like to sit down?"

THE WOMAN BURST INTO TEARS, and Sharon rushed to her side, repeating, "It's all right" as she escorted her to the restricted entrance. The security guard who arrived to work the metal scanner confiscated a folding knife. "Me and Luna gotta protect ourselves against crazies," the woman snapped. Sharon nodded over her shoulder that the detectives should follow.

Sharon's office, like her clothing, was soothing mauves and lavenders. On the walls hung photos of the Resource founders, which included pro football and hockey players, along with a federal judge who was African American. Sharon faced the three, Deb on one side of the woman and Erik on the other. He jiggled a leg until Deb gave him a look.

The woman finally gave her name to Sharon, who started the questioning. "Protecting your granddaughter is important, Mrs. Kearns, and we're here to help. Tell us more about Luna."

The only sound for a minute was the squishy one of Mrs. Kearns kneading her gray bag. She regarded Deb suspiciously and eventually addressed Sharon. "I ain't all young and good-looking. People don't pay attention."

Sharon knit her eyebrows. "That's why we're here at the Resource, to listen to everybody. Go ahead."

Mrs. Kearns hacked a smoker's cough. "Luna, she's a good girl, mostly. Had a tough time with school, when she'd be all anxious and buzz around. The doctors say she got fetal alcohol problems because her ma drank when she was pregnant. I can't brag on my daughter." Mrs. Kearns took a tissue from her bag. "Luna's mom was so goddamn sexy by the time she was twelve, she wouldn't listen to me. Like her boobs stopped up her ears. Had all the attention she wanted from men. I can't say where she is right now. She had Luna with her second husband, and what the hell, she ran off and left him with custody. He's all right, saw that Luna had doctors. Except he remarried a few years back and moved to Illinois. Luna couldn't hack the stepsisters, flat-chested snots. A high school here had a program for her, so I took her in, and she'd visit her pa regular. She's graduated. She's employed, like I said. She's worth something, you know."

"Yes, she is, and so are you," Sharon said. "Have you checked to see if she's with her father?"

Mrs. Kearns wiped her eyes and mouth with the tissue. "She took the bus some, in a tiff. But he calls me if she shows up, so's I don't worry."

"What did Luna say about coming to this location?" Sharon asked.

More bag kneading. "Luna talked, ya know, like this place was over the rainbow. She could learn to act fancy for one of those 'livable wage' jobs, but why'd she have to act different besides not getting twitchy anxious?"

Deb, twisty anxious herself, said, "Mrs. Kearns, you mentioned an ex-policeman."

"Why should I talk to you?" Mrs. Kearns gave Deb a flat stare.

"Detective Metzger is an expert on protecting women and children," Sharon reassured her.

"Guess I can see that. Luna works at a café place in Dinkytown, by the U. University I guess I should say. She don't earn much because students don't tip a rat's ass. A man—there were two or three talking to her for a while—one of 'em told her about 'The Resource,' said he could see her doing better. Luna talked like she wanted help, but I give her a roof and food. Why she need help?"

"Let me answer that," Sharon said. "First, a former policeman, Dan Routh—"

"Wait, the murdered guy? Christ, do I need to be worrying?" The bag kneading restarted.

Deb said, "We're here because of Mr. Routh's death and to protect anyone who might have had contact with him."

"Someone has Luna?" Mrs. Kearns wheezed.

"We know nothing like that, Mrs. Kearns," Erik said. Deb had almost forgotten he was there. "It could be a coincidence that your granddaughter spoke of him."

Mrs. Kearns warmed to Erik, with his damn soft clothes and blue eyes, and asked him, "You at camp programs with the kids here? I bet the kids like you."

Deb zipped back to the topic. "Mrs. Kearns, do you know where and when Luna last saw Dan Routh?"

"I dunno, that café? Dumb name like Café Café."

"The Kafka Café?" Erik asked.

"Yup, that's the one. I came here because"—Mrs. Kearns appealed to Sharon—"you take people in."

"At a related facility," Sharon said. "I can check if she registered there. However, because she's over eighteen, I can't say anything without her permission. As for Mr. Routh, people here trusted him. He approached young people having problems with sex-trafficking, drugs, or alcohol. I'm sorry to ask, but have you seen signs that Luna was involved in anything like that?"

Mrs. Kearns kneaded her bag. "Luna might have a little fun like anybody. She, uh, has been staying out lots. Kinda checks in, and she knows her mom screwed her up with the booze. She bums rides from friends or takes a bus. She's got a new boyfriend, didn't mention a name, just said he was 'ma-ture' so don't worry. Weekends she hangs with friends doing music stuff. They all caterwaul. Her thing's the drums. It was therapy when she was little. When Luna couldn't deal with crap, she'd bang it out." The tissue Mrs. Kearns put to her eyes had dissolved into shreds. Sharon pushed a box across her desk. Mrs.

Kearns took a fistful and cracked her neck. "Arthritis. Luna would get my pills for me. She found a discount supplier and their generics are better than the brand ones."

"My grandfather has arthritis. He's ninety-seven, a farmer," Erik said.

"Real work. Did a number on his back, I bet."

"When Gramps has a flare-up, he uses a Tylenol-opioid combination. Is that what you use?"

Mrs. Kearns nodded and patted Erik's arm. Deb squirmed. Usually tough-time women connected to her. Where was Mr. Sensitive Erik last night, with Brenda Hilbert?

Mrs. Kearns took her hand off Erik, rummaged in her bag, and held up a bottle. "When Luna brought me the generic, it kinda gave me the flu at first but then it worked better. Cleared my head. Is this like your grandpa's?"

Erik put up a hand to keep Mrs. Kearns from giving him the bottle, and Deb pinched her thumbnail into her finger and asked, "Mrs. Kearns, what you said about Luna and anxiety, did she have a prescription?"

Mrs. Kearns went back to kneading her bag into the shape of a collapsed lung. "Luna don't take them all the time, what they charge. Adderall got her through school. Like I said, she'd get her pills and mine, for that discount. What, seems dark in here all of a sudden. What's wrong?"

Luna possessed drugs with street value.

After that, the interview soured. Erik convinced Mrs. Kearns to hand over one of her pills to check if it was on the up and up. Deb had to explain that Luna might be "exposed" to drug dealers and that they needed to track down Luna for her own safety. She avoided sharing the worst-case scenario: that Dan Routh attempted to rescue Luna, and that, strung-out, she had run and hidden in a dumpster, and when Dan tried to help, she lashed out in panic. Grandmother and granddaughter had this in common: each carried a knife because of the crazies.

While Sharon reassured Mrs. Kearns that every effort would be made to find Luna, Erik signaled Deb to a corner for a confab and announced that he would scope out the Kafka Café. "Go for it, Mr. Sensitive," she said, which threw him off guard, and she hurried to add that sure, she'd hang with Mrs. Kearns to learn more about Luna. Usually a break like this in a case thrilled Deb and she would dynamo ahead. With a vulnerable girl as prime suspect, this one dragged her down.

CHAPTER 7

Eighteen-year-old Jaylyn Dudek was surrounded as she rode shotgun in the Nissan Cube. She ached to be alone in her head with Beethoven's *Moonlight* Adagio, its poignant arpeggios reaching one over the other. Instead, buildings closed in on her while Cousin Lionel, owner of the Cube, yammered on.

The U surrounded them. Jaylyn adjusted her pointelle sweater. The pointelle, in a peach tone that made her brown skin glow, slipped from her shoulder. Jaylyn had been on the fuller side of medium, but this summer of unknowns had cut into her appetite. She buttoned the top button over the matching camisole and stared out at University of Minnesota grounds, its class buildings, student housing, administration offices. All told, 60,000-plus people worked and studied on the Twin Cities campus. Jaylyn should be one of them in the fall, music major—*performance* major, if she got her act together—but she hadn't graduated from her west Minneapolis high school (it was practically Edina). Nana, her mom's mom, said Jaylyn was born to receive joy and return it amplified. Instead, Jaylyn's life was on hold, a fermata that wouldn't end.

She tuned in to Lionel, seventeen and related on Jaylyn's African American side. He was swearing that they'd never find a parking spot in the U's Dinkytown, even on a Tuesday, and that their destination, the Kafka Café, was nothing but a mirage. Then he returned to his favorite pastime, opining on the news. Lionel, not yet a high school senior, followed the news and opined. He repeated that police wanted leads on the killing of a St. Paul officer, ex-officer, known for rescuing kids off the street. "Killing the good guys, that's screwed. Least it was a white guy this time. I suppose if you're police, you got to figure somebody wants you dead."

Jaylyn plucked again at her sweater. "You don't mean that. Not with Uncle

Ed next door." Uncle Ed wasn't an uncle, though he was an Ed, a neighbor, a policeman, and an African American. On her dad's Polish American side, there was a Wisconsin sheriff, but he was a second or third cousin seen only at Dudek reunions (he brought home-made bread), and they didn't attend those much since the cancer took Dad. Dad, missed every day. Still, so many dead people thanks to idiot police with guns.

Lionel said with mock fervor, "End the violence. We need to interconnect, to release our positive intuitions. We need *inter-connec-tu-ivity*."

"We *need* to leave in time to pick up Gabe at Little League." Guilt always stabbed Jaylyn at the thought of her ten-year-old brother. Green-eyed Gabe would do fine with Lionel cheering him on to excel at excelling. Dark-skinned Lionel was more like the agreeable middle child than a cousin since he spent so much time at the Dudeks and attended Jaylyn's school. Lionel's mom and hers were sisters on the Fowler side. Although the Fowlers had known success against the odds for generations, Lionel's mother had partied her way down and out of the middle class, and his father had never been in the picture. Dwell on that and Lionel would flip to disagreeable.

Lionel, stymied by parking and traffic, was about to flip anyway.

"Try the next left, Li." Jaylyn leaned on the window and worried that once in the café, her friend Retta would tease Lionel. Jaylyn had tried to explain once that too much teasing wasn't flirting, but a micro-aggression against a Black boy. Retta shrugged that *macro*-aggressions "like hitting and kicking" had been her life, the reason she had developed a "rhino hide." Jaylyn wasn't so sure that Retta, who teetered between sympathetic and snappish, had that tough a hide. She also worried that Lionel and Retta's boyfriend Ramon would throw themselves into a dog fight. Handsome, white, and twenty-three, Ramon appealed to women, which made other men—or boys, in Lionel's case—resent him. The mother who abandoned him must have had some Hispanic in her to name her unwanted child Ramon. Jaylyn watched billboards pass for not just *any* apartment but for *clean* apartments. Retta and Ramon needed one of those. Both adults, both stuck with a shit-for-parent.

Jaylyn's friends fell into three groups: the high achievers who'd gone through school with her; musicians, who made up the closest, brilliantest, most supportive cutthroat group you could know; and the rehab kids, many but not all from a rougher social set.

Jaylyn had met Retta at teen rehab sessions three years ago, when she was fifteen and Retta a year older. Retta Mazzi, with a pale olive sheen to her skin, could be in an Italian Vespa ad, the girl on the blue scooter with streaming tresses. Back in rehab, Retta had the dead hair and blotchy skin of alcohol abuse. "Grew up with booze," she sneered that first day in therapy circle. "That's how you're screwed when your parents are crazy drunks." Jaylyn felt the power of Retta's case and knew her own excuse wasn't much. When her turn came, Jaylyn struggled to speak of her father dying the year before of pancreatic cancer. She couldn't get it all out. The oxy pills left behind when Dad died, her wrist broken when she tried to help her grieving mom by vacuuming the stairs, the doctor who set the wrist saying that Jaylyn's own grieving body had betrayed her by falling, more pills. She choked up over "my dad," and Retta reached for her hand.

Ramon Jaylyn met in a nighttime math course at a community college. Ramon, whose quasi-criminal father had moved them all over the place, was working on a GED while Jaylyn was catching up on course material missed during last fall's bout with mono. (Mono, the kissing disease—blame the *ex*-boyfriend.) Ramon had liked Jaylyn first, before she'd gone and introduced him to gorgeous Retta. People said of Jaylyn that she was "graceful." Graceful didn't keep the guys.

"Are we going in circles?" she whined to Lionel.

"You asked me to come, remember? You didn't wanna be the third wheel? How come you're sweetness and light to everybody but me?"

"You're *fam*-ly. Eyerolling, case you can't see it."

"What I see is a spot." As Lionel signaled to parallel park, a Mustang revved up to his bumper and laid on the horn. When Lionel waved him on, the Mustang gunned past. Lionel muttered as he reversed that the Mustang would've been towed because he wasn't the kind to pay the parking fee, whereas Lionel was a man of honor.

He dressed like a man of dorkitude in his Best Buy knit shirt and chinos, his job uniform, but he asserted his self-proclaimed "awesometicity" with his hair. Jaylyn had a stylist who wove her natural hair into a chic take on French braids and cornrows. Lionel insisted she bring him along last time, and he requested a style "too fly for accounting and too trad for pimping." The stylist flared his nostrils at Lionel, yet he jived out with a not-bad do.

As Jaylyn opened the car door, her cousin bragged, "Notice, Cuz, our perfect position re the curb, perfect. Sheila knows just what to do." Lionel had a Cube, a used Cube, and he called her Sheila.

"You need a woman, mooning over the Cube like that." Jaylyn wound around people on the sidewalk. It suddenly felt hot. "When you going to get over that gal dumping you?"

Lionel caught up. "You mean the gal who oohed, *Lionel, he's the answer to everything*? She didn't dump me. She was all graduated. She *intuited* I wanted to release her. She was *older*."

"You and older women. Your crush on Retta, so obvi."

Lionel purpled. "You women think you can turn poor deprived Ra-*moan* into James Dean."

"Who?"

"Get some cultural literacy, Cuz. Rebel without a cause, fifties film star." Lionel held the café door for Jaylyn.

What the Bach, Retta and Ramon were first for once, at a high-top table. They had a fuzzy bedroom look about them—sex with an alcohol chaser?

Retta waved. "Hey, Jaylyn, Lio-*nel*, we gotta figure out how to save Ramon." Retta air-kissed Jaylyn, who hopped on the stool next to her and across from Ramon. That put Lionel between Jaylyn and Ramon at the round table. She nudged Lionel for gawking at Retta's plunging top and then looked around the Kafka Café. The maze-in-a-maze pattern on the walls was dizzying, and that dizziness resurrected the feeling of having the bejesus scared out of her.

IT HAD BEEN YESTERDAY, a chilled Monday morning with the wind sweeping across St. Anthony Falls and over Mill Ruins Park. Jaylyn waited in the Minneapolis postcard setting of the Stone Arch Bridge and shivered in her twill jacket. Retta had texted that she absolutely had to meet Jaylyn before Jaylyn's 10:00 piano lesson at nearby McMillan Academy. But it was Ramon who had grabbed her from behind, and both staggered with shock. His father had tried to kill him.

SEEING RAMON AGAIN, PALE AS a movie vampire, the shock iced back into Jaylyn's veins. His dad had barged into their rundown condo Sunday midnight, Ramon had sobbed, "so high he thought I was three demons. He had a knife, it was bloody, and he charged me. I ran. I ran all night." Then Ramon had collapsed against her at the park. Jaylyn grabbed the café table edge and found a focal point, the lemon wedge on Retta's glass. "What are you drinking?"

"A Virgin Collins. You have to order at the counter." Retta's breath hinted that she'd frontloaded on a stronger brew. She shouldn't have alcohol, of course. Ramon, of legal age, could do whatever. Street-smart Ramon could be trusted when things got rough, which made his trauma yesterday more distressing.

"*Jaylyn*, you've drifted off." Retta grabbed Jaylyn's arm. "Ramon and me like *have* to find a place. You won't believe the gross laundromat we have to use. Ramon *has* to have decent rags for work." Jaylyn had seen that even with jeans and tees, Ramon had an eye for quality. Give him a chance and he'd rise like cream. Retta released Jaylyn to wave her hands about. "Ramon, he can't stay with his crazy-shit dad and I'm done with my mom and her badass boyfriends. No way we can save for college by sponging off our pa-rents. Stupid if we end up dead."

Ramon cringed. "It'll be fine. Retta's ma's like yours, Lionel, with her boyfriends."

"My mom's being independent," Lionel snarled. Jaylyn should not have filled him in on Ramon's story.

Retta shuddered. "Anyway, Ramon wants back in the apartment for stuff. He called his 'dad,' who might, like, finally be sober. No answer, nothing." She pronounced "nothing" with a ping on the end.

"I thought you left your phone," Jaylyn said to Ramon, making him cringe again. "Duh, you had to replace it."

Ramon stared into his glass. "The window AC unit was running. He only does that if he's there, but no sign of him. He was with a woman last week, a young one. Maybe he's hanging with her. Maybe I can find where he hides the spare key in a bush or something. What really sucks—my delivery van was gone."

"Could be dear old dad's dead inside," Lionel mumbled.

"*Lionel*," the girls chorused.

"C'mon. What if someone knifed his dad, or his dad knifed him, and the knifer caught up with him, and, you know, and then the knifer peeled off in the van?"

"*Lionel!*"

Ramon swore and people at the next table stared. "Shit, that man's a shit, but he kept me alive, hell he saved my life twice, when my mom couldn't hack it. I get that I got to move on. Back when I met you in that math class, Jaylyn, when I was about to give up, you made me see there was another way. I saw how easy it would be for me to sink to Dad's level, and I saw that it didn't have to be that way. Because of you, Retta, I got a future."

Jaylyn teared up. She had nailed the math concepts because she had to talk Ramon through them, and also talk him through what a normal life should look like. When Ramon passed, he was stunned that the world allowed advancement. "I can't believe I did it," he said. "I honestly did it." Then she took him to celebrate at the restaurant where Retta worked, ha.

Jaylyn had been relieved, though, when Retta finally showed at the bridge yesterday to take charge of Ramon. Retta had now shifted from worry to smiles. "There *is* good news about Ramon's job. Let's celebrate. Lio-Nelly, pretty please order us yummies?"

Lionel despised "Nelly." Jaylyn distracted him by calling for limeade as he schlumped to the counter.

"Here's the problem." Retta put her hand on Jaylyn's. "We can't get a place together 'til we get those stupid two-month deposits."

"We don't need to beg, Retta." Ramon rubbed Retta's shoulder so he, Retta, and Jaylyn formed a chain of limbs. Retta had not repaid the last fifty bucks Jaylyn loaned her. With Ramon, Jaylyn had to force him to accept a favor when he realized that advanced math books cost hundreds and she offered to rent one for him. He paid her back. At the moment, he was reassuring them, "I worked out stuff with my boss. Insurance will cover the missing van. It's not the first time one's disappeared. He needs me full time. The future's home delivery, prescriptions, everything."

Jaylyn nodded like it didn't make her nervous that Ramon delivered prescriptions while his father probably dealt drugs. Second thought, that was how Ramon set himself apart, like in HBO shows when the son of a crime boss becomes district attorney.

"How'd your lesson go, Jaylyn, after Retta rescued me?"

Jaylyn stiffened.

"Jay-lyn?" Retta sing-songed. "You in there?"

"Oh, canceled. My teacher's husband had an accident and there might be brain damage." Hearing the news at McMillan, she'd felt totally screwed on how to move forward with the University audition repertoire. As an afterthought, she realized what her teacher was going through.

"Aah, too sad." Retta touched Jaylyn's arm again. "Didn't that teacher say you were too sweet to compete?"

Ramon was confused. "Compete in sports?"

Lionel returned to clack down an order number and ran off at the mouth like a thirteen-year-old. "You ain't seen 'compete' if you ain't seen music geeks. Piano keys are *teeth*. Chopin groupies would *eat* each other over whose scales are evenest. Singers . . . sopranos and Rottweilers, they're the same breed."

No one chuckled. Jaylyn stewed over the frenemy who said she was too sweet for youth piano competitions because they shook her up so much, and Ramon asked what Lionel had ordered.

"Veggies, pita, and hummus. You can pay up." He slapped the bill down.

"You got dip, dip?" Retta derailed the conversation.

"Is it only prescriptions you deliver, Ramon?" Jaylyn re-railed it.

Lionel derailed it again. "Painkillers and opioids?"

Don't talk pills. It was visceral, Jaylyn's memory of nausea smoothing into warmth, of feeling safely folded away. Ramon was talking about delivering adult diapers.

"Most deliveries are prescriptions for disabled customers," he went on, "based on computerized orders. To keep it safe, everything's prepaid and the van is unmarked. This company, Bailey's, is ultra-careful about sourcing, uses pharmaceuticals from the U.S. or Europe, nothing from China. No fentanyl, no carfentanil."

"Did you know"—Lionel cracked a carrot—"that in one state, they had so many overdose deaths that they stored bodies in refrigerated trucks? Get high, die."

"You're talking illicit drugs." Ramon was patient. "Deaths are down this month."

"This month," Lionel said. A woman tattooed with roses put down limeades and platters, and Lionel watched her twist her hips around a chairless table. Eyes on her, he added, "Remember the bill," and shook salt on a celery stick so hard that grains spilled onto the table.

Ramon shook his head at this childishness. "Shouldn't you toss a pinch of that over your shoulder for luck, Li?"

Lionel freaked out. "You're joking, right? Why would I do that superstitious crap? You pick that up in a book like *Huckleberry Finn*? I opted to read that and wrote an 'A' paper about Huck as an abused runaway who couldn't hack foster care and felt at home with marginalized folks. Today Huck would be trafficked. *Ow*."

Jaylyn had pinched him. It was Retta who extended an olive branch. "Since my Rav 4 died, I'm stuck with bus passes. I need a Cube like you, Li."

"You still driving that lunch box?" Ramon asked.

"Ever see police pull over a Cube? No, man. Sheila's innocent. This dude isn't getting stopped by *police*."

Ramon smiled slyly. "Not going to see the Cube stopped by a woman either." Retta and Jaylyn burst out laughing, and Ramon kept on, "Oooh, Lio*nelly*."

Lionel waved celery-stick dip in their faces. "Least I'm not picking up women to traffic them. Trafficking, think your father's involved, Ra-*moan*? Killing ex-cops like that Routh guy in the news?"

Ramon stood, his stool clattering, the skin blanched tight over his cheekbones, a *ffft* escaping his lips. The whole restaurant stared. Lionel stopped mid-bite. "I pay attention to the news, that's all."

Ramon cooled, and Jaylyn released a breath, but he did not sit. "I can't be around when Dad's devils catch up with him. I gotta rescue my computer before he pawns it. Retta, you stay. Be safe." Ramon kissed her hair, reached into his jeans pocket, and threw a rumpled twenty on the condensation from Lionel's glass. Lionel snatched it up. Ramon wormed his way to the café's alley exit.

Retta slipped off her stool to follow, but Jaylyn held her back. "He means it."

"It's *awful*." Retta sat.

Lionel dropped his eyes to Retta's breasts. "I'm sorry. Tell Ra-*moan* I'm sorry. Say, we can give you a ride, Retta."

"Nah, but thanks, sweetie." Retta patted Lionel's arm.

Lionel had not totally chilled. He was proud to carry cash from his job, and yeah, they hit him up for stuff. With deep trouble, Retta would come to

Jaylyn. Retta had been Jaylyn's biggest cheerleader when her "regular" friends
shied away during her rehab stint. Time for Jaylyn to return the support. She
lived in a nice house cleaned by a nice cleaning service with nice people, and
everyone figured that meant nice safety cushions everywhere. They'd be right.
The noise level in the café dropped like a rock. Police had entered.

CHAPTER 8

THERE WERE NO PROMISES IN POLICE WORK. You couldn't promise your son that you'd spend time with him on schedule, or swear to your father that your life was fine. You could pledge to do your utmost at home, at work, but when-where-how could you make your utmost kick into gear? Erik's outlook on life would be less gloomy if the air conditioner in his Highlander hadn't petered out this hot afternoon three traffic lights away from the Kafka Café.

He used to be young and fun and hang out at the Kafka. He had started at the University of Iowa but transferred to Minnesota after one year. Erik was a clever boy, clever enough to realize that if he wanted to have fun with fellow students full of ideas and empty of sense, then he shouldn't stay at Iowa where his father ran security. Distance and a judicious ignorance on both sides allowed a father/son bond to blossom.

How freeing, if this Tuesday happy hour task led to resolution of the case. Erik had little confidence on that front. When he'd called the café earlier, the manager reported that Luna worked the slow times. "She gets flustered," the manager said and louder to the side, "Watch the grease. Luna hasn't shown since Saturday. These orders shouldn't be sitting here. Doesn't answer her phone. I can fire you." Erik decided that the obscenities that followed weren't aimed at him. Next there was the ordeal of parking. Erik had been promised a space by local patrol. That promise was fulfilled as a burly officer directed him to a side-street garage. Because his name sounded like "one," Erik thought of him as Officer One. Waiting as well was St. Paul Officer Dahlberg, from the discovery of Routh's body. Luna and her grandmother lived in Dahlberg's patrol area, and Dahlberg remembered dispersing Luna and a cluster of friends for essentially "being high in public." She could identify Luna if she appeared, and as Erik spoke to Dahlberg, she brightened. He and Officer One would canvass the café clientele while she questioned staff. The uniformed officers adjusted their Kevlar vests. Erik slid the magnet part of a body camera under the placket of his shirt and caught Dahlberg watching his hands. "Be careful, sir," she said with a low breath as he clasped the camera to his chest.

The din of chatter met them as they entered. Show a badge, though, and the party stops. The college-aged workers at the counter, sweating under the brim of their Kafka caps, sputtered at Dahlberg: *oh, yeah, Luna, haven't heard squat from her, everything okay, eh?*

A threesome by the window was transfixed by Erik's entrance, good place as any to start. The closest person, a woman with lustrous hair, kept her back to him. Across from her sat a wide-eyed African American boy, high school age, in a computer-nerd outfit. The graceful girl beside him could be his sister, except her skin was shades lighter. Then again, genetics takes weird turns. Erik had his father's dark hair while his sisters were platinum blondes, and his mother's shade depended on her hairdresser.

He worked around a table that had lost its chairs until he stood next to them. A drained glass suggested a fourth had recently left. The three called attention to that space by deliberately pretending not to notice it. Erik could draw them out on that, but it didn't serve his immediate purpose. Better to start straightforward. "Good afternoon. I'm Detective Erik Jansson with G-Met."

"I'm Lionel Fowler, Detective." The teen held out his hand, and Erik shook it. "My cousin, Jaylyn." Lionel nodded toward the girl next to him, who glanced downward. "That's Retta." Retta's body language conveyed that Erik was a lying bastard who could plummet through the floor into a pit of fanged vipers any second, and what would she care.

"We're concerned about this woman who works here, Luna Johnson." Erik showed a photo on his phone. Lionel peered at it, Retta barely glanced, and Jaylyn drew back with a quick intake of breath. "Luna's been missing since Sunday." Nothing. "She may be connected to this man." He swiped to the DMV image of Dan Routh. A middle-aged white guy that the young and hip wouldn't recognize.

Only, Lionel did. "That's the dead man in the news, the ex-cop." The Italian girl choked but Lionel kept on. "Isn't it? He rescued addicts and stuff?"

"The man is Dan Routh. His body was found early yesterday." Erik stalled on the memory, the spittle on the man's brow. "Routh formerly served in St. Paul's eastern district." Erik switched back to Luna on his phone. "Luna is also a musician. She sings and plays drums."

Lionel piped up, "Jaylyn's a musician. She *kills* it with Mozart."

"Oh? What instrument or vocals?"

"I study piano at McMillan Academy." The girl's tone stung. As if to make up for it, she added quietly, "Do you play an instrument?"

Erik laughed. "I had a guitar phase."

Then a chain of events: as Dahlberg questioned employees and Officer One worked the café, a dude with his hair in a topknot angled in from the back and a counter worker put out an iced coffee to go. When Topknot saw Officer One, he charged toward the front. People squealed as Topknot pushed them aside and shoved the empty table out of the way. The table hit Erik's hip, sending a jolt of pain up to his teeth, and he dropped his phone. He vaulted the table and blocked the door. Topknot spun around, pushed a screaming girl off a chair and threw it at Erik, which he dodged. Topknot grabbed a fork from a table to use as a weapon, but Erik caught that wrist and twisted. The fork dropped. Erik blocked a blow from Topknot's free hand and caught the other wrist. Disable the hands and prepare for a headbutt. Topknot, too dumb to know headbutts only worked with goats, went for it. Erik jerked to the side and Topknot jutted his beaky nose back and forth. Erik twisted Topknot's wrists to pull him down, Topknot bumping against him, and the body cam hit the floor. Officer One shouted that people should stop shouting, and Dahlberg was there with cuffs.

"It's not mine," Topknot rasped.

"What's not yours, Topknot?" Officer One knew him.

"It's medical," Topknot said.

"There's no such thing as medical meth," Dahlberg said. "You've been in my neighborhood. The dealer with cut-rate prices and cut-down products. There's a warrant out for you." The male officer pulled a packet from the side pocket of Topknot's cargo pants.

"Topknot, this might help you. Do you recognize her?" Erik grimaced as he picked up his phone to show Luna's photo. There was a chance Luna had connected with the dealer.

The chance was way off. Topknot gave a stupefied, "Huh?"

"We're familiar with the situation, and anything we find on Luna I'll pass on to"—Dahlberg hesitated—"Erik." She smiled, and as Officer One trundled Topknot away, she grabbed the iced coffee.

Hip pain brought tears to Erik's eyes as he stooped for the body cam. He went to the counter to request an ice pack. The café crowd was busy posting video of the incident, and Erik concentrated on not limping as he headed back to the trio. There had been a second when the piano player appeared to recognize Luna.

He uprighted the table that had fallen next to the threesome. "Is everyone all right? Can I get anyone a glass of water?"

The long-haired one masked panic with attitude and snapped, "Are you a waiter?"

Erik had pretended to be one on a past case. "A busboy in high school. I can fold napkins." Taking one from the table, he twisted it into a pinwheel shape and set it by the pianist. "You seemed to recognize Luna. We're concerned about her welfare."

"Like you were concerned about that guy's . . ." the hostile girl began, but the pianist spoke over her.

"I'll look again." She took Erik's phone with agile fingers and for a moment lost herself in the image.

Erik offered a hint. "I have the impression that Luna's style is headbanger music and rockabilly."

"The jeans skirt and Doc Martens, a singer friend of mine has the same style, that's all." The girl returned the phone without making eye contact.

Erik decided he could push a little more, but not much. "Might your friend know Luna? I'd appreciate any help. I'll leave contact cards in case anything comes to you." He put cards down.

Lionel picked one up and used it to salute Erik. The long-haired girl flicked one to the floor as if by accident. The pianist looked at the last as if it were a disgusting stain on the table. Erik would worsen matters by lingering to see if she picked it up.

He gave in to the limp as he headed to the door, when a girl from the counter came after him with a supersized cup.

"Your Ice Whack," she said. "On the house, sir."

"Sir" and no icepack. Brimming from the cup was a snow cone, dripping pink, blue, and green over Erik's fingers. Outside the door, Erik was about to trash the cone when a small boy oohed at the sight. With the mother's permission, the boy skipped away with the cone, leaving Erik to rub his hip with a sticky hand. Nothing for relief of pain, nothing to help solve the case. Unless someone, like that girl, remembered Luna.

CHAPTER 9

LATE WEDNESDAY AFTERNOON, the digital pursuit of Dan Routh's killer continued.

For Deb, the pursuit was supplanted by a shoulder war. She charged toward the G-Met cyber unit door while checking her phone, Erik charged from the other direction checking his phone, and their broad shoulders jammed between jambs. Her shotput muscles against his kayaking ones. He seemed surprised that she existed. She was surprised he was surprised. He burst out with "sorry," she parried with, "excuse me," he perked up as if that was his name, slid by, and she tripped in.

Cyber Paul had stepped out.

Deb rolled her head around on her shoulders and the HVAC system's whined. "Brenda Hilbert's off my suspect list."

Erik frowned. "Your reasoning?"

"Are you challenging me?"

"I'm thinking."

"Is that why you're staring at the ceiling like there's a cockroach there? Have you turned into a cockroach? Stop with the bug eyes. I've done some checking up. It's that"—a neck muscle spasmed—"it's a daddy thing. Brenda's furious that her father died on her before they could fight more or work it out."

"You mean, Routh died before something not quite imagined didn't quite happen."

"If you want to be all cryptic, yeah." Deb kneaded her neck. "Broken families, you know. They think they're after peace and quiet and then the quiet's just a blank. What a person like Brenda wants is her childhood back, all patched together and shiny."

"Like an Airstream trailer?"

The question was funny, though her partner's tone didn't convey humor. Erik was mad at Brenda and he had no right to be. Deb had developed a Look for Erik, a special glare she shot at him now. "Meanwhile, 'partner,' Nancy LeClerc is dumping emails on me. She doesn't send them herself. Her assistant does 'as dictated by N. LeC.' Dictator is right. She wants me to check out rumors that a drug-and-sex distributor is bouncing around hotels offering a bargain package. So I reply asking for details and hear back that it's on me to find the good stuff. What to do?"

"Forward the information to the drug units."

"Oh right, like I hadn't already done that." Deb wanted Erik to *listen*, not advise. "Still leaves Dictator LeClerc. What am I to do with that?"

"Treat her like she's human." Erik was disgruntled. He was the kind of guy who could be disgruntled. If he didn't get off his high horse soon, she'd pull him off. His tone shifted, "Oh, afternoon, Paul."

Cyber Paul stepped between them, thank god. He was shorter than Deb and Erik—not hard to be—and the true Golden Boy of Greater Metro, thanks to the glow of his Danish and Dutch-Polynesian heritage. "Good afternoon, guys, Detectives. I apologize for being late, a, um, meeting with the FBI." Paul seemed to have frequent meetings with the FBI. He directed them to chairs at a computer station and sat between them as a buffer. Paul was a shy soul, like Clark Kent before he got the S on his chest, except as far as Deb knew, Paul made no dramatic wardrobe changes out of his oxford shirt with rolled-up sleeves. She wondered if Paul rolled up the sleeves in emulation of G-Met Chief Ibeling, though the techie lacked the musculature that rendered Ibeling's casualness a bulging threat.

"Here's where we are." The vent above Paul rattled, then lapsed into a hot silence. "As you know, the preliminary autopsy report shows no alcohol or illicit drugs in Dan Routh's system. There did not appear to be a prolonged fight, since bruising was minimal. Routh stayed in moderately good shape, and at five feet ten and a hundred ninety, he could've held his own if he had the tactical advantage. Cause of death was multiple stab wounds by a small blade that nicked the thoracic aorta. No wallet on Routh, no phone, no keys. No watch either, but the skin indent around his left wrist suggests he wore one. Using the plate number for the van Gordon Omdahl loaned Routh, I found the vehicle on the traffic cams. I can't trace an entire route because it's night, the cameras are scattered, and they don't all function."

"For shit's sake," Deb interrupted him. "I mean, for shuck's sake."

Paul leaned into the monitor. "Well, there are a few clips near the *Celebrate!* station. Routh came from the north following a white Ford Econoline through East St. Paul around Wheelock Parkway and Arcade Street. Nice neighborhoods up there. The speed varies. The Econoline may not have seen

Routh at first. The Econoline plate is muddied over, and the driver seems familiar with the area and stutters into the *Celebrate!* station from the rear alley, avoiding cameras. The Econoline could have run out of gas or had engine trouble. The Chevy Express Routh's in pulls up behind and out of sight. Seven minutes elapse, and at one thirty-three a.m., Routh's Chevy is backed out and disappears down a side street. Two hours later, a small tow truck, no signage and another obscured license plate, arrives to haul away the Econoline."

Erik wiped sweat from his brow with his forearm. "Our working assumptions could be that, whether or not the killing was premeditated, the person or persons in the Econoline have experience in avoiding surveillance."

Deb undid a button of her shirt and fanned it away from her throat. "Thanks, Paul. What about cellphone records?"

"Dan Routh had a cheap cellphone carrier, and we get what he paid for, slow service. The carrier should've responded already."

Deb, despite feeling swampy and swamped, forged ahead, "No sign yet of this Luna who disappeared on Sunday and who had mentioned Dan Routh to her grandmother. We don't even know if Luna had been in any contact with Dan recently or intended to meet him. The Resource says Dan gave burner phones to the skittish kids so they could contact him rather than him forcing them in. These kids—because they're users, because they deal a little to cover their next fix, because they're prostituted—they back off from anything that appears official. Maybe Luna's like that. According to the Resource, Dan tried not to look like he was collecting information to use against the kids. Kept what he knew about them in his head. Dan even wore old jeans because chinos looked like a uniform. I figure he knew St. Paul well enough from his cop days that he didn't use GPS."

Paul considered this. "I use GPS all the time because you never know what roads are closed for construction."

"You find out anything about Gordy Omdahl? He calls every three hours, repeats things, wants to help." Erik pulled his shirt away from his sweaty chest. They might as well be playing strip poker.

"Owns the Omdahl auto-repair shops."

"Chop shops?" Deb perked up.

"I hope not. I take my Jag to one."

"Wait, you have a *Jaguar,* Paul?" she stammered.

"XJ6. But it's old."

Erik cocked an eyebrow. "Doesn't that make it more valuable?"

"Lots of guys get hand-me-down cars from Grandpa." Paul tucked a leg under him and swiveled back and forth.

Deb took the cue. "Thanks, Paul, we'll stay tuned for updates." Erik urged her out of the cyber steam bath with a sweep of his arm. They paused in the hallway under a vent blowing frigid air, and their phones beeped.

Updates from the tip line: the first said that Dan rescued girls "for his own use"; the second reported that a few nights before his death, Dan Routh had a shoving match in a bar with his old police partner, Jack Meshbesser. The second tip had been leaked to the press. Consequently, the press demanded to know if the cops were doing in their own.

"Aaah, couldn't we stick with a simple killing and not this, this *intrigue*?" Deb shivered and rubbed her goosebumpy arm. "Tip One, I'll see if the Resource can put me in contact with Routh's rescues. The cop fight, your lead." Erik had frozen under the vent. "It's your job."

"Thank you for the obvious."

"I breathe sarcasm, caught it from you. It is your job, partner-with-seniority."

Erik buttoned up his shirt. "I have Ben again."

Drat, he'd played the dad card. Deb waved him off and turned to call over her shoulder, "So start tomorrow!" His glare burned her back as she walked away. She figured Erik wasn't satisfied about letting Brenda off the hook. She hadn't killed her dad, Deb was sure of it. She just needed the woman's digital alibi.

Brenda had not called back.

CHAPTER 10

THURSDAY MORNING, AFTER DROPPING BEN AT DAY CAMP, Erik changed into chinos too nice for yard work to visit Meshbesser's Minneapolis precinct. Erik's older sister, the banker, had called him last night after seeing *Duel at the Kafka Café* on YouTube. She offered unsolicited advice that he should make an épée standard equipment and that for an interview where he hoped to soften a combative mood, he should dress business casual. How casual could that be, he wondered, since this sister ironed denim. Then she dunned him for his contribution to a Father's Day gift for their dad.

Erik received an unwelcoming welcome upon entering the Minneapolis 5th Precinct. The receptionist, in a voluminous dress with a swimming shark pattern, recognized him. She had worked at the precinct where Erik started as a police officer, was always on the cusp of retirement, and smiled with weasel teeth. "No longer the adorable rookie, are you, Jansson? No more happy face? You want the third door on the *right*, bet you'll be sorry you wanted it, and you're not as *right* as you think you are." She used to cozy up to Bob Uhle, the partner Erik "disgraced" in accusing him of sexist behavior. Uhle relied on off-color flirtation to butter her up, and she never refused butter.

Erik entered a room that was a notch above G-Met's maintenance in having a recent paint job. It was still a box, and Erik had hoped for a friendlier atmosphere to set up an interview rather than a grilling.

Meshbesser, *Sergeant* Meshbesser, swelled into the room in his uniform, vest, and armed duty belt. He fudged a tale about being geared up for training maneuvers and nixed Erik's idea that they switch to a walking interview along Lake Harriet. He let Erik sit and stood over him as if here in the Minneapolis 5th Precinct it was a war zone. Serious crimes did occur in the 5th; meanwhile, many neighborhoods received an A+ for schools and safety.

Erik, for example, resided in Linden Hills, which was practically Edina.

"Thank you for agreeing to see me, Sergeant," Erik said. Although stocky Meshbesser could do a body plenty of harm, it would cost him, and he creaked as he sat. Most officers of similar education and experience had moved beyond sergeant rank or retired; he'd paid for making a lateral move from one city to another.

Meshbesser plopped down. "Jansson, heard you're a Scandi mix. You're not blond."

"I'm Nordic Noir." Erik skipped over the Swedish-Sami-Viking Raider concoction he was. "I realize it's been over ten years since you and Dan Routh were partners in St. Paul."

"Get to the point, Jansson."

"You were seen talking to Routh in Bar SuzyBill the Thursday evening before he was killed."

"He had no business being there"—the *b*'s exploded from Meshbesser's mouth, a girlish pucker set in an oversized jaw. "He gets himself in trouble. Maybe he picked up the sauce again. You try working with an alcoholic partner. The mean sots don't have your back because they're puking on your front. Sober, and their hangovers screw their judgment." He tilted his head back. "I heard you have a female partner. That must sweeten the deal."

"Like vinegar. That's a compliment."

"Oh, you pay compliments. Here I thought you were all about being hero by taking the shortcut to glory—ratting out your fellow officer." Meshbesser used the cleanest of Uhle's names for Erik. "Well, 'Officer Lambkin,' you of all people should know how some cops get holier than thou."

Erik struggled to remain cool because if he flushed from neck to temples, it would be painfully evident against his white shirt. "When he was on the force, Dan Routh was reported twice for use of excessive force. He was cleared, but—"

"Past is past, nothing there." Meshbesser pursed his tiny mouth. "Don't. Waste. My. Time."

Erik didn't scare. "Partnerships are tough. Tough because of what's on the streets, tough on the home life."

"Didn't I hear you divorced? From that sexy wife?"

Erik ignored that dig to commiserate and bait, "Partners are tough on each other. They get drunk and embarrass each other, fight. They think they help each other, but they mess up." Meshbesser flinched and Erik took a guess about the relevance of notorious incidents. "They shoot each other in the foot. They sleep with each other's spouses."

"What the . . .? I never touched that she-cat of his, not before the divorce, not after. She was super-sexed when they married, and it turned to bile. Don't be such a shit."

"If I were that, this place would smell even worse. Look, I'm doing my job, Sergeant. It gets coldhearted, you know that. I need to determine if anything Routh said or did at any time led to that dumpster."

Meshbesser fidgeted with his weaponized belt. "There's bastards that rat out their buddies like Dan did before he scrammed with his pension. What the hell was he up to? Bleating about junior officers using excessive force? Taking out his guilt on scared kids trying to stay safe on the job. You wanna know about the bar that night? I hadn't seen Dan in years and he's in my face bragging about being 'redeemed' by this rescue act of his. 'Redeemed,' my ass. And it sure as hell smells like shit in here."

Erik abruptly raised himself then quickly realized what was happening. This was Brenda Hilbert all over again, hate and want and loss with nothing left to patch up and save. He sat. "Sergeant, Jack, Dan had a lot of good in him. You saw it."

Meshbesser stared at a wall. The corner of his eye was crusted with eczema. "Hell, I didn't kill him. Up in Canada fishing Saturday through Tuesday. Can't beat my alibi, border crossing. Border patrol takes your photo, nice lot of mug shots they have."

"It appears that Dan followed another person into the dumpster, likely a person he was trying to bring in off the street."

"It don't surprise me. A strung-out kid is your killer." Meshbesser scrubbed his face with his hands. "Stuffy in here."

"Did he mention any names that night you met? Was he upset about a St. Paul officer?"

"Give your fellow officers a rest, Jansson. Wait 'til you get some dings on that slick exterior of yours." Meshbesser stood.

Erik didn't. "I was in that dumpster. Staring into the dead eyes of a man who wanted to do the right thing. Yes, a strung-out kid could be the killer. But there was coordination, too." Erik didn't want to say too much. He believed Meshbesser to be honest, more or less, but gossip could spread to corrupt quarters. "We're looking for eighteen-year-old Luna Johnson, who was supposed to meet Routh on Sunday. Also, a Chevy Express and a Ford Econoline van were at the scene. They're missing."

Meshbesser took his time sitting. "Gangs of all colors work in that area. An up-'n'-comer saw a way to score vehicles." He narrowed his eyes at Erik. "I still have friends on the St. Paul force. They're all fussed up about a home-grown zero, Vernon Grimes. Born in St. Paul, knows the area like the back of his greased hand, has a nice split-level in a safe area away from his own dirty work. Worked himself to the top of the heap. Grimes has a mobile 'business plan' for drug and sex trafficking active in that part of St. Paul and along the interstate corridors. He's got action in Minneapolis, too. Nobody's pinpointed it yet."

"G-Met has undercover—"

"Take my advice. Grimes and Associates are above your paygrade. Let the friggin' FBI have them. Grimes is a brutal snot who considers himself an en-trep-e-neur with style. His henchmen—you'd be peanuts to them—drive Mustangs, Corvettes. You better pray they're not involved. Find this 'Luna.' If she did the deed, let the prosecution figure out her 'social needs.' Kids want the world handed to 'em then wreck it."

"Is that why you moved to Minneapolis after Routh left the force? For your kids' sake?" Though the move could have been to avoid investigation by St. Paul Internal Affairs, Erik chose the positive spin.

"What? Oh, the schools. This area has decent publics. It's practically Edina." Meshbesser stood again to leave.

Erik also stood. "If you think of anything . . .."

"Uh, thought of something right now. Grimes, his selling point's 'the thrill without the chill.' Drugs that get you high and you don't die. Could be docs and pharmaceuticals supply his 'safe' product. Maybe Grimes blackmails them or sends out a Mustang to run over their toes."

"Thank you." They had reached the door, and Erik held out his hand.

Meshbesser didn't take it. "You think you're too clever, Jansson, for death in a dumpster. None of us is. The smart ones like you bitter up and see the world sour. Or they go for fake sweetening. You can smile and smile—you got the face for it—and you'll get your way. You'll be pleased with yourself until you realize there's nothing anymore behind that smile. Get out of Dodge while you can. Go into advertising. You're phony enough for it." Hands on his duty belt, Meshbesser swaggered down the hallway.

Erik had to hurry back to G-Met to check updates with Cyber Paul. He jogged to his Highlander, always packed for a camping getaway, and rummaged around for a change of shirts. His white one felt soiled.

CHAPTER 11

A HEAVY-METAL BEAT POUNDED IN JAYLYN'S HEAD as she drove her Jeep, inherited from her dad, through the industrial area west of the Mississippi River. She kept imagining that missing girl from the café drumming out a manic solo. In the detective's photo, the girl had attitude. People weren't as keen on rescuing girls with attitude. It was the attitude that had reminded Jaylyn of her rehab friend Teddi, though Teddi had switched from headbanger whiplash to retro swing and blues. Possibly Luna had been with Teddi at a McMillan music jam, and the girl never came back because Teddi, not yet eighteen, could cut down an unpracticed musician in a hot sec. Teddi had, Jaylyn hoped, stopped cutting herself with safety pins, paring knives, and random scrap. It made Jaylyn queasy.

She drove past the neighborhood where both grandmothers tsk-tsked "the unfortunate Blacks" lived. She crossed the Lowry Street Bridge to Minneapolis's blue-collar Marshall Terrace, which was guarded by a rusting forest of energy-company pylons. Over the river and through the woods to Grandmother's Tudor-trimmed house she went.

No wolves lurking at Gran Dudek's—scared off by her wiry mane and hydra-headed chore list. A few years back, Jaylyn and her brother Gabe started calling her White Gran, like Red Queen and White Queen, because Gran was the color of bleached flour. Her mom put a stop to that, admonishing, "She loves you, in her way." Gran's way was a challenge, but loss was behind it, and loneliness. Jaylyn couldn't let her gran be lonely. At the sound of the Jeep, Gran popped out and snapped the screen door shut. She wore a retiree's summer uniform of a glittery t-shirt, pedal pushers, and white sneakers. Short and thin, except for "bloat," she pulled 5'5" Jaylyn down to kiss her on the cheek. "Come inside quick, honey, so the cat don't get out. I'm taking care of

Thea's cat whilst she's in Des Moines. Her grandchildren *asked* her to visit."

Inside no cat appeared, though a saucer of milk sat on the kitchen floor. The saucer matched the doll tea set that Gran gave Jaylyn for Christmas when she was five. Instead of buying a toy set, Gran went to the St. Hedwig's Church bazaar and bargained down donated dishes to a dollar, and Jaylyn was thrilled to have real china made in China. The pink flowers on the cat's saucer clashed with the orange Formica counter. The kitchen had mostly been redone when the harvest-gold stove stopped working, and Dad saw to it that the appliances gave way to stainless steel models. It was his rule to never do all Gran's chores at once because that generated more. With the kitchen he came close to violating that rule, but before Gran made up her mind about a new counter, Dad was diagnosed with cancer and the project stopped. At the sight of that orange counter, it hit Jaylyn that her dad, sensing his grim future, had rushed to finish things for his mother.

"Jaylynnie, you're in one of your dazes. I s'pose you go into fugue states since you play fugues. You must be working too hard."

"I have that part-time job with music camp program, that's it, and—"

Gran grasped her arm. "You haven't been the same since that nice white boy left you. Joseph—"

"Josh."

"Had a nice head of hair, that Josh. Older, weren't he? Nice boy."

Not that nice, ghosting Jaylyn after they separated last fall during their mutual mono phase. "Gra-an. I wish you wouldn't say 'white boy,' and remember, you told me there are other fish in the sea?"

"Minnesota ain't on a sea. You don't eat regular. I have us some brownies. Thea baked them, insisted I have the whole pan. You know how she is." No, Jaylyn didn't know. Gran busied herself cutting brownies and Jaylyn pushed aside junk mail on the dinette table to set down iced tea. Gran put a big brownie in front of her. "How come Gabe and Lionel aren't with you?"

"I dropped Gabe off at little league, and Lionel's at work."

"Ach, I'm being a dumb Polack. Don't you *ever* let anyone call you a dumb Polack. That's right, Lionel told me. He calls all the time, you know. He said you were in an incident with the police. I bet you had to use your shooter training. Least that Edina High School taught you something useful."

"A man was arrested, no guns, and you know my high school's in west Minneapolis."

"Same crowd, practically."

Jaylyn squished brownie crumbs with her finger. She'd been through active-shooter drills for years, practicing lockdowns. The new video this spring was an upsetting reenactment. You did not see anyone shot, but you saw cornered kids, and the biggest threw a backpack, a weapon clattered to the floor, and the rest scattered in different directions. A green-haired white girl hid under a computer desk. A police officer barged in, rifle ready, and barked at her. Crying, she held out trembling hands to prove herself harmless. He wasn't there to calm her. He rushed off, gun leading, to take down a man. The acting was too good. The officer's eyes were hard.

Gran was nattering on, "Thea and Flo brag on their grandkids, think they're the bee's knees. They haven't heard someone like *you* at the piano. Too bad light rail flattened your teacher's husband. Your aunt Lyndsay will get that genius teacher for you. Lazar, the Jewish one."

"*Gran.*"

"Oh, he's Polish like us. Nazis went after Polish Jews and Catholics. Now don't go thinking there was hanky-panky between Lyndsay and Lazar." Lyndsay was the prodigal daughter who escaped to NYC presumably to be a pianist. Instead she became a Wall Street whiz. She and Gran got along best at a thousand-mile distance. "Jaylynnie, you're finishing your credits, 'course you are. You be careful picking up those boxes in the garage."

"*Ow!*" Blood beaded around Jaylyn's sandal strap. Blood made her woozy. "The cat got me."

Gran dropped her white mane beneath the Formica and scooped up an orange kitten, the harvest-gold kitchen reincarnated as a vicious mini-beast. "Snippet, stop that or I'll pin you to the clothes line. Jaylynnie, you better get help."

"I'm fine."

"Not for addiction because you're sober now. I mean loading the boxes in that Jeep of yours to drop at the church. This house, I should sell it. Flo is selling hers, so's we're on the top of the senior apartment waitlist. Call that nice white . . . that boy? The boxes, I'm talking about."

Jaylyn's mouth had gone dry with Gran's badgering. She was asking now if Jaylyn's *graduated* friends were too good for hard work. What they were was hyper-scheduled. And she could not call, had no current number, for that disappearing act, Josh. Retta . . . no, Retta had multiple waitress jobs, but Ramon might be free. Gran's junk might include useful stuff they could use for an apartment. Kill two birds with one stone. She shouldn't have thought about killing—it reminded her of Ramon's dad almost killing him, the missing Luna, the way the hard-eyed policeman in the shooter video merged with the café detective—only there was a difference she couldn't catch.

To her relief, Ramon responded to a text saying he could help.

IT TURNED INTO A TRIAL, getting Ramon to Gran's. He had to leave the delivery van at a drug store for another driver, take the bus, etc., etc. Ramon liked cool clothes and wore chinos from a smart label. Jaylyn worried he'd stain them.

Then she worried that Gran would eat up Ramon's terrible stories about his past and work herself into a state and then everyone else into a state trying to settle her down.

The opposite happened. Ramon charmed Gran as they crowded into a garage built for a Model T and not the storage of a lifetime. Of course he did. He served high-needs people all the time with his deliveries, and he was determined to make something of himself. (Retta needed more of that determination.) Ramon dodged questions about his background and played up how great it was that the family supported Jaylyn's music (though he had yet to hear her play). Gran rattled on about how she never finished high school, her husband and son died young, her daughter in New York was a finance hotshot and too busy to come home, and just so you know—Gran hugged Jaylyn at this point—she spent years building up a nest egg for the grandkids' education. She touched Ramon's arm. "I was a receptionist at Tool and Die. Those men, the filth out of their mouths could tar a road to Mexico." Then Gran's friend Flo drove her Buick LeSabre almost into them. Gran stage-whispered to Ramon, "Flo will talk your nose off then start in on your ears," and left for a Walmart shopping spree to replace the stuff she was giving away.

Ramon backed the Jeep up to the boxes. Jaylyn was about to compliment Ramon on being so sweet with Gran when his mood plunged and he half-sobbed, "Is there anything good here?"

"We don't have to deal with it all today. Oh, I forgot how much you've moved." Jaylyn didn't mean to trigger the trauma of constant uprooting.

Ramon changed the topic. He had curious streak, which helped him educate himself. "Retta told me that the cops attacked people at the café. I shouldn't have left you guys alone." He held up a rusted iron skillet.

"That can be saved. They arrested somebody who had drugs, that's all. No one was hurt." No one, she recalled, but the tall detective. She felt it when the table hit him.

"They were going to arrest a girl?"

"She hadn't been home, that's all."

"Retta thought you recognized her. You're sure you're fine?"

Jaylyn shrugged it off. "Retta exaggerated about the police."

"They didn't pay attention when her dad beat her and her mom. I can't believe a cop tried to suck up to you guys."

Jaylyn bent over a box of dishes. "This set's good." She felt confused.

Ramon sounded confused. "I thought your gran had a big place."

"That's Nana, in Golden Valley."

"Huh. I could use a drink."

"I'll get it. We can't let the cat out."

"I need to pee." He made a "need-to-pee" face.

She giggled, "All right, go ahead."

Snippet made a dash for it. Jaylyn caught her, and when Ramon returned, she tossed the cat back inside. He had to hurry. He reached for a box high on a storage shelf, spilling Grandpa Dudek's old clothes. Sweeping up a fedora, Ramon angled it on his head. Jaylyn laughed until she noticed the mouse poop on the brim, and Ramon threw the hat away with a mock screech. Jaylyn set aside the boxes she would take to Ramon and Retta when they had their apartment, delivered Ramon to the bus stop and the other boxes to St. Hedwig's. She'd done her good deeds for the day.

But as she headed home, queasiness returned. It could be the old Jeep making death rattles, or anxiety over that Liszt étude she had wildly decided against her teacher's advice to use as an audition showpiece. Usually it was music she couldn't shake from her head. This time it was images of Ramon in the fedora, the hard-eyed policeman, the girl with attitude.

Jaylyn felt a slash across her heel and veered from her lane. Snippet, hiding under the seat. Back to Gran's it was. Just when Jaylyn should move forward, it was three steps back.

CHAPTER 12

DEB ASSUMED ANY ACTION she would get on a lovely Thursday evening would be online progress on the Routh case. If only she had been right.

She toiled late in the G-Met office, where an asthmatic dragon had wrapped itself around the building to wheeze hot air through the vents. Cyber Paul had forwarded Dan Routh's phone records. There was the land line, used to call the drugstore, daughter Brenda who never picked up, the stepdaughter who did, and Gordy Omdahl. Two calls last week went to Dan's former police partner, Jack Meshbesser, with a duration of seconds, and three more with the same duration, suggesting a transfer to Meshbesser's voicemail. The cell number showed more calls to Gordy and many to the Resource. There were calls to burner phones, presumably kids Dan wanted to help. Gordy Omdahl, who called G-Met a few times a day, making him more nuisance than help, told her that the street kids used burner phones so they wouldn't be tracked. She homed in on two numbers. Dan's cell showed erratically recurring calls from the same number for two weeks prior to his death. Sunday of the murder, Dan called that number at three in the afternoon, received a call back an hour later, and then received a call about 11:30 p.m. Since Luna Johnson was supposed to meet Dan, Deb speculated that the recurring number was Luna's burner and that Luna put Dan off until a late-night panic call.

Deb dropped her head to her desk and mentally replayed an earlier phone call with Luna Johnson's father, who stayed in Missouri but took over from the grandmother Mrs. Kearns the job of harassing her. He threatened to hire a private detective, and Deb begged him to hold off because it could interfere with the G-Met investigation. It might well come to hiring a PI who could pin down people in literal ways, muscle on concrete. Deb assured Mr. Johnson that G-Met was watching Luna's bank account. The girl had depleted it Sunday morning before disappearing, but Luna's father routinely transferred several hundred dollars into the account. The next transfer would occur at 12:01 a.m. next Tuesday, and they might track her to an ATM. Mr. Johnson hung up without saying goodbye.

Deb lifted her head to yawn, startled herself with the realization that it was well after 8 p.m., and jumped into action. She had a pressing, or depressing, errand. Last week she succumbed to the inspiration that she would not only bike to work during summer months, she would do that famous weeklong trek across Iowa, RAGBRAI. Hyped up, she bought a special alloy design for thousands of dollars, not to mention cool gear. Then her credit card bill arrived, her Prius needed repairs, with the result that the new bike waited in that Prius to be returned to REI. RU Crazy to spend so much and work so late, she scolded herself.

Deb returned the gear to the Bloomington location off I-494, the southern loop of the Twin Cities beltway. Edging to the 9:00 closing, the clerks didn't drag on about how they could serve her better and other non-helpful helpfulness. She then drove over the interstate to a noodle restaurant, because noodles she could afford. Closed. Too famished for pride, Deb ate alone at a taco place. Cucumber vodka in the freezer at home would have to be her vegetable for the evening. She drove away from the sunset onto I-494 east.

A dispatch call startled her, and she pulled over into the breakdown lane as passing trucks rumbled her car.

A warped voice addressed her, "Yo, Metzger, task-force gal. Undercover officer Code Name Squeegee here. Heard you're interested in the LeClercs. There's an ongoing incident at the Airport LeClerc Simple. I'm linking you into the Bloomington police line."

"I'm there."

"What?"

"On 494, the exit's in a mile."

Squeegee ended the call with "Cool to be you," and in a minute Deb was wending through the service roads into the back lots of hotels. Behind the neon, the landscape dropped off darkly into the wildlife refuge that edged the Minnesota and Mississippi Rivers, where bodies were occasionally found. At the far edge of a parking lot, she saw a van parked at an angle, two women with skirts up to their butts clinging to each other, a figure heaped on the pavement, and two men up in each other's business. Sirens blared and arriving Bloomington officers dazzled the group with their headlights. Deb jumped out first. The two women—girls—screamed, "*Back off, back the fuck off!*" The men were aware of nothing but their determination to kill each other. The squat one—Deb could see his clenched face—yelled, "*I'll slice your fucking throat,*" and reached to his shin. The other, back to Deb and in a polo shirt of all things, shoved the squat man's shoulder—"*Leave.*" Squat man regained his footing to punch a fist into his adversary's mouth, who to save himself from falling, grabbed at the squat man's shirt, and both went down.

One officer drew a Taser, the second his Glock. One girl reached toward the fighting men, while her companion drew her away in a push-me-pull-you maneuver. "*Police. Stop,*" ordered the Glock officer. The squat man raised his arm to strike polo shirt.

Deb shouted, full power, "*Raccoons, rabid. Rabid. They bite. There.*" Everyone froze, until the squat man started to rise, the girls shrieked, the Taser popped, and Deb flinched with shock at the prong's impact. No, she hadn't been hit, she realized in a gasp, but she'd been Tased during training and her body never forgot. The two officers hauled up the squat man, limp from the jolt, and back-up cruisers arrived. Two more officers ran to the screaming girls still standing, and the third girl raised herself up from the heap. It was Luna.

The man on the ground stirred and Deb was on him, securing his hand with plastic cuffs. *To keep you out of trouble,* she was about to say when she realized who he was. "Geoff? Mr. LeClerc?"

"Excuse me, do I know you?" Blood running from his mouth, Geoff remembered his manners.

"Detective Metzger, Deb Metzger. We met . . . never mind. What are you doing here?" She pulled him up with a vise hold on his right forearm. He choked and spit blood. No prep school Lacrosse game had prepared Aunt Nan's boy for this level of violence. "Medics will be here ASAP, Geoff, Mr. LeClerc."

He raised his pained eyes to hers and said tightly, "Can't you people stop this? I thought you were stopping this." He jerked his head toward the girls and the movement was followed by an *aah* of pain. The squat man was escorted away, and Geoff spat, "*You watch it,*" which set off more pained *aahs* until he turned back to Deb, hissing, "*This, this—*"

Deb spouted a cliché, "We'll get to the bottom of this. Ambulances are here, Mr. LeClerc. You've got some abrasions, and that jaw"—that smooth pampered jaw didn't hang right—"they might want to x-ray that."

The evening would stretch into exhausting interviews. The van, the presence of girls, the knife holster that the squat man strapped around his leg, it all had to connect.

"Detective Metzger?" A back-up officer interrupted her process of deduction. "I'm notifying DNR about the raccoons, only"—Deb prepared to fess up that the critters were imagined as a ploy—"I see tracks for one and my light caught one pair of eyes at the edge of the refuge. Where did you see the other?"

"Same place," she lied.

CHAPTER 13

Friday morning was no better than Thursday night, when Deb and Erik first questioned the squat man from the hotel scene, Charles Monteiro. Last night, the man had the smugness that came with hiring an overpriced lawyer who didn't bother waking up. With eyes closed, the lawyer nodded approval with every "no comment" Charles made. Monteiro preferred to be called Charles, and he revealed nothing about his shenanigans with three women in the hotel lot. Charles was in holding when a Minnesota Bureau of Criminal of Apprehension special agent called dibs on him. Deb's plans for the day had not included being stuck in a G-Met conference room with a brooding Erik and Mr. Condescending Special Agent.

"We have the resources to track down information on Monteiro." The special agent refused to sit in the rickety G-Met chair. Special agents were supposed to keep in tip-top shape: this short one was bottom-heavy with duck feet. Even his voice was kind of a quack. "We're close to having a court-ready case on an assault on another man from three weeks ago. Our forensics will sweep Monteiro's van and check for a match for Luna Johnson's DNA. You've already had a go at the women, Detective Metzger. They recalled nothing about your Luna or Dan Routh."

"They're still coming down from their highs," she grumbled. Her hopes sunk miserably last night when she realized that the youngest girl did not have Luna's bewitched eyes. Hers were a drugged brown.

The agent persisted with his royal 'we.' "We'll release the suspect but will be following him and have a warrant to tap his phones. Your man Greg—"

"Geoff," Deb corrected.

"Did not wish to press charges. The women and Charles said he started the fight near the LeClerc Simple and Embarrassment Suites."

"'Embarrassment' was Geoff's name for the rival hotel, not the real—"

"Before you interrupted," Special Agent chided her, "I was about to say the hotels don't want to be involved, and your Geoff does not want to press charges."

"He's not *my* anything. He doesn't want to upset his elderly aunt, who might—"

"Let it drop. We'll keep you apprised. Nice to meet you both." The BCA special agent left them to the stale G-Met air.

"How come he's 'special' and we're not?" Deb groused to her too-silent partner. She was in a mood. A Big Dark Broody mood.

"Because we're originally from Iowa? Generic Midwest, pigs and people."

Despite his wisecrack, Erik was in a tight-browed funk. They couldn't both be in a mood. They needed to schedule that out, take turns. "Something's bothering you, partner. Try expressing a feeling."

Erik struggled with that.

Deb resumed, "Look, the girl that collapsed is sixteen and at the hospital detoxing. There's a charge there somewhere against Sir Charles, *who they're effing releasing*. He sure looks good for the Routh killing."

"His arms are short."

"His arms are short. That's bothering you, his arms are short. Not everybody has windmill blades for appendages."

"Really short, even for his five-four height. Hardly an elbow." Erik pushed his windmill arm down on the wooden chair, which cracked.

"This offends you because . . .?"

"The dumpster. I had trouble getting up on the dumpster. Forensics used ladders. Dan Routh was muscular, impulsive, and five-ten. Spiked with adrenaline, he could get in."

"What about Luna?"

"If someone pushed or threatened her and she's panicked, yes. At five-six, regular proportions, Luna wouldn't be forearm-challenged. Your man Charles—"

"Charles is not my man. Geoff is my man, only I don't want a man. I want a woman, personally speaking."

"Well, the BCA's man Charles doesn't run from trouble—he fights back. Punches below the belt because he's there already."

"So you're saying we keep searching for a killer because of his arms."

"Because of his arms." Erik rubbed his face. "What I really don't understand about the incident is why the Department of Natural Resources is messaging me updates on raccoons at the wildlife refuge not being rabid."

Deb shrugged like she didn't know. She needed away from raccoons, men who weren't hers, released suspects, the case, her partner. She needed to whack a golf ball hard and high.

CHAPTER 14

Late night Friday, Erik wanted action and he wanted sleep. He lay in bed, progress made on the latter account. Rapid resolution on the cop-rumor side of the Routh case would have made a great sleep aid. Before being released by the BCA, Charles Monteiro from the hotel incident said he had 'friends' in St. Paul who would vouch for him. Were these friends associates of drug lord Vernon Grimes, police officers, or police officers who were associates of Grimes? A review of Routh's financials showed that eight years back, he invested in the Omdahl garages. Where had that initial sum come from? Erik's clock flashed 11:30 p.m. He slept well when Ben was in the house. However, the boy had graduated (!) from preschool, and as recognition of his class's achievement in learning not to bite each other, they were rewarded with a sleepover at the Apple Valley Zoo.

It went without saying that the best cure for insomnia involved a woman and a little imagination. Very little imagination.

There was no woman. That left reading.

People persisted in giving Erik mystery novels—morbid Scandinavian tomes in which it never stopped raining and antidepressants existed only as an overdose option. He received other types, which he rarely finished. He selected one set in Minnesota. A broodingly handsome bad boy-investigator had women *throwing* themselves at him, begging to have his babies. Erik threw the book at the wall.

That left the ultimate remedy, *The Song of Hiawatha*. Erik picked up the volume of Icelandic sagas overlaid with Ojibway lore as rewritten by a New Englander. He typically fell into a stupor at "how he lived, and toiled and suffered, / That the tribes of men might prosper." Erik couldn't face Heroic Hiawatha sacrificing for his people. He hustled himself up and pulled on his nighttime running gear. With the reflective shoes and vest, he could be a lighthouse on the shining Big-Sea-Water.

He did not make things easy on himself, having decided to drive his Highlander from his Linden Hills apartment to the dumpster site in St. Paul, forty minutes to an hour, depending. Rough eastside bars like Paddy Wagon were favorites with gangs, and Erik had reached out to undercover agents to listen for tips. He would focus on activity around the *Celebrate!* That store did not operate 24/7, because two years back, street kids hung out for night dealing and drinking. The area remained questionable.

If only Erik knew what questions to ask.

SLEEP WHEN IT DIDN'T WANT TO COME could be darn ornery. Gordy placed a sock over his eyes to block out his clock's neon numbers, no good. He put the sock over the clock itself. The blinking 12:47 showed through. Ellie, lying on his feet, sneezed, and Rainbow on the floor twisted onto her spine and farted.

That did it. Gordy got up. The dogs padded after him and woke up Dorothy in the kitchen. She'd been exiled there until it was certain that her barfing episodes were history. Ellie yipped. She must need to go out. Gordy should've gotten Dan a dog.

Ellie and Rainbow hopped around as he reached for the leashes and his jacket. Dorothy had to stay behind and whimpered her resignation. Outside, a half-moon softened the night. Tomorrow flower buds would open, and Gordy would see his grown sons. They'd come through his early drinking days and the divorce all right. Despite this reassuring thought, Gordy's chest tightened. Why do you get mad at people when they die? Dan had turned his life around the hard way. He had left the police force before they made him leave, and after a few weeks of burning through his severance pay in bars, he'd come to an AA meeting to state, "Hi, I'm Dan and I'm an alcoholic." He'd reminded Gordy of himself, a good-enough guy except for demon drink, so Gordy became Dan's mentor.

It looked good at first when Dan found a job as a security guard. But habits are habits. Dan had a temper and any little thing set him off. He would drop by a bar, *just this once*. It was never just once, and Dan quit his new job during a hangover.

By then Dan was desperate for money, and Gordy loaned him thousands on the condition he go back to AA meetings. Gordy rearranged his schedule at his auto-repair shops to prepare Dan for job interviews, and Dan picked up a security job in a medical suite on the evening shift. Gordy escorted Dan home until Dan had the habit of *not* picking up a bottle at happy hour, *not* taking a swig before bed. He wasn't sure Dan would make it. Then Dan began attending AA meetings on his own and connecting with groups that helped young addicts. There were still stretches when Dan could not be reached. Gordy should have asked what's up, only it probably had to do with him convincing people on the sly to leave behind a gang or a pimp-boyfriend. Dan never had a miracle, the can't-miss road mark that life had changed for the better. Gordy had.

The dogs sniffed at smashed poop on the sidewalk. Gordy pulled a bag from his windbreaker to scoop it up and realized he'd walked the mile to Dan's house with its police tape. A man slipped around toward the back door. That detective, whose name was . . . Rick? "Hey, Rick!" he called out. "Oh, Erik!"

It was not the detective. The man held a thing straight down in his hand and came at Gordy fast. The dogs jerked at the leashes and Gordy, heart ka-thumping, tripped.

GORDY OMDAHL'S HAND SHOOK AS he handled the knife. Erik, sitting in Gordy's kitchen, didn't volunteer to help because he had a towel on his lap and on the towel a massive Newfie rested her head. With each stroke of Dorothy's fur, Erik's blood pressure dropped a point. The kitchen clock hands pointed to a Spitz and a Collie, AKA 2:30 a.m. Below the clock hung a framed Gandhi quotation: *in a gentle way, you can shake the world.*

Gordy fixed a ham sandwich, and Dorothy's eyes followed the sandwich as it went to Erik. He talked as Gordy fixed another. "It's not unusual for people to case out empty houses. Whoever it was disappeared fast. Do you know if Dan's keychain had an address attached?"

"They took his keys?" Gordy staggered at the counter.

"The patrol will stay in the area." Erik had been pulling up to check Dan's house when Gordy stumbled into the street, and Erik slammed his brakes and flashed his lights to make an oncoming car swerve away. He caught the barest glimpse of a midsize man. He calmed Gordy down and offered to take him and his pets home. Rainbow gagged all the way.

"I was rattled. Thought it was you, investigating." He handed Erik the sandwich. "You, eat. Dan, I should've been watching him. I had a miracle happen. I wish Dan did."

The sharpness of Erik's hunger hit him, and he bit into the ham. He took another bite. Thick Sunday-dinner ham, butter, homestyle bread—a farmer sandwich like the ones Erik's Grandfather Jansson ate coming in off the tractor. "Absolutely nothing that happened is your fault, Gordy. You helped Dan find a purpose." Erik swallowed another bite. "For example, take—"

Dorothy grabbed the sandwich out of his hand, down in a gulp.

"Dorothy! Sorry, I can't punish her because you said the T word." Gordy held out a bread crust and said "take" and Dorothy took. Rainbow and Ellie crowded in for their share. "Here, you have the rest of mine. You need it more'n I do. Dan and I were walking in the park last week. Wish I could remember what he said."

Erik chewed this over, along with the rest of Gordy's sandwich. "You could try writing everything down. If you start writing without worrying about what's important . . . I didn't mean right now. You can rest."

But Gordy had pulled a notebook out of the counter drawer and started writing in loose loops. He breathed hard with his head close to the pen. Erik glanced around as he waited. Was Gordy's miracle winning the lottery? He had the Rolls Royce of toasters, and Erik could fall into a sleep coma on the luxurious leather in the sitting area.

Erik had almost dozed off like the three dogs when Gordy gave him the notebook. "Can you read it?"

Erik read aloud:

Dan was meeting a woman he had been meeting before. Skittish. She was afraid of a man. Her name sounds French and another thing was French. Her name was like a song. The song was in a movie about stealing from a casino. It was a good movie. I like George Clooney and he was in it. A piano plays the song which is like two names. It's a French song like that Saint Paul street Saint Clair. Clair-de-Luna or like that. They were meeting at a French place but it wasn't a restaurant and I asked and Dan said he shouldn't of told me. I should forget it. I forget things then I remember. A young man was in trouble. Dan had helped him before. Dan helped people. They shouldn't of killed him. Dan wanted to travel. The dells are in Wisconsin. That's a good place to go with kids because of the water slides.

"You're a good reader," Gordy said. "You must've paid attention in school."

"Had to. My mother was a teacher and is now a superintendent."

"These kids on the street could use a person like that. There's something else."

"You don't need to write more tonight, Gordy. This is a big help." It confirmed that Dan interacted with Luna, not much else. "I can see myself out."

Gordy ignored Erik's words to limp after him. Outside, he repeated that there was something he had to remember. With his good night, Erik promised Gordy that he would check in with him again and opened his Highlander door.

Gordy had his hand on the door handle. "I got it. I'm offering a reward. That's it. I'll set it up first thing in the morning. That'll speed everything up for ya."

Or bury Erik under false leads.

CHAPTER 15

Eight thirty Saturday morning and G-Met Chief Ibeling had gone fishing, so no brownie points for showing up at the office. Deb tripped around a figurine on the floor outside the chief's door, a white-tailed deer with bluebirds perched on the antlers. The eighteen-inch Bambi sported a sign around its neck: THE BUCK STOPS HERE.

Deb stood and the HVAC system whinnied. Could be a red Swedish Dal horse trapped up there, a friend of Bambi's. The whinny followed her as she passed the office of Erik's nemesis, Drees. Drees, that tool, imagined his shiny self to be the department wunderkind and likely had a pedestal in there to stand on. She passed the office of a female detective and speculated that in another dimension she and her might be the same person since they were never in the same place at the same time. She paused at a cracked door decorated with the royal lion-and-unicorn coat of arms, the office of Jimmy Bond Smalls, AKA the Black James Bond. Smalls claimed he was hired for this stereotypical reason: G-Met needed a handsome, smooth-talking African American to be cool. Deb chided herself that she had no time to chat. She entered her office—no Erik. How could he get off not showing up? With a murder and a missing girl, you work 8-12 days straight. Maybe he was out being transcendental with a tree somewhere. Pre-Bambi, there had been a circulating G-Met plaque that announced PASSIVE on one side and AGGRESSIVE on another. What had happened to that plaque? PASSIVE/ AGGRESSIVE would be perfect for Erik's desk.

Deb updated notes on the Luna side of the case. According to her grandmother, Luna burned through cheap Tracfones and had a special one for her new boyfriend. Deb did not tell the grandmother that the morgues were keeping an eye out for Jane Does. The friends said Luna had been making herself scarce ever since meeting that new boyfriend. Like maybe Deb could find Luna where they serve chunky monkey ice cream because she wouldn't give up chunky monkey for the world. The frustration made Deb's overheated head buzz. No, that was the HVAC.

Autocorrect was altering "Luna" to loony when Deb's cellphone said, *the queen calls*, the notification that Nancy Leclerc demanded attention. Multiple messages, as dictated by Nancy to her assistant Jude. Would Deb keep Nancy informed on the Routh investigation because Nancy was most disturbed by the tragedy? Would Deb stand in for the previously scheduled Routh at a LeClerc fundraising golf outing? Would Deb schedule this coming week a meeting with the LeClerc CEO, Luis Peña, on developing advanced anti-trafficking training for employees?

Deb had the damn right to procrastinate. Nancy's demands did not constitute a G-Met priority, and she had to be at the Resource to interview people Dan Routh rescued. It was strange that Nancy made no mention of Geoff's scuffle in the parking lot. Geoff had explained to Deb that night that recently the hotel board had discussed "problem party behavior" around the hotels. A few lax managers were fired, and Geoff had taken it on himself to do spot checks "to keep up the standards." He had expected drunk teens, not thuggish Charles. Deb scrolled through Nancy's demands again to make sure she hadn't missed anything life-or-death. Huh, below each demand, sexy Jude added emoji: a winking face, an "oh-no" face, and a golf bag with a thumbs-up. Interesting. Deb typed a reply *on a hush-hush case, shhh.* Too dorky, deleted. She retyped *on the case*, followed by a cartoon Snoopy carrying a golf bag. She hit send.

Going out the door, she tripped around the buck figurine. THE BUCK STOPS HERE, right. She rolled her head back, the HVAC horse whinnied, and grit fell in her eye. Deb bolted.

CHAPTER 16

SATURDAY STARTED WITH JAYLYN BEING JARRED AWAKE at ten by a phone call. Lionel wanted to know if Ramon's last name was Kenney, Kinney, or Kinny; then he could run a background check on Ramon's dad during his work break, for fun. Lionel, who *thought* he had the answer to everything, got it into his head that Ramon's dad killed the former policeman, Root or Routh. Without a word, Jaylyn turned her phone off. Lionel had not glimpsed the hollowness behind Ramon's eyes, a hollowness carved out by loss and pain. She turned the phone back on to have a word with her cousin and saw a new message: Fritz Lazar would see her at eleven. She tizzied herself around gathering sheet music, and then the Jeep engine would not turn over at all.

That put her on an Uptown bus desperate for relief. In the past, pills floated her there. Pills would do her no good, reason lectured. Yet moments like this, with a white woman glaring at her from across the aisle, she had a rush of unpleasant memories, recalling all the slights that had come her way. She worked at convincing herself that the slights were hardly a blip compared to the insults and assaults examined in her mom's magazine, *Minority Nurse*. For Jaylyn, many involved music—why not play jazz, blues, funk, why music by dead white men? Classical types weren't all white, weren't all men, weren't all dead, and Jaylyn did play *un peu de tout*. She didn't understand it herself, how she found passion in scores that teemed with sharps, flats, accidentals, *decrescendo, crescendo, dolce, agitato, furioso*.

A chaperone. Should Jaylyn have a chaperone to be alone with this man? Aunt Lyndsay hadn't needed one. Lyndsay, though, had a core of steel. Jaylyn had a core of butterflies. She shouldn't wish for a field of poppies as she rang the apartment buzzer for genius teacher Fritz Lazar, but she did. She crossed the threshold.

Following notes stuck to doors, she passed by an arched opening to a Euro-styled kitchen and through another arch into a room where a grand piano sat atop layers of Persian rugs. Opposite was a leather sofa adorned with brocade pillows, and next to that, an overstuffed chair flattened by an oversized man behind a newspaper. He swore hoarsely to himself. "Sue those Big Pharm bastards. Stuff their own damn medicine down their throats. Let them OD themselves to the grave." He threw down the paper with its opioid lawsuit headlines and boomed, "What's this?"

"I'm Jaylyn," her voice trembled. "Lindsay Dudek's niece."

"Obviously I'm Lazar." He hauled himself to unsteady feet. Once handsome, he had mottled skin that lacked red corpuscles; once tall, he hunched. He drank his career away, they said, a star turned addict. He seized a few breaths. "Well, Ms. Dudek, you better have more talent than Lindsay did. Though it wasn't talent she lacked or will—she had an abundance of will—it was musical imagination. Don't look shocked. I don't bite." Lazar grabbed the back of an ergonomic chair on wheels positioned by the keyboard. "Pull up the bench. Begin with the usual modulation of scales."

Jaylyn sat and raised her hands.

"You should know better. Adjust the bench. Your hands have a good span. No complaints about reaching notes."

Could she trust him? A figurine on the piano seized her eye, Minnesota's purple Prince. After Prince died from a fentanyl overdose, Nana and Mom had mournfully placed similar figurines in places of honor. She started the scales.

She was stopped. "Mechanical. Even scales should be musical. Do lyric." Lazar shambled across the room to a cabinet, pulled out yellowed music, and placed it on the piano. "Play."

Claire de Lune. Debussy's too-familiar piece had to sound as if it had fallen fresh from the sky. Jaylyn teared up with the strain of playing for this strange man.

"Breathe. Wish me away."

Jaylyn closed her eyes. So much to wish away—her stalled life, Retta and Ramon's drama, this strange man, an ominous dread she didn't understand. She played from memory. After letting her hands lift from the last chord, she opened her eyes.

Lazar was studying the Prince figure. "There's potential. I'm to be paid in cash." He named a stunning amount, and Jaylyn flashed with anger.

"How much again? You didn't say over the phone!"

"I had to know if you were worth it. You'll not need to pay for today. Unlike medical professionals, I do not charge for mere entry of my space. By the way, if you ever have a movement issue, find a sports doc who understands the mechanics. Be wary. Believe me, it's a *pain* to change docs. So you missed your University audition slot because of illness, and completing that is your aim. I understand you have a Beethoven sonata, this piece, and you want to add a showstopper. You have selected one, committed the notes to memory?"

Jaylyn tried to sound easy about it. "Oh, the Liszt *Étude Number Six*, the one based on Paganini."

"Yes, yes, I know the one. *Pum—ta-didididi-Pum*. Don't waste your money. Some Mendelssohn? No? Wait, did one of your piano compatriots claim he, or maybe it was a she, could play the Liszt while you weren't capable?" Lazar peered down his nose. "And you want to knock them from their high horse?"

Her legs in shorts stuck to the scratchy bench pad. "Um, there was this violinist . . .." He'd been a cutie and she was rebounding from the disappearance of her "mono" boyfriend Josh. "And I thought we could collaborate on pieces and instead . . .." The violinist wanted suck-up adoration. He'd shoved aside the Bach duo, a rhythmic disaster for them both, and insisted on impressing her with the Paganini *Caprice 24 for Solo Violin*, the theme and a few variations. She knew the variations were too slow and he'd skipped the hardest ones. To top it off, he'd made a pass at her.

"Finish sentences, Ms. Dudek, and ignore pissant violinists. The Liszt after all, play like the devil. Come back daily next week." As Lazar stood, his hand slipped from the chair back and he pitched forward. Jaylyn caught him under the armpit with her shoulder, a move perfected when she had assisted her cancer-stricken dad. Lazar groaned and reached for his chair, which rolled away.

"Get your balance first." Jaylyn couldn't hold him up much longer.

"The couch," he wheezed. With her support, he lurched in that direction and twisted to go down on his back.

Jaylyn propped a tasseled pillow beneath his legs. "I'll call 911."

"No, just a pill," he hissed. "Shouldn't have changed meds. In the kitchen, over the sink, brown bottle."

Jaylyn ran to the kitchen and opened cupboards until she found the pharmacy of a madman. Ancient antihistamines, Motrin, Midol (Midol?), baby aspirin, herbal wraps, green bottles, pink, emetics. She picked up a Percocet bottle, five years out of date. She shoved it behind everything. It was worse than her dad's medicine cabinet at the depths of his suffering. A locked cabinet for Dad; she knew about the key. Then he was dead. After the first round of pill use, she'd relapsed and hidden pills high in her closet. Her brother Gabe, five at the time, got hold of them and went running to their mother. Mom screamed and screamed at Jaylyn, "Gabe could have swallowed these, *all of them*, *every single one*. How could you, how dare you? Don't you love your brother? Don't you love us?" Her mother sobbed, sobbed harder than she had at the funeral.

Jaylyn wiped her eyes, grabbed the bottle and water. Ramon had told her that a pharmacist could come in and overdose-proof a home. It took legal waivers, a physician's cooperation, and a fee. Then the measured doses could be delivered in a proper fashion.

Lazar had propped himself up, his mottled face like a dead fish belly. He took a pill and returned the bottle to Jaylyn. "Back where you found it, Ms. Dudek. Liszt," he gasped, "practice it slowly. Remember, fast playing is slow playing done fast." Exhausted, he fell back.

Jaylyn took the pills to the kitchen and rushed to the bus. The loud hip-hop coming through her earbuds couldn't quell the anxiety. She had no wish to roam the Twin Cities carrying wads of cash to pay a weirdo. Ramon didn't carry cash on his deliveries for safety's sake. She should work up the nerve to tell Ramon, get his pharmacy on the case. She was certain Lazar's pills were opioids, or Lazar had an irregular supplier. Black-market pills in a brown bottle, a terrifying temptation.

CHAPTER 17

At 2:20, DEB SWALLOWED TYLENOL and consumed her lunch of a yogurt drink while sitting in her Prius on the public golf course lot. After, she opened the hatchback to change into her gecko-soled golf shoes and grab her rolling bag. She wished she could play the course through Hole 15, which featured a bunker in the shape of Charles Schultz's Snoopy. She couldn't take the time because she was itching to pop into hotels along the I-494 corridor. Luna, whether being trafficked or partying on her own, might be hidden at one. A few drives would put Deb in a take-charge mental place.

She took a spot on the driving range, set the tee and ball, and wiggled her toes. She raised her driver and with a whoosh swung through. A slice. She switched from her driver to an iron, shifted her shoulders, and sliced with a divot.

The man next to Deb cursed so vigorously that his gut jiggled, "*Damn.* This range is for people who have a clue about the ball."

"Sorry." Deb switched back to the driver. Her next ball went farther into her neighbor's territory.

"Stop hitting like a dyke-bitch. Find a beginner's course."

"Find a walking course yourself."

"*Ahem*, some of us are concentrating," a woman to Deb's left said. When gut-man dropped his head, she mouthed to Deb, "Don't take the bait," and left.

Oh, Deb took the bait all too often. She took sunscreen from her bag and rubbed it on the back of her neck where a muscle twitched. The morning's Resource interviews ate at her. Several young women and men called Dan Routh a savior. He would go to their hangouts—convenience stores, public parks, hotels, bar parking lots—and strike up small talk. A boy recovering from meth addiction talked about how Dan's face "showed he'd been to hell and back." Dan had told him, "When you're sick and tired of this, and you will be, here's places," and gave him information on addiction clinics. Dan provided bus passes, meal vouchers, in a few instances a cheap phone with his number on it. The women were won over when Dan showed up with a little dog or came with a friend whose dog was "a gigunda teddy bear." A woman with tracks on her arm made the point that "perverts" couldn't take care of a dog like that. "She's a mountain rescue dog," she said, "but no brandy keg."

For that, Dan was dead. Deb swung hard for a straight-ish drive. Club suspended behind her, she thought of the one dissenting voice, a girl who ragged, "He was coming on to me. He touched me. No way I'd go with that freak."

Deb's next swing missed the ball entirely. Gut-man jeered, "Let a real golfer have that spot."

"I have a space," answered a familiar voice to her left. The sensible woman had been replaced by Geoff LeClerc in his hornrims. With his face puffy from Thursday night's tussle, his friendly grin was lopsided. He spoke loudly for gut-man's benefit. "It's Detective Metzger, isn't it? Geoff LeClerc." Then for her ears only, "I want to say, kudos to you, you impressed Aunt Nan. That's not easily done lately."

"Because she's worried about trafficking?"

"Deb, your swing indicates you're tense. I'm a sports doc when I'm not busy calming down Aunt Nan, and let me guess," Geoff sighed, "she's the source of the tension. I didn't tell her about the 'scene.' Security knows, obviously, but she tends to blame the wrong people." He teed up, only to stare sullenly at the golf ball. "What I don't get, Detective, is the difference between sex workers, who want their choices respected, and sex victims. I read about sex workers, ever present in human history, in *The Atlantic* . . . think it was *The Atlantic*. The kind that work in places like Amsterdam. That toad of a man who slugged me should be imprisoned, but the woman who lied that she was his girlfriend, weren't you just interfering with her chosen career?"

Deb reddened and kicked the divot back into the sod. "She was held for questioning and released." *Without saying a damn helpful thing.* "The girl who collapsed was sixteen."

"Bastards."

"Mr. LeClerc, Geoff, do you have children? Are you married?" There it was, her foot in her mouth again.

"Marriage . . . why, hmm, I enjoy marriage so much that I've done it three times. As for children, I content myself with playing uncle to Aunt Nan's grand-brood." Though his teasing tone returned, Geoff appeared worried. That made his swollen face resemble Porky Pig's, and Deb rolled her lips in so she wouldn't laugh. He went on, "Lately I worry that Aunt Nan fixates on her issues. A Marriott could be burning with babies inside, and what would she care. If LeClerc Hoteliers were a public company, not family held, she might be forced out. Don't misunderstand me. Aunt Nan is mostly sharp and means well, despite her polished claws." He grimaced. "It's not dementia, I don't think. If she bothers you, let me know. Heard anything from Jude? Excuse me, we shouldn't hold up these eager people. Would you like to get a drink?"

"Thanks, but no. I have to get back to work." Deb noticed Geoff's top-of-the-line shoes. "Do you usually golf on public courses? I would have thought a championship course—"

"Give me a little credit, Deb. I'm a man of the people. You should know you have to change up courses to stay on top of your game." Geoff compressed his lips, his seriousness again undercut by the puffiness. "Tell me if Aunt Nan . . . you know."

If Nancy came between Deb and her work. She gave him a wave-salute and was heading toward her car when Geoff caught up with her. "My card, in case." He handed her one, done in an intricate script.

The heat and humidity were rising, and Deb's car was a suffocating heat box. It closed in on her, the dead ends of the case, the live problem that vulnerable Luna remained missing. She blasted the AC into her face and tossed Geoff's card on the passenger seat. Its script resembled music notes. A light popped in Deb's brain—or was it the ball whizzing past to crack an Impala's windshield? Luna would show up for music.

THE SMELL OF GRASS WAS ENOUGH TO MAKE YOU HIGH. That rainwater aura made pungent with greenness did little to soothe Erik. He muscled through a U-turn because the Sears lawnmower, aged 100 in mechanical years, failed to self-propel. It was 3:40. If he had no G-Met updates by 5 o'clock, the chances of a weekend arrest in the Routh case became nil. He was dedicated to his work with its prolonged hours, but work had cost him his marriage to a dream woman—who'd *cheated*. That was not the whole truth, but as much of the truth as he could bear. Erik shoved the mower ahead. No new information, and he could join his father and little Ben at the campsite near Marine on St. Croix. A sunrise kayak ride, a bracing dip, eggs and sausages sizzling outside—great moments for his son to remember, contingent on his dad frying up full pork Iowa sausage and not the vegan alternative. Erik believed in vegetables to the point of eating them, but they didn't lend themselves to olfactory memories. He stalled out by a bush fragrant with pink roses. His interview with Routh's former partner Jack Meshbesser had left a rotten taste in his mouth. Meshbesser was mean, and mean could cover fear. What did Meshbesser fear? St. Paul Officer Dahlberg, whose blonde hair seemed natural to Erik, had reported that the Topknot dealer recognized Luna's picture as a Kafka Café employee but had never talked with her. Erik yanked the lawnmower's pull-start and yanked again. Life would be a piece of pie (apple and rhubarb were Erik's favorites) if Kristine, if he, if they had stayed together. If only he hadn't driven her to *him*, that base duplicitous bastard mentor—

His phone buzzed with a message. It was William Fridley, an investigator with Minneapolis Police Internal Affairs, who had worked with St. Paul IA when Dan Routh was on the force. William Fridley had not attached Dan's files from a dismissed excessive violence case; instead, he recommended a discreet meeting on Monday.

Erik shut off his phone and about-faced toward the house. A figure stood on a rise, arms crossed. Erik removed his ear protectors and pushed the mower to a confrontation.

"Bond, James Bond. James Bond Jr." The brown boy, seven years old, dropped the British intonation for Midwest flatness. "Mr. Jansson, why are you mowing our lawn?"

"TENDING A LAWN IS WHAT MAKES A MAN A MAN IN THESE PARTS," Jimmy Bond Smalls said to Deb as he poured iced tea in his kitchen. "Erik was pacing a rut into my office floor, so I dispatched him here for a constructive break." Deb followed Jimmy and the tea out the back door to behold grass badly sculpted into waves and dirt patches. Jimmy's eyebrows lifted in dismay as he handed over a glass. "Man, Erik. You're usually such a *perfectionist*."

Erik cooled his cheek with the perspiring glass. "Moles."

"At G-Met? Drees?" Deb knew it. Drees has gone rogue as a mole.

"No, the moley-mole kind."

"Varmints?" The boy, Jimmy Jr., looked up from the dead lawnmower he'd been poking with a stick. "How come you didn't use the new electric mower? It's like a race car. Oops, Dad forgot to charge it. The moles, can we kill them?"

Erik chewed an ice cube and surveyed the disastrous lawn. "You can poison the grubs they eat, but that has an environmental impact on surface water and birds."

"Thank you, Erik, for that prairie sage advice." To his son, Jimmy Sr. said, "Jimmy Jr., google earth-safe mole control." The boy took off at a run for the house.

And Deb took off with Erik. "You know, partner, I have this idea. So we have a missing person announcement out to the authorities on Luna Johnson, probable witness or participant in Dan Routh's death. Nothing. But we know she's into music. There're all these music events this weekend, and we can check them out since she might figure she's safe in a crowd. I've generated a list, and for outdoor stuff there's a country bash, a picnic with the classics, the fundraiser Hirsch Fest, which is a big deal."

"Can't find the iPad, Dad," Jimmy Jr. yelled and his father trotted to the house.

Erik set his glass on the mower and picked up a rock. "Too much. This is Minnesota. Throw a rock and you hit a musician."

"And if it ricochets?"

"It hits a writer. You could contact the music venues' security teams."

"*I* could? Think those bouncers would pay attention to one girl?" Deb stomped a divot.

"But we, who've never seen her, could pick her out of a crowd?"

"We could check the drummers."

"I'm *thinking*." Erik threw the rock. It hit a tree and bounced out of sight into the yard to the west. Someone yelled, "*What the f—?*"

"It's all right, that guy's not the bass player he thinks he is." Jimmy Sr. returned, followed by Jr. with his eyes on a tablet. "The Luna thing, my two cents worth—"

"Yo, Dad, there's tons of traps. See." Jimmy Jr. held up an image of a dead mole, pink claws dangling, caught in steel pinchers, which was exactly how Deb felt.

"Traps, huh," Jimmy Sr. said. "Your gramps used to attach a hose to the car exhaust and stick the hose down their run."

"I thought your father was a peaceable pastor?" Deb said with a harshness not meant for Jimmy. She'd lost Erik's attention. Throw a rock and you'd hit a rock-brained partner.

"O deliver us from plagues," Jimmy Sr. chanted. "Erik, show young Dr. Death here where the mole horde is the worst."

Erik walked the boy to a hedge at the end of the lawn.

"It's about his son," Jimmy said to Deb. "He wants to be with Ben. And he's right, the music venue check is a long shot."

Deb scuffed another divot. "I *hate* it when girls—kids—go missing."

"I get that. Think of what keeps kids from running off. Knowing their parents care. You plan on having kids?"

"Not by sperm donor." Deb watched Erik point to a mound and Jimmy Jr. jump on it, followed by a karate kick and "ay-*yuh*." She inhaled. "So your moles are headquartered under your lilacs, Jimmy."

"I have lilacs? That'd explain the purple—"

"I guess I can make calls to the venues that might appeal to Luna," Deb conceded.

Jimmy Jr. bounded back, trailed by storm-cloud Erik.

"Compromise," Jimmy Sr. said. "The moles get a reprieve, Deb can contact venue security providers and check out the country bash, and Erik can stop by the big Hirsch Fest since it's halfway to Marine on St. Croix."

The village was on the St. Croix River, divider of northern Minnesota and Wisconsin. Deb was curious. "Marine on St. Croix. How did the 'on' get in there?"

"Because, it wouldn't be 'in' the river. Jeez." Jimmy Jr. passed judgment on the grownups.

CHAPTER 18

Jaylyn zigzagged the Jeep, battery replaced, through construction. To follow the detour to the Hirsch Fest, she had to make a left onto a multi-lane road and then a right.

"*Watch it!*" her high school friend Audrey screamed from the passenger seat.

A horn blared, and an Expedition sideswiped the Jeep. The driver flipped the finger while Jaylyn's phone GPS insisted that she make a legal U-turn.

"He was *speeding*. Road rage can be *lethal*. Do you want me to drive, Jaylyn?" Audrey, blonde, bronzed, and graduated, slurped her monster drink. Maybe she wouldn't see how much Jaylyn was shaking. She did see. "Seriously, I can drive."

Jaylyn shook her head no.

"Breathe, girl. Remember, you're empowered by Bach, Beethoven—"

"And Beyoncé," Jaylyn said. She took the next exit too fast.

They had several miles of country road to go. Audrey, daunting in her confidence and competence, grilled her, "Who are you in love with now?"

"I'm not 'in love' with anybody." Jaylyn pretended it was funny.

"Whatever happened to that cutie who grew up on a farm? Was it out this way?" Audrey gave Jaylyn a cautious side eye. She meant the disappearing act, Josh.

"Don't think so." Jaylyn shrugged it off.

"Didn't you meet a cool dude in your remedial classes?"

"They were 'make-up' classes, after the mono." Which she caught from Josh. "That guy's Ramon, he's going with Retta."

Audrey followed with a polite, "How is Retta?" Jaylyn's school friends and rehab co-survivors didn't mix. Audrey bitched that Retta put on a street-cred act, and Retta bitched that Audrey was a résumé whore.

"Oh, wait, that virtuoso beat you out at the piano competitions. Flying-fingered Franklin." Audrey put her hand to her brow. "Oh, Franklin, Franklin, wherefore art thou, Franklin?"

"Quit it," Jaylyn giggled. "Franklin and I have said ten words total to each other."

"See, you're counting." Audrey tilted toward Jaylyn. "He's waiting for you at the U." Franklin—skinny, funny, dark eyes and light Afro—had already begun piano studies at the university.

Jaylyn bumped across a field and parked within a chalk outline. She hopped out and tugged down her dress, a floral pattern that would disguise sweat stains.

Audrey slipped from the Jeep. "What's the pee situation?"

Jaylyn pointed behind the performance shell. "Porta potties."

"Ew! Wait, are those food trucks? I hope they have lots of ice. My shorts are sticking." Audrey pulled the material away from her taut legs. "Think there are Jell-O shots?"

"We're underage," Jaylyn channeled Gran's bluntness. "Besides, it's a dry event."

"Non-alcoholic Jell-O shots?"

"That would be, like, Jell-O. Hey, you're messing with me." Jaylyn whapped Audrey and then took her arm. "Come on, you child. We'll find you a potty and refill your sippy cup."

Audrey laughed herself free. "I'll manage. Ta-ta." She jogged off to grace the porta potties with her beauty.

Jaylyn picked up her musician pass and wandered. The fest was a circus of recovery with peaked tents and side acts. A slope formed an amphitheater that ended in the main stage, with woods framing the back area. She searched the crowd for Teddi, neither pretty nor ugly but magnetic. No one knew Teddi's full story—except Teddi, if she let herself remember.

They had both benefited from rehab and wanted to show support because, like Jaylyn's Nana said, when you've been given much, you give back more. Teddi overlapped with two of Jaylyn's groups, the rehab group and the music group. In the sharing circle, not the one where Jaylyn met Retta but the insurance-covered Hirsch one, the teens had been joking about sex when deadpan Teddi announced, "Sex gets old fast when you've done it since you were four." Teddi was a cutter. She pulled up a long sleeve to display neat scars above the left elbow. "Those on the right are crooked," she'd said. "I can't pass as a lefty."

An incredible mimic, she could pass as many things. Besides nasal white pop stars, Teddi could channel soul singers and once, instead of speaking, she sang, "Cry me a River." Real crying Teddi didn't do. Everyone else in rehab cried, if only as a hand off to the next person in the break-down line. Teddi never did. She told foster-care stories: the goody-goody life savers, the dumb and dumber shits, and the outright poisoners. Lots of harm, no one fouled. A joke, she'd reassure the circle. "It's all good. I'm here contrary to my parents' worst intentions."

After the group ended, Jaylyn invited Teddi to a weekend at Nana's. They listened like the possessed to Grandpa Fowler's vinyl collection. Ella Fitzgerald, the Andrews Sisters, Sarah Vaughan, Rosemary Clooney, John Lee Hooker, Ray Charles, The Cleveland Symphony, gospel, gospel, and gospel. If only Grandpa had been alive to jangle on about his faves. Six months after Jaylyn's dad died, an aneurysm took Grandpa Fowler.

Since then, Teddi hadn't kept in touch except for a few McMillan jams. Then, yesterday, she texted to say her keyboard player had a wisdom tooth implode, and could Jaylyn play backup? Easy noisemaking, good exposure.

Where was she? On the stage, a coffeehouse duo sang woe-is-me lyrics that made Jaylyn want to suck lemons. The growing crowd ignored the performers' life lessons to catch up with rehab roommates: hey, looking fine, wonder-of-wonders. Families spread out blankets for a picnic. She'd asked Retta and Ramon to come, but Retta had picked up a shift cocktail waitressing (don't sneak drinks, Jaylyn prayed). Ramon said maybe and was curious about Hirsch programs. He confessed to Jaylyn that he wished his father had money for rehab. That night his dad had come home crazed to kill—would it have worked if Ramon called an ambulance? Though cops might order medics to inject a fighter with ketamine, elephant anesthetic. If someone was boozed up, the dose could kill.

Teddi . . . there she was, in a polka-dot blouse and high-waisted shorts. She had rolled up her magenta hair into a 1940s do. At the same time a prowling horn player laid eyes on her. "*Ow*, Teddi, you bombshell. Seeing anyone?"

Teddi shook her head *nuh-uh* and, adapting an Irving Berlin standard, sang with a seductive burr, "I've got my clothes . . . to keep me warm." She hugged herself, and the dude took the hint and picked out another chick to hit on. Teddi slipped into Marilyn Monroe at seeing Jaylyn, "Thanks ever so for saving my sweet butt, and my butt looks terrif in this outfit." She dropped Marilyn. "Hey, gal. You look kinda shattered. Where's your family support? Little bro, that cute cousin?"

Teddi, seventeen like Lionel, managed on her own. At a past jam, Teddi said that she was e-man-ci-pated, no more fosters. Jaylyn wanted that kind of tough. "Gabe's with his ten-year-old buds, beating on each other. Lionel's working." Jaylyn's voice tightened. "Mom had a funeral to attend. Her coworker at the hospital had a daughter die." She could tell Teddi. "The daughter was twenty-five, overdose."

"Hey, that's hard." Teddi put her arm around Jaylyn, who sniffled and saw that a tattoo camouflaged Teddi's old cuts. The half-hug lasted one second because Teddi wasn't a toucher. "We'll run through things in the warm-up tent. First, I gotta hit the falafel stand. A body needs what a body needs." Teddi worked her hips as she walked away.

There was Audrey again, the only school friend (Jaylyn thought) who knew about her pill thing, at a table loaded with brochures. Seeing Jaylyn, she thrust forward a basket of lumps smothered by white goo and a brown gelatinous substance. "Tater Tot Poutine?" Jaylyn took the last soggy tots. Her friend tossed the container and picked up brochures. "Duh, addiction's bad for you. Wait, this is touching, from Lily—*the pill took me home inside and the bad went far away.*"

Jaylyn's words—had she given permission?

"You okay?" Audrey asked. "A lot of people abuse for a bit but aren't addicts."

A man the color of dishwater took shape out of nowhere. "Don't you ever think that. Addiction's the Devil." He leaned his ravaged face into Jaylyn's. "Satan waits at the crossroads." He turned on them—a skeleton played drums across his back—and wormed into the crowd.

Audrey dangled the brochures like she'd forgotten what they were. "Who made him the profit of doom? Okay, Jaylyn, don't look so shocked. You warm up your piano chops while I prowl for hot guys. Oh, remember, you got gobs of talent, gobs."

Jaylyn gave a shaky thumbs-up as Audrey went off. The butterflies started as a woman behind her gasped, "Guess anyone can be saved. That's my old dealer."

Dealers, here? It was like finding spit in your glass. Jaylyn stood on tiptoe. Near the stage where a rock group adjusted amps, she saw several men. Was one Ramon? No, Josh. Thinner, harder. In rehab world, thinner meant using.

CHAPTER 19

THE HIRSCH FEST DREW IN ALL SORTS because trouble hit everybody. Gordy set up his "Therapy FUR You" tent away from the stage to give the dogs a bit of peace and quiet. Ellie and Dorothy's ears still twitched in distress when a high lonesome voice crooned "In the Pines." The song made Gordy shiver in the heat. It was too much like last night's dream of Ghost Dan in the Chevy Express driving the two of them over a cliff again and again. If only they could find that telltale van.

Gordy had put himself in a high lonesome mood when Ellie and Dorothy barked like crazy at an approaching dog. A Belgian Malinois—those dogs could jump into trees—pulled a man toward the parking lot. When another man in a Twins baseball cap came from that direction, the dog man made the Malinois sit. The men talked and separated, and Gordy recognized the one with the cap. "Hey there, Erik, good to see ya so soon!"

Dorothy bounded up to Erik, and Gordy and Ellie joined them in the sun. "Dorothy's soft on you. What brings you out?" Oh no, the young man couldn't be a drunk. Gordy backpedaled. "I mean, are you working?"

That Erik had a great smile. "A bit. It looks like your dogs are doing their jobs." Ellie perched on her haunches and waved a paw to attract a passing couple's attention. "Where's Rainbow?"

"You remember! Rainbow's a therapy case herself if the bands get loud, but she's a good reader. She'll sit with schoolkids, and when they read out loud, she tilts her head so's they know she's paying attention. Say, any tips because of the reward yet?"

"In due time. Did Dan ever mention this girl, Luna Johnson?" Erik showed him a photo on his phone.

"Yeah, that's the one who wanted to go to the Dells."

Erik tilted his head like Rainbow would.

"I told you, didn't I?" A tremor shook Gordy. "Wait, I got it now. She liked the Dells, it's where she wanted to go. I took my boys there when they were little for the rides in the 'Ducks' on the river. They loved that. My boys're off fishing. You should meet them. I mean, you didn't find her in the Wisconsin Dells?"

"It's fine, Gordy." Erik put a hand on Gordy's arm to steady him. "Could we sit in your tent?"

As they sat, Erik texted on his phone. He wasn't smiling. Gordy asked, "Are you all right? Did I screw you up?"

"I hit my hip the other day, sore when I sit. You're always helpful, Gordy."

"I never seen her. Dan was talking out loud to himself about Luna, and I asked what's up. He said she was a girl who put off coming in, saying her boyfriend would take care of her. And Dan, he made her mad when he said she could learn to take care of herself. So he switched to a happy thing, like where did she like to go. She said the Dells."

A friend of Gordy's dropped by, and seeing they had business, took the dogs for a walk.

"I must've told you about the Dells. But you'd remember. Since the Miracle, my memory needs practice. Better than most people's if I keep it exercised, the doc says." The salt of tears ran into his mouth. "If I'd been drunk when I had the accident, I woulda been blamed, I, I—"

"Take you time. Your accident . . . was Dan there?"

"Nah, nothing to do with Dan, except it was why I could help him. Don't you want to hear music?" On stage, a woman sang like she was being punched in the gut.

"Not that music."

"I was a plateau drinker," Gordy began. "My dad was, and he acted like a fun guy. Never did squat, which made my mother a sourpuss. I wanted to be like my dad, maybe not the best thing. I did auto repair, got married, me and the wife had two boys. I had a good time with beer, fishing, what guys do." Gordy wished the dogs would come back. "Me being a so-so guy wasn't enough. My wife divorced me. That's when I went to AA. It wasn't the higher-power stuff so much as it was other people's stories. The way they yearned."

"Life without yearning is nothing. I guess it's what you yearn for."

"You've got the brain. I bet you can quote Shakespeare."

"'What fools these mortals be.'"

"Ain't that the dog's dish. Want lemonade? I like Gandhi, 'My life is my message.' I buy inspirational posters for my garages and like the Gandhi ones best. I also got the mechanics coffee mugs. They say, 'Be strong, be brave, and clean up after yourself.'" Gordy retrieved a gallon jug and plastic glasses from a cooler. "Ten years ago, I was vacuuming out the Yukon I had at a truck stop when this eighteen-wheeler pulls in and the driver goes for the air hose." He drank lemonade to wet his throat for the hard part. "Now, you don't just inflate a commercial tire. You gotta allow for screwups and faulty models. You inflate them in a cage. I ran up to warn the driver, not trained like he was supposed to be, but he had the air going, and it happened."

"The tire blew."

"Catastrophic zipper failure. Exploded at the seams and killed the guy. I had three surgeries to reconstruct my face bones. Hey, the girls are back." His friend released the dogs, and Ellie jumped in his lap while Dorothy flopped down and drooled. "I tell ya, Erik, all those educated doctors, nurses, therapists, knowing what to do and doing it. I was born again. Carol, my ex-wife, helped. When I was healing, I tried real hard with my sons—scared 'em at first with my stitched-up Franken-head. I couldn't even think of drinking. I went to AA anyway, and the lawyers and accountants drying out helped me with the settlements. I gave Carol a million and she married one of the accountants. We barbecue together. I set up my own shops, started with the rescue dogs. My boys, one's at the U and the other's starting Normandale Community in the fall. Can you believe it?" Gordy had worked himself up and was embarrassed.

"It takes a special person, Gordy, to see all that as a miracle." Erik dragged the back of his hand across his eyes. "Excuse me, I have to leave. Security people are making the rounds, asking about Luna Johnson. You can say you talked with the G-Met guy."

"I shoulda remembered."

"It all works out, Gordy." Erik waved bye.

Gordy watched as Erik ran into the Belgian Malinois guy again, this time the dog wore a working vest. The handler said, "*Zumbro, sit*." The dog obeyed, though his every cell wanted to leap. They disappeared into the crowd. Erik yearned too much, and Gordy had let him down. Darn it, he'd forgotten to ask if the vans had been found.

Gordy could hear gospel, Ezekiel seeing the wheel way up in the middle of the air. If only he had seen things earlier. Dorothy woofed at a man who paused outside the tent. His black t-shirt had a skeleton on it, and his skin was more creased than a Rolling Stone's after sex, drugs, and rock 'n' roll. He patted Dorothy without smiling.

It couldn't hurt, could it, to ask skeleton man? He sure needed comfort. Gordy called out, "You look like you could use a seat in the shade and a lemonade."

The man sat.

JAYLYN GLOWED FROM THE PERFORMANCE. Before going on stage, she'd been in the warm-up tent slow breathing over the portable keyboard. Teddi said screw that, play Little Richard's "Tutti Frutti." They danced on stage singing that, Teddi hitting a tambourine, and Jaylyn picking up the chords on reaching the piano. Later she riffed on Gershwin's "I Got Rhythm" with bars of "Rhapsody in Blue" thrown in. Teddi rocked the audience with her Janis Joplin tribute, declaring, "We could've saved her!" When they shimmied off, a man who booked local gigs drew Teddi aside. Jaylyn came out the back of the stage to be met by a baby-faced man in a security uniform.

"Hey, miss. I loved your piano-playing, you, um, swing. Wow."

"Ooh, thank you." Jaylyn smiled. Put her in a dress and she flirted. He was holding paper, like he wanted an autograph.

"Uh, yeah, um, have you seen this woman tonight? She's a drummer. Luna Johnson?"

Jaylyn's jaw dropped—the missing girl from the café in a different photo. She did seem familiar.

"Do you know something?" the guard asked. She mutely shook her head no.

"If you think of anything, call this tip line." He gave her a card, moist from his hand. "You can have one of mine, too." He dug into his pocket, came out with one, and mumbled, "Bye."

Heat roiled in her gut—poutine! With her backstage ID, Jaylyn slipped past barriers to a less public porta hellhole. She emerged quickly, rubbing a gob of disinfectant into the webs of her fingers. Though away from the stage, she could hear a woman perform covers from Joni Mitchell's *Hejira*. The ascending wail drove Jaylyn up the hillside. Shifting clouds dimmed the pre-sunset sky. Beneath the trees, a bunch of men milled around, a mix of colors and ages, none with ID badges. She heard rough edges of talk. Either a judge had sentenced them to rehab, or they came for the aging bad-boy headliner. The bad boy's career had three stages: the rebellious high, the agony of relapse, the delight of being clean. The rebellious high songs sold best. One man stubbed out a forbidden cigarette. A jug-eared punk made fun of the Joni wannabe by yowling, "I'm meno-pausal." Another slipped into the woods, unzipping his fly on the way. Then, to the left stood Josh, two-faced in the shadows.

They greeted each other in a bump halfway between a hug and a kiss.

"You're looking fantastic, Jaylyn, the dress, everything." When his smile ticked up, Josh looked damn fine.

"Mmm, thanks." Jaylyn twisted bewitchingly and was reminded of a Rodgers and Hart song, *horizontally he's at his very best.*

Josh Miller had been a volunteer peer-counselor when she came to the Hirsch Center a year ago for support sessions. It sounds heroic to ward off temptation by yourself, but Jaylyn's mother said over and over, if you ever, ever, feel need, forget pride, forget doubt, find support. People don't win wars alone. Josh was two years older—maybe she did have a thing for older guys, which had *nothing* to do with losing her father. His cheeks had a rosy flush and Jaylyn teased him then that it was his farm-boy wholesomeness, and he laughed. In conversations after group sessions, he admitted being bored out of his skull with heifers and soybeans. His father, "rigid as a barn door," expected him to work constantly, and his mother "specialized in being sad." No one smoke or drank. Neighboring farm kids participated in school extracurriculars, but Josh's father wrote those off as a waste. At fourteen, Josh started with beer. Too much evidence, so he switched to a drug he never specified. His younger brother ratted him out to their mother. She handed down her rusted pickup so Josh "could hang with friends." But Josh would party alone, 2 a.m., on the porch, with weed, and his father caught him. He shouted and hit Josh, waking up his mother who intervened—"He loves Mom but that doesn't help her." A school counselor badgered an insurance company for the family, his dad sold heifers earlier than planned, and Josh went to Hirsch Rehab for a month. He was the turn-around kid, graduated from high school, and had become an intern counselor when he met Jaylyn. When her session ended, he said he wanted to know more about music, and that's how it went. Until mono.

The headliner's crew took over the stage to adjust the amps they'd brought, not unusual for groups to trust only their own sound equipment. Against testing squeals, Jaylyn prattled about her music pieces before asking Josh what he was up to. He frowned at his shoulder as if something had landed on it. "I came to help out new sober buddies." He nodded back at the group. "Keep them away from these dive-bar jerks. Anyway, what did the security guy want to know?"

Jaylyn batted away mosquitos that had come out to feed. "I thought he wanted my autograph," she giggled. "Turns out there's a girl missing. She plays drums they say—Luna Johnson."

Josh didn't respond.

"Josh, everything okay?" Jaylyn probed. "You're thin." She slapped at a mosquito, missed, and it bit her neck.

"Lost my baby fat. No, uh, I relapsed last fall. After getting over the mono, I, uh, needed a boost, and I went the wrong way with that." Josh ran his hands up and down his ribs. "Anyway, you know the drill. Relapses happen, move on."

He wanted to tell her something more. Jaylyn touched his arm. His body leaned closer, but he stared at the woods. "I was on the verge of dealing to afford my own fix, and I saw how young the kids were—oh, there's the kids. I got to head them off. Find you later." The band took the stage and played warm-up strums, and Jaylyn, all wired over Josh, ran to the audience side around the amps.

A snare made a rim shot and a dog rushed her.

THE GIRL FELL INTO ERIK, and the flounces of her dress tickled his arms as he steadied her. "It's all right, miss. The dog, Zumbro, finds drugs. He didn't mean to knock you over." Zumbro plopped down by the amps and barked. The girl seemed in shock. "You're the pianist from the café. Are you all right?" Security, patrol officers, and state troopers swarmed the area amid screams and shots. Erik suspected she had answered him and he hadn't heard. "Your cousin Lionel has been emailing me. Is he here to escort you home?"

A whispered no, then the comment, "You're fast."

"I doubt I'm as fast as you on that Gershwin."

She appeared stunned—active movement would help. Erik walked her toward the parking lot. "Did you see something suspicious?"

"Men."

"Well, men as a lot are suspicious."

The girl smiled faintly. She seemed too vulnerable to leave alone, but she surprised him by making eye contact. "That girl?"

"Hey, there you are!" A glorious-looking girl in short-shorts backtracked from the exiting crowd to take charge of the pianist. Erik returned to the backstage round-up to check in and check out. With a bevy of officers to take statements, he could leave, finally, and meet up with his father and son.

"Detective," he heard a girl call after him—the pianist. "Josh Miller, rehab counselor, might know Luna." Before he could thank her, she pivoted and ran, a graceful figure in the dusk.

CHAPTER 20

Saturday night had been a bust. By Sunday morning it seemed that Deb had marshaled all her talents into *not* finding Luna Johnson. Deb hunched in her Justice RBG sleep-tee over the kitchen table and moused through messages on her computer. Erik had texted from the Hirsch Fest yesterday that Luna might be in the Wisconsin Dells, crowded with tourists at this time of year, and Deb had alerted the authorities. Nada. She had the name of an addiction counselor several people, including a security guard, had mentioned to Erik: Josh Miller. Nada. No answer, no voicemail. She slumped at her table—*not your table*—in her sublet—*you'll have to move someday*—and reviewed her computer updates from Cyber Paul.

Cyber Paul had devised an approximation of Routh's route the night he died, and though Routh had entered the *Celebrate!* station from the north, at the time of the panic call he was near the I-94/35 interchanges in St. Paul. Cyber Paul speculated that Routh's caller gave him the *Celebrate!* address because a chase was not probable though possible if . . .. Deb skipped over Paul's "if" and clicked on the map insert. A hospital occupied the northwest side of the interchanges and a liquor store and churches to the southeast. There were hotels and parking lots where one could hang out and take off like a shot in several directions.

Deb scratched her tingling arms. Sunburn. At the driving range, she'd put on sunscreen too late. She went to the bathroom for aloe lotion, and as she slathered it on her hands, her cell rang. She wiped her hands on the face of the justice and answered.

The Eau Claire, Wisconsin, Police Department reported that Luna Johnson was in custody.

The woman officer said Luna had wobbled into an emergency room crying that her heart had gone crazy, used an insurance card on her father's account, and the system picked her up. After her exam, the girl volunteered to the officer that she'd had a panic attack due to skipping anxiety meds, and she was scared she'd die before reaching the Wisconsin Dells. According to the officer, "Luna thought the waterslide would wash all her troubles away." The doctors restricted Luna's right arm to a sling. Luna claimed she fell when she arrived in Eau Claire, courtesy of a truck driver. She didn't know the driver's name. She ran out of meds, that's all. Eau Claire officers would feed her and transport her to the Twin Cities. Deb gave the address of the Resource—a setting less threatening than the G-Met station with its poltergeist HVAC. The travel time would be about ninety minutes. Deb emphasized that the girl might have been the last person to see Dan Routh alive and added that she would inform Luna's family of the good news. She ended the call.

After a half sandwich and full shower, Deb discovered that, as usual, the laundry hadn't done itself. She picked up from her dresser a brand-new top meant for presentations. Presentations—when you present to people like Nancy LeClerc who expect miracles from your puny mortal being. Anyway, the sleeveless wrap top would class up a blazer, and the color was cream—no bonding over drippy ice cream with Luna. Deb wriggled into the top, which sent her breasts in different directions. As she adjusted everything—this could be a date-night top, where are you, woman of my dreams?—Sharon Nordin called to say she would be at the Resource with security and a lawyer. Deb called Erik and reached his voicemail. Either he was in a Northwoods dead zone or balked at the caller ID.

Everyone, excluding Erik, arrived at the Resource at the same time. The Eau Claire officer reported, "Luna phoned her grandmother before we left, and she had a good nap in the car."

Sharon used a more adult tone. "I'm Sharon Nordin, director at the Resource. I'm pleased to meet you. Do you prefer to be addressed as Ms. Johnson or Luna?"

Luna obsessively rubbed her thumb against the fingers of her right hand. Her black hair hung in tangled corkscrews, her scoop top strained over flesh, and her glittery flipflops revealed toes with peeling green polish. She spoke in a mouse voice. "Luna works. Can I have a pop?"

"I'll find you a beverage soon, Luna. This is Detective Deb Metzger with the Greater Metro Unit," Sharon said.

"Am I in trouble? I didn't do anything. I wanted a break, that's all. Did my job call you?"

"Your grandmother missed you. She was worried. We were all worried," Deb replied. She didn't mean to slip into talking to eighteen-year-old Luna like she was a child.

"She knows, like, I'm okay." Luna rubbed her eyes, which were bright blue with dark rings around the irises. Any number of types would go after her.

Sharon introduced the woman lawyer—Deb didn't catch the name—and a froggy bass welled up from the woman's petite frame. "I'm here for you, Lena. Luna, I mean."

Sharon directed them through a locked door to a meeting room. The barebones décor centered around a table where a water pitcher sweated through a paper napkin. Everyone but Luna took a glass and poured water. Sharon went to a corner fridge and brought back a bottle of iced tea for Luna.

She took one sip. "Can I have a cup and sugar?"

Sharon took a coffee mug, bowl of sugar packets, and container of stirring sticks from the top of the fridge. "Will this do?"

Luna poured the tea into the mug. She tore open six sugar packets, her slinged arm clamped to her side, and stirred vigorously with her left hand. She took a few gulps and stared at Sharon. A delayed response kicked in. "What's *that* on your face?"

Sharon's birthmark remained a constant pink. "A sign that I'm not perfect. None of us are, yet we thrive."

Luna sat up straighter. "Oh, right. You help people get good jobs and the right clothes. In the information thingy there was a blouse with big red roses?"

"We'll discuss the jobs program later," Sharon said. "As for the clothes closet items, there's a lot of turnover. Are you comfortable enough, Luna, with your arm?"

A shrug. "I fell out of a truck, that's all."

Deb opened her mouth, but Sharon continued softly, "Luna, you knew one of our helpers at the Resource, Dan Routh."

"Yeah." Luna rocked back and forth in her chair.

"We understand he had plans to meet with you last Sunday," Sharon said.

"I don't always remember things right."

A fib. Treat Luna like a grownup and maybe she'll behave like one. Deb went to the heart of it: "The body of Dan Routh was discovered Monday morning in a dumpster. He'd been stabbed to death around midnight Sunday, last week. Did you have plans to meet with him that day?"

"He's not dead. He can't be dead."

"When did you last see him, Luna?" the lawyer asked.

"He can't be dead. I *know* him." Luna rocked harder.

"People we know die, Luna," Sharon said.

Luna stopped rocking. "He carries this dog sometimes, a friend's, in a pouch on his chest, like for a baby. He let me pet her." Her voice rasped, "Was Ellie with him? They found her in Dinkytown and that's why she's Ellie and that's so confusing."

The lawyer took it, "Dinkytown's mascot is Dinky the Elephant, so she may have been named Ellie for Elephant."

"That doesn't make *sense*." Sobs wracked Luna's whole body. They gave her a minute.

Deb spoke in her smallest voice, which wasn't that small. "Luna, I've seen Ellie. Ellie's fine." The sobbing subsided. "I'm not here to pick up people for having marijuana, pills, or a beer. What can you tell us about meeting Dan?"

"I dunno. I met him a couple of times, once, um, outside the hotel with the ducks inside? The pond in the lobby? He said I could do better. Said hanging around could feel scary and hopeless. He knew about scary and hopeless. He said it was great to control your life. With this fetal alcohol thing they say I have, people won't let me decide? I'm not that bad, just need my meds, that's all. He knew women who could help who weren't all snobby and blonde, not blonde like you, like money blonde."

So, cheap dye job was Deb's look. "You're saying Dan wanted to arrange a way—"

"Men like me, they do." Luna snuffled. "I have a boyfriend. He has plans. His dad's psycho-abusive. My boyfriend's super sweet and cool. We just had a little fight, ya know? I took off, so like he'd get I'm independent."

"Were you with your boyfriend Sunday night?" Sharon asked.

Again, Luna was wracked by sobs.

It was awkward, not to mention against policy, for Deb or the lawyer to hug Luna. Deb offered her blazer, which the girl ignored. Sharon unwound her neck scarf, Luna took it, and kneaded it with snotty hands. "I wasn't sure about coming here, ya know. I wouldn't have time for my boyfriend. S-Sunday Dan called and said we should meet . . . another time." She stalled. "I went to hang with my boyfriend, only his fucking ugly boss showed." She abruptly stood. "I need to pee bad." She charged the door and Sharon hurried to her escort her out. The scarf dropped to the floor.

The cop in Deb went crazy. She jumped up to rescue the scarf. *What boyfriend, boss of what, what the hell was everybody doing, where?* She stretched her back and popped a joint. The lawyer glared and Deb snapped, "Could be a trafficking setup," and the lawyer snapped back, "I'm well aware." The lawyer stabbed a finger at her phone while Deb grunted through another stretch. The door opened and the two slipped back into good behavior.

The girl sat, looking like death. The lawyer croaked, "We're stopping, Luna, so you can rest. We'll arrange for a squad car to take you home."

Luna panicked. "I can't go home in one of those, *no*. Like I was in *jail*? Can't this Deb person take me?"

Beep beep beep—Deb's phone alerted. "Sorry, that means urgent." Luna stared with her strange eyes. "*Super* urgent."

Update text, huge news: Vernon Grimes, regional crime kingpin, had been arrested at one of his Minneapolis party houses, based on information obtained from the Kafka Café and Hirsch Fest arrests. The mug shot inspired Deb.

"Luna, do you recognize this man?" Deb held out her phone.

"It's upside down," the lawyer croaked.

"Is it?" asked Sharon.

"Wait, can I see?" The kid in Luna perked up. "It's like the IQ tests they made me take all the time. See, the face is the same upside down and right side up."

Sharon leaned in. "You're right, Luna. That crease in his forehead like a mouth, the squashed nose, cauliflower ears. He's as ugly upside down as right side up." She leaned back in amazement.

"Is that the man you saw that night, when you were supposed to be meeting Dan?" Deb asked.

"You don't have to answer that, Ms. Johnson. I advise that as a lawyer. And take it easy, Detective Metzger."

Everyone tensed. Luna lifted her chin, defiant, stalling, and Deb's phone beeped with *Urgent Update*. She pressed it—

"*Ding Dong the Grimes is Caught!*"—the drug squad pretending to be Munchkins with a dead witch. "*The Grimes' with Feds, the Grimes' with Feds.*"

Sharon laughed, and Deb barged ahead. "Luna, could Grimes be your boyfriend's boss, or his dad?"

"Too ugly to be his dad. Ray's handsome. Can you play the song again?"

"That's an interdepartmental communication." Though a few bars couldn't hurt, and Luna had handed over a name, Ray. Deb hit play then stopped the song on a falsetto "*Hi Oh*" when she saw a new message. Erik, caught in traffic on his way back from camping, would arrive at the Resource soon.

Time to be tactical. She scrolled for a picture of Erik and Ben that she'd taken for him once. She cropped out the boy to leave the doting adult. "Luna, my Greater Metro partner and I can escort you home." Deb showed Luna Erik's photo.

Luna tilted her head. "He's kinda sweet."

The lawyer gave Deb the I-know-what-you're-up-to squint as Sharon said, "Luna, before you leave, we'll set up an appointment to discuss your future."

Deb got the message that she was dismissed. From the Resource entry, she could see that the day's forecast was coming true—light rain building up to torrents. She texted Erik, *bring on the sweet*.

CHAPTER 21

E YES SPEAK THE LANGUAGE OF LOVE.
Unless the eyes belong to a pair of detectives, then their language goes wonky. Deb and Erik had a vocabulary of squints, stares, and sidelong glances. Loosely translated as "what the," "you're joking," and "back the hell off."

Rain poured outside as the two steamed in Erik's Highlander and waited for Sharon to bring out Luna. He exuded the plant-mineral smell of lake swimming and wore a Twins camo cap. When Deb dashed out, soaking her new top, he remarked that she looked dangerously armed. She thought he meant packing extra weight around her hips, like strapped-on guns. She retorted that her pants flattered 'natural curves.' He meant the sunburn that bisected her arms. Tractor tan, she retorted, and asked where's Ben—at his mother's? No, her parents' house. What happened to his mother? Do I know who she's sleeping with, is that what you're asking?

Erik gave Deb the finger with his eyes and she was about to flip a real one when he blurted out, "Why was I supposed to bring dessert?"

"I meant be sweet, deploy that smile." Deb watched the rain fill the dings in Erik's Highlander.

"Wouldn't that be phony?"

"You're not usually averse to tooth display."

"Our job involves plenty of fakery as it is."

"Duh, yeah, we have to dance it out with the suspects. What's going on?"

His answer was to gaze out his side window.

"Partner, you're too moody to be fake. You is You. Has Drees been at you? Now Drees has the smile of a snake, if the snake had an orthodontist. Luna likes good-looking guys and you're the only one in this vehicle. Smiling's not fake, um, if you want the best for her. I want the best for her. She might be Dan's killer, and maybe the best for her is our understanding what she went through. Then we can send her to prison, happy."

"She's happy or we're happy?"

Deb pulled on her hair.

Sharon and Luna appeared in the doorway. Erik slid from his seat, grabbed a rain poncho from the back and held the poncho over the women's heads as they trotted to the Highlander. Deb stepped out and stood by as Erik sheltered as many heads as he could.

"We have a plan for the week." Sharon touched Luna on the arm and walked serenely through rain back to the center. Deb urged Luna into the back seat and joined her there. When Erik slammed his door shut, Deb made introductions and strangely slipped into the Muppet-chef Swedish accent. "Luna, this is Detective Erik Yansson."

"You're not very blond, are you?" Luna coyly bit her lip.

"Well, I, uh, try to be." Erik pushed back his damp Twins cap à la Humphrey Bogart.

Deb squelched the repartee. "Yansson went to Sunday School."

Erik flipped the AC to high to suppress a fishy odor and flashed his smile. "There's cookies in the back, and a flannel shirt if anyone's cold."

Deb had forgotten her blazer inside, leaving her uncomfortably, if not dangerously, armed with goose pimples on top of the sunburn. Luna reached over the seat and grabbed the flannel from the camping pile. "Oh, so sweet, you brought me supper." Erik sent Deb an 'it's my supper' look, but Luna had already taken the compostable fork and dug into the container of ziti. "Mmm. Is health food healthy?"

"That's the idea," Deb said. Luna had an adolescent illogic, only Luna wasn't adolescent. While Minnesota law treated trafficked women as the victimized, Luna was eighteen, and if involved in drug-dealing, recruiting girls, or murder, she could be tried as an adult. Deb's gut sensed that Luna didn't kill Dan. Deb's gut was useless in a court of law.

Luna ripped open the cookie sack, and the Highlander filled with the aura of butter and chocolate. Deb took a melty one and bit in. How had Erik acquired warm cookies on a Sunday afternoon? Anything he would ever do, she forgave. Luna, mouth full, garbled, "Sharon says anything I say in this vehicle is inadmissible."

"This vehicle is pretty inadmissible," Deb agreed.

"I admit that I'm annoyed that ninety-four is closed, again," Erik said. "We'll have to wend our way to East St. Paul and your grandmother's."

Luna batted her eyelashes and handed him a cookie. "I like food. Instead of being a server, I could be a cake baker. You're not on the clock in the same way, Sharon says."

"What about music, Luna?" Erik asked before biting into his cookie.

Luna twitched. "I could be in a lot of bands. I'd just have to sleep with the dudes. That's exploitive, Sharon says."

"How about girl bands?" Deb asked.

"Sharon says if women would cooperate and not call each other bitches, it'd be better. But, like, there are so many bitches? Hey, there's the corn stand. It's run by a Hispanic family."

Deb wanted to move past the Sharon Says game. "Do you go to the stand with your boyfriend?"

"My boyfriend says we got to support people like that, the working people, not the rich creeps. If I was rich, I wouldn't be a creep."

Boutiques that announced neighborhood pride alternated with closed storefronts. Erik drove coincidentally toward the block where the dumpster was located, the one where Routh had been stabbed. Luna was staring out the window and shutting down. Deb sent Erik a 'be fascinating' look. He frowned, she raised her eyebrows, and he lunged ahead. "You're right, Luna. It's a challenge figuring out what to do."

"Ray's smart and a badass—sorry for the language, Mr. Yansson. Ray says you need to please people. His dad screwed him up and people took advantage of him and that's why he gets me." Luna rested her head against the spattered window. "Insurance sucks. Ray knows doctors that do right by you, and he can upgrade cheap generic pills from drugstores. The fucking stores—sorry, Mr. Yansson—they only care about money with all that crap they sell."

The rain became heavy, and the wipers whumped against it. Erik kept his gaze riveted to the street. Luna fidgeted, and Deb edged around the inadmissible. "I'm impressed by the way you protected yourself and made it to Eau Claire."

Luna ignored the comment. "Hey, over there. I remember this place because they do African hair, braids and rows. Pammie should go there—my friend. She's got the frizzies. Ray says mean dudes would call her a dog."

A lane closure stopped traffic. Erik bumped them through a flooded rut to a different street.

"Are you married?" Luna asked.

The pounding rain trapped them in a floating confessional, and Deb wondered if she meant married, period, or married to each other. She was trying to come up with a joke—married to each other only if forced by space aliens—when Erik cleared his throat and said, "Sadly, I'm divorced."

A few beats passed. Luna leaned forward. "Did you fight?"

Erik bent over the steering wheel. "Never physically. We . . . I learned too late that there are ways to fight that can push toward coming together and ways of fighting, and not fighting, that seal off what shouldn't be sealed."

Deb was about to reassure Luna that she shouldn't worry about understanding Erik when Luna spoke again. "You probably didn't swear when you fought 'cause of Sunday School, but most people swear, and say someone calls you a fucking moron and a whore and pushes you. That's just being mad, right?"

Deb struggled against going ballistic. "There's mad and there's aggression. That kind of talk is a red flag and it makes Yansson squirm."

Water sluiced around them into the gutters. Luna fell across Deb to look out her window. "Wait, where are we? This is near Phalen." She became frantic. "This ain't near the hotel?"

"What hotel?" Erik asked.

"The simple one?"

Deb, heart in mouth, choked out, "A LeClerc Simple? Is that where Dan was to meet you? No, don't tell me. Tomorrow—"

Erik slammed on the brakes, and they all bounced back against the seats. A muscle car caught his rear bumper, blared around him, and there was a sharp yelp.

"A dog, why I stopped." Erik switched on the siren, portable beacon, flashers, and jumped out. The chilling rain blew into the back seat.

"Ellie?" Luna banged herself back and forth against the seat and made compulsive hitching sounds, "eh, eh, eh." Deb put a hand on her shoulder and pushed a phone button with the other.

"Animal down!" she shouted at dispatch.

"You mean officer down?"

"Animal," she repeated, "and send an ambulance. A woman in shock." Luna slobbered into hysterics. Deb leaned over Luna to see. "It's not Ellie. She lives blocks away." Not that she could tell.

Soaked Erik poked his head in. "It's alive. Luna. Deb will help you, and I'll call—"

"Emergency vet. Or Gordy Omdahl." Shoot, Deb shouldn't have said Gordy's name in front of Luna, involved in who knows what. Erik stepped out again to direct traffic around the stricken dog. Deb put her arm around Luna, an anti-shock measure. "Yansson is an expert pet rescuer. He's done it before. This is just an accident, a mistake."

A whine escaped. "*I made a mistake.*"

A mistake—stabbing Dan Routh? Deb's gut lurched, but not as much as Luna's. She puked up Erik's supper all over the Highlander.

CHAPTER 22

MINNEAPOLIS ROSE UP LIKE THE EMERALD CITY OF OZ. Erik drove over the rise on I-35W northbound to see the deep green of the Minnesota River Valley and beyond, a cluster of buildings aspiring to the sky. In the Monday morning sunshine, he could pretend to follow a yellow brick road. The lush tree canopy obscured the valley businesses, though glinting roofs were like so many poppies. Poppies in a city littered with opioids.

Erik had slept the sleep of the exhausted after settling as best he could last night's incident with the stricken dog. The EMTs in the ambulance addressed Luna's anxiety with a blanket and a trip to the hospital. The dog, its organs punctured by broken ribs, breathed its last. Erik took its collarless carcass to a night vet to check if an identifying microchip had been implanted. He had received no updates and wasn't sure who would foot the bill. At seven a.m., he'd stopped by the G-Met station and requested traffic cam footage on the Mustang, not that he had much confidence in availability or clarity. He swapped out his scraped and puked-on Highlander for a G-Met Taurus and headed to Burnsville to interview the perennial suspect, "my brother-in-law, Vince."

Vince had been reported yet again on the tip line about Dan Routh's murder. Vince's wife feared that her brother, who had schizophrenia, had called it in before he disappeared from his group home. Erik asked if the brother might have insight into the Routh murder. The brother would occasionally seek "medicine" from drug dealers, be rounded up, and spout names like "Squeegee," "Hairpin," "Ringo Raymo Dingo," and "Colette." The Colette came from a movie, and Vince noted that peculiar things became 'real' for paranoid schizophrenics. Erik did not reveal that Squeegee and Hairpin were undercover officers. Finally, Vince, an importer of fine foods, provided brioche and an array of cheeses and jams.

Vince's record remained clean. Erik's own record would soon be a matter for discussion. A message came over the radio from Deb: Luna remained in the hospital being treated for dehydration and anxiety. Her time alone might have been more traumatizing than she let on. When doctors cleared Luna, Deb would schedule a follow-up meeting with a lawyer present. Erik dreaded his next meeting, and the tip line had tipped Erik into dismay.

Anonymous sources persisted with the corrupt-cop angle on the Routh murder. Before leaving Vince's cul-de-sac, he called Ibeling. The chief, his clipped words a Morse code, said, "Seek a pattern." When Erik asked for elaboration, Ibeling beeped out, "Red herrings swim in schools." A red herring Erik understood as a false lead. The last thing he wanted to do was consult with his younger sister, the poet, on the full meaning of the phrase. She had sent him an email after the café incident urging him to develop "negative capability." He googled that: it was a poet's idea of holding multiple ideas and uncertainties in mind without "irritable reaching after fact & reason." Ibeling, despite his use of metaphor, expected fact and reason in every report.

Interstates and surface streets were a changing tangle of closures and detours, the Minotaur's maze. William Fridley of Minneapolis Internal Affairs wanted a rendezvous at the Wilde Café in the St. Anthony and Main neighborhood. Meeting outside the office was a trigger warning, a hint of conspiracies within conspiracies. Erik desperately wanted Tyvek he could wrap around his moral sensibilities to protect them from deceit. He also desperately wanted to dodge Carpocalypse. He exited east toward the university, doubled back to West River Parkway, and crossed the Mississippi River. The café honored the Irish-English wit Oscar Wilde (*Be yourself; everyone else is already taken*) and had a lovely view across the river toward the Mill Ruins Park and the Stone Arch Bridge. There was a music academy over there, and Erik had associates who had started toddlers on lessons with violins the size of a man's shoe. He and Kristine should agree on a squeak-proof instrument for Ben.

Erik spotted Fridley at a table under the trees. Fridley, who shared his name with a northern suburb, was in his mid-forties. His gray suit said company man while his paisley shirt defied pigeon-holing. A long nose gave Fridley a melancholy mien.

He stood and extended a hand. "Fine to meet you on this fine day, Detective Jansson."

"You can call me Erik." They sat at the table.

William Fridley quoted a childhood poem: "'My mother calls me Willie, but the fellers call me Bill.' Skip the 'Bill' and go right to Frid. Life's easier when I answer to what people call me. You order inside. I already had a chocolate croissant and washed my hands of it."

Erik secured a large coffee and returned to see that Frid had taken papers from a messenger bag and that good-looking women were jogging by.

"Great scenery." Frid noticed the direction of Erik's gaze. "Sitting out here, people watching, the pressure eases. But you're itching to get down to business." Frid put his hand on the papers but took no action.

Erik initiated it. "It's necessary that I investigate anything in Dan Routh's past that might be relevant to his murder. His former police partner has been cleared as a suspect."

Frid nodded. "In a nutshell, Routh was charged several times with using excessive force early in his career. Officers covered for him, and later he covered for them. One case before body cams involved a female officer shooting off a suspect's elbow. The case review suggests she panicked in a non-threatening situation. Routh's testimony exonerated her, and she left the force to become a Lutheran minister in Texas. After that, Routh did an about-face and became witness for the prosecution, and his testimony led to judgments against two officers. His peers did not take kindly to that. Routh was about to be investigated for being impaired on the job when he left. I have found nothing that suggests current cause for friction."

Frid tracked a stroller pushed by a pretty African American woman. "What I want to discuss today is this. We need more officers in Internal Affairs. Positions are opening. You should apply."

"What?"

"Not your dream job, Erik? I know the image. IA guys are soulless snitches addicted to filling out forms and dotting people's i's and e's. I guess you don't dot an e, but people forget accent marks on names that aren't Anglo. The reality is that our work protects citizens and exonerates decent officers. I admit, not every case is handled appropriately, careers are ended, personal lives upset. The consequences of officers' bad behavior, not yours."

Erik couldn't think of what to say except the expected: "Would this mean a promotion and raise?"

"Not much of a vertical move, more of an incline."

"Do you work with partners?" Erik hadn't touched his coffee. Too hot.

"That depends on the final job description and the complexity of the cases. It's not lonely."

Erik took a cautious sip.

"What I mean, Erik, is that I have a good life. Not all buddy-buddy with the union, not everybody's favorite person to see. Never was, with this sad horse face my ancestors gave me." Frid illustrated with a droopy smile. "I live in a friendly neighborhood, my wife's a pharmacist, three kids in school doing great as long as there's high-speed internet. I keep bees. Don't laugh, bees are fascinating. Maintaining an apiary is a science and an art." Frid pulled nearer with his phone. "Here's a video of me and my oldest, smoking the bees."

It was a HazMat situation, a blur of dots shuttling over the screen, an incessant *bzzzz*, and two figures in moon suits. The big figure assured the little, "Don't worry, they're docile." Tending bees and dealing with cops under suspicion had its parallels.

Frid smiled fondly at the video before turning it off. "I've heard through my various channels that you're the straightforward type"—Erik gave him a straightforward look—"with a gift for deceit."

"That would make me capable of negative capability."

"You read John Keats! I love the pulsing warmth of that poem about his living hand. Wait, Sonje Jansson, is she related? I devour her poetry, the eroticism—"

"She's my *sister*."

"Right. Understand this." Frid weighted his words. "The move to Internal Affairs is best made when you're young."

"Before police work makes you jaded?"

"While your record is clean, Erik."

Erik sat back.

Frid pulled forward. "I'm not saying you're heading into corruption, but you've experienced how murky situations can be. What seemed the right action in the moment appears horribly wrong later. What I'm saying, you're in the profession long enough, your record can be questioned."

A future of black marks. "I've already been taken to the mat over my former partner, Bob Uhle."

"That case shouldn't have been as messy as it was."

"Isn't that true of most IA investigations? Messier than they should be?"

"Touché. Erik, you've got guts. I wanted to give you a heads-up about those openings. We can't serve justice if we don't keep our own house clean." Frid stood. "Good talking with you."

Erik mumbled a pleasantry. They stood and shook hands, and Frid added, "It seems highly improbable, Erik, that fellow-officer angle with the Routh murder. But the world is full of the improbable. Good luck."

"Thank you."

"Of course, they say you make your own luck. Stay sharp. You could marry again in a minute, if you wanted to. You're in my prayers, Erik." Frid walked away, but like many Minnesotans, he was stymied as to how to say goodbye efficiently. He turned back. "I suppose being duplicitous, if you are, is an advantage, as long as it's not outright deceit." He peered into Erik's blue eyes as if searching for a soul.

Bees also took a deep interest in Erik and buzzed around him. With or without capability, he was in a negative space.

CHAPTER 23

DEB WAS DRESSED TO PROWL, with a leopard-print scarf around her neck. The scarf made her feel less exposed in her V top since she'd left her blazer somewhere. She did have the presence of mind last night to tell the hospital to secure Luna's street clothing while a warrant to test them was in process. Thus far this Monday, Deb had prowled through case notes without pouncing on a thing. Erik was not there to distract by jiggling a leg or staying silent until he uttered a *non sequitur*. She hadn't known the term *non sequitur* until he used it to describe a suspect's statements, and she remained unsure of it. He had made the good point that while Luna may have been physically capable of killing Dan Routh, she did not appear organized enough to arrange the hauling of the abandoned van. Deb's computer dinged with messages, and she returned to her predatory focus.

The drug squad: if you received a video *attributed* to this unit, delete. Do not repost *Hey oh, the Grimes is Caught*. For reference, see attached clip.

The Resource: *blazer in custody.*

Foster: *see attached forensic report: Routh on anti-anxiety, blood pressure meds.*

Jude: *Nancy desires a meeting. Fill out a time slot.*

"Fill out a time slot"—imperiouser and imperiouser. Deb filled out one for late next week, when, if pigs flew upside down and backwards, the Routh case would be solved. The mention of Nancy and the memory of Luna saying a "simple" hotel stirred an idea, which the jangle of the office phone knocked from her head. Chief Ibeling's temporary assistant—the regular, Celeste, was out—barked, "Come to Ibeling's office ASAP, immediately, right now." *Click.*

The predator had become prey. If Deb had anti-anxiety meds, she'd take them ASAP, immediately, right now. G-Met operatives were rarely summoned alone to Ibeling's office. He would stalk the hallways in rubber-soled shoes, catching people deep in case analysis. Also catching them in the middle of trash-can basketball, Bollywood dance moves, and the all-time standard, snoring. Ibeling had earned the moniker Allwise, almost.

Deb entered the chief's suite to face a man with the pointy face of a devil. He sneered, "You're wearing *that*?" She yanked the leopard print from her neck and stuck it in her pocket, knocked, and heard "Enter."

The cold bureaucratic surfaces of Ibeling's office were overlaid with a shrine to grandchildren. The chief stood behind his desk, unrolling and rerolling the sleeves of his shirt. "Sit," he commanded.

That meant Deb looked up to mid-height Ibeling who wore authority like an epidermis.

Ibeling grasped the chair back. "Jansson off with that investigator or lawyer? Skip that. Progress on the Routh case?"

What lawyer? "We've located Luna Johnson, the woman Routh was presumably meeting that evening. She's been hospitalized for anxiety and it may take time for her to be, um, forthcoming. Vernon Grimes may have been in the area with Routh." She avoided defining the area until she had a smidgen of evidence. "That makes Grimes a suspect."

"You'll have to take a ticket and wait in line to interrogate Grimes. Do you have physical evidence that connects him to Routh? I see not. Make progress."

"LeClerc . . ." Deb began.

"Yes, Metzger, you made an impression on Nancy LeClerc. Prioritize Routh—no slacking—but cooperate with Nancy LeClerc within appropriate boundaries."

Deb didn't have slacks, she had trousers. Prioritizing the Routh case if it involved a LeClerc property would drop her in a vat of boiling oil. True, it would be perfumed boiling oil.

"Metzger, there's another matter." Ibeling grabbed his chair hard and it banged against the desk.

"Are you feeling all right, sir?"

"Never reference my feelings. Make sure Jansson gets to the Empathy Workshops."

"The what?"

"Empathy. You should have it. Learn the English language while you're at it."

"Sir, I don't understand."

"Empathy, E-M-P . . . second thought, don't overdo the language. Take Jansson. Draw him out."

Deb bobbed her head and moved to leave.

"Close the door."

Deb closed the door. The outer office Beelzebub droned, "Have a super-nice day" and handed her a report with a big sticky note, REDO.

DEB FUMED BACK TO HER OVERHEATED OFFICE. Erik, holding a cup that said *Wilde*, circled the desks.

She attempted civility. "Morning, partner. Most people drink coffee, not take it for a walk."

"Oxygenating it improves the flavor." He took a sip. "Eck, cold."

"I'm supposed to deliver you to Empathy Workshops."

"Second part of the order is you stay to supervise me." Erik set down his undrunk coffee.

"Is your failure to attend workshops legendary?"

"If I'd gone to Ibeling's office first, he'd have said the same for you." Erik sat at his computer.

Deb sat at hers. No Empathy in her emails. She read a message from the hospital liaison reporting that Luna had been sedated to ensure rest. Luna was exactly the vulnerable type Deb felt compelled to protect. She was within an inch of believing that Luna was totally innocent, but it *infuriated* her that Luna could instead be a lying killer. Deb opened her mouth to annoy Erik when a bang at the door made the two of them jump.

Drees stuck that Adonis head of his into their space. "I'll forward the Empathy Workshop information. It's important." If only he'd shut the door on himself when he left.

Erik put his head on his desk.

"Detective E. Jansson," Deb said loudly. "Do you consider yourself big-hearted?"

"What do you mean, Detective D. Metzger? Enlarged heart capacity? Running is good for the heart, but over-training causes stress."

"No, you strange person. Like care for people, feel their pain, that crap."

"I serve the public, there's my family, I like dogs."

"What about your 'they could die' list. Not that you'd 'kill' kill anybody, but there are *people*. People who say, you're wearing *that*?" Deb drew her leopard scarf from her pocket with a flourish. "People who say, 'I'm telling you this as a *friend*.'"

"They could go away."

"Criminals who lie bold-faced with a cherry on top, swear they'll stop cooking the books, beating the wife, taking money from the offering. Then they rinse and repeat the same dirty behavior."

"You mixed metaphors." Erik was dropping paper clips into his cold coffee, the expression on his face illegible.

"I lack empathy for people who judge my metaphors. Wait, I got it. People who claim to be true empaths."

"Drees," Erik stated.

"Drees," Deb echoed.

Erik capped his paperclip coffee. What *was* he going to do with it? "Are you implying that our metaphoric hearts are shriveled?"

"Dried peach pits covered in mold in a stomped-on shoebox with a dead mouse. Speaking of shriveled hearts, were you meeting with a lawyer this morning?"

A sudden anger came over Erik and he jumped up to pace. "I have to appear in court later this week for an old case." Deb went for a distraction. "Speaking of empathy or the lack thereof, Ibeling said you had a revenge fantasy. What is it?"

He controlled a smile. "One is that I slam a guy, 'Ray' for example, against a wall and he dribbles down into a puddle, which I suck up with a Shop-Vac. For some reason, the Shop-Vac's important."

"You know, that's weird. I think of suspending him from a bridge by the toenails. The bridge is important. Romantic fantasies, on the other hand, obviously there's a golf course."

"Obviously?"

Drees appeared again. "Forwarding the workshop registration. Complete ASAP."

"Want iced coffee?" Erik asked.

"Sure." Drees took the covered coffee with paper clips jangling like ice and disappeared. Erik waved bye to Deb and vamoosed in the opposite direction.

Deb's computer popped up a new message: she had botched the LeClerc appointment form with the result that Nancy set a meeting time at her private residence for Wednesday, 8:30 a.m.

Next came the workshop items from Drees. So he hadn't gagged to death on a paper clip. Deb ignored them and checked for updates on Luna. The girl had given them such a runaround about Ray that Deb could wring her neck. Hypothetically, that is, and with empathy.

CHAPTER 24

MAYBE TODAY WOULD DO IT. Today would solve Dan's killing. Gordy rubbed grit from his eye and adjusted his St. Paul Saints baseball cap. A midday breeze kicked up dust in the South St. Paul Service Plaza, and the constant traffic up on the multi-lane Wakota Bridge over the Mississippi River made hearing difficult. He watched his friend Leif motor in with his rig. A trucker leaving the plaza honked at Leif as he jumped down, and Leif waved with his knit tam. The tam was red, Gordy's non-colorblind friends said, like Leif's hair. Leif's signature look was to wear the tam on a slant, with the crush held in place by a sunburst pin. Why the big guy needed a signature piece baffled Gordy. Leif was already a bursting sun with his bushy beard, bushy hair, and a face scalded from the outdoors.

As they walked into the store section of Truck Corral Diner, packed to the gills with merchandise, a magazine on the rack caught his attention: *The Animal Mind*. The cover showed a real pretty Golden Retriever.

"Yup, they sell the raunchy ones."

"Huh?" Gordy tilted his head back to see at Leif's level. A sexy brunette winked down at him from an adult magazine. A paper liner hid her torso but not the top roll of her breasts. Gordy dropped his eyes back to the animal magazine. Its neighbor was a publication on human mindedness and stress relief. These stores, you could get it all.

"How about that booth." Leif tucked his tam in a pocket and eased his bulk through the diner section. It wasn't crowded at one o'clock on a Monday. Leif plonked down in a booth, and behind him, yellowed foam peeped through the Naugahyde. "The service place off I-35 at mile 69 doesn't sell smut. Devotionals is what they got. I picked up a brown one for me and a pink for Maeve, cute shirts for our girls, three and five now. Franchise food there, though the hotdog buns are made with potatoes."

"For gluten-free truckers?" Gordy asked as a puckered woman with gray hair wound to a point plopped down menus. Her shirt read MARGARET on the front and on the back, CHOW DOWN, GAS UP. She asked about Leif's girls, and he showed pics of them in princess costumes.

"Gordy?" Leif broke into his thoughts. "I was tellin' Margaret here you're my guardian angel, keeping me sober."

"Keep him safe for those girls. Coffee?"

Leif said yes, Gordy no because he could feel a headache starting. A coffee mug and water glasses appeared in seconds, and Leif had Margaret stay.

"The hot roast beef sandwich will do me. One would set you up for the rest of the day, Gordy, ten-buck special."

Gordy saw BLT on the menu, but in June the tomatoes would be hothouse. Margaret tapped the pen against her pad.

"We don't want to rush Gordy," Leif explained to the server. "Tire blew a few years back, nearly split his brain. You'd never know it. Sharper than he looks."

"You got two hemispheres, hon." Margaret put a hand on Gordy's shoulder. "You can get by on one, or is it you have two, but they don't have to talk to each other, like an old married couple? Anyway, a half a brain's more that our cook has, right, Sam?"

Sam, behind the counter, showed no sign he'd heard her. Gordy ordered the hot turkey sandwich.

"You been following that Vernon Grimes case?" Leif asked.

"Huh?"

"In the news. Grimes is a verticalizer. He runs drugs and girls at different levels. He has an elite line for snob perverts, a middle line for guys who want a quickie or a hit on the way to work, and then there's the bottom feeders. 'Cause he's diversified and gives his 'facilitators' leeway to grow the business their way, the cops are having a time of it figuring out all his schemes. He might get away with it."

The sandwiches arrived: meat between slices of white bread, mashed potatoes on top, all drowned in golden gravy. Leif shoveled food in and spoke with his mouth full. "Gravy's house-made, has flour lumps. Izz good."

Gordy dug into his. The potatoes tasted pulverized, but the turkey was thick and the bread mushed into the gravy, and that gravy was go-od. He might've become a food snob. That's what being rich did to you when you try to impress a woman like Tamra by taking her to a place in Minnetonka where the food had a pedigree and came with pea tendrils.

It was like Leif read his mind. "How's that gal, Tamra?"

Gordy swallowed. "She's in Rapid City. Her niece is having a terrible time with a pregnancy. Tamra called to say they're going ahead with the gender-reveal party anyway."

"The what?" Leif swished water in his mouth.

"Before the baby's born, they surprise everybody, is it a boy or girl. It doesn't make sense to me, gender-reveal. These days kids are just going to change it up anyway."

Leif leapt to his big feet, held his phone like a gun, and faced the entry. A trucker came to a standstill where the booths started. "Take it easy, Leif," the man snarled. "You need to stay out of other people's business."

"You watch yourself." Leif tilted his head back. They had a stare-down, the other diners keeping their traps shut. Then the man turned slowly to the cashier, said "Ham and Swiss to go," and slipped around to the store side.

Leif sat. "We don't need the likes of him in trucking."

"How come?"

"Trafficking," Leif said in a low voice. "Like that Grimes' stuff. Those big oasis places and rest areas, at night these vans sneak around, lights low, to 'service' the drivers with drugs and sex. Back in my drinking days, when I'd curl up in the compartment with beer and a girly mag, didn't notice, didn't care. Now, with Maeve and me having the girls, I'm on the hotline like you wouldn't believe. Called on that dude once when someone was dragging a kid to his rig. Us truckers, we get training on how the girls act if they're being 'escorted.' We all got a light, you know, a little light, and we all gotta let it shine. Say, Gordy, you all right? Pack away too much turkey there?"

Gordy hyperventilated. He put a napkin over his mouth and nose to stop the dizziness.

"Z'it your brain? I can call medics. They have to know this place in case of food poisoning, right, Sam?" Sam ignored them.

Gordy exhaled to a count of six, inhaled to a count of six. "My friend was killed. It's why I wanted ta talk to you. Dan, he rescued girls from traffickers."

"The ex-cop? Didn't know he was your friend."

"I was his sober mentor." Gordy's eyes leaked.

"Oh jeez, that's fricking rough. You save a guy's life, keep him off the sauce, and *blam*, something takes him down. Hey, man, you need to go outside for air? Except it's diesel exhaust."

"On the house, hon." Margaret put a ginger ale in front of Gordy and refilled Leif's coffee.

The ginger ale prevented the gravy from becoming gut sludge.

"Take your time, Gordy." Leif sat back against the foam. "That plate I ate has to settle. Then I got serious business, you know, with the 'amenities.'"

Gordy's brain flipped on. "Leif, what do you know about Larimer's Body Shop? The van I loaned Dan was stolen, and that's the best evidence. The detectives haven't found it. They're Great Metro folks."

"Like special agents?" Leif put down a couple of twenties on the table and wouldn't let Gordy contribute.

"I don't know if they're special. Dorothy likes them."

"Well they're all right then. Here's the thing, Gordy. Don't mess with this stuff by your lonesome. I know a guy who can help. He's in with these G-Met types, helped them solve a big case, three, maybe five, six murderers. Here." Leif pulled out his wallet, waterproofed by grease. He handed over a bent card, the name on it, Bent Nail. The flip side showed a contraption made out of birch branches, like a chair in a horror movie with arms that came alive and trapped you.

"Bent Nail? That's his name?" He looked to Leif.

"Yup, Bent. Call him, he'll know what's up."

Gordy's brain was cooking now.

Margaret reappeared with a witchy cackle. "Hon, this time I'm giving you the tip. Larimer's has been shut down. Grants is still out there, you be careful around there, and these ones." She wrote names on a ketchup-stained receipt. It was Siracha ketchup on the table—Trucker's Corral was *ketching up* with the times, which Gordy pointed out to Leif and they had a good laugh.

IT HAD BEEN A HORRIBLE DAY. Jaylyn was stuck in traffic on Monday afternoon, and the Jeep sounded bronchial. The morning had been percussion fun at her part-time camp job, and her ears still rang with kindergarten heavy metal. Then there were hours of Lazar drilling her on trick endings in music, known as deceptive cadences. But the past hour was the worst. She should never have said yes to couch-hopping Ramon and Retta. They wanted her help moving Retta's stuff from her mom's place to an apartment Ramon found near the Washington Avenue bridge. The bad things listed themselves in Jaylyn's head.

First, Ramon said that he ran into his dad, found out his own belongings had been pawned, and slipped away with his dad's vintage watch because in Ramon's view he was owed it. Second, Retta had shaved half her skull over the weekend because she was fed up over men grabbing her tits and ass. The consequence—nasty-looking Retta was fired from that waitressing job when she needed money the most. Third (it kept getting worse), Retta with her sore scalp was woozy and blamed it on allergy medicine she'd taken—more like angry medicine. Fourth, at Retta's mom's place, her mom was not there and they'd had to wade through unwashed laundry and empty booze bottles. Fifth, Jaylyn went into the bedroom Retta had used and a naked man was passed out from a noon drunk. His butt cheeks were tattooed with "grab" and "here."

That's when Jaylyn screamed and the man woke up and came at her. Ramon rushed in and slugged him. He got the two women to the Jeep and drove to a McDonald's, where they stepped out to catch their breath. Retta went to the bathroom to be sick. Jaylyn acknowledged to Ramon that Retta could be difficult and was in danger of cycling downward. Ramon touched Jaylyn's shoulder and promised that he'd work on helping Retta and that he was *done* with his father. He looked her in the eye the whole time, and she saw the blankness of pain. "Good news," he added. Due to a shake-up at work, he had an increase in earnings. When Retta came out with a fizzy drink, Ramon said he'd take it from here and sent Jaylyn on her way.

Traffic budged, and the Jeep coughed itself into the faster left lane. The lane stopped being faster. Jaylyn had the sudden urge to spend the rest of the summer with school friends, relaxing in their swimming pools and privilege. Saturday's Josh sighting at the disastrous Hirsch Fest messed with her head, as did Retta's funk and anxiety over Ramon's father. Though the vintage watch Ramon took would go with the fedora they found when moving boxes from Gran's.

The hat made her remember. While driving to a music thing in May, Jaylyn had seen on the street a woman—girl—in a fedora arguing with a man. She realized seconds after driving past that the man was Ramon. She asked him about it soon after. He couldn't remember. Jaylyn described the hat, and he frowned. "Oh, not good. A girlfriend of my dad's, fussing that he dropped her. I said stay away from him."

Fedora girl resembled that missing girl, Luna, that's why the image was familiar. What was she doing with a man like Ramon's criminal father? Jaylyn hadn't heard anything about the girl, but Lionel had told her after the Kafka stuff that the authorities kept some cases quiet. Her cousin blabbered on about secret investigations and protecting runaways from bad people. Jaylyn couldn't report Ramon's dad because she didn't actually know anything. There was nothing she could do.

Jaylyn switched on classical radio and was easing her mind with the quiet spaces of Satie's *Gymnopedie* when she was rear-ended.

CHAPTER 25

ERIK FLINCHED WHEN DEB SWUNG TO HIT THE BALL. Since Deb was playing air golf in the G-Met office, the ball was imaginary, his distress real. It was Monday dinnertime and they had made not an inch of progress. "Was that a hole in one?" he grumbled. She didn't hear and swung fast several times. At Iowa State, she'd been a Cyclone. It made sense.

Erik picked up his coffee cup, which was rimmed with a green slick. It had been a fresh cup hours ago, retrieved after he had foisted off his first cup on Drees. Then Erik forgot about the coffee when Frid forwarded him archived files of IA investigations. He had spent the afternoon poring over them. A phone call from Gordy Omdahl should have been unburdening since Gordy promised not to pester the detectives anymore. However, the reward Gordy offered opened a Pandora's box of wayward leads. The tips piled up into a work overload. Deb came and went, spouting things about Luna that clarified nothing. She switched from talking to herself to playing air golf. Deb swung again, and the imaginary ball must have landed in Erik's coffee because its depths stirred.

"I've been slicing," she groaned. "So, partner, wither go we with this Routh mess? Did you see that I forwarded updated case notes?"

"My inbox is clogged with tips." Erik found Deb's email and scanned the updates. "Where's Brenda Hilbert's alibi?"

"C'mon, you can't think she did it?"

"Procedure."

"Since when are you all hot about procedure? Look, Dan Routh was a bad dad. He paid for it, and he tried for, what's that thing with carbon, you know, what to do about releasing carbon in the air?"

"Sequester?"

"No, like buy and sell?"

"Offset?"

"That's it, offsets. He offset his bad parenting by helping others. All right, that still leaves serious damage behind, and Brenda's not big on forgiving." Deb pounded something into the floor with her imaginary club. "But you gotta give her an effing break." She scowled at Erik. "Not everybody grew up like you did with preachers and teachers, everybody so do-goody, that you hang out with murderers for relief."

"I don't *hang* with murderers. I catch them." Erik wished that when he and Deb were first thrown together, he had never told her that, surrounded by goodness in his youth, he ran to crime. "You're sore because you said your father—"

"This has *zilch* to do with my dad. The way you look at Brenda . . .." Deb humphed and sat.

He stood. "All right, she's not my favorite person."

"You're fixated on your first negatory impression."

"When I first saw her, you were dallying at the LeClerc event."

"On your order. Well, your ordery-type suggestion. Scoping them out for what they knew about Routh, which was a total dead end."

Erik sat and pounded hard on his keyboard. #@#$% flashed across the screen.

His pounding didn't stop Deb. "You know, partner, it's in my job description to draw you out."

He got up fast and turned away. He could explode. "When the chaplain and I met Brenda, she spit on me. Somebody spit on Routh. On his eyebrow. I thought she was going to spit on him, or worse, at the mortuary." He was pacing himself into a corner when Deb startled him by leaping up and making a perpendicular hand signal.

"Whoa, time-out." Deb's red cheeks mirrored his own burn. They'd reached a standoff.

After a beat, she sat. He returned to his chair while she sighed, "You know, I know, that we're not going to encounter Miss Manners out there, and yeah, it's good you didn't let Brenda at the corpse. Somebody spit on Routh? I don't remember saliva from the autopsy report."

"Gunk on his eyebrow." Erik stretched back in his chair and rubbed his face hard enough to pull on the skin. "I should see if the substance has been positively identified." He put a hand on his keyboard and did nothing. "Routh had thick, wiry brows."

"And that reminds you of a person you know. And it sucks to be on the receiving end of spit. I'll get on Brenda about her alibi. The best she can do is Alexa."

"A friend?"

"A bot friend, internet login records. While we're getting things off our chests—"

"We are?"

Deb was up again, swinging her air club like crazy. "Drees. He stopped me in the hall to say that Nancy LeClerc is Ambition in Chanel, savaging the women who work for her. Then he says to my face, to this face—"

"Would you rather Drees address a different part of your anatomy?"

"*To my face*, he says, 'Deborah, you of all people should know that certain women lack empathy.' Why isn't he busy with his own crime-of-the-century? You could get your workload off your chest."

"After Grimes's arrest and Gordy's reward offer, tips have flooded in about Routh's killing. They fall into two groups. The smaller set blames corrupt cops, that's soul-sucking research, and the bigger group names rival dealers. Schools of red herrings."

"Aren't red herrings really pickled kippers? The dealer tips you can delegate to precinct officers. Do you have a real ball?"

Erik took a stress ball from his desk drawer and threw it hard at Deb. When she caught it, it slapped her hand, and grains of sand drizzled to the floor. She threw it back just as hard and then the tosses slowed for a game of catch, a thin trail of sand mounting between them. "Have you read *Tom Sawyer*?" he asked.

"Was there a cat?"

"There's always a cat. I was thinking of the fence-painting part."

"You want . . . to paint a fence?"

"If Drees has time on his manicured hands, he could chase down corrupt-cop tips."

Deb paused to tape together the leaking ball. "Oh, it would take you out of the hotseat. Playing Drees, that's deceitful."

Erik was about to say *duplicitous*, but *duplicitous* was how he described his wife's, *ex*-wife's, base bastard lawyer mentor. "I'd say honorably strategic."

"'Honorably strategic.' Huh." Deb tossed the ball. The tape spun off midway, opening the seam wider. The ball, having lost its sand, fell with a *plap* between them.

Erik brushed up the sand with his hands. "It may be too low?"

"You need a vacuum. What behavior do you want to model for your son? Would you want a sweet boy like Ben to con Drees? Or are you morally bankrupt enough that you have no problem with that?" Deb seemed fine with moral bankruptcy where Drees was concerned.

"You think Ben is sweet?"

"So sweet he gets away with playing you."

Erik dropped the ball into the wastebasket and leaned over it as he brushed off his hands. He didn't want Deb to see him smile.

When Deb packed up her imaginary golf clubs and departed, Erik left the door open and fidgeted at his computer. The office was dim until Drees chanced by and the ambient light glinted off his blond hair.

"Jansson, did you give me coffee with paper clips in it?"

Erik gawked at him blankly.

"Guess not. No progress on the Routh case?"

"There's a pattern I'm not quite seeing in the tips. They've increased since the arrest of . . . hmm, slipped my mind."

Drees barged ahead. "The arrest of Vernon Grimes, you should be aware of that. Rivals and his terrorized gang are taking advantage to report activities that they were too scared to report before in order to undercut each other and make their own share bigger."

When Drees invaded his personal computer space, Erik suppressed a shudder and pointed to his monitor. "Now, um, there are calls about corrupt officers."

"Which by law we must follow up."

"They could be misleading leads. I mean—"

"You mean criminals are seizing this opportunity to undermine officers investigating them by calling in false tips." Drees jiggled the spare change in his pocket.

"Of course. I have a court date coming up and prioritizing what to do next, well . . .." Erik shook his head.

Drees ran his hands up and down the outside of his legs. "Jansson, this requires serious thought. I can't finish my last case report until other people provide data. I'll try to make sense of it for you. I'll talk to Ibeling."

"No need. I'm sure Ibeling will see what must be done."

Like that, Erik cut down his workload.

BUT HE HAD CUT THE EASY HALF. Erik wanted to attend to one last item for the day. He headed to the Cyber Unit, mulling over an observation received from undercovers Squeegee and Hairpin: an Eastside patrol officer was sniffing out dealers but had taken no action. In a cubby one over from where the forensic accountant, a woman, worked on another case, Erik spoke with Ms. Mahdi, one of the interns. Cyber Paul wished to hire her on a permanent basis for her sharp eye. "Ms. Mahdi, using records available to us without a warrant, check these names in this district for injuries or sick-leave absences. I'm operating on a hunch. I'm looking to see if these officers were or are coping with injuries and chronic pain."

"Because they aren't reaching out for help, are they?" Ms. Mahdi, earnest and discreet in her hijab, sat at a computer to pull up databases. "We talked about Post Traumatic Stress Disorder in a class and how law enforcement officers can be reluctant to ask for help. They might require an intervention."

Erik had been thinking of the fallen as corrupted, not as in need of help. Thus the need for the young and idealistic to counter the cynicism of experience. "Yes, you're right. If that's the case, we'll contact the appropriate support system. Also be aware that people might seek pain relief in illegal forms."

"Oh." She was crestfallen.

Erik regretted her disillusionment. "Ms. Mahdi, you might google 'negative capability.' How to be openminded *and* suspicious. In our jobs, you have to be willing to entertain the best and worst while suspending judgment. Not really humanly possible, but we try."

She clicked open more databases. "The Quran tells us that while we may deserve disaster, Allah pardons much."

"There may be nothing in it."

"There's always a need for help."

Erik left the intern to her assignment, unsure if he wanted her to succeed.

CHAPTER 26

BROKEN ROMANCES RUN RAGGED.
    "Could you button me up?"
"But I'm better at unbuttoning."

This banter occurred in repeated dreams, so when his ex-wife asked, "Could you button me up?" on Tuesday morning during the Ben pickup, Erik's reply came on cue. Kristine immediately stepped away and hurried to their, no, *her* bedroom. When Erik had seen her loving up Ben, wearing that curvy sheath with the back buttons, his heart forgot that they had divorced in a fury. She'd cheated. Being a lawyer, she knew cheating had consequences. So what if the cheating happened after one of his homicide investigations intersected with her labor-issue case? A remark she dropped by happenstance turned into a major clue for him. He never meant to cause trouble with her firm. Erik's mouth tasted bitter as he packed up Ben's lunch in a Jedi backpack. Kristine returned, her foxiness subdued by a suit, her curly hair pulled into a bun, the vitality of her face erased. She hugged Ben without a word. Was Erik supposed to apologize? She still had that bastard-mentor-lawyer-seducer "boyfriend," a cad older by at least ten years. Erik had squat.

That wasn't true, and he knew it. He had Ben, blessedly too sleepy to be upset by his parents' spitefulness. Erik also knew that he couldn't move on until he confronted all that had driven them into opposite corners. Maybe he wasn't trying. Maybe he just shut down.

And he had an open case to confront. Having left Ben at camp, Erik returned to Linden Hills for a run along the Lake Harriet Trail. He pounded his way practically to Edina. Having pawned off tips on Drees, Erik spent his running time figuring out minor characters. His speculations would be moot if Luna revealed enough to put the Routh investigation to rest. But was there indeed a larger context involving a network, Grimes's for example, of traffickers and dealers? Several people at the Hirsch Fest mentioned a counselor, Josh Miller. Would this Miller have interacted with Routh and therefore have information? When Erik called the rehab center yesterday, Human Resources told him that Josh had not done peer counseling since February. The DMV records listed several Josh Millers, none with a Minneapolis or St. Paul address. One young and attractive enough to be remembered by girls had a rural address an hour southwest of Minneapolis.

Erik backtracked to the north end of Linden Hills. His phone buzzed—the G-Met intern had news.

IN THE CYBERUNIT, WITH THE HVAC HISSING, Ms. Mahdi asked if she had retrieved the right time sequence for the traffic-cam footage, last week Sunday. Erik realized his error. Instead of Sunday with Luna and the dog, that devil autofill had submitted the window for Dan Routh's murder the previous week. It turned out to be exactly the right sequence.

The intersection where the Mustang hit the dog was a street over and several blocks west from the *Celebrate!* dumpster. The intern hit play at the 11:50 p.m. time marker.

A boarded storefront darkened the area; a trash receptacle and mailbox stood at the southeast corner. A traffic cone indicated a dip in the street by the storm drain. A few vehicles drove through the intersection, not slowing for the red light if no cross traffic appeared. Then the cross street filled, likely people leaving the same drinking hole, and a white van jerked in from the south and slammed the brakes for cross traffic. A shape fell street side and rolled to the curb. The intersection clear, the van stuttered off. Then a second van appeared as if tracking it.

Ms. Mahdi paused the video at time marker 12:17 a.m., Monday morning. "Replay?"

"No, hold it." Erik checked case notes on his phone. The first van's plate was obscured, but that of the second van matched the plate from Gordy Omdahl's missing Chevy Express, the one loaned to Dan Routh. "Okay, continue." The shape stayed in the dip of the street. "Speed it up," Erik directed the intern.

At 12:49, the shape stirred. The full hair and figure suggested a woman. The figure scurried behind the mailbox. Three vehicles passed. At 1:01 a.m., the person, crouching, moved east along the cross-street sidewalk and out of the picture. The footage would be enlarged, reviewed, and more would be requested from adjacent intersections. Erik knew what he would find. Luna had been in the first van and escaped.

THIS JOB PROMOTED HAIR LOSS. Deb stopped tugging her hair spikes and forced her hands into her pockets. Through the one-way window she watched Luna fidgeting in the interrogation room, and next to her sat a different lawyer than the frog-voice from the Resource, an older man who cut his teeth on clergy-abuse cases. Eleven o'clock and Erik was stuck on the phone about a court date. Neither wanted a dragged-out wait for Luna, though with hardened suspects, a prolonged wait worked as a cruel and not unusual punishment.

How to proceed with an eighteen-year-old diagnosed with an FAS-related anxiety disorder? Few victim-survivors were telegenic paragons. As a general rule, life did not produce telegenic paragons. The nature of trafficking and drug use fostered complicity, compromise, and contamination. The hardest case Deb had when she worked in Iowa—not the hardest to crack but hardest to bear—involved a woman who had been done very wrong. Then she did the worst, her own child dead. Rabid victims biting back.

"Thoughts on your tactics?"

She jumped. *Dammit*, when had Erik slipped in? "What we know: Luna was supposed to meet Dan Routh Sunday night. Luna shows up next week Sunday in Eau Claire, presumably on her way to the Wisconsin Dells. She has injuries consistent with a fall. Luna gushes on about a boyfriend. He may be using her, but Luna *yearns* for love. In your Highlander, after the Mustang hit the dog, she goes absolutely hysterical that she 'made a mistake.' I couldn't question her in the ambulance—that wouldn't hold up in court, given her condition. My gut, once it recovered from—never mind, I hope you've having your Highlander detailed—still finds it improbable that she could fall from a van and limp several blocks to climb into a dumpster and knife Dan."

"We can't close out that possibility."

"No. We—"

"You. A woman should take this one." Erik was serious. "I'll follow your lead."

"Until some whacko idea pops into your head and you speak in strange tongues."

"That's strategy."

"All right then." Facts, a good place to start. A better place would be Luna's perspective.

Luna didn't look up as the detectives entered and seated themselves. The lawyer shook hands.

"Luna . . ." Deb almost followed with an assertive "I believe" but switched to neutral. "It seems you were in a dangerous situation. Dangerous enough that you fell out of a van to save yourself."

Luna picked at a red cuticle. She wore a sundress with a ruched neckline and a scarf for modesty, probably on the recommendation of Sharon at the Resource.

"Luna, telling the truth reduces anxiety. It drives me crazy to hold things back. Situations can be messy." Deb flashed on the evidence photo of murdered Dan atop garbage. "And I like to help people get out of them. Erik, Detective Yansson, likes to help. First, we need a place to start. You got into a van. Where?"

The lawyer prompted, "You can answer, Luna."

She did not make eye contact. "In a parking lot."

"Where was the parking lot, Luna?" Erik asked.

She shrugged. "Don't know. I might make a mistake."

Her lawyer signaled he wanted to talk with his client in private, but Deb barged in, "Sunday, after the dog was hit, you said you made a mistake. In the ambulance."

"In the ambulance, you said you're the queen of mistakes," Luna filled in.

"I said I was an expert witness when it came to mistakes. Women make mistakes, terrible ones. Men make mistakes too. Even Yansson makes mistakes."

"I should have traded in my Highlander months ago," he corroborated.

"Just because we make mistakes doesn't mean we don't deserve justice. There are still good outcomes. Post-it notes started out as a mistake."

"Detective Metzger, your *point*?" from the lawyer.

"You said in the ambulance, Luna, that someone said you *were* a mistake. You are not a mistake. You have value. Who said that?"

The lawyer had his hand on Luna's arm and whispered. She blinked wet-ringed eyes at Deb. "I don't, um, remember the ambulance. I remember the parking lot had trees around it, kind of sloped down. It was near one of those interstates and the hospitals in St. Paul. We were hanging out on the lower end, me and Pammie. The hotel was supposed to have a fun bar. I'm not old enough to drink but I can have fun at a bar. Like I thought there were ducks inside? But that's a different place. Ray said the hotel was simple?"

The name "Ray" again. Deb was damn good at moving fast and cornering her prey, but at cautiously pacing herself, not so much. She breathed slowly. "Do you remember more about the hotel?"

Luna looked at the lawyer, who nodded an affirmative. "Kind of French?"

"A LeClerc Simple?" Erik asked. "One is in the location you describe."

"Maybe." Luna picked at her cuticle until it bled. The lawyer handed her the beverage napkin from under his water glass.

"What was your plan for the night?" Deb asked.

Luna wrapped the napkin around her finger. "Hang out."

"You had arranged for Dan Routh to meet you there."

Deb overheard the lawyer advise Luna, "Remember to breathe." What was it about the human race that it had to be instructed to breathe?

Deb repeated, "You were in a dangerous situation, Luna. Someone, his notes suggest you, called Dan Routh from a burner phone."

"My boyfriend and me, we had a fight earlier, and I was mad and called Dan and, uh, later, um, forgot to call him to tell him don't come."

"Could that be because you *did* want Mr. Routh to come?" Erik asked. "Was that the mistake?"

The lawyer put up a hand. "Luna, would you like to talk in private?"

She didn't react and Deb filled in the space. "You mentioned a fight. About what?"

It spilled out. "He wanted me to bring more girls 'for fun,' and I just wanted to be with him. I figured Pammie would come. We were going to meet in the parking lot. Pammie had another girlfriend, they were late, and my boyfriend, Ray, he'd been so nice but he was pissed at everybody being late. I was getting the shakes, and he said I should take one of my pills—he got me better pills through his job. I took one and maybe he did too because he got strange. Then that man drove in, the upside-down-head guy. He's, like, Ray's boss for a bunch of delivery jobs. He didn't see us right away because he was on the other side of the lot, and Ray grabs my arm and says, 'You gotta do me a big favor. Help me, my boss is pissed.' Then, like, Dan pulls up next to us in a van, and I see his face. Like he doesn't know what the hell is going on. Ray's super strong and pushes me into his van. Maybe he thinks Dan works for his boss and will hurt us. I kind of flop around in the van when it takes off, no seats in the back, and my heart's beating like crazy. Ray's yelling 'the fuckers' in front, and I can't sit up. Like I'm getting those palpitations now. I need my paper bag." The lawyer came prepared with one, which she grasped and held to her face while her breasts heaved and her breathing rattled. Deb was about to say slow exhales worked better than a bag but held her tongue and did slow exhales herself.

When Luna put the bag down, the lawyer asked if she needed more time. Instead of answering, she stared at Deb.

"You're on my side, right?"

"Yes." Deb was. For now.

Luna unwrapped her cuticle and took a bite at it. "Ray's calling me a whore, saying it's my fault, saying he was promised that the hotel was good. He says I'm supposed to help. He says I told and calls me a fucking bitch."

Erik said slowly, "I'm curious how Ray—I don't believe you've said his last name—how Ray wanted you to help. Did he ask for money?"

Luna pushed at her cuticle, which oozed blood, and rewrapped it. "He wanted to take me and Pammie to a party, that's all."

"Did he say anything about meeting men or partying with drugs?" Deb asked.

"Luna, you don't have to talk about yourself," the lawyer directed. "You can talk about the people arranging the party."

Tears drip-dropped to the table.

"Luna," Deb sighed, "parties can be scary when strange men drink and get high. Terrifying. If I'd been in your position, I'd call Dan. I'd get out of there any way I could."

"Detective . . ." the lawyer warned.

Deb wouldn't shut it down. "It's hard, I know. But the more we know, the safer you'll be, Luna. You were in the back of the van, Ray yelling at you, and upside-down-head man or Dan Routh chasing you, maybe both. You escape."

Luna screwed her face so she could barely speak. "Ray said it was a good hotel, he knew people. I was torn, you know. I liked what Dan told me about the Resource and I kinda hoped Dan would come, see Ray, so we could talk, the three of us." She squeezed her eyes shut. "I, I didn't think . . . there'd be *killing*."

The lawyer took over. "Which you did *not* witness. Luna, you've been very helpful to the detectives."

"Yes, we'll get you back to your grandmother," Deb said. "But I'm worried about Pammie. It would help if you could describe Ray so—"

"*You* wouldn't understand," Luna burst out. "Not somebody like *you*. He *loves* me. You don't get it. *He loves me.*"

Deb got it all right. She was lesbian and wouldn't "get" man-woman love. Luna's breath hitched.

Erik put his arms on the table. "I'm thinking that you're worried about Ray. Maybe he's running the show, maybe he's trapped in the system."

"So he's innocent?" Luna asked Erik before the lawyer could stop her.

"I'm thinking there's a dangerous system out there—"

"You think he's hurt?" Luna interrupted him. "I don't want him hurt. He loves me."

"There's love and there's acting lovingly." Erik held her with those blue eyes of his. "The system . . . when someone tries to get out, people like Dan Routh are hurt. The helpers are hurt."

"Like in that TV show, with Fred Rogers, *Mr. Rogers' Neighborhood*," Deb butted in. "The helpers are important. A helper was—"

"Detectives," the lawyer rolled out his heaviest sigh. "While we all admire Mr. Rogers, may I remind you Ms. Johnson is an adult."

"I like Daniel Tiger." Luna settled a little. "Mr. Rogers would say I could go now."

"This is about justice and protection for you." Erik borrowed a line Deb used. He'd taken her lead. Deb would be furious, but she was shaking with frustration and all she could squeak out was, "Take care, Luna."

The lawyer escorted Luna from the room, and Deb shook it off and schemed. She would consult with the lawyer again about putting Luna with a sketch artist to identify her "boyfriend." The captured Vernon Grimes might provide information about his traffickers to reduce his own charges. That was a pipe dream. Did pipe dreams involve opium? Anyway, in her meeting with Nancy LeClerc, Deb could gather information about the LeClerc Simples. She was tempted to send Erik, since hetero women took to him, except Nancy admired tough women and Deb could ferret out the inside scoop.

Speaking of Erik, he was catnapping in his chair.

CHAPTER 27

I**N THE NAME OF DUTY**, Erik had his second workout of the day. It was late Tuesday afternoon, and the gym unofficially referred to as the Testosterone Zone was overrun by women. The women checked out Erik in his shorts before moving on to their spin class. Why did it require a class to sit on a bike and pedal nowhere? Erik might as well do the same, since the Routh case was heading nowhere. Luna's account of events lacked significant details: Ray's last name, Pammie's last name, phone numbers. Erik was at a standstill—he had to be to spot Undercover Agent Hairpin who was bench-pressing two hundred pounds. Hairpin appeared to be Afro-Latino, and his tight waves were held back by a fanged snake pin. Erik guided the barbells into the stand, and Hairpin, who investigated the drug supply chain, mopped his face and ranted.

"What's with Twin Cities law enforcement? What kind of laggards are we?" Hairpin moved to dumbbells and Erik joined in with the biceps count. The undercover's cherub tattoos sucked in and puffed out with each rep. A closer look revealed that they were temporary. Hairpin huffed out, "Check it out online, Jansson. Norfolk, Virginia, did 'Uptown Funk,' the choreography totally down. Bangor, Maine, PD, s'got 'the duck of justice.' Apple Valley force, zoo animal karaoke. Dakota County, skate boarders, and an Elvis impersonator. And they're throwing the book at us for one song."

A background Munchkin piped up, "*Ding dong the Grimes is caught.*"

"Cut it out over there." Hairpin rubbed his face with Erik's towel. "What did you want to show me?"

"Your first impression." Erik displayed images on his phone: a police sketch of "Ray" based on the description coaxed from Luna and a DMV photo of Josh Miller.

"Generic white guys. How do you tell yourselves apart? Brothers? I don't think they're the same guy. The one in the drawing looks older. 'Course, it's a simulation. The second looks more familiar. What does your source say about the two?"

"Our source, a recovered girl, needs rest spells, and we haven't shown her the DMV photo of Josh Miller yet. I have a tip that Miller might be familiar with young users and suppliers east of the University area."

"Huh. Can't think where I mighta seen him."

"Miller's done peer addiction counseling with Hirsch Rehab and attended seminars at the Resource. The drawing is of 'Ray,' who was being followed by Dan Routh the night of Routh's killing."

Hairpin swigged vitamin water. "Lots of Rays, Ricardos, Randy, Richard. Names change on the streets. The guy could've been christened Julius for all we know. I mostly track the Spanish speakers and the transporters across state lines. You want street-level knowledge, I'll message my partner Squeegee to reach out."

"Do I meet up with him, her?"

"Squeegee? Squeegee's so deep undercover that I don't know what 'he/she' looks like."

Erik and Hairpin circled the gym to cool down, and they paused by the clear partition with the spinning class beyond. Hairpin admired a brunette's pumping calves. "Have you reviewed everything on Grimes?"

"I heard he prefers the delivery model."

Hairpin rubbed a towel across his sweaty neck. "He picked that up from operators out of Xalisco, Mexico, working the West Coast in the nineties. Grimes likewise uses decent-looking kids, and he's convinced his team that they're a class act with high-end products and customers. Promises rewards."

"Honor among thieves?"

"Wouldn't go that far. His low-level facilitators don't carry a lot of product. If a kid's randomly picked up, he can't be charged for much. Grimes expanded by throwing sex services in the mix, which raises the legal stakes. His abuela must have read him Machiavelli at bedtime. Yeah, he'll 'upscale' his lieutenants and facilitators with a little cash and a neighborhood that's an upgrade from a sewer. That's the diamond-crusted carrot. Then he comes at 'em with a bloody stick. He gets something on them, like 'I know where your sister hangs out.' A brute when he loses his temper. He's killed a few; we just haven't found the bodies yet. I'll say this, his organization's been damn shaky since his second in command died."

"A drug-war killing?" Erik walked toward the lockers before the spin class cited them for visual harassment.

"Grimes's second had business sense but not the common kind. Common sense, I mean. Thought he'd try heli-skiing last March. He didn't get the memo that the helicopters set you down on the alp. You don't jump out, skis first. Say, Jansson, can I ask you something?"

"Yeah." They reached the entrance to the lockers.

"What's your story? Single, I hear. You like kids? I've got this cousin, gorgeous if you don't insist on your women being underfed. How do you feel about Catholicism?"

They were ambushed—Drees pushed through the locker door. The hair on his arms was groomed. "Gentlemen, did you have a good workout? Jansson, you haven't broken a sweat. By the way, I saw your ex driving a great new Audi."

Erik made an excuse that he had to prepare for an upcoming court appearance and would shower back at the G-Met station. He'd have to rub himself down with disinfectants, given that shower's mold status and the film that coated him after any Drees encounter. What he couldn't explain to himself was his anxiety over Josh Miller.

KNOWING THE WORST OF PEOPLE CAN DESTROY THEM; knowing the worst can be the only way to help them. Under the steam of the G-Met shower, Erik entertained the faint hope that Josh Miller might have witnessed Luna consorting with the mysterious Ray. Josh was scarcely active on social media. Before coming into the station to shower, Erik sat in the parking lot and called Josh's father. Mr. Miller was annoyed that Erik interrupted him at chores and became downright angry over Erik's assurances that Josh was not in trouble: "Why would the law call if he's not in trouble? Is Josh using again?" Mr. Miller cursed as Erik repeated that this was simply a request for Josh's contact information, which Mr. Miller was not required to supply.

"His mother's here. She'll tell you," and the phone was handed off. Erik succeeded in upsetting a second person. Mrs. Miller began crying. His dread increased as he asked if there was reason for concern. She answered shakily, "No, Josh has never had *real* trouble with the law. Except a DUI. You probably know he used drugs. He raised himself up out of that and I was so proud he wanted to be a counselor and then I worried about what he exposed himself to, to temptations." She cried harder. Erik was about to volunteer to call back later when she provided an address and a cell number. "I wish he'd be better about keeping in touch. His number changes, and we haven't spoken in over a month. Our younger boy, Stuart, might know, but he's not back from Chicago until tonight. If you reach Josh"—she swallowed a sob—"tell him to call his mother?" Erik, still in his Highlander, called the numbers. Josh's had a full message box, so he left a message with Stuart. How far did Stuart go to be his brother's keeper?

Out of the shower, Erik rubbed precautionary antiseptic between his toes and speculated that Grimes & Associates had their hooks in Josh.

TUESDAY WOULDN'T END. Deb sat at her desk trying to hang on until 6:00 p.m. After the session with the lawyer, Luna took a burrito break and watched a Mr. Rogers episode on a G-Met monitor. Deb then worked on convincing Luna to describe Ray. In doing so, Deb revealed too much. "I know what it's like," she said, "to be the odd one. To know you have skills when people won't see that or convince themselves they don't like what you've got. To think you've found love then lost it." True, Deb delivered her message like she was announcing truck arrivals at interstate dispatch. As Luna picked at herself, Deb reminded her that her dad and Gammy loved her, that she had a friend in Pammie. With Pammie, Deb applied the screwdriver and twisted. Had Luna heard from Pammie? What made Pammie vulnerable? Where did she hang out? Luna began to weep, Deb backed off, and after another Mr. Rogers break, the girl met with a sketch artist sitting at his CGI computer only to balk at describing Ray.

Ding from Deb's attention-hog computer. A reminder of her meeting with Nancy LeClerc tomorrow, *be sharp and prepare on these topics.* The phone rang, Lola Scheers of the task force. She said her husband was recovering and that she had checked regional reports and, yes, there had been an uptick in suspicious activities at LeClercs. Raids were in the works for two of the Simples. Trafficking stings worked in different ways. In one approach, women officers under sexy pseudonyms used the internet to set up "dates" with pimps and johns. When the men arrived, they were arrested. In another, investigators acted as johns to show up at assignations to arrest the pimps and pull in the girls. Lola had planned that second option, and morning was a good time because trafficking "clients" figured a morning meet-up was less likely to be noticed. The hotels were routinely forewarned of planned police activity. However, if hotels were being deliberately blind, Lola argued, the forewarning was last-minute and cryptic. In other words, Deb should stay mum about the plan.

After the call, Deb slumped down at her desk and felt like bread turning to mold.

ERIK NUDGED HER ELBOW AND DEB ROUSED HERSELF to take the paper towel he offered. She rubbed her eyes with it and wiped up the drool on her desk. As she shook off her grogginess, Erik scowled out their filmy window. His damp hair stood up in tufts. "Well, partner, thanks for the towel. Did you comb your hair with porcupine quills?" Nothing. "Rebooting here. How goes the case?"

"I reviewed the last forensics report. The substance on Dan Routh's eyebrow was soap gel from a dispenser in a broken garbage bag." He leaned his back against the window as if in pain. "It's good it's not saliva—no one spit on him—but saliva would have provided DNA. Beyond that dead end, I've become fixated on this kid who probably has nothing to do with anything,

Josh Miller. People at the Hirsch Fest mentioned he might know Luna or her street crowd. He bears some resemblance to the sketch of 'Ray.'"

"Airbrush your worry lines and *you* resemble that sketch. Oh gosh, when the artist asked Luna to describe the shape of Ray's eyes, she said 'eye-shaped.' Yeah, we—by we I mean me—have to pace ourselves with Luna. After lunch I pressured her on her friend Pammie. She gave me an out-of-service number, and then had a panic attack. Those are no fun to have, or watch."

Erik sunk into his chair. "Can't even have a decent revenge fantasy with a no-show villain."

Deb double-yawned, "What was yours? Oh, a Shop-Vac. No Shop-Vac sucking up perps? Ugh, what did Sherlock Holmes do when he was in a slump?"

"Shot himself up with cocaine and played the violin."

"I can get my hands on an alto sax. Expired Aleve." She pawed through a drawer, but Erik didn't even look. "Something's eating you." Something was usually eating at Erik, if he himself wasn't busy eating.

"What?"

"Something's eating you."

Erik stood and paced. "My wife, ex-wife, bought an Audi."

"Oh, Audis, sleek. Fun for Ben to ride in." Deb wondered what car would be best for a joyride with Nancy's assistant Jude. She had checked Jude out on social media, and dammit, her accounts were closed to outsiders. Deb hated being an outsider. She picked up on Erik saying that a Subaru used to be good enough and chimed in again, "She's a lawyer, she can afford it. You're letting the status thing get to you?"

"Drees told me. How the hell would he know." Erik fumed at their streaky window. "Why not a BMW?"

"*That's* the issue?" Deb threw up her hands. "If your ex is going to sell out, why not sell out for the make you like? You realize, legally speaking, the two of you are totally over."

"I drove her to him."

"To *Drees*? Oh, you mean that bastard dude. Look, police life—stress, schedules, sleeplessness—that drives people away."

"In the Subaru. I drove her to him in the Subaru."

"*What*?"

"I drove her to the airport. They had the same flight, same hotel, same conference." Erik closed his eyes and thudded his head against the window.

"Hey!" Deb pushed herself up from her office chair. "Stop beating yourself up, don't crack the window, good *riddance* to the Subaru, and move on already."

Erik stared daggers, bayonets, and lances at her. "Like you did?"

"*Not fair.*" So she ended her last relationship. Somebody had to.

Erik resumed pacing. "Sorry. I shouldn't have said that. But you *pry.*"

"That's my specialty." She sat down hard. It would have been authoritative, if not for the whoopie cushion sound. "I pry. I detect. I could leave you to wallow in that dark space that's your head." Erik was breathing rapidly and she began to sweat. "Look, *sorry* about prying. *Someone* has to flush you out. And you should go home and rest." Now she'd done it. He stormed out the door.

Deb banged at her computer. She should up and go home. *What's this?* Drees was forwarding practice empathy tests from an online site. If online lists are *listicles*, are online tests *testicles*? Deb wanted a sense of accomplishment for herself before calling it quits. She clicked open the empathy exam: match the image of the man to the description of the mood. Should be easy.

IT WASN'T. DEB WAS FAILING THE EMPATHY TEST when Erik stormed back to stand over her desk. She quickly closed the site.

"Sorry again," he forced out. Then he stood there, all hang dog.

"Partner, for reals, are you okay?"

"I would like to ask a strange favor, hypothetical." Erik gave her an aggrieved look then returned to his desk.

"A strange hypothetical favor?"

"Forget it."

"No, no, I may need a strange hypothetical favor one day. Heck, I probably need one every day. Like, do you have a love potion?"

Erik answered slowly. "If I find one, you'll know. But if I'm ever found dead in a dumpster, or dead, period—"

"I should solve your murder, hypothetically."

"I was thinking more on the lines of keep the photos from Ben." He squirmed miserably.

"Jeez, yeah, but lighten up. You're a smart guy out there, we got each other's backs when we aren't too busy yelling at each other's fronts. And there's gotta be good news out there, from someone."

Like that Erik squirmed with anticipation. "Have they contacted you?"

"What who where?"

"Squeegee and Hairpin, the undercovers. I've been assuming that this 'Ray' stabs Dan Routh and drives away in *Dan's* van, which actually belongs to Gordy Omdahl. Then Ray panics and calls an associate, says help a guy out, my van broke down, haul it away from this *Celebrate!* station. Within twenty-four hours, the location of Routh's body is all over the news. Ray's associates figure out what he did and say nothing because they're all part of the Grimes ring. Later Gordy's reward doesn't tempt them because they all have something to hide."

"You can take a break to breathe," Deb inserted.

"An alternative—Ray dumps the stolen van somewhere and drives back with the tow himself. What if it leaks out that Ray's saying, 'I know who killed that ex-cop. Grimes is in custody and can't touch me. I'll rat out the killer and get the reward.'"

"Hold it, you're saying 'Ray' didn't kill Routh?"

"No. I'm saying guilty Ray sets up a scapegoat. Or *we* make it look that way, have the undercovers put out the rumor that 'Ray' is going to call in a name and collect the reward. Then his worried associates flush him out."

"There's no honor among thieves."

"Exactly."

"See? If I annoy you, partner, you do good work."

Erik stormed out again.

CHAPTER 28

Tuesday at six-ish, Jaylyn was rushing to hell and gone, not that St. Paul was hell, despite what they said in Edina. Her Jeep was a goner, and to borrow the Cube, Jaylyn had to bribe Lionel with a promise of a date with an adorable cellist. Ramon and Retta were waiting at a pizza joint off Como Avenue, and after pizza they'd sit in on her McMillan jam. The plan allowed Ramon to make his last delivery and surrender the van to another Bailey's driver in the area. The plan failed to allow for Jaylyn's lesson with Lazar running late, because in his words, "inspiration transcends time." *Not on I-94 West, it doesn't.*

Jaylyn pulled into the parking area way late, and Ramon, messenger bag over shoulder and pizza box in hand, ran from the entry and hopped in. "Retta's boss rehired her"—he snapped his fingers—"if she could show pronto. She took an Uber. You'd better move it."

"Great." Jaylyn hoped that Retta had tamed the weedwhacker haircut. "Could I have a slice?" Ramon opened the box and Jaylyn grabbed one. She took a bite—onion topping—and dropped it back in the box, which disgusted Ramon. Well, he could've taken an Uber to McMillan. She maneuvered with angry jerks from one-way back to two-way streets. Her mood must be showing because he looked stricken. He shot her a glance. "I'm losing Retta, I feel it. When I'm free, she's not. When we're together, she's hostile."

Jaylyn regretted her pettiness and her mood sank lower on recognizing Retta's pattern of withdrawal. "Have you checked for signs of drinking?"

Ramon jammed the pizza box under the seat. "Fuck, her being pissed off and sick. Are those signs? You're right, we need to watch out for her." He rubbed his eyes. "This is too heavy. So what's up with your music?"

"My friend Teddi wants to practice for a bluesy gig. Cool stuff, you'll like it. I'm behind because my lesson with Lazar started late." When Lazar admitted he had become too slow to run his own errands, Jaylyn was about to recommend Ramon's service, but she didn't have the nerve. "Anyway, Lazar has musculoskeletal issues. He's, like, a genius on movement. And he talks a lot, spouting off wacko ideas."

"Didn't you see the detour sign? This street's two-way during construction. Do you trust him?" Ramon, the case with every guy when a woman drives, watched the road in terror. "Can you trust a wacko?"

Did she, with those tempting mystery pills of his? "I'll see if his ideas work. He kinda works through pain to help me. That says something. Lazar has this theory. He says Johann Sebastian Bach *loved* a god, Beethoven *was* a god, Stravinsky *acted* like a god." Ramon mumbled merge left. "Dvorak heard happy angels all the time because even his sad music is happy and—"

"*Jaylyn!*" Ramon grabbed the dash as a Lexus swerved around her, horn wailing, and an oncoming Suburban rode the curb to avoid a collision. "*Turn right. Right.*"

Jaylyn jerked the wheel and teared up. "This stupid Cube, no pickup at all."

"Pull over."

"By the hydrant?"

"I'll drive. You need to calm down." Ramon opened his door as she jerked to a halt and they switched.

A fortunate switch, because the McMillan parking garage was closed for structural repairs. Ramon dropped her off and said he'd find her. She dashed into the building, breathless and happy. Musicians everywhere, the jazz hipsters and classic nerds who morphed into each other, teen stars mimicking each other's riffs. Little kids skipped along with fairy-tale violins while Muggle adults hulked behind them. The assigned place was a recital room.

"You're late, Jaylyn." Teddi tapped her Doc Martens as Jaylyn came up the aisle between chairs.

"Fifteen minutes is nothing in blues world," Jaylyn laughed. Months back, Jaylyn had introduced two of her music friends to Teddi, who enlisted them for the gig. The bass player was Wolfman, a dark-skinned African American. He raked his facial hair with his long nails and grunted, "Hey." The drummer, a redheaded African American, curled over his set like a bass clef. He greeted her with a rim shot. He was called Oboe because of his reedy tenor. Jaylyn rifled through the music in her bag and raised her head to see Ramon come into the back, wave his phone, and step out.

Teddi started them off with "You Go to My Head." Jaylyn sight-read her part, the bassist improvised, and the drummer brushed his snares when inclined.

Teddi stopped. "Bleh. Everyone agrees, right, that it sucks to suck? Let's give 'Sinnerman' a try. Piano player, count it off."

The words were from an old spiritual. The trippy rhythm, Jaylyn adapted from Nina Simone's 1960s piano arrangement. "One two, one two." The drummer came in with rapid clacks. Teddi entered a half beat late, raised her hand, and they stopped.

Second try, syncopation right, Teddi came in, *sinnerman, where you gonna run to . . . we got to run to the rock please hide me . . ..* "Stop. That likewise sucks." Teddi took exaggerated cleansing breaths and they started over.

Thrust after thrust, the rhythm tripping over itself to get away . . . *I can't hide you, the rock cried out don't you see I need you rock Good Lord, Lord all on that day . . ..*

"Oh god, please hide me, ugh." Teddi stomped about. Back in group therapy days, if Teddi lost her detachment she turned mean as shit. That's when the tough-love counselor would say, "You got outta hell. Don't let attitude drag you back." She spit into that counselor's face, "I've a right." He said, "You've a right to seek legal action and reparation. You've a right to grieve, a right to take time to heal. No right, none whatsoever, on making others suffer." The counselor had suffered, the result an artificial leg because he'd drunk-walked in front of a drunk driver. If Teddi still sulked, he'd start in with dumb jokes about you can't run and you can't hide, knock-knock I know you're in there, life is tough but it comes with ice cream. Nobody could hug Teddi because of the sex abuse thing, but the counselor's slant worked. He had a different dork tactic with each kid. He instructed Jaylyn to get pushy, to push her palms hard against his and resist, resist more, with all she had.

Jaylyn had daydreamed her way through Teddi's instructions. The piano part was basically frantic repeats. Another attempt.

Teddi stomped her foot. "*Jaylyn*, you're *rushing* me. Get rid of the boyfriend. He's a distraction."

Ramon must've returned. Not Ramon, Josh. Jaylyn's heart missed a beat. "Give me a sec."

Instead Teddi gave her the stink eye. "Here to rehearse!"

The drummer squawked interference, "Don't be such a hormone, Teddi."

She relented with a roll of purple-lashed eyes. "The Great Oboe has spoken." She took from a music stand a small hourglass, a joke timer for Chopin's minute waltz, flipped it, and in a witchy falsetto, declaimed, "You have three minutes, my pretty." Jaylyn ran back to Josh.

His "hey" was overridden by her hiss, "You didn't call."

"I'm in trouble, Jaylyn." His eyes skittered about the room and he moved sideways toward the wall. "I thought I was doing the right thing. I mean, I was doing a wrong thing but thought I could, um . . .."

"What are you talking about?" The musicians behind Jaylyn fooled around with a version of "Stand by Me."

"Someone I know died. That counselor, the one with the bionic leg, he's moved on from teen rehab and I want to find him. I thought you might know."

"Why would I know? I'm not using." When she saw how her tone stung, Jaylyn downshifted from Gran's sharpness to her mom's pragmatism. "Do you need to call a doctor?"

"They give free samples to kids. I know about this undercover . . ." Josh broke off when the door opened and Ramon slid in. Ramon blinked at the two and slid out. The surprise threw Josh. "Who's that guy?"

"A friend's boyfriend." Behind Jaylyn, Teddi and Wolfman argued.

"Jaylyn, I'm sorry. For a sec I thought I knew him, maybe. Look, I need to check out stuff. I'll call. No, meet me tomorrow by the Stone Arch Bridge, your favorite spot, noon." Josh darted in to kiss Jaylyn on the cheek and rushed out the door. Jaylyn hung in a pocket of empty air.

Until she saw the trio watching her. They finger-snapped their approval.

RAMON WAS SLOUCHING IN THE BACK OF THE ROOM when the session ended with a bang and Teddi's whimper that everyone had to freaking practice. He walked Jaylyn to where he'd parked the Cube in the North Loop neighborhood. The streets had been polished by a gentle rain, a gentleness lost on Ramon. He stopped dead at the crosswalk, despite the signal being in their favor. "I'm trapped." He stepped off the curb, stepped back when the light turned against them. "My jerk boss wants me to work *nonstop*. We're competing with *drones*, *robots*." He was crying, soundless. The light signaled they had twenty seconds to cross and he took fast, long strides, Jaylyn trotting to catch up.

Halfway, she grabbed his elbow to ask if this was really about his dad because Ramon had hinted about reporting him for drug possession. It never got out of her mouth. Ramon moved even faster to the other side. "Retta's covering up something. I hate to put it on you, Jaylyn. It's just you're, like, the first reliable person I've met." He sniffed. "I found this in the bathroom." He took a bottle from his pocket and pressed it into Jaylyn's hand.

Deciphering the script under a streetlamp sickened her. "It's hydrocodone with acetaminophen, you must know about that from your deliveries, a narcotic-Tylenol blend." Jaylyn reached for an excuse. "Did Retta sprain her wrist at work?"

Ramon hustled down the sidewalk. "You take it before she washes 'em down with alcohol."

"I can't take a prescription. It's illegal." Jaylyn fought panic and hurried again to stay with him. "Take it back, Ramon." She indelicately stuffed the bottle into his pants pocket.

He slowed. "It's like someone's trying to get to Retta when I'm not around.

I can't be around all the time. You can't be around her all the time. She has to watch out for herself. *She has to.*"

Jaylyn had missed something. Ramon's dad? Was he after Retta too for money? It had to be hard for Ramon to completely break from the man, to lose his dad forever. She didn't dare ask about that outright. "Who would be out to get Retta?"

Ramon shook his head. They were almost to Hennepin Avenue. She'd joke that he might as well have parked the Cube in South Dakota if his expression wasn't so grim.

He read her mind. "Sorry it wasn't parked closer." He fished the pill bottle out of his pocket to dig for the fob. When he handed the fob over, Jaylyn gave him a quick hug. If they'd been a couple, it would have been romantic, with the soft evening air, the gleam of the streets, the sun tinting the skyline pink. "I shouldn't have worried you. I'll catch light rail. Bye." He squeezed her hand. Then he was gone.

In the Cube, Jaylyn flung her bag on the passenger seat and shivered. There was a dissonance. Must be the idea of the pills. What a relief to go home, to bed, the same bed she'd slept in since learning to say her prayers. She would fall asleep to the lilt of Bach's "Sheep May Safely Graze." Bach had a god, Bach loved a god.

CHAPTER 29

TUESDAY EVENING WOULDN'T END. For his third workout of the day, Erik did another run around Lake Harriet, this time through a misty rain. He returned to his apartment in a Zen state, ate reheated pasta, and showered. Wearing his boxers, he slouched back in what Ben called his Papa Bear chair (no Ben tonight) and opened a crisp pilsner to quench his thirst. He took a few swigs and closed his eyes. Naturally, the phone rang.

Undercover Squeegee had worries.

It took a minute for Erik to adjust to the adapter that disguised Squeegee's voice. It then took time to patch in Deb for a conference call. She yawned that she'd fallen asleep watching a show about siblings on the verge of croaking each other over the family succession plan. Squeegee swore at himself for missing that episode because the show was his fave. Deb asked how he became "Squeegee." It was a role, he explained, like in that sci-fi series *Dr. Who*. The main qualification was that you could act cool while staying alive among those who, if they knew, would have you dead.

Erik broke in, "On that 'dead' note, Squeegee, you were having doubts over planting rumors about Ray."

"A potential death sentence. Put it out there that Ray's cheating on Grimes, and Grimes might make Ray grave fodder. That would be rough justice, if Ray killed Routh."

"So you can't predict how a rumor will play out," Deb said.

"It might flush him out alive, like you're hoping. He'd come to us for protection or someone will rat him out through a tip. When you sent me that sketch of 'Ray,' I thought for a sec it was an informant of mine, a dark-haired guy in his twenties. Coinkydink or not, that informant just left me a need-to-contact message. I don't know what name he goes by on the street. I'll suss him out."

"You have no idea at this point if he's connected to Routh, right?" Erik asked. "Right."

Erik released a weary exhale. "If your informant is *not* Ray, that returns us to the rumor tactic. I don't want to set off a street killing. But . . .."

"But what?" Deb yawned.

"But what do we think the Ray that Luna described is doing right now?" There was a crackle over the conference line and Erik feared the connection was lost.

Then Deb said, her anger muted by exhaustion, "With that profile, a controlling type. He'd be sweetening up a new girl. The sweetness stops when he needs to force a 'favor.' Then he moves on to victim number whatever. He'd save himself before he'd save any of them. No honor among traffickers."

They ended the call with the plan that Squeegee would reach out to his informant, and if that contact yielded little, the undercover would spread rumors about Ray cheating the Grimes gang.

What was left of Erik's beer stank of stale grain. He dumped the tepid brew down his bathroom sink and crawled into bed. His Zen state had evaporated.

A FORKED TONGUE CRACKLED THROUGH DEB'S MORNING DAZE.

She had been thrashing through a nightmare that she stood before an audience shouting. The more she shouted, the more they couldn't hear. She came to the part where she would say the words that would make everything clear, but the words stuck in her craw and she woke gagging on the sheet. Was it fear of meeting with Nancy LeClerc this morning? Or was her dream about experiencing what abuse victims feel? That no one understands the insidious harm they've endured? That no one understands how they're burdened with guilt when their tongues fail?

The phone call shaking her out of it should have been a relief if not for the demon timbre. Deb, on the edge of her bed, interrupted the caller, "Squeegee, can you turn off your voice adaptor? It's worse than last night and I can't make out what you're saying."

"I can't run the risk of you recognizing my velvet tones at a Whole Foods." After a squeal, the undercover agent asked, "Better?"

"You still need an exorcist."

"That's what this job does to ya. 'Bout my informant, the kid's spooked and I couldn't get a feel from a burner phone confab if he's your 'Ray.' Didn't feel right to ask him direct about that, but I convinced him to meet up with your dude Jansson."

"Not my dude."

"He's his own dude then, except he was with his boy, so I kept our conversation to the meet-up details. I'm passing on to you my Grimes knowledge. Listen good. On the drug trafficking, what I can tell you is that his people piggyback on top of legit delivery services. In a few cases, the delivery dude hasn't a clue of what's in the box—thinks it's laxatives. Most figure not to ask. Some of 'em are duped or trapped in it. If any of these facilitators loses a delivery or creams some from the top, they find out pronto the boss is badass." Squeegee inhaled a death rattle. "Me and my partner Hairpin are trying to figure out how Grimes's people can offer pharmaceutical opioids, not contraband knockoffs. Who's writing those scripts and who's picking them up? On the sex side of things, drugs can slip past a public lobby easy, but sex workers? I'd be asking which hotel managers turn a blind eye."

"Keep me informed. I've got an appointment." Heaven forfend that Deb be late for Nancy.

"Right, except I have a tip just for you, Metzger. I hear you golf."

How'd he know? A phone alert cut the tip short: officers were about to descend on the LeClercs as Lola had planned. Deb had to shower, caffeine up, and dope out what to say to Nancy. Squeegee squeezed in before she switched to the alert that rumors were going out about Ray, a Grimes gang traitor.

DEB SWERVED THROUGH CONES AND lane closures as she pushed the G-Met vehicle six miles over the speed limit. No need to get into trouble as she headed west to Wayzata, the reverse direction of the usual Wednesday morning commute. The sooner Deb whizzed through this meeting with Nancy LeClerc, the less likely she was to get steamed. As for Nancy's many questions about the Task Force charter, it was not on Deb to explain every comma, commas not being her strong suit anyway. Besides, the woman had Jude to figure out details, and Jude might be there, sexy and intriguing. Deb's pulse ticked up.

Most indubitably, she would not inform high and mighty Madame LeClerc that her hotels had been implicated in a trafficking setup. Collect evidence first. Deb should have pushed Luna harder on Ray and his goings-on. Luna might call her names, but Deb was used to being dissed as a lesbian and generally had no problem laying out that a dude is a cad, a bounder, a dick, a trafficker, and very likely, a no-good killer. So why did she hold back from quashing Luna's illusion of love? During the rainstorm, when they had been trapped in Erik's Highlander, Erik expounded about love like it was all he'd been thinking about. Maybe that was all he had been thinking about. Maybe Deb was all nerves because that was what she wanted to be thinking about too.

Deb took the 394 Exit—this westward-ho adventure was eating up time. She should have worn her black suit for Dan Routh's funeral at 1:00, rather than auto-dressing in chinos, a pink button-down, and a blazer. Nancy would be quick to hit the nail on the head, though, and Deb should be back to St. Paul in time.

She drove to Nancy's street. So this is what a swanky zip code looked like. Houses of 10,000 square feet and more with landscaping that belonged in *Town & Country* magazine. During a surveillance camera discussion, Cyber Paul said there were few police cams in neighborhoods like this because a) residents, with lawyers backing them up, would complain about violations of their privacy; b) the areas were low crime; and c) the low crime was due to private security systems better than those any taxpayers could support.

A paneled wood mailbox displayed the number. Deb angled around towering oaks onto a drive of crushed stone, which made an oxbow curve in front of the house. Geometric shrubs filled in the oxbow, so different from Gordy Omdahl's psychedelic peonies. The house was pale-yellow stucco with cream-toned shutters on the windows. Deb figured the architectural style was not castle, not ultra-modern, so French traditional? Renaissance? The Italians had a renaissance. Did the French, or did they just have fries?

Deb pulled up to the central entrance. No doormen popped out. She pulled ahead, where high hedges obscured the garages except for their solar-paneled roofs. She turned off the car and walked up the massive steps to a door knocker and a bell. She tried the bell and then the knocker. Nothing. Was anyone alive in there? Was anyone *dead* in there? This couldn't be where Nancy's father killed her mother?

Tires crunched on the drive and a beauty of a red Tesla pulled up. Nancy LeClerc, in workout tights and jacket, levered herself out. She pressed her phone pad and the Tesla parked itself by the hedges.

"Your mouth's agape, Detective," Nancy said as she stepped past Deb to the door.

"I like your car," came out numbly.

"It's convenient. Please come in." Nancy opened the door, which had been unlocked, and walked in. That rich, you didn't need to lock the door because ninjas drop from the trees should anything happen. Nancy cleared her throat. "Excuse me. I'll step in and out of the shower. To the right you'll find a guest bath, and beyond that, the kitchen. There's coffee, juice, and water there if you wish." She trotted up the curved staircase, leaving Deb to the complimentary beverages.

Deb followed black-and-white tiles to the kitchen, where there was an elegant beverage station. The cupboards, like the outside shutters, were white-paneled wood, the countertops black granite. Rather than a counter-island, a large table with curved legs stood in the center. Its white tablecloth had a border pattern of green vegetables—parsley bunches, peapods, celery. Trompe l'oeil, that was the term. A bowl of green apples, real, sat in the middle. No other signs of food. Thin Nancy might take sustenance from gazing at the tablecloth. Wouldn't it be lonely here? Nancy could adopt Deb as an adult daughter, and she could inherit the Tesla.

A corkboard by a pantry displayed family photos of beautiful people at the beach, beautiful people with skis, beautiful people at graduations. A departure from the trend was a bald man in a hospital bed surrounded by children. Deb remembered from an online profile about the LeClercs that Nancy's husband died a decade ago. A few photos dated back to the Kodak camera era. In one, a young woman wore a peasant shirt, headband, and bell-bottoms. Her fingers signaled V for peace, and over her head was the Haight-Ashbury sign. Nancy LeClerc was a *hippie*?

On the counter, a newspaper lay folded and next to that a book, *Yoga for Inflexible People*. *Click, click, click* in the tiled hallway—Jude in heels? Deb, her heart fluttering, checked the doorway. No Jude, more clicks. She dropped her eyes. A baby goat maa'ed and clicked over to the tablecloth, where it started in on the faux celery.

At that moment Nancy entered, dressed in Bermuda shorts, a fresh jacket, and sandals. She had slicked her wet hair back from her lined face and looked as good as a septuagenarian could look.

"Excuse me, your goat?" Deb said.

"What?" Nancy stared at her in disgust before she saw the animal chewing away. "Where did *that* come from?"

"It's not a comfort pet?" Deb knelt by the goat and hoped it would release the cloth long enough for her to grab it.

"Believe me, when I've had pets, I'm the one providing comfort." Nancy scooped up the kid, but the animal wouldn't let go of the cloth. Deb poked it in the tummy to make it maaa. It didn't maaa.

"Ms. LeClerc, um, you hold tight and I'll grab the cloth—though it might rip. We could cut away the chewed part with scissors."

"While the goat's chewing?"

"Wait." Deb grabbed an apple and put it in the line of chewing, and the animal transitioned to the apple flesh. Nancy carried the kid to a French door at the end of the counter, where she placed it, apple in mouth, outside.

"The gardener brought in goats yesterday to eat invasive weeds by the lake. This one must have escaped. Look at that cloth, all slobbery and tattered." Nancy surprised Deb with a pleasant laugh. "That's what I get for ordering it all the way from Provence. *Merde*."

"That's the word I was looking for," Deb said. "Not *merde*"—French for shit—"Provin-*cial*." Deb accented the last *shil* sound.

"Provençal," Nancy corrected. "We don't *look* for words, we remember them. Help yourself to coffee and we can move out to the patio and enjoy the morning. With the tragic loss of Dan Routh, we'll need a new spokesperson for the task force. Best combination would be an articulate woman who's been

rescued and a persuasive investigator working the cases." Nancy opened the
pantry, took out plate, and removed a tea towel to reveal pastries. She helped
herself to coffee and a bran muffin and opened the door to the patio. Deb
fixed a coffee with cream, took a croissant, and followed.

Across the expansive lawn, Lake Minnetonka shimmered. Chairs arranged
around a bistro table faced the lake, and the goat dozed in a sunny spot, a
comforted animal. Deb stumbled into small talk. "Your home is lovely. Have
you lived here long?"

"My husband found this place, and my daughters grew up here. After
his parents died, Geoffrey was here for his teens. I should downsize, but the
grandchildren love this old place for the holidays. At Christmas, they take
over the decorating."

Deb would love having Christmas in the mansion if it meant a stocking by
the chimney with a Tesla key in the toe. Did Teslas have keys?

"In the summer," Nancy went on, "they come to swim. It's weedy out there,
no thanks to the goats, so they bike to a public beach. Minnesota winters I
can't stand anymore."

"Do you go to California?"

"Hmm?"

"San Francisco? I saw the photo inside."

"Oh, my Flower Child days," Nancy laughed again. "Those didn't last.
Turns out I didn't believe love should be free. You have to earn love. You're
born into it as family, I suppose. A few men win it with a smile."

Nancy sipped her coffee and gazed at the lake. Remembering her husband,
perhaps. Deb didn't figure she could win love with a smile. People took to Erik
(even she did, a little) when he smiled. Then again, a smile alone hadn't kept
his wife from divorcing him. Deb's former partner, Cee-Cee, had a fun grin,
but they competed for who had the stronger stubborn streak. Deb won, not
a win to make her proud. Maybe Nancy was right that you had to earn love.
How? Deb needed to tune in because Nancy was speaking.

"You're a busy person, Deb." She said Deb! "I don't want to take up your
time, but I believe that in the wake of Dan's death, we can honor him and still
make a plea for our cause." Loud ringing in her jacket pocket interrupted and
she set down her muffin, one bite consumed, to check her phone. "Goodness,
hotel security. Excuse me." She hurried inside.

Deb was in an excellent position to observe Nancy's reaction if the call
was news about the raids. She speed-ate her croissant, shedding flaky bits.
The kid woke up, made *merde*, and scampered over for the crumbs. Before it
could start on her pants, Deb picked it up, a female, and began petting. The
kid almost dozed off then caught the scent of Nancy's muffin, lunged and took
a chunk in her mouth. Deb stood, the chair clunking behind her, and held the

goat away from the table.

A door slammed, and Nancy stomped toward her, waving her phone overhead. "What is this, Detective, about routine trafficking at a LeClerc? We don't tolerate that. Yet here it is. My CEO's on the phone telling me police are *invading* while guests are attempting to check in and out. Are you here to distract me?"

"No, you asked me here, and the officers will question managers—"

"Our managers?" Scarlet streaked Nancy's cheekbones.

"There are suspicions of a pattern of trafficking and drug-dealing incidents at . . . ." The kid kicked Deb's stomach.

"At my hotels and you didn't have the grace to inform me?"

Before Deb could reveal that Geoff LeClerc likely suspected what was happening, the goat butted her chin.

"Put the poor thing down," Nancy commanded.

Deb did, and the kid bucked over to the lake weeds. *What to say, what to say, what to say?* She glanced at Nancy, whose cheeks blanched from scarlet to ashen. The older woman put a hand on her lower back. "You okay?" Deb asked.

"That's not your concern. Leave. I have to go into crisis mode, thanks to your professional ineptness."

"Let me explain."

"Go."

Deb bit back her humiliation and cut across the lawn toward her car. She could overhear Nancy on the phone. "Jude, call the goat wrangler and come at once. I'll be on the lawn in child's pose."

A yoga pose to relieve lower back pain—Deb considered returning. But if Nancy hurt her back stomping after Deb, she could hurt her throat screaming at her to leave already. Deb's steps turned into determined strides. She had no reason to apologize. The law was right. So Nancy was thrown by the raid, that was the effing point of raids. Ms. Earned-Love had no right to attack her.

At the drive, Deb checked over her shoulder. Nancy was heading inside, her spine held stiff. The goat pranced on the patio table, and from its mouth dangled a muffin paper.

CHAPTER 30

JAYLYN IN A SWINGY SKIRT TWIRLED on the sidewalk in a Mary Tyler Moore pirouette. She hummed a song about meeting the man you love on a Monday or a Tuesday. Why not on a Wednesday? A photographer at the Mill Ruin intersection snapped pictures of her and mouthed, "Want one?" She mouthed back no, and he returned to posing a couple. The backdrop of the Stone Arch Bridge—old mill silos, the blue cantilevered Guthrie Theater, waters rushing over Saint Anthony Falls—made the site the "Best in the Twin Cities" for engagement photos. Not that Jaylyn was *in* love, but she twirled again at the fantasy that two men might fight over her.

The bus ride hadn't been bad, and she had her music mojo back. She had run through the Liszt cleanly if not rapidly that morning. Josh had texted that he'd meet her around 11:30 by the Lock and Dam No. 1 interpretive marker. He probably assumed she'd be going to the McMillan noon recital series. She had a twinge of doubt because Josh had disappeared on her before. The bench by the marker was free, a sign! She dashed across West River Parkway, claimed it, and took out her phone.

The phone turned e-vil. A frustrated text from Lionel: *Pizza under Sheila The Cube's seat? Ya coulda gassed her up.* Jaylyn would give him a twenty later. Time for Josh. Jaylyn checked her phone again and noticed a message she'd missed from Retta: *feeling awful, Ramon working, went to Mom's.* Why did Retta go back to that soul-killing squalor? She had always talked Jaylyn out of backsliding when a frantic Jaylyn couldn't share the temptation with her sheltered high school friends. (Truth be told, they had addicts among them whose parents would wrangle mood-altering prescriptions out of doctors.) It was Retta who insisted that Jaylyn was better than pills and shoved her into the future. When Jaylyn would reciprocate by telling Retta to aim high and pick a college, Retta would protest that kids with school smarts were wrong in thinking anybody could have school smarts.

"*Jay Jay!*" A screaming gull startled her. The clouds were flocculent—an ACT test word, woolly like sheep. "Sheep May Safely Graze" was easy compared to the speedwork in Bach's *Well-Tempered Clavier* and nothing compared to Liszt. A school bus rolled up into the parking lot of the Army Corps of Engineers building. It discharged chaperones with set smiles and ten-year-olds for a lock-and-dam tour. Jaylyn put her bag on her lap and shifted on her butt. The weight of her bag didn't stop her legs from trembling. She chewed her thumb. The Liszt, she'd taken on too much. Lazar must know about beta blockers for musicians overcome by stage fright. She needed to pee. What the hell was with Retta, and why was Jaylyn wasting her life waiting for a guy who stood her up again and again? Josh seemed considerate and consistent. He wasn't. She needed a restroom. She texted, *mill museum lobby*. This was Josh's last chance.

Then motors revved and people screamed.

THE PICKUP TRUCK SAILED OVER THE EMBANKMENT and into the river with a sonic-boom splash. Erik, only a hundred feet away, missed it.

His day had started placidly. He picked up Ben early for a picnic breakfast and watched his ex in an unexplained panic drive her new Audi over the curb. Not so long ago, he'd have seized on any vulnerability as a possible opening of her heart, a chance at reconciliation. Now—let her be well and let her solve her own problems. He and Ben went to the lake, where they sat on top of a picnic table and ate cereal from red and blue bowls. Ben leaned against Erik, swinging his legs and chomping. The boy began chanting to entice a squirrel closer, and when the squirrel started to crawl into the bowl, Erik whisked Ben off to camp.

After switching to a G-Met SUV at the station, he'd driven to the rendezvous point in the parking lot below Lock and Dam 1 and the Stone Arch Bridge. He sat in his car, reviewing the plan. When Squeegee, calling at the crack of dawn, requested a recognition trick for "Informant A," Erik said he'd be in a national-parks logo shirt sunning on a Taurus X. The whole thing sounded iffy. Squeegee's informant *might* be in the Stone Arch area before noon, and he *might* approach Erik if he felt safe. Safe from being accosted by couples who wanted their photo taken? Erik enacted the plan and left the vehicle to lie on its hood. He stretched out a leg and put a forearm over his eyes. He dozed off.

To be wakened by a sonic-boom splash. Disoriented, Erik caught on from the screaming that a truck and a horse had plunged into the water. The horse turned into a Mustang car that roared away, and a man was in the drink.

An African American woman who'd been eating an early lunch in her Civic grabbed Erik's arm. "Dang, he went over right there. Dang. You got a rope?" He hit 911 and an alarm sounded in the Army Corps of Engineers building. He grabbed a rope from the emergency stash in the Taurus and tied one end around a concrete bench and tossed the other where the Civic woman directed. A gasping man in the water floundered close enough to grab the rope with one hand. Water gurgled up from the sinking truck and the sinking man lost his hold. Behind Erik, people shouted, *Pull him in, jump in.* "Don't," the Civic woman said. Erik didn't have time to see the huge man barreling up from behind who slipped and crashed against him.

The cold water seized Erik lungs and the flailing man pulled him under.

WHEN SHE REACHED A SEVERE BRICK BUILDING—the JDC, Juvenile Detention Center—Jaylyn stopped running. After the truck sailed into the water, she'd run to the museum and hidden in the restroom for five minutes of eternity. Then she slipped out and ran across Park Avenue and continued running. She hadn't *really* seen who was driving the pickup. Now here she was at the JDC, "Go to Jail" on the Monopoly board, catching her breath. She would never end up in there. Too old.

Jaylyn's legs wobbled as she backtracked to the corner by the Vikings Stadium. She could order a ride from its lot, where it wouldn't look like she'd been released from jail. When she pulled her phone from an outer pocket of her bag, it dropped to the street and the screen shattered. Her hands shook as she picked it up, dropped it in the cavern of her bag, pulled out a tissue, blew her nose, dropped the tissue, put her hand back in the bag and hit something— Retta's bottle of oxycodone. Ramon must've dropped it in her bag when she hugged him. An early Ella Fitzgerald song ran through her head, "When I Get Low I Get High." She dry-swallowed two.

CHAPTER 31

IF ONLY THE POST-IT ON DEB'S OFFICE DOOR WAS A MISTAKE: *Det. Met, See Ibeling ASAP*, with a death's head instead of an exclamation point. She yanked off the note and strode toward High Command. She should have stood up to Nancy. The rich could get away with murder with *noblesse oblige*, and working-woman Deb would have to "oblige." She should look up that *noblesse* phrase before she tossed it at Ibeling, in case it meant something closer to *merde*.

Erik, meanwhile, was chasing a lead. More likely lolling in the sunshine, stuffing his face with sustainable ice cream. Deb could use a blob of Chunky Monkey right now.

On approaching Ibeling's suite, Deb moderated her walk. Next to the door lurked the Bambi figurine with its label, THE BUCK STOPS HERE. Deb entered. Beezlebub the assistant was nowhere, and on the inner door hung a sheet of paper with tiny script reminiscent of LeClerc signage: *Knock. Enter.* Two knocks and she entered.

No one behind the desk. Deb swore, "Dammit."

"Metzger, down here," came a growl from the floor.

She stepped to one side. Ibeling lay on the floor, face up, hush-puppied feet pointed toward her. Propped under his knees to relieve back stress was the three-dimensional fish plaque from his wall.

"Remain standing," Ibeling ordered. "We can dispense with eye contact."

"Yes, Chief." Deb felt she'd whooshed up in height as she towered over a shrunken Ibeling. On Ibeling's desk, she glimpsed his notepad. NANCY underscored three times. Drat, first-name basis. Deb attempted civility. "Should I call someone, sir?"

"Nancy LeClerc called *me*. Metzger, do you have two left feet? Are they both in your mouth?"

"I—"

"Where's Jansson?"

"Lunch?"

"Don't sound like you're asking a question unless you're asking a question. I'm asking the questions. What did you say to Nancy?"

"Nothing. There was a goat."

"A goat."

"As, um, Lola Scheers will report, officers are scoping out LeClerc sites, kind of like a raid, and Nancy got pissed—took umbrage."

"Metzger, you're off that case for two days or forever. Good time for your empathy training. Nancy stays true to her word." Ibeling squeezed his eyes shut so the lids resembled wrinkled pits. "Paul will check the hotel reports. I'll have to smooth things over with . . .." A gasp. "No contact with anything LeClerc. None."

"Sir." Deb couldn't stand being mealy-mouthed. She firmly addressed the wall shadow where the fish plaque had hung. "We're doing exactly what Nancy LeClerc wants, stopping trafficking. Just because she's rich doesn't mean she can interfere with justice."

"No whining," from the floor.

That wasn't *whining*. Deb chewed her lip. How could she argue when her superior was virtually under the desk?

"Metzger, leave."

"Are you sure you don't want me to—"

"Go." Ibeling pushed at the fish prop, which yodeled. Ibeling whapped it into silence then grasped his lower back.

"Sir?"

"Out."

Almost Allwise Ibeling. Today's emphasis fell on *Almost*. Deb backed through the administrative office and heard sounds at the outer hall door. She opened it to catch Cyber Paul whispering to Jimmy Bond Smalls, "There must be painkillers in the evidence room."

"What, taking narcotics from evidence? For Ibeling? Are you crazy?" Deb fumed.

Jimmy Bond Smalls reached behind her to pull the door shut. "Desperate times, desperate measures."

"If we don't do something"—Cyber Paul scanned the corridor—"Drees will take over."

Drees, that tool. "Can we call the missus?" Deb asked. Greta Ibeling, former black ops turned deluxe caterer, must know how to manage a husband.

"Shhh," from Paul. "A spy. No, it's Medford."

Coming down the hall was Detective Medford, sometimes confused with Detective Metzger, except he was Black, stocky, and male. "Softball sign-up." He posted a sheet on a board next to the door. He almost tripped over the little buck. At the bottom, the sign-up sheet announced in red letters, THERE'S NO EMPATHY IN SOFTBALL.

Jimmy Bond Smalls slipped into Ibeling's suite for a few moments, slipped back out, and squealed a whisper, "What did you do to him, Deb? He can't lift that knobby head of his."

"What did you do?" Mild Cyber Paul turned on Deb. "And why is the whole LeClerc review being dumped on me?"

"Can you pitch?" Medford demanded. "You got those shoulders, and you haven't signed up yet." He jerked his head back to the softball sheet. No one had signed up yet. This was persecution.

"A-*hem*." One of the mailroom Julias snuck up on them. She spoke down her hawk's nose. "Have any of you checked your alerts?"

Jimmy Bond Smalls said, in self-defense, "Coast Guard stuff."

"A-*hem*" was repeated. Julia apparently had the ability to silence her heels or make them sound on demand, because she walked away with authoritative clicks.

"Say Metzger, did your partner drown?" Medford held his phone overhead. "I was planning on him for first base."

Deb's heart thumped and she checked hers. "Well, then he's texting from Davy Jones's locker." She read on that a man was trapped underwater in a truck and Erik was being rushed to the emergency room.

"*Scatter*," Paul hissed. Beelzebub was returning, and progress had been made on no accounts. Deb was out with the LeClercs, Erik was out of it, period, the softball roster was blank, and Ibeling groaned from within.

On the floor, the buck had fallen.

CHAPTER 32

JAYLYN WORKED SALIVA AROUND HER SOUR MOUTH and shrunk into the bus seat. The National Honor Society president at school taught her the trick. Twist your fingers like this and you'll gag it up. That friend was heading off to the Ivy League, where they must be familiar with high-strung bulimics. Back at the stadium, they would think there'd just been another upchucking drunk.

She had no idea what was going on. She stalled on sending Josh a text. She wanted to call her mom and say, "I'm sick," except her charge-nurse mother would know at once it was bad. Lionel, too young and at work. Nana, out of town. Gran, no.

That left the Great Weirdo Lazar. Hurrying off the bus in Uptown, Jaylyn checked her phone's cracked screen: a Ford pickup with a man's body was being retrieved from the Mississippi River with no further information at this time. She was two hours early for her lesson, yet she had to do something or end up in a puddle. She buzzed Lazar's apartment. She shouldn't have given Josh's name to that Hirsch Fest detective whose eyes yearned to help. It couldn't have been Josh, and police wouldn't use muscle cars to chase people. She buzzed steadily. The outer door clicked. She entered and saw Lazar in a sleeveless tee, a wife-beater. One hand gripped his apartment doorknob, the other held a Hawaiian shirt decorated with hula girls. How dare he hold a lesson dressed like this? Her face contorted.

"Enter, play Liszt." He staggered free of support to push an arm into a sleeve.

She couldn't respond.

"Ms. Dudek, play the damn thing. Sit down, hit the notes."

She could kill him. Jaylyn sat and pounded.

In the sixth measure of the sixth variation of the sixth étude, Lazar said,

"*Stop*," and applauded heavily. "Brava, Ms. Dudek! Missed notes, but the spirit's there, the virtuosity. Don't be afraid of what you are, and if you want to have a nervous breakdown, have it after a performance, never before."

Jaylyn's phone sounded out with Beyoncé's "Put a Ring on It," the tone she'd set after seeing Josh again. She grabbed it from her bag and rushed into the kitchen. This would be Josh. She hadn't recognized the truck. Glimpsed a silhouette, that's all.

A cut-off call followed by a text from Ramon, *Retta's doctor*? Jaylyn texted back a clinic name and a question mark. No reply. The counter edge dug into Jaylyn's hip.

"Is all well?" Lazar was behind her, his shirt buttons misaligned by one.

The crying started with a great heave.

JAYLYN SAT IN AN OVERSTUFFED CHAIR sobbing herself dry. Lazar, with walker and without walker, shuffled here and there with a glass of water and then a Kleenex box with one tissue left. He played a Bach piece pianissimo and afterwards groaned his way into his support chair.

"Ms. Dudek," Lazar sighed theatrically, "if I had known you were upset about *death*—that you saw, or imagined you saw, a friend die, I wouldn't have pushed. When one's ancestors died at Auschwitz, one becomes accustomed to ghosts. I erroneously assumed by your haunted expression that a worthless boy dumped you, you'd gotten a traffic ticket, or whatever else upsets your hypersensitive generation." He waved away her generation's sensitivity. "Death . . . you can cry about death. Though death can be inspiring, opera, the great Requiems. If we didn't have death forcing us to be, to do, we would be silly creatures without meaning."

Jaylyn's red eyes popped. "That's very Svengali of you."

"Svengali?

"An impresario"—she checked her phone—"who seduced and hypnotized an Irish lass into becoming a great singer."

"If hypnotism were that efficacious, we'd be bored into nirvana. I tried it, pain relief. The hypnotist moaned moon tones and then screeched at me for my recalcitrance. I lacked faith, she said. I do lack faith in charlatans."

"Is it true your grandmother escaped Auschwitz by seducing an SS officer?" That was the rumor at McMillan.

"My grandmother invented lovers the way most people invent excuses. You do what you can to save yourself, so very few could save themselves. A million dead at that one camp. A goy delivered her to London, and she married him for a minute. Husband Two, a proper Jewish banker, brought her to the States when she was nineteen. We won't discuss how she comported herself after that."

Jaylyn was goading Lazar and herself. "A girlfriend of mine might be drinking again and another . . . friend, using."

"Can't you people take care of yourselves?"

"Can't you?" She shouldn't have said that.

"We all need coping strategies," Lazar flatly stated. "Breathing slowly from the diaphragm, sipping herbal tea, smiting one's enemies hypothetically, smiting them directly."

For coping, Nana did church and attitude. Mom did yoga, and after tough shifts, a goblet of chardonnay. Lionel would dream up networking schemes. Gran didn't cope. "My family talked about how to cope after my dad's death." After she'd been caught with pills. "My little brother Gabe wanted mice."

"Mice?"

"So he could be like Little Bunny Foo Foo, picking up field mice and bopping them on the head."

Lazar roared with laughter, and Jaylyn smiled through tears. She dug through her bag for more tissues. She came out with the pill bottle.

Lazar spoke in staccato. "What. Are. Those."

"They're, um, my friend's. Her boyfriend wanted me to take them."

"He tried to save her by hiding them on you? He doesn't know about drug disposal boxes at police stations? Do *not* use them."

She hit back. "Are you an addict?"

"A fair question." Lazar lumbered about. "There's a terror in success. I drank when I was a top performer. The drinking I controlled better after a car accident. Then the spinal stenosis set in, my vertebrae crushing each other. My medical history . . .." He brushed it away with another wave of his hand. "Chronic pain grinds down your everything." Lazar flapped down on the piano bench and slammed out the opening bars of Verdi's *Dies irae,* a horror-movie soundtrack proclaiming the wrath of God. "Opioids without addiction, alchemist's gold. Bah!" He rolled into the calming arpeggios. "You look like you could use sustenance, Ms. Dudek. There's ice cream in the freezer. For both of us?"

In the kitchen, Jaylyn found a half-full carton of dried flaky crystals and a box of ice cream bars on a stick. She also got bowls. They held the sticks and ate over the bowls.

"The runaround I get from doctors," Lazar said, chocolate dripping down his chin. "No opioids, more opioids, substitutes like methadone, suboxone, that don't get you high while they retrain the brain off the addiction. Two years ago, I found a movement specialist who was generous with the scripts. I felt wonderful, then not so wonderful. I ordered a refill, and a new pharmacist demanded a consult."

"Nurses often ask for med checks."

"Isn't your mother a nurse? I recall Lindsay saying that her younger brother married one, a woman who was the opposite of their mother."

He rattled on with more hand waving. But Jaylyn had frozen on Lazar's remark that her mother—warm, brown, open-hearted, nurturing—was the opposite of White Gran. She felt a great clearing in her.

"To finish my tale, Ms. Dudek. If you're thinking you need anti-anxiety medicines, I doubt it. You quietly absorb everything, go to the edge of the cliff, and become nervous not because you're scared to jump but because you know you will. I've talked to your old teacher. Don't looked shocked—she's brilliant if people pay attention. She said you go very shy and let drop that you'd already begun a piece beyond your capacity, and she'd rework the plan so you could, in essence, throw yourself off the cliff again. Back to the pharmacist, he insisted, 'Try another physician. This one has you orbiting Pluto.' I had a challenging transition to a different doc and new meds."

Addicts dream, hope, beg, and lie; Jaylyn bet he stayed in touch with generous doctors. She picked up the bowls. "Why the unmarked bottle?"

"Easy open." Lazar didn't make eye contact. "You don't need to pay me today. We'll sort it later."

Jaylyn left for home, drained except for peculiar surges. Surges of what? Anxiety, anticipation? Her high school scheduled her make-up final for next week, meaning that for the next few days math and music were her everything. After all, Josh's pattern was to promise and not deliver. Retta and Ramon could take care of each other. She was carrying hundreds in cash; Lazar never asked for it. She should have persuaded Lazar to take checks while he was in a sharing mood. And she still had the pills. They had to be legit, not laced with carfentanil because, even having them in her mouth, she'd be dead by now.

CHAPTER 33

Down and out, their G-Met partnership was down and out on this Wednesday evening. Erik was down in a hospital bed and Deb was out of the LeClerc side of things. Deb checked at the nursing station for Erik's room number. On her way to his room, she nearly collided with earlier visitors who introduced themselves as Ben's grandparents. Great, her partner's ex-in-laws, the Rosens. The woman, her bobbed hair silver, was a sophisticated variant of the middle-aged Lutheran woman. The features of the man next to her suggested Jewish heritage, and his springy salt-and-pepper hair brought him up to Deb's height. The woman asked politely if Deb would keep an eye on Erik. Then her husband went into inquisition mode and asked what was up with his daughter Kristine. His wife intervened saying he couldn't expect Detective Metzger to know that. The Rosens said goodbye with the expectation in their faces that Deb would keep an eye on everybody.

"Nice haircut." Deb pulled Erik's attention away from his phone. "Aren't you supposed to be in a butt-less gown?"

Erik, in a clean shirt from out of nowhere, track pants, and socks with a hole over one toe, lay propped up on the bed with the side bars pulled up. The pillow stopped short of a patch on the back of his skull. His submersion was reflected in his fishy pallor. He alternated closing eyes.

"Have you been cloned?"

"You're concussed. Where's Ben if the grandparents are here?"

"At a pony with sleepovers."

"You're concussed. You have heard the news, haven't you?"

"Global warming's over?" came faintly.

Deb sucked in a big breath. "Brace yourself, don't stand up. The driver of the submerged pickup drowned and is being identified. The man who jumped in to rescue the driver—while you were snoozing—is being examined. You must have done a deep dive to escape him because Coast Guard thought they'd lost you for a minute. Coast Guard's also sorry they banged your head against the boat. You got dope-slapped good. Speaking of dope slaps, the man who pushed you in 'by accident' is recovering from being whapped silly by a witness who kept yelling at him, '*Dang* you're stupid.' Now what's this?" Deb picked up a digital tablet from the bedside table and tapped it. "A menu?"

"Room service."

"Have you tried the burgers? It's dinnertime."

"Concussed. Can't stomach anything."

"How about toast for you, soup for me, ginger ales, oh look, eggrolls. Mmm, a brownie. Done."

"That goes on my bill."

"No worry. Are you in pain?"

"They injected my head. Stop moving."

"I'm not moving. Close your eyes."

"Makes me dizzy. I hate this."

"You're easier to understand concussed. It untwists your mind maze." Deb had the panicked notion that she should keep him awake. "What's with the phone? You're not trying to work, are you?"

"A teen, Lionel. Meeting. Had to postpone." Her partner released a *sssszt* of pain.

"I'm taking over the lead on the case." Ibeling didn't need to know. "Put your phone away, dammit. They gave you pillows for a reason."

Erik sank into the puffery, and Deb dragged over a chair. Except for the blip and hum of monitors that freak out if you kick the bucket, it was cozy. She leaned back. "You know, this is, like, our special place."

"Hmm?"

"You know, hospitals. Our place where we can relax. Chill together."

"One of us has to be out of commission for there to be peace?"

"Yeah."

The conversation died up, blip-less.

A nurse entered and smiled at Erik. "Well, Detective, how are you recovering from the slings and arrows of . . . what was it?"

He pulled himself up in a show of fortitude. "Slings and arrows of outrageous fortune."

So Erik could flirt and go all literary. He'd heal. The nurse had him lean forward, a vein popping from his forehead, and she checked around the bandage. She joked, "No oozing brains," and departed.

Erik relapsed into a zombie stare. "If it makes you feel any better," Deb said, "Nancy LeClerc never wants to see my cheerful face again. I'm the pain in her back, which she wrenched. I'm wondering if I should reach out to Ju— Nancy's assistant, make amends."

He looked a question.

Deb screwed up her lip. "Hard to know what to say. I mean, your kid sister's a poet, your mom's a teacher type, you quote that slinging stuff. Don't goggle at me cross-eyed. I, I can't get started."

"To say what?"

"Sure as hell hope Nancy didn't bitch at you because of stupid me."

That got her another goggle.

"Her assistant's hot," Deb admitted.

The head hit the pillows. "'I'm very sorry to have caused distress to Ms. LeClerc. Please let me know how I can assist her, or you, with the situation. Feel free to contact me anytime.'"

Deb thumbed away at her phone. "All righty. Next prob. Ibeling would have spanked me after the LeClerc mess if he could've gotten up off the floor."

"Ibeling's down?" the pillow mound asked.

"You know that wooden fish he has on his wall?"

"Large-mouth bi, bi—"

"Bass, not bitch. Propped under his knees."

Erik was speechless. Deb kind of liked him concussed.

The bedside tablet beeped, and Deb's phone dinged simultaneously. She checked them in that order. "Okay, food in ten minutes. You're going to love this. The guy who pushed you hurt *his* back and wants to sue for police brutality."

Erik dropped the f-bomb.

"Okay, your Sunday School inhibitions are down. Not your fault it's all embarrassing. Speaking of embarrassing, you know you're supposed to wear clean socks and underwear in case you end up in the hospital."

Erik glared an f-bomb at her.

"Is this not the time to mention that Drees wants practice drills on empathy?"

"Drees . . . makes me want to be a worse person."

After that utterance, Erik rolled onto his side and pulled a pillow over his head. He reached a hand back to drag the blanket over him. Since he already lay on half the blanket, he was taco-wrapped with a toe sticking out. The nurse returned, and Deb asked if it was safe for Erik to sleep. The nurse pulled from her pocket a techie clip and attached it to the exposed toe. She showed Deb how her watch tracked Erik's vitals and left again.

A muffled voice came from the taco as a hand extended a phone. "Text this number, Ibeling down."

The number had an Iowa City area code, Erik's childhood home. Deb entered the Ibeling message and added, *Erik concussed*. She pushed send. The tablet on the bedside table beeped. The ordered meal had been successfully delivered to Room B-232. Too bad this room was D-323.

JUNE JUST DIDN'T GET DARK. Nine o'clock on a Wednesday and dusk was only beginning. The dogs stayed behind, sleeping, and Gordy headed his van north out of St. Paul. Pretty easy the way 35E and 694 came together and you ended up in Little Canada. Little Canada was the baby of a French-Canadian who started it with a mill, so there you had it, a Twin Cities suburb with the logo of a fleur-de-lis on a maple leaf. Gordy had considered moving to Little Canada two years ago when a neighbor complained about Gordy's lawn being messy, with naturalized tulips and violets popping up all over. That neighbor moved away six months later and left trash in Gordy's cans. So much for Minnesota Nice. Then there was that real, good, Canadian Nice.

Gordy wished he had Dan along for company, except the whole reason for this nighttime tour of auto shops was that Dan had been killed and the van Gordy loaned him stolen. He was glad Dan's funeral had gone well, that people came, people who thought Dan a good man, people he helped. Dan's daughter sulked, and the stepdaughter cried. That Big Deb came for the funeral part, only her head was in someplace like New Zealand. Gordy exited toward an industrial park. Sometimes they named places after sweaters, like Cardigan Junction over there. The pond off the surface road was like greasy camouflage. Colorblind people like himself, according to trucker Leif, made good snipers because camouflage didn't fool 'em and they caught movement. That's why Leif badgered Gordy to go grouse hunting with him, only then you'd have dead bony things with feathers, and Gordy had a poster that said hope was a thing with feathers.

He saw Vadnais Lake, where a Hmong fellow caught a record-breaking bass with a minnow. Maybe Gordy should've called that guy Leif knew, Bent Nail. Gordy drove along an industrial park. He had that lonely feeling that bothered him in his drinking days—sitting by your lonesome, telling yourself you're making it better and cooling everything down with a beer. Then it's all empty like your glass, and filling it again gets you nowhere. It had taken a long time, a dark, empty time, for him to learn that you couldn't put your faith in a glass. He shouldn't have put his faith in money because the reward offered about Dan's death hadn't done a thing. People wouldn't do the right thing for money, but they sure did bad things for it.

Why was he driving around here? Oh, he remembered. After the funeral he watched TV news about a crackdown on chop shops south of the cities. Gordy couldn't say why that didn't sit right. Then he got it. They'd missed that Grants place, the one that Skeleton Man at the music fest said was secretly linked to Grimes. It also made more sense that the van Dan drove would have been hidden in east St. Paul. It could've been parked in a garage and then hauled to a shop later with the hauler avoiding traffic cams. Gordy had thought that through before he left his house. He reached a point where his thinking got stuck. He doubted Gandhi had anything helpful to say on chop shops. Instead, Gordy went into his bathroom and picked up the book he kept by the toilet, the sayings of Confucius. He flipped through and came across, *To see the right and not do it is cowardice.* That's when he decided to scope out Grants. Gordy, who knew body shops, could spot what wasn't right.

He drove past industrial places and noted their camera eyes. Figures if you ran a dirty shop with vehicles coming in at night, you'd doctor the footage. Lots of buildings had motion-sensor lights that might alert a passing patrol. The sensors could be dirty or malfunction, but Gordy trusted them more than he trusted automatic faucets and toilets. People should just learn to flush.

He shouldn't have been thinking about toilets. He squirmed in his seat and rolled down the front windows. Wasn't the freshest smelling air here. If anyone wanted to know what he was doing, he could say he was remodeling his garages, and at night he had time to check out other designs. Not that garages had much of a design, being boxes with parking lots.

Ten minutes later, he pulled into the street entrance of Grants, which had no windows except in the office area. Then he saw the building was L-shaped, with a raised roof section in the back that could handle a semi-cab. He poked the van down the alley by the ell. He heard the thrumming of air handlers. Although wire fencing protected the rear parking lot, the big gate was open. Gordy edged in.

Repainted paneled vans lined the perimeter under security lights. Pretty darn ordinary. Confucius also said: *The hardest thing of all is to find a black cat in a dark room, especially if there is no cat.* It never made sense before to Gordy, who didn't care for cats. It came to him now that he was looking for something not there—a van with a big sign that read *contains evidence of murder.* He might as well pack up his screwball notions and go home. As he backed around, he faced the buildings with their vehicle ports. Vertical banners blocked the adjacent entry doors. Usually a banner stood out front to announce a sale or serve as a seasonal decoration. These looked dull tan and gray. Gordy blinked. A fellow had come out of the door and was lurking behind a banner.

Gordy held his breath and pulled forward toward the repaired vehicles, like he was checking to see if his was in the row. He made a show of shaking his head in disappointment and angled his van toward the exit. Only he felt light-headed and his foot misbehaved—he gunned the engine, spun gravel, screeched past the gate, and bumped down the alley too fast.

Merging onto 694 South, Gordy saw in the mirror a black car, a Ford

Mustang, keeping a distance behind him—too dusky to make out more. He passed vehicles to lose sight of it. *Jesus*, he was pushing eighty. He slowed and motorists zipped by. The Mustang reappeared. He drove past his usual exit, took the next, and snaked his way home. When he entered his neighborhood, he overshot his place, a Volvo behind him but no Mustang. He doubled back to his driveway.

Inside, Gordy worked up the dogs to be jumpy and noisy. A stranger couldn't know that they'd never harm a flea, which reminded him they needed summer pest treatments. Ellie, Rainbow, and Dorothy gobbled extra treats and Gordy microwaved a glass of milk to take to bed.

The milk didn't do any good. The dogs quieted except for Rainbow's twitching, but Gordy's heart ka-thumped through the night.

CHAPTER 34

S TARS AND SPARKLES FLASHED when Erik opened his eyes. He refreshed the washcloth with hot water, returned it to his eyelids, and leaned back in the tub with his head bump resting against an icepack. A Thursday-morning bath that ran hot and cold was not the usual order of things, though it beat staying in the hospital with its bleeping monitors. Back home, Erik had no choice but to relax. His father had confiscated his phone.

Half an hour earlier, as soon as he'd entered his apartment with his dad and collapsed on the couch, his phone rang. Even without the speaker function, his dad could hear the man scream, *Why did you call me, Detective, if you didn't know Josh was in trouble? Why didn't you save my son? I'll not waste the Lord's name on you. There's a place for you in hell.* Dazed Erik had no answers and asked the man to repeat his name and number. *Don't give me that runaround.* The man hung up.

His dad reminded Erik that his messages should be forwarded to dispatch. That was overridden if he answered, Erik explained. That's when his dad pocketed the phone with the instructions that his son should have a soak. Erik ran a bath and poured in Epsom salts. The pain from being battered against the Coast Guard boat flared when he settled into the water. He must have groaned, since Dad knocked to ask if he was all right. "I'm a big boy, Dad," he joked. A big concussed man who shouldn't fall asleep in the tub. The drug counselor Erik attempted to reach days back about Luna, Josh Miller, was that who drowned in the river? Was he Squeegee's informant? The Epsom salts stung.

He could hear his dad searching for items in the combined kitchen/dining area. The apartment was pleasant, with teal walls, a few marathon trophies, framed art of Ben's, and family pictures. It lacked a dog, and Dad was never quite at home without one. Nor did it have land. The senior Jansson felt trapped in a place where you couldn't step outside and at the very least survey the domain of a lawn.

Dad knocked. "Where's the ladle?"

It took effort to speak. "I use a cup."

"I'll pour oatmeal right from the pot."

"Oatmeal, June?"

"Your larder, son."

Was bare. Also on the food front, his dad had told him that Ibeling's wife was on the road, judging baking contests. Greta Ibeling, former black ops, instilled terror in amateur bakers by rivaling British judges for bluntness paired with infinitesimally fussy distinctions. Before retrieving Erik, his dad saw to it that Almost Allwise was home on ice and his daughters informed. Would Ibeling take Vicodin or Percocet? Erik had been limited to Tylenol because drugs that impacted brain function were out.

He tossed the washcloth aside and twisted the faucet to the hottest setting. His muscles unkinked and his thoughts dissolved. His dad faintly whistled a fishing song. The whistle became a song about love. Erik hazed over and sunk deeper in the tub. A steamy image rose from the past—Kristine in snug shorts, walking backwards during a campus tour for the benefit of Erik's younger sister. The sister did not crystallize, so Erik was walking into the flushed face of Kristine, her lips full. She, the nice nurse, the blonde St. Paul officer with the sweet smile, one of them, all of them, were sliding in with him.

Enough with brining himself. Erik doused his body with cold water. After toweling off, he slipped into loose athletic pants, beach slides, and a white tee. He padded to his kitchen area.

Dad was wearing the gag shirt never worn in public: "Fish Fear Me, Women Want Me." He was too shy and devoted to Erik's mother to pursue women, even if a high-school crush once blurted to scrawny, adolescent Erik, "You're kinda cute but your dad's like a movie star." His dad, still handsome in a weathered way, looked concerned. "Take it easy."

"In my prime, Dad." Erik winced as he sat. A man in his prime should have a home, a woman, a family, and a ladle.

The senior Jansson sliced crusty bread and smeared it with homemade jam he'd brought with him. "Ben's eager to see you. He'll want a story about you rescuing the man who jumped in. I'll pick him up when he's done at camp."

"Aren't you supposed to be at work?" Campus security was the job.

"Practicing for retirement."

Erik raised a brow.

His father added cream to his heart-healthy oatmeal as an answer. Apparently, the larder did have cream.

Erik's cheekbone ached, and he touched it gently. His father seemed about to ask how Erik was feeling. What came out was, "Where do you hide the sugar from Ben?"

Erik nodded at a high cupboard. "He knows how to reach it."

"'Course he does." His dad poured sugar on the oatmeal. "Your face is fine."

"Other officers aren't keen to see it coming through the door."

"I expect not." The senior Jansson added more oatmeal to his serving, having over-sugared it. "Eat a good breakfast and you'll feel more like yourself. Somedays, being yourself is work. Hard work when your mind's going every direction. I was investigating goings-on in a university department, and this tenured professor says to me that I look like my spirit animal is a Kodiak bear. I guess because they're tall. Then he says that my animal is really a sheep because I do the administration's bidding."

Erik hid a smile by sipping coffee.

"Professor Pfeiffer shows up"—his dad's duck-hunting buddy—"and says, 'Course Sven looks like a sheep. He wears a pelt to hide his claws."

"And I'm to believe this?"

"I'm your father," he said.

Erik's low laugh was cut short by his phone ringing in his dad's pocket. Reading glasses gone AWOL, his dad held it out to check the ID. He asked with suspicion and hope, "Are you seeing a woman named Susie?"

"It's an undercover agent named Squeegee. I'll take it."

Cold steel struck Erik's heart. The shock: Squeegee reported that the drowned man from yesterday was Josh Miller, twenty-two, the peer addiction counselor that Erik had been seeking. Miller had Dan Routh's contact card in his pocket and heroin in his system. Was there a chance he was Luna's Ray after all? Had the rumors Erik set in motion sealed Josh's fate?

THAT AFTERNOON ERIK AGAIN HELD AN ICEPACK to his head, only this time he was leaning back in a police cruiser passenger seat. The cruiser driver, Minneapolis Detective Patkus, had been assigned to the suspicious death of Josh Miller. With their cases overlapping, they headed together to the Miller farm west of the Twin Cities. Upon receiving Patkus's call, Erik had recommended that they dress for outdoor work. To get a farmer to open up, talk to him over chores. Patkus, a former Gophers fullback, had the bulk of two men and would be welcomed to lend a hand.

During the drive, Patkus reviewed with Erik the current information on Josh Miller, whose name had not yet been released to the public. The M.E.'s preliminary report said that Josh did not show signs of recent heroin use and that the injection site was his shoulder. Supposition: he was stabbed with a hypodermic. Because the drug was not injected directly into a vein, the young man did not experience an immediate rush and may not have realized a drug was in his system. The heroin eventually skewed his responses and undermined his efforts to save himself after the plunge into the river. The M.E. surmised that the victim had been attacked elsewhere and escaped in his pickup. No one had any clue why Josh drove to the bridge.

Last fall Josh had gotten sick and dropped out of community college courses. Over the holidays, he picked up part-time jobs as a stocker at chain pharmacies. Not a good job to combine with drug use. Patkus added that his partner was canvassing Josh's Seward neighborhood where he shared a house "with young males oblivious to each other's doings." Surveillance cameras were being checked.

Squeegee sent via computer more information on Josh and the Grimes group investigation, which gave Erik slight relief. The Ray rumors were planted about the time of the drowning; they could not have incited the attack. Josh had been an off-and-on informant since last fall concerning where and when drug and sex traffickers appeared at youth hangouts. The young man hadn't reported much during the winter, having either stayed off the streets or fallen deep into use again. He made contact a month back—he and Squeegee had a system for changing up text numbers—about a new group of slick dealers. Josh had several phones to be checked, and the one he'd had with him was drying in a bag of rice.

Erik's phone rang.

The caller, a special agent with Minnesota's Bureau of Criminal Apprehension, wanted a word with Erik. More than *a* word, and Erik could only listen dutifully for so long before bursting in.

"You're calling *me* about Deb Metzger? Call her again if she doesn't answer her phone the first time. What do you mean she's a problem?" Erik spoke sharply and Patkus gave him a surprised side-eye. "You mean the chatter out there is that Grimes's organization *sees* her as a problem. On top of that, you were supposed to track Charles Monteiro after that incident at the Airport LeClerc where Deb arrested him. You said he'd lead you to Grimes's supply chain. Instead, you lost him. I bet a wolf's eyeteeth that Monteiro is spreading the word that Deb's trouble. I bet Monteiro drove the Mustang that hit my Highlander last Sunday when I was transporting a trafficking victim. 'Your Charles' is probably the Mustang driver who forced Josh Miller into the river. Cameras picked up that vehicle. The driver was short and the license plate stolen. Sure Grimes is in custody, but his peeps still play rough. Go after the Mustangs."

Erik, after being forced to listen again, heated to boiling. "You can't do random road stops on Mustangs because that would be *profiling*?" Erik repeated the last to Patkus, "That would be 'profiling.' "

The agent justified himself. Erik paid more attention to his soggy icepack, which had slid down his neck. He tossed it in the back seat. "No, *you* listen, Mr. Special Agent. A Mustang, when it's not an equine, is a make of automobile. It's a car. It doesn't have rights. How about you find Charles and you warn my partner Deb *now* that she's of interest to the Grimes gang. Then go out and profile a few Mustangs." He ended the call in disgust.

Patkus pulled over to the side of the country road. "Hope you never want a job with the BCA. Why don't we get out for a bit." Outside, Patkus tossed him a Gatorade bottle. He guzzled it and watched robins hop around a berry patch. Patkus wondered out loud if a farm stand close by sold rhubarb pie. *Ah, pie.*

The men returned to the cruiser, as prepared as they could be for the grief they would encounter.

THEY ARRIVED AT THE FARM to find that Mrs. Miller had shut herself in the house, and her husband wouldn't let anyone near her. The detectives and Mr. Miller ended up in a bottomland field with a stuck tractor. Miller did not lay into Erik because Patkus's size was a deterrent and because Erik knew how to drive the twenty-year-old John Deere 6310. Along with Miller's younger son, just back from the University of Chicago, they debated removing the tractor's front spike, which was used for lifting round bales. Deciding instead to pull the Deere out backwards, they attached a chain to Miller's GMC pickup. Erik put on the baseball cap he'd brought and adjusted it to fit over his bump. He ignored the rule that one should not operate heavy machinery post-concussion and climbed into the tractor cab. Patkus stood by to give a wheel a push, the younger son shouted *whoa or go from the sides*, Erik shifted into reverse and eased down on the gas when the chain engaged. The tractor came out with a *thuck*.

The son took Erik's place and drove off to spear a bale for livestock. The three men climbed into the GMC, and Miller bounced them back to the farmstead. "Won't get a thing done tomorrow with rain predicted. I knew when I was out on the Deere, saw the trooper pull up, and the wife came screaming"—he choked out the rest—"that it was Josh." He stopped by the barn, eased himself out, and leaned against the pickup as if every bone was in agony. Patkus talked to him quietly.

Erik clumped through muck to the side of the barn where the son was forking apart the giant bale. Despite his reedy muscles, Stuart was the egghead type, an egghead who rubbed his eyes as snorting heifers tore into hay clumps.

"I don't know why Josh and Dad couldn't just get along. They were always at each other." Stuart tossed a clump toward a lanky Holstein. "Too thick-headed, both of them. Dad wanted Josh to be a farmer. Josh was too 'outgoing' for that. Me, everybody pegged me as the kid who should stick with school. They wanted Josh to stay put, keep him safe."

A collie released from the house came barking up to Erik and then settled by the silo. "Whatever you want to talk about, Stuart, I'll leave a card." The shadows of eagles crossed over them as they flew to a nest in a lone tree a hundred yards away. Erik watched one eagle perch as its mate soared to the field's perimeter by a stand of oaks. The view reminded Erik of his grandfather's farm. Erik was last there at his grandmother's funeral, where his grandfather pulled him aside to say, "Don't outlive your woman." The pit deeper than that was to outlive your child.

He had to re-engage Stuart. "My dad became a policeman to get away from hogs."

"Hogs stink." Stuart blew his nose into a dingy handkerchief. "Stink up everything. Josh could be so *stupid*." Erik held out a sheaf to a runt heifer. "What I don't get about Josh, he could be so easygoing and then he'd get all hard. When he was in recovery from meth and pot, he couldn't just walk away. No, he had to be a drug counselor. Like he always had to fight a demon."

"I think for former addicts, a demon is always around a corner. The struggle is daily. It sounds like your brother tried."

"Oh, he tried lots of stuff to get high. Yeah, Mom believed he'd turned himself around." Stuart scooped leaves out of a watering trough. "He hid a lot from us. For one thing, he called me three weeks ago and said he wanted to get a kid away from a dealer. Except, the dealer found out about him squealing, so Josh was staying away from everybody until he figured it out. Dumb paranoia, I thought." Stuart, wet-eyed, glanced toward the house. "Mom thinks she failed him. I tell her it's a sickness. With treatments. But you have to stick to the treatment. That last call, I told him, 'You're a counselor, you *know* you need help.' He said he'd go to a guy named Dan."

Stuart stopped messing with the hay. "I suppose he tried to stay sober, worked at it. Though Josh didn't get 'work.' I mean, he worked, he didn't get *discipline*. He wanted to get by on liking people and they like him back. I kinda think he didn't really believe he had potential. He sold himself short, you know?"

Heifers with hay in their mouths nodded. Erik adjusted his cap over his sore head. "Was selling himself short connected to any recent activity or being stupid, as you say?"

"Well, he broke up with his girlfriend for stupid reasons."

Josh could've sought drugs after that loss or became suicidal. "Did you meet her?"

"No, he kept his sweeties to himself." Stuart checked a small tear on a heifer's ear. "Out of the blue, Josh texted me a couple of days ago, *what would you do about a rival?* I sent back, *duel to the death, ha ha*. No idea what girl he was talking about. Maybe the same one. Don't know her name. He kept her away from us. Didn't want our dirty subsistence life to scare her." Stuart bitterly stabbed the hay.

"Do you know why they broke up?" Erik rubbed a watery eye.

"This is the stoo-pid part. Josh went to hear that girlfriend play piano or something and after that it was like, she's too good, I'll drag her down. Why couldn't Josh try that level?" He sobbed into the hide of a heifer, and the heifer shuddered. "*Why couldn't he try to live?*"

The returning eagle squealed overhead and the babies in the distant nest chittered. From her talons hung a dead fox. Hay wisps clung to the fur as evidence of death by mowing machine. The eagle wheeled and banked toward the nest, the red foxtail streaming.

CHAPTER 35

The Thursday afternoon call saved Deb from cleaning her sublet's closet in a fury. Erik wanted her to see Luna and put to rest the already dubious theory that Josh Miller and Ray were one and the same. Deb had never received an official G-Met cease-and-desist order after Ibeling's scolding yesterday. Either "Almost Allwise" was only venting, or it was impossible to send statements while reclining on a fake fish.

A cute St. Paul officer, Dahlberg (straight, dammit), had been escorting Luna from her grandmother's to the Resource. Luna's re-connected phone number and media accounts were being monitored. She whined that Ray might really love her but was too scared to get in touch. In Deb's view, if Ray loved Luna, she wouldn't have needed to escape a moving vehicle.

Deb waited in a room until Resource Director Sharon showed Luna in. Luna's amazing ringed eyes showed how pleased she was to have hair stylishly pulled back and an office-appropriate blouse. But after Sharon left, anxiety tightened her every feature. Deb had to put the girl at ease. Nothing profound popped into her head, so she was reduced to, "That blouse looks great on you, Luna."

Luna lit up again like that donated blouse would change her whole life. Maybe it would.

"They're giving me training about stuff. Like, don't fuck up a job interview by saying *fuck* all the time. I like that it's about helping here. I like to be helped and I like helping."

"I see."

Luna squinted at Deb. "You know, I think Ray needs help. Don't you feel bad about not helping people?"

"Well, I do have an important question. Do you know this man?" Deb put down a photo of Josh Miller.

Luna's new confidence wavered.

"Luna, is this Ray?"

"No, his face isn't tall enough, long enough, whatev." She chewed a fingernail.

"Do you recognize him at all?"

Luna made a leap that Deb had not predicted. "He's dead, ain't he, uh, *isn't* he? Because you're only interested in dead people. Is he dead?"

"We're not sharing information with the public yet."

"Am I the fucking public?" She began shaking. "He's *dead*. Go away. *Go away!*"

When Sharon entered the room, Luna was in complete meltdown.

Deb went away.

ALL RIGHT, DEB HAD BOTCHED IT with Luna yesterday, a follow-up to the day before's botching with Nancy LeClerc. The suspect "Ray" seemed to be a figment of the case's overheated imagination. According to special-agent jerks, Grimes's people might be onto Deb. She determined that the best thing to do this Friday morning was to go where no thug would follow. The Mostly Lesbo golf outing.

The outing could untangle the LeClerc knot. The group's organizer, Maureen, had crossed professional paths with Nancy LeClerc. The raid on the LeClerc Simples had rescued preteens and caught two pimps who did not one bit resemble "Ray." Nothing indicated that anyone at the hotels was actively involved in trafficking or dealing. Nothing yet, that is. More had to be uncovered about the hotels. Showing up today was Deb's duty. Especially on a morning that pinged with perfection.

Deb pulled into the public course lot, which lay immediately west of Minneapolis in Hopkins. She loved the incredible exhilaration of a golf swing. Sports had been Deb's salvation since puberty, when it was the way for an oversize girl with no interest in boys to fit in. Her heart still thumped for the angelic straight girl who broke the barrier and asked Deb to go out for volleyball. Deb remembered less fondly how her dad (pre-divorce) doted on her older football-star brother and barely noticed her. Deb overheard him say to Mom not to blame *him* with his sports interest for making Deb "bent." Good ole Mom retorted, "The thing to blame is your attitude toward your talented daughter." Which reminded Deb, she hadn't replied to her mom's last phone message.

Deb rolled her cart toward the small group of women who had played hooky from their jobs for golf. She wore the powder-blue tournament pants given to her by her ex-girlfriend Cee-Cee. Their color should have warned Deb that while she viewed the world in black and white, Cee-Cee saw pastels.

Wearing them today was meant to be an *ironic* gesture toward country-club style. However, the stares she received on arriving suggested the pants were more of a fashion oops. And despite their sisterhood, the group spent the next hour bickering their way through the holes.

The possible Nancy source, Maureen, worked in a high-end accounting firm. She arrived crabby because she had to leave her wife behind. "Wrecked her ankle tripping over our schnauzer," she complained. "Stuck in a boot." She ignored Deb's quip. "Someday we'll all get the boot." There was Priya, a psychology professor and Maureen's friend, who argued with a straight golfer, Kate, about whether Kate's grandfather in assisted living was being conned by a volunteer. Kate had a concussed look about her. "Mother of triplets," she yawned to Deb. "I sleep standing up, like a brood mare."

Listening avidly to the grandfather/con debate was Kate's college-aged cousin who had arrived late and was catching up at Hole 7, Chance. Chance was a beautiful being with an androgynous figure that could carry off golf knickers and an argyle vest. Chance's hair was like a British schoolboy's, with a hank angled across the forehead. Deb took her eyes off Chance to pay attention to Priya.

"Ask the investigator here," she was saying to Kate, "if this sounds like a scam in the works. This 'friendly' volunteer offers to check things on Gramps's computer."

"Wait, who's the investigator?" Chance asked.

"Deb there," Priya answered. "I didn't catch the details. Insurance fraud?"

"No, I'm criminal. I investigate crimes against women and children, homicide."

"Murder?" someone asked. "Have you killed anyone?"

"Not yet," Deb joked. Her companions fell silent.

Until Chanced picked it up. "Say, I like your pants. Designed by that Swedish golfer, Annika? And are you like 'officer' or 'inspector'?"

"The kids call me Detective Deb, got attitude, got cause." Deb confidently prepared her shot.

Chance tossed back the forelock. "This woman told Gramps that she knows Kate's dad from high school, only he doesn't remember her."

"Stop right there," Priya barked. Deb missed her swing and did a double step to catch her balance. "It's a con. This woman is taking charge of your grandfather's life by claiming connections that aren't real."

"But she offers to take him on daytrips, which he's actually not up for."

Deb might as well contribute, since her game sucked. "Cons do small favors and promise big ones they never intend to deliver. It could be this woman isn't totally honest with herself about taking advantage, but it's more than charity."

"Speaking of charity, do you know Nancy LeClerc?" Maureen made a great shot. "It was on the news as I drove over. She's come out with another big anti-trafficking statement, how it 'stops here, stops now.' Sounded like she arranged with law enforcement an ambush at her own hotels to make a point."

Deb looked skyward to hide her burning face. "I met her at a meeting."

Maureen put a club behind her neck, weight-lifter style. "Those LeClercs have a temper. Nancy was quite the wild child back in the day, ran away to San Francisco after her parents killed each other. I heard an uncle caught her in an LSD den and dragged her back. She fought him tooth and nail. So much for family love."

"Ooh, don't talk that way." Triplet Kate shuddered.

"Her father killed her mother and then himself," Priya set the record straight. "Nancy tapped the trust fund for college, stabilized the family business, picked up a few husbands along the way, had children of her own."

"Daughters who can't stand working for her." Maureen nodded that Deb should take her turn.

She readied herself. Club up, swing starting—

"A real bitch," burst from Maureen, and Deb caught the ball with the toe of her club and sliced it over a wall of arbor vitae. Maureen continued as if she hadn't ruined Deb's shot, "Nancy can't stand other women in the C Suite."

"She's cool to me," Chance said and everyone stared. "What? I'm friends with Sutton and Blair, her grandchildren. She loves *them*."

Deb repeated Erik's words to Luna, "There's love and there's acting lovingly."

"Detective, you have depths," Priya oohed. "Depths."

Deb wished to heck someone would find those depths and explain them to her. She squinted in the direction of her mishit ball. "Is that another section of the course?"

"That's Wunderlyn. To get in"—Priya waved a hand skyward—"you have to be nominated. If nominated, you're put on the waiting list. If advanced to the top of the list, you hand over one hundred thousand."

Chance pointed. "Critters have made a break in the hedge. Maybe one of us can squeeze through with Deb. Kate?"

"Nuh-uh."

They left Deb alone to try her luck in Wunderlyn.

BRANCHES CRISSCROSSED THE UPPER HALF OF THE HEDGE, and Deb had to scooch to peer through the lower part. A bank dropped down—all she could see. She'd hit her way into the humiliation trap.

Stashing her golf bag at the hedge base, Deb wriggled through. Her wriggle turned into a slide. As she righted herself, two women came tilting over the rise in a cart. Short and squared off, they made a matched set: one in a red visor, white shirt, red shorts, and the other in a white visor, red shirt, white shorts. Wiry hair exploded from the top of the visors, and their chins drooped as they glowered at her under now lowering skies.

Deb rolled back her shoulders. "Detective Metzger, homicide. May I help you?"

With lifted noses, they hissed, "Wicked thing." The twosome retrieved their balls and drove off like royalty, heads as high as their squat necks could carry them.

It was like Deb had landed in the wrong story. The ball left behind must be hers, in a fantastic position for a putt into the seventh hole of the wrong course. At that moment a ball spun over the rise, she ducked, and another ball whizzed after it. A golf cart whirred, and Deb straightened to see Geoff LeClerc and Jude bouncing toward her.

Geoff hit the switch and his face contorted. Jude slipped off her seat to stay by the cart. She was chic—in a blue sport skirt and blue-and-white saddle shoes—yet appeared subdued, not what Deb expected of her.

"It's Detective Metzger, isn't it? I didn't see you play through." Geoff's childish cheeks, the blue and white of Jude's outfit, the fish-frown of the red and white women—it was like those *Alice in Wonderland* books. Deb made herself beam through embarrassment. "I fell through a rabbit hole chasing a White Rabbit. He was running late."

Geoff broke into laughter. "And now you're in Wonderland, Wunderlyn properly. Where are your clubs or are you using . . . what did they play with in those books?" He looked to Jude as answerer of needs.

"Flamingos." Jude frowned. Upset with Deb for Nancy's sake?

"My clubs are back at the hedge."

"I'll get them," Jude offered.

"You don't have to," Deb said to Jude's passing shoulder.

"Oh, she contends with much worse," Geoff said. "If that's your ball there, it's in great play position."

"My swing is off today. That was a slice—"

"From the public domain," Geoff finished. "Your shoulders are uneven from knots in your trapezius. I'm a sports doc, remember? If you ever heard that to remember. Do you mind if I check?"

He pivoted her so her back was to him and when he pressed a spot beneath her right shoulder blade, it seared. "Oww!"

"A few seconds of pressure and it'll release. There. You've angered trigger points." His thumb dug in where her left shoulder merged with her neck, and again an intense burn was followed by a softening.

"I can't believe it, looser already."

Jude pushed the clubs to Deb, whose back re-tightened at the possibility of a thing between Jude and Geoff. Jude could be ... ambidextrous?

Geoff was lecturing her. "Watch out if you go to a doctor. Too many medicate the pain away. Likely cause of your bad form, Deb—stress. Forget the job. Otherwise, time off is no good to you."

Jude did not look like she was forgetting. Deb wished they could talk in private, though it probably wouldn't advance her detecting agenda and might kill her romance agenda. Clouds bunched over them, and Deb remembered a surveillance video gathered in the raid. Geoff was her way in. "Thanks. If you could put in a good word with, um, you know."

"You're a problem, Deb. That's how Aunt Nan sees you," Geoff lamented. "You're done there. Believe me, she doesn't treat people as they deserve to be treated. She's not a criminal, to my knowledge." He chuckled. "It's in her business interests to keep everything on the up-and-up. I'll have a chat with the CEO, Luis, about whatever the issue was."

"Serious goings-on at a Simple," Deb said. "There's video from three weeks ago of you shouting at a man, similar to the incident I interrupted."

Jude started. "What incident?"

Geoff overrode her. "You have a video of me, Detective? What the *hell*? Are you trying to piss off every LeClerc?"

"No, no, no. I was just hoping you could come down to the station and . . ." she trailed off.

Geoff dropped his chin to his neck to practice a putt. Jude studied the darkening clouds. Geoff lifted his head, scowling. "I drop by the hotels. I see bad behavior. I make it go away. I don't hang around young fools to become acquainted. Look, Detective, do you have this video on your phone, or did you lose it down the rabbit hole?"

Deb took her phone from a powder-blue pocket and hit play.

Geoff shaded the screen with his hand. "Christ, I don't remember. I've broken up more than one party. That rude young man, I can't see his face. I don't make a point of remembering that type." He squeezed his eyes shut. Please remember, Deb hoped. No such luck. He peered at her. "Have you identified him?"

Deb was about to say it could be a suspect in a murder, Ray, when Jude sneezed hard. "Bless you!" Deb said and reached into her golf bag.

"Detective, are you listening?" Geoff asked.

"I, um, was looking for this." Deb drew from her bag a bandanna for wiping sweat and gave it to Jude, who sneezed into it discreetly then mumbled "allergies." Deb stood off balance. "That scene, on the phone? You're right, Geoff. It's nothing."

Geoff's smile returned. "Tell you what, if I hear anything from Luis, I'll get back to you, or Jude will." Jude knocked invisible dirt from her saddle shoe.

How many times did she end up being Geoff's errand girl instead of Nancy's factotum? Geoff checked his phone. "I'm afraid we have to leave you." He nodded to Jude, who got into the cart too obediently. "Deb," he put his hand on her shoulder, "take care of that tension. It distorts everything. I could drive you to your car but this cart, two only, as you see."

"That's all right, I barged in." Deb was oddly sad. "I'll sink my putt so I can say I was below par on the seventh hole. How should I make my way back, main entrance or rabbit hole?"

No answer. She was alone under a menacing sky, the perfection of the morning ruined.

CHAPTER 36

Eʀɪᴋ sᴀᴡ ʜɪs ᴏᴡɴ ᴅᴇᴀᴛʜ. Scratches gouged from eyes to chin, shirt ripped open, baring his chest, teeth clamped. All self-inflicted.

Instead of solving the Routh murder, he would die right here, on a Friday afternoon, in the tunnel that linked the Hennepin County Courthouse to Minneapolis City Hall. Death by boredom.

He couldn't think straight, he couldn't think crooked, he couldn't think in circles. The back of his skull throbbed, his sinuses hated the incoming storm, his heart tightened from the pressure of others' grief. If he had Ray in his hands, he wouldn't be led off track by bits and pieces about Grimes's operations, by the coincidental death of Josh Miller. If only his court session would finally begin, an end would be in sight. He could move toward life.

Erik had been leaning his forehead against a vending machine in a vile little room off the main part of the tunnel. He straightened and squeezed his Styrofoam cup. He should toss its bitter dregs, quoting Hamlet, whatever Hamlet said, and try a cup from elsewhere. He could leave this catacomb and return to a chain eatery in the main underground thoroughfare. That would mean being Out There, With People.

He'd already been Out There, With People, cooling his heels in a line for lattes when two old men in front of him began complaining. The shorter appeared to have a dead rodent on his pate. The taller moaned that last weekend's yardwork seized him up. As he yammered about hot joints, his ear hair wriggled. "Keep popping those oxys," short rodent head urged. That's when Erik chose isolation with vending machines. He surveyed the snack cakes restrained by a coiled bar. A Little Debbie hung, suspended between shelf and release.

He could blame Deb for not breaking through to Luna Johnson, convincing her to tell all. But he had to acknowledge the difficulty of drawing out a girl in all kinds of uncontrollable pain. On the Routh killed-by-irate-former-colleague front, Erik had antagonized fellow officers and received that job offer from Internal Affairs. That would be a promotion downwards to hell. Beneath it all, his ex-wife Kristine was being hyper cheery during the Ben handoffs. It wasn't the Kristine he knew, and there's the rub—he hadn't made her happy. *Ding*, his phone. Another hour delay on the court case, which brought it dangerously close to the judge's martini time. Erik suffered the pangs of despised love and the law's delay.

The investigation behind today's case dated back to when Erik was a greenling at G-Met; he merely had to confirm timing points. Case notes provided his script, stick to it. Court was supposed to be an unsurprising bore with no sudden witnesses rising up from under the floorboards. The ghost of Ibeling's voice haunted Erik: if a testimony goes off script and that spawns an idea, keep it to *yourself*. Make notes for *later*. Anyway, his case wouldn't receive much attention today. Vernon Grimes, the big catch, was being arraigned before another judge for his drug running.

The vending machines buzzed. Erik was being bored out of this mortal coil. With the Dan Routh investigation, people wanted to put him on a set track. Be the self-righteous snitch cops could hate. Be the straight-ahead do-gooder. Be the nice guy without needs of your own. Narrow tracks that let others predict where he'd go. He preferred all terrain with diversions.

Bringg . . . Bringg bringg bring. The alarms didn't stop, and the tunnel vibrated with people stampeding. Erik rushed to the central passage. His phone beeped, 10-98, code for prisoner escape. A tattooed man with white hair was steamrolling through. Erik stuck out a foot. The man thwapped flat against the tile floor and belched an *ouf*. Erik jumped to straddle and secure the runner, but instinct screamed *roll away*. He threw himself toward the wall to escape the grasp of a large man who, balance thrown, fell on top of the first man. It became a rugby scrum with security guards and husky volunteers adding their weight to the heap. The oxy-popper popped pills and threw himself on top, spider-like. Erik recorded the scene with his phone as evidence until his phone *beep-beep-beeped*. This melee was a diversion. Vernon Grimes had escaped through another door.

Triple-hell.

CHAPTER 37

*A*H, HECK, CLEANING OUT THE FRIDGE did not make for a tasty snack. Deb, hunger-starved and love-starved after the futile golf trip, pinwheeled cheese slices over old bread. The cheese's dark dry edges made a nice pattern. She spooned on the last teaspoon of relish and nuked the combo. She took a bite. She spit that bite down the garbage disposal, flipped the grinder, and fed the disposal the bite's mother ship. Why had she stopped buying Pop Tarts?

She needed sustenance to confront Luna again, to figure out why the subject of Josh Miller upset her. She also had to be on the alert for the escaped Grimes. Before Deb's cheese fiasco, Erik had called to report on the courthouse fiasco. Neither of them intended to catch Grimes—that was sport for an armored SWAT team. Grimes couldn't hide in his tarted-up split-level in the burbs. There'd be terror on the streets, since the unfaithful in his ring had exploited his lockup, and Grimes would carry a lethal grudge. When Deb told Erik of her LeClerc golf-course mishaps, he said they sniped at her because she was the messenger they didn't want to hear. Then he asked about Luna. "She's still not telling all, and our relationship's circling the drain," Deb moaned. "With the traumatized, you have to give lots and expect shit in return. She wants sweet support and that's not me."

Deb thought she'd lost Erik on the other end, until he finally said, "Think about how your strengths work for her."

On the way to the Resource, Deb chomped on a carrot and wondered if she should have clued in Geoff about Ray back at Wunderlyn. Deb couldn't figure out if she was shielding Ray from public knowledge out of allegiance to Luna or out of a sixth sense that didn't make sense.

Luna came into the room wearing grungy sweats and accompanied by a tired lawyer. First thing was a complaint, "They're telling me how to act."

"Um, they're modeling behavior."

"It's all cookie-cutter." Luna chewed her thumbnail. She stopped and stared at the offending nail. "See, see what I'm talking about? 'Leave your hands alone.' I'm not supposed to touch myself? I'm with me all the time? Cookie-cutter."

"Cookie cutters come in all shapes now." Deb almost added, *including erotic ones.* "Luna, something's making you feel bad and it's not the people here. You talked about helping. I need your help, Luna, on *anything* you remember about Dan Routh, the man I showed you yesterday—yes, he's dead. About Ray."

Luna chewed harder on the nail.

"Luna, helpers aren't all cookie-cutter. I help in a tough way. I'd like to help your friends on the street, like Pammie. Get between the mean men and her. There are men who want 'help' and expect a woman to be that help. I've seen enough of them to know that if one woman can no longer help, they forget her, get rid of her, move on to the next one."

Luna scrunched up her face. "I wanna go."

"Luna, this place is full of nurturing angels. When you need protection, when you need justice, I'm your avenging angel."

Deb had her hand on the doorknob when Luna said, "Ray's dad stalks him. And I think his dad works for upside-down-head guy."

Grimes. Through his father, Ray connected to Grimes.

DEB RETURNED HOME FURIOUS. Luna couldn't provide a description of Ray's father except to say he was a gorilla she'd seen at distance. Deb dusted for about the third time in her life, swishing the feather thingy over the folk masks and paintings. Too bad she didn't own any of it. She needed a place beyond this sublet, because she'd received an email timed at 3 a.m. from Botswana that the owners were returning in two months from their mission. She'd be forced to tackle the closets if a break in the case didn't happen ASAP.

Her private number, AKA the Mom Line, rang. Deb forgot that she'd shared the private contact with Jude "in case of emergency," though more as a hint for the future, since Jude should have the good sense to call 911 in a real crisis. On answering, Deb learned that the number had been passed on to the LeClerc Hoteliers CEO, Luis Peña. He had called Deb at G-Met, been transferred to dispatch, and ended that call because of the "delicate nature of the situation." He wished to meet in person, discreetly. Deb could be so discreet that she wouldn't even tell Almost Allwise Ibeling.

That put Deb on the roadways at 4:00 on a Friday. It rained off and on. She wended her way west through stop-and-go streets because I-494 traffic west moved like a constipated python.

The LeClerc administrative suites were part of the office towers of MN-100 between downtown Minneapolis and the western suburbs. On the eleventh floor, Deb stepped out of the elevator to see through a window a sprawl of buildings and beyond, the urban wilds of woods and wetlands. She entered an imposing suite and took a seat as directed by a no-nonsense receptionist. She picked up a business magazine to read a feature article on CEO Luis Peña.

Peña's family had migrated from Cuba, and his great-grandmother was Swedish-Minnesotan. In the first years of the twentieth-century, Minneapolis doctor Alfred Lind decided Cuba was the place for warmth and sugarcane riches and convinced a number of Midwest Swedes to follow. Deb skipped over the exodus from Cuba to the last paragraph. Peña's favorite novels were by Minnesota writers: O.E. Rølvaag's *Giants in the Earth*, which Peña admired for its account of the struggles of Norwegian immigrants, and F. Scott Fitzgerald's *The Great Gatsby*. "Gatsby would have been a happy man," he stated, "if he'd gotten over the trophy wife quest and focused on family."

An interior door opened and Peña, somber in dress and manner, shook her hand. "Detective Metzger, good of you to come. Call me Luis, please, and we'll work on sorting out these circumstances around the Simples. The LeClerc group has integrity."

Deb had been advised multiple times to make an effort to connect with "elite" people, i.e., suck up. "Thank you for reaching out, Luis. I was reading about you in the magazine. It must suit you and your values to work with a family-owned company."

Luis demurred. "You must understand this, Detective, about family companies. They're bat-shit."

"Excuse me?"

"Absolute bat-shit. Think of a regular board with its egos. Add to that lingering resentment over who lost the kitten, who pushed who off the sled, who inherits the Jaguar, and you get the picture. I want to emphasize that our security team is cooperating with your cyber unit on reviewing surveillance. The rest we'll discuss in my office."

Like Ibeling's, Peña's office was a shrine to family, only instead of toddlers posing with fish, girls posed in billowy confirmation dresses. Waiting was a Hispanic woman, middle-aged, in a trouser suit that appeared to be in Deb's price range. She introduced herself as Carolina Huerta.

"Carolina is in a unique position," Peña said. "She worked in housekeeping at LeClerc hotels, earned a business degree by night, and she's been substituting in reception to learn front-house operations." Peña said to Carolina in Spanish, "Please tell the detective, even if it doesn't make sense."

"I speak a little Spanish," Deb said in English. "In investigations, many things don't make sense in the beginning."

Luis indicated that they should sit in a circle. Carolina clasped a crucifix she wore and began hesitantly. "It's a different world, cleaning the toilets and greeting guests. We're all trained to watch for signs of trafficking—men who pay cash for the rooms and handle all the transactions. Drugs get by more, and drinking is always there. Generally, a manager intervenes if people are terribly drunk or high in public spaces. But . . .."

Deb filled in. "People are on vacation, meeting family and friends, having a good time, and that spills over into those spaces."

"Exactly," Luis said. "There are security cameras, but the content isn't scrutinized unless we suspect a problem. Go on, Carolina."

"When I was working housekeeping last fall, I noticed bad things. Many condoms in the trash, a stink to the room I'm not going to explain, more blood than usual." That begged the question of what was usual. "There were vouchers from the loyalty program, perks for free drinks or free room-service breakfast. The loyalty people, that *L'Étoile du Nord* program, they're usually rich or business travelers. That's terrible, I thought. Those people should know better." She glanced at Luis.

He poured water for her. "Please continue."

"This summer, I check in loyalty customers. If they're families, they come to the desk because they often need something extra, like a crib. The business guests wave and proceed to the best rooms, which with a credit card on file they can unlock with a phone app. Like a Tesla."

So Teslas don't *have keys.* Luis interjected that the company needed to rethink phone-app entry, and Carolina went on, "If the app doesn't work, which happens, people show me their loyalty ID, and I run a key card. Maybe I'm being too judgy, but many of them look too scruffy to be loyalty types."

"How do they behave?" Deb asked.

"They want the key quick. They're nervous or they're bold."

"Do you notice young women, teens, young boys with them?"

"Usually just a man comes up and wants help at the busiest times, when I can't notice much."

Luis sounded weary. "With this week's police check on suspicious behavior at our hotels, I had accounting look into the payments behind the cards. Though the cards look the same, some have a source other than the LeClerc group. I found an online site that mimicked ours and found I had to input a code. The site was fuzzy on how to access that code. That didn't sit right."

"From what you're both saying," Deb summed up, "a way to avoid raising suspicions about trafficking is to use an 'accepted' loyalty card. Carolina, this has been incredibly helpful. Thank you for coming forward."

Carolina teared up. "Blessings on the poor children. Catch those bastards,

Detective. They should see hell." She shrugged a burden off her shoulders, they all stood, and Luis escorted Carolina out.

On his return, Deb remained standing. "Your loyalty system could be hacked." He pulled back like he wouldn't hear more.

Deb couldn't let him bury it. "Look, Carolina has caught on to something. People, kids, are at risk."

Luis, displeased, put his hands in his trouser pockets and rocked on his heels. "Your digital security—"

"Yes, Detective. Our security firm is looking into breaches as we speak. There's also"—Luis made eye contact—"a matter that may be completely unrelated. Why don't we sit?"

They sat stiffly.

"Our loyalty system . . ." Luis resumed. "There is, was, an intentional override. Previously, board members could gift a high-status card to select people like a celebrity or well-positioned business associate. That practice was stopped a few months back." Luis closed his eyes. "Detective Metzger, what I'm about to say is confidential between the two of us." He opened his eyes and sighed. "Last year Nancy LeClerc quietly underwent treatment for breast cancer. During that period, perhaps concerned that her time was limited or under the influence of medication, she made liberal gifts. That didn't come to my attention until . . ... Anyway, I didn't recognize the names."

"Oh." Deb had no other response for a minute. Then she fumbled over a question, had Luis asked Nancy about the gifts? There hadn't been adequate reason to stir her up, he replied, until Carolina came forward today. That dumped the issue on Deb. Nancy had been vulnerable, and somebody had sniffed that out like blood.

Deb headed back to G-Met. She was inching along in 494 traffic and more rain when Cyber Paul sent a video downloaded from LeClerc security. The car idled and her heart raced as she watched it on the vehicle screen. At Luna's hotel, a week before Dan Routh's death, *another* video of Geoff LeClerc yelling at a man to leave the property. The man was in full view—Luna's Ray. Deb had reason to go back to Geoff.

Back at her sizzling office at dinnertime, she put off reconnecting with Geoff until she had a plan. She added information about that video and the loyalty cards to the Routh case murder boards. She and Erik had a digital version they could project on a drawn window shade, and a sticky board on wheels that got bumped around the room. She had the hologram to her left and the craft project to her right. The thing about crimes that involved criminals, as opposed to murders that involved tweedy Brits in quaint villages, is that they were embedded in a mess of illicit activities and the boards displayed too many loose threads.

Hearing a knock at the door, she clicked away the digital board and kicked the solid one around.

Drees, all smiley faced. "Deborah, are you set for the empathy tests? By the way, how's Erik? Is he upset?"

"We all are, over the Grimes escape."

Drees thrummed his fingers against the door frame. "I meant the ex-wife going through a breakup?"

Oh, frick it. Deb gritted her teeth. Drees must mean Erik's ex was no longer with the lawyer-mentor-bastard who had seduced her away. She had no idea what Erik knew, or felt, not that she would admit that to Drees. "He manages."

"Well, it's come out that 'The Mentor' has done this to women before. He takes up with the promising ones, and when he tires of them, moves on. Oh, does one of us need to step in for Ibeling? His back pain is worse."

"It's Friday night, Drees. I'm closing up."

Drees hissed goodbye, or maybe that was the HVAC.

A sudden whoosh, and the HVAC ceased its sibilance, the temperature fell to a comfortable level, and Deb dropped her head to her desk. Another knock on the door, and a deep voice said something like, ". . . is Jansson."

"He's out." She rubbed her eyes. It was a retired hero in a bomber jacket—Gregory Peck in *Twelve O'Clock High*. No, Erik speed-aged by recent traumas. *Duh, no.* "It's Mr. Jansson, isn't it?"

"*Sven.*" The way he said it, she wasn't sure if Sven was his given name or simply what everyone called him. You couldn't tell a straightforward Scandinavian from an ironic one. He went on, "Ibeling will be home through the weekend, possibly longer. Blake's in charge." Blake was a senior officer who liaised—what a word—with the courts, but how did the senior Jansson know this? "I'm picking up Erik's windbreaker, which I see fallen behind the door here. He's tied up giving statements over that courthouse escape. Is there anything he absolutely has to know for the weekend?"

Erik's father had a stern bearing. No way of getting around a man like that unless—*oh, right*—you were the ultimate charming trickster. Deb woke up her computer, mincing through an update, and so switched to Erik's. "The cyber unit will not have records on the drowning victim's phone and internet use for several days or longer. Oh no." Updates reported that surveillance cams showed Charles Monteiro at Josh Miller's apartment before he fled. Find Charles, and then you'd find Ray? Deb experienced brain overload and Erik was supposed to be resting after his river dunking and courtroom adventures. "Um, it can wait."

Mr. Jansson came over to the desk and waited thoughtfully. "Detective Metzger?"

"Yes?"

"I'd appreciate a Kit Kat bar."

She opened Erik's secret drawer—not that secret after a fight between them—and handed 'Sven' a bar. She surmised from the tilt of his brow that she should take one for herself. He may have smiled.

At the door, he returned to serious. "Please remind Erik that he does not have to be a martyr."

Deb would, if she knew what that meant. She was exhausted by trying to figure out what anything in the case meant. Exhausted by what felt like a problem surrounded by problems.

She stood to leave, and her work phone dinged, *urgent*.

CHAPTER 38

THERE ARE PEOPLE FOR WHOM a Sunday brunch reservation is urgent. Nancy LeClerc's grandchildren fell in that category. Having heard of Deb from their friend Chance, they were eager to share, at their convenience, what they had seen as LeClerc interns. That had been Friday's message. Saturday—yesterday—time had stopped.

Saturday morning, Deb and Erik had rushed to the G-Met station to watch, via streaming video, the drug unit question young male suspects who provided opioids as part of pizza and grocery deliveries. Their known whereabouts did not line up with "Ray's" activities. The officers did learn that Grimes's dispensing lieutenants kept the delivery facilitators on separate schedules so, if caught, they couldn't snitch on each other.

Then Erik busied himself at the computer searching for the latest news on criminal justice programs, reparative justice, and career opportunities. He explained that he was forwarding the information to a teen he'd met at the Kafka Café, "This Lionel—seems like a good kid, lots of curiosity—sent me his transcript and wants to know how I got where I am." Deb pointed out that where Erik had gotten was this dim office.

At that, lightning flashed, and punishing rain slammed the windows. The overhead lights crackled to their demise, and eventually a generator kicked in with jaundiced lighting. The computers gobbled up their battery power. Annoyingly, the office phone continued working. Deb answered and could barely hear over the thunder. It was a guy named Frid asking if Erik had made a decision. Erik stalled him with a "later." Then she and Erik amused themselves with implausible theories. It had been nearly two weeks since Dan Routh's murder, and "Ray" remained invisible. When the generator lost oomph, they dozed at their desks as the best use of the black hour.

In the morning the rain stopped, and Deb left for the brunch appointment. It was grasping at a single straw. Nancy's grandchildren—The Sibs, as they called themselves—had arranged to meet Deb at their Minneapolis country club.

The Sibs weren't "LeClercs"—Nancy had no sons. They were Stevenses. Also, Betty Danger's "country club" wasn't a proper club at all. It was a parody with mini-golf. On her way, Deb drove by Ukrainian and Polish neighborhoods, saw a rainbow arch over the Tiki thatches of Psycho Suzi's Motor Lounge, and spotted the small Ferris wheel at Betty's.

For once, traffic had been light, and Deb entered Betty Danger's twenty minutes early. In the interior space of ornate Victorian wallpaper, three honey-haired people chatted by the host station—the toned brother and sister and a woman who had to be their mother. She was Nancy, fuller and softer, with a figure that could carry off gaucho pants. She hugged each sib and approached Deb. "You must be Detective Metzger. I'm Glenda. Sutton and Blair won't admit they're so excited about being 'consultants' that they rushed off early. They're ready to save the world, now that I've dropped off the forgotten phone charger." She laughed and touched Deb's arm in parting. According to Deb's intel, Glenda ran a cookware company specializing in unusually shaped cake pans.

The Sibs stepped forward with extended hands. "Sutton." "Blair." Deb was pretty sure the male was Sutton and the female Blair, but she didn't want to be tested on it. Both looked like they were born to wear tennis whites, and their current dress wasn't far from that.

"Chance called us because she guessed you wanted to know more about the hotels and we were interns. Do we call you Detective Deb, like the kids?" the girl asked.

"Deb's fine. Could you repeat your names?"

The girl took it. "That's Sutton, my darling bro. I'm Blair. If we'd had another sibling named Hedley, we could be a law firm."

"As it is," the brother said, "we're an English soap."

"We should sit and order before the detective bashes us in the face to stop the sib act." Blair flashed a pearly smile that Deb was indeed tempted to bash.

They went to outdoor seating, where the employees had dried the chairs. The Ferris wheel remained off limits because it was slippery. They ordered family-style servings of scrambled eggs, bacon, and biscuits. After the first few bites had taken the edge off everybody's hunger, Deb started in, "So, the two of you interned with management at the LeClerc hotels. When?"

The brother—Sutton?—took it. "Part-time last summer, spring break, and this year two weeks at the end of May. We make more money as lifeguards, and Gram didn't give us any loyalty points for our work—that *L'Étoile du Nord* program."

"So you know how the loyalty program works?"

"Spend more, save more," the brother said.

"She gets that, Sutton." The girl layered eggs on a biscuit. "With points, you can use a phone app to bypass registration. I think Gram was afraid we'd 'abuse our privileges' and party. When we were in high school, she made us work in housekeeping and food service. Gram believes everyone should experience working at the bottom."

"Don't say 'bottom,' it's demeaning," her brother said. "Positions in maintenance and customer service."

"Basic idea, hard work, low pay." Blair went on, "On the managerial side, we learned procedures for medical emergencies, active shooter situations, fire alarms. Like your job, only we have to keep our customers happy, while your customers are—"

"Dead," Sutton concluded.

Time to speed this up, especially since the Sibs had hoovered the food and Deb might need a second meal elsewhere. "Did you witness anything suspicious?"

The Sibs exchanged inscrutable glances. Their lives were too easy to foster suspicions. On the other hand, their rich great-grandfather murdered their great-grandmother and killed himself. Sutton nodded. Blair said, "There are bizarro people out there. A few times the manager made 911 calls on people who overdosed in their rooms."

Deb crumpled her napkin. "You're holding something back."

More inscrutable glances. Sutton took it. "Gram had us submit reports, saying we could alternate who wrote them. Except we kind of wrote them together."

"I wrote them," Blair revised.

"Gram was always approving when 'Sutton' signed and critical when 'Blair' signed," Sutton said. "Biased against women executives, one reason why Mom left her job with Gram's company."

Blair continued, "Uncle Geoff survives better than Mom did. He's kind of a personal consultant to Gram, her Zen master. We called him before coming to see if he had ideas about what's up. He said he already talked to you and didn't know if it was worth your time, but hey, everybody has to have brunch, right? Uncle Geoff doesn't like to upset people, except he gets on Mom's nerves, maybe because he's not really her brother but acts like it."

"That's not it. Mom's cool that he's like a second or third cousin adopted. It's like their chakras aren't aligned. The only time I saw him really worked up was at Thanksgiving two years ago when Gram announced her will."

Blair wrinkled her nose. "That's private."

Sutton faked an upper-crust accent, "Oh, but the servants shall talk." He dropped the act. "Most of Gran's personal wealth will go to foundations like the

Resource. The company, our mother and aunt might have to duke it out over how they'll take it over. I guess Uncle Geoff gets a share. He made a big protest that Gram was cutting off her descendants. Does he get the house, Blair?"

Blair shrugged. If personal assistant Jude acquired it, Deb could visit.

"Anyway, Uncle Geoff handled so much for Gram when she had cancer treatments last year. Don't poke me, Blair. Oh, I'm not supposed to discuss her health either."

Blair said, "When we interned, Uncle Geoff would make a game of it. He'd check into our hotel to make a surprise inspection. The managers probably tell him more than they'd tell Gram because, um, Gram can be a, uh, witch."

Sutton frowned. "Uncle Geoff doesn't always follow through. He might not see what's going on. He has fun being a divorced dude. He doesn't always get back to me."

"You're jealous because he pays attention to me because I'm the girl." Blair stuck out her tongue at her brother. Deb would have to pressure Geoff—baby-faced, naïve Geoff—to remember more about hotel incidents and to be brutally honest about Nancy. "Pressure" wasn't the right approach—Deb had to "sway" him. Swaying was harder.

A server bent to remove plates, and horns blared down the street. Diners stood to gawk, shouted *look out*. An Econoline van crashed through the barrier fence, people screamed, dishes clattered, and a couple dived out of the way as the van stopped. The airbag trapped the driver and Deb rushed over. The couple moaned on the ground by their upturned table, and multiple calls went to 911.

Thank god the Sibs had trained for emergencies.

CHAPTER 39

*T*HIS IS A DAY OF REST, JAYLYN WANTED TO SCREAM.

Sunday at Nana's in Golden Valley had started peaceably, with her mom, brother Gabe, cousin Lionel, and Gran all present. The kind of day to remind them of their blessings. But it was so wet in Nana's yard that the after-church barbecue had to be moved inside, and pan-grilling the pork chops set off the smoke alarm. Next Gran got in a dither when Lionel tried to FaceTime Aunt Lyndsay and was disconnected. Gabe pestered Lionel to take him to the zoo, only Lionel was invited to a party for a *female* co-worker, which explained his daisy-print shirt. Jaylyn said she couldn't take Gabe because her Jeep was in the shop. Her mother then remembered that the Omdahl shop had left a message on the landline that the Jeep wasn't worth saving. Like a three-year-old, Jaylyn ran to the basement.

She sat at the old upright down there. The Jeep had been Dad's. She picked out a few notes, which turned into Beethoven's *"Für Elise."*

When Jaylyn was ten, they had been returning from a trip to Disney World and their luggage was delayed. She skipped up to the grand piano by the carousels and was stopped by a white couple. They pointed to the sign on the piano: IF YOU PLAY, PLAY. IF YOU DON'T, DON'T. Then her dad, with his blond eyebrows, was there. He asked politely like he didn't know her, "Can you please play me my favorite song?"

She soothed herself now with that same piece, *"Für Elise,"* then returned upstairs.

Gran complained she had a headache and needed to go home. Lionel packed Gran in his Cube and said he'd head from her place to his party in St. Paul. Jaylyn volunteered to take Gabe to the zoo if she could borrow Nana's Buick. "Later, please," Gabe wheedled since he had picked up a digital game.

Mom and Nana dozed off sitting down, and Fifi the dog yapped for a walk. Jaylyn had no choice in the matter of Fifi's needs and changed from her church dress into shorts and an off-shoulder top she'd brought along.

A full rainbow arched across the sky, mirrored by the colors of flattened peonies that brightened the lawns. Jaylyn's phone pinged. She'd just now received a two-day-old message from Retta: *call me, sick*. Retta probably failed to charge her phone or pay her bill. Another message from Ramon— *on special deliveries, can't raise Retta at her mom's. Is naked guy there?* Jaylyn wanted to emoji Munch's scream face—*what am I supposed to do*. It became itchy hot, and Fifi hadn't done her business yet. Another text was incoming, maybe Mom reminding her to hurry back to take Gabe to the zoo.

It was not. One word from Retta's number—*help*. Retta playing the drama queen. Jaylyn texted, *busy*. An immediate follow-up, *dying*. Yet another, *91*. Jaylyn stopped under a shade tree. She called Retta—nothing. She texted— nothing. Jaylyn called again, no answer, and experienced a sickening vision of Retta's phone buzzing across the floor.

She punched 911. When the dispatcher answered, Jaylyn couldn't speak until prompted. Then it came out—a friend overdosing, Retta Mazzi. "I'm Jaylyn Dudek, sober buddy, here's the address, I forgot the apartment number. No, I'm not there, Retta called to say she overdosed"—a lie. "My mom's Rose Dudek, a charge nurse at—" The dispatcher stopped her, said the situation was being addressed, was there anything else about Retta? Drinking, yes, sexually active, yes, history of abuse, yes, access to drugs, yes.

Call ended. Fifi tangled herself with a passing French bulldog. The yapping set every dog in the neighborhood howling. Jaylyn, filled with dread, extricated Fifi and apologized to the human walker.

AT DEB'S SHOUT, *HEY, DUDE*, men along the Lake Harriet shore grinned at her until they calculated her height and her inclination. These men did not include Erik, whose attention she was hoping to attract without calling him Detective, partner, or late-for-dinner. He stood in the lake, baseball cap covering his banged head, utility pants rolled up to his knees. He contemplated the opposite shore as Answer to All Things. Deb had changed into the golf shorts she kept in the car, while in the car, because on leaving Betty Danger's, she realized she didn't have egg on her face but she did on her trousers. She kicked off her shoes and waded out to Erik.

"Partner, you need obedience training. Come when called. Are you totally unconcussed yet? Can you follow my finger?"

"Depends on where the finger is going."

"Matter settled. Question: is vehicular misadventure rampant in Minnesota? People are constantly run off the roads—a past case, this case.

Eighty-six-year-old dude claimed a Mustang forced him to drive into a restaurant that wasn't a drive-in, and so on and so forth."

"Automobiles kill more deer than—"

"Skip the Ranger Rick stuff. So there I was, debating the mini-donut option, pumping Nancy LeClerc's grandkids for information . . .. I see your look. They didn't need much pumping. Turned out to be dangerous at Betty Danger's. When this old guy plowed into the restaurant, I swear Sutton and Blair, or Blair and Sutton, were about to rip off their clothes and go all Captain Underpants."

"You mean Captain America?"

"What you said. Nancy LeClerc has the Resource as a beneficiary, and CEO Luis Peña has tech geeks searching for a leak in their loyalty program, and none of this sounds like a solution to Dan Routh's murder. Grimes is on the lam, we can't identify Ray, I'm a 'problem,' maybe I'm being followed by a Mustang, you're the walking wounded, and here we are." Deb ran out of breath. She left out what a fool she'd been on the golf course with Geoff and Jude. Deb had hoped Jude would send a cute follow-up text. Nothing, and she'd been an idiot to put her foot in it again. She realized that she'd left her sunglasses behind. The top of her head was hot, and the afternoon light glinted off the water to sear her eyeballs.

"Are you all right?" Erik asked.

What the hell, she wanted to cry—howl like an electrocuted cat. She pressed her eyes shut and opened them to see that her toes underwater were broken by refraction. "Hmmm, well. Hmm." She thought she heard Erik repeat the question. "I'm BOMO," she sobbed and let it all spill out because that was better than more sobbing. "BOMO, Born Missing Out. I haven't seen the musical *Hamilton*, I haven't been to Iceland, I haven't eaten at the Bachelor Farmer, I don't know who Lizzo is."

"I can sing one song from *Hamilton*. Hasn't helped a bit," Erik said.

Kids dashing into the water splashed them. Two dueled with swim noodles before bobbing away. Despite her constricted throat, Deb managed to say, "So, partner, what are your aspirations, crime-fighting wise?"

"To be to law enforcement what Roger Federer is to tennis."

"Hell, I'll be to social justice what Meryl Streep is to movies."

Erik burst into laughter and Deb joined in until she couldn't breathe. Right, she'd have the range of a brilliant actress and he the quality of a world-class tennis genius. They sighed *oh my* and wiped tears from their faces. "Well, then," Deb sniffed back moisture, "Routh is dead. Our number one suspect is a vague concept, Ray. Anything on that corrupt-cop angle?"

"Yes and no. Leads have come in that an eastside patrol officer has approached dealers, to scope them out. He hasn't acted on anything. A year ago, that officer had his right scapular and upper arm broken by a baseball bat during an attempted arrest. I'm reaching out." Erik didn't expand on how he was reaching out.

"Meanwhile, back at the LeClercs—I'm cat puke to Nancy—Ray decided that the Simples were a good site for nefarious activity. Be great if we can get to Ray before Grimes does. Grimes gets there first, we might never find the body. What Luna recalled in our last chat is all over the place, not unusual for what she's been through. She had a plan for independence, love, and a thrill—eloping with Ray. The opposite happens—he abducts her. She makes Ray's dad sound dangerous. A real boogeyman."

"Technically, a boogeyman isn't real." Erik splashed water on his arms and face.

"Well, Dictionary Dan, there are horrific parents." Deb dampened her hands and put them over her closed eyes. "And con artists invent the most amazing stuff to cover their tracks."

Erik jumped to a different track. "After the Hirsch Fest, I thought Josh Miller, as peer counselor, might know how to find Luna, but then she showed up. We also played with the idea that he might be Ray. No, but maybe they connect. Half an hour ago, the detective on the Miller case forwards me data recovered from the kid's debit card tracing where he parked last week. Tuesday night he parked a few blocks from the Stone Arch Bridge, not far from where he drowned the next morning. Was that a regular rendezvous with someone? On one hand, I sense I'm not making a connection. On the other, I feel that Josh Miller is Not Our Case."

The boys on noodles circled around them, splashing hard with their feet, until an adult yelled. Deb splashed back. "By the way, where's your fam, Ben and your dad? Not that I'm prying. Okay, I'm prying. You're out here alone being neither fish nor fowl. What would Tennis Roger say? Does Roger ever even grunt?"

"Ben's off with his grandpas while I 'fully' recover." There was a hitch in Erik's voice.

She didn't speak. Maybe they were thinking the same thing, that not every award went to Meryl, and Roger did lose. The sun glinting off the water made it hard to tell if Erik was tearful. "They're still the GOATS," she said.

"What?"

"Roger and Meryl, Greatest Of All Time. I caught Nancy LeClerc's goat, ha-ha—a little weed-eater that escaped the herd. Don't look at me like I'm crazy, the irony wasn't concussed out of you."

Behind them, a mom yelled, "Sasha, don't drown your brother!"

Sasha wore a pink flamingo suit. "You know, partner, I was a swimsuit model in college. A sports magazine featured a pic of my butt as I was springing from a starter board. Nice to know what people find attractive about you. My competition suit was 'burnt cardinal.' These kids come in every color."

"Every color, hmm," Erik said. "It seems like it's about relationships. Luna can't give up on a relationship with Ray."

"With trafficking, it's fake. People are commodities."

"Josh had a girlfriend, a pianist, when things started going bad."

"Where's this going?"

"Not sure."

Erik was on his phone, leaving a message, "Lionel, Detective Jansson. Call me at your earliest convenience." To Deb, "This kid, Lionel, might be the answer to everything. What if Josh Miller's old girlfriend is the pianist I saw at the Hirsch Fest? She's related to Lionel. I remember now that she was one of the people who mentioned Josh. That parking spot of Josh's is near the music school she attends. She could know more than she realizes."

Deb's phone alarmed in her pocket and sent them both splashing to the shore. "Oh, jeez, unknown caller on Luna's line. This should've—" She was interrupted by a new call.

"Luna?"

"Detective Deb, don't be mad! I just wanted to see Pammie. She texted and I took Gammie's car and she's not here and I'm scared and—"

"Hold it." Deb slid into her Prius, Erik joining her. She handed him the G-Met wireless tablet that was in the car. "I'm with my partner, Yansson, Erik? We're listening. Take a breath. Okay. Tell me where you are."

"The park? Lake Phalen?"

Big park, urban park.

"Luna, are there lots of people?"

She sobbed, "I'm parked illegally."

"Not an issue. Tell me—"

Her voice hitched every other word: "I got here . . . got a text, it says go someplace else . . .. I don't think Pammie sent it."

"Luna, do you see a golf course, the activity center?" Deb watched Erik pull up patrol activity on the tablet. They were running a race and sitting still.

"Uh, I see the sign to the center."

"You're by the parking lot, right? You stay. We'll track that text. Erik's requested a car to meet you in"—he held up three fingers—"three minutes."

"No!" Erik was transfixed by the patrol activity.

"No?" Deb asked.

He said, "Luna, two minutes, Squad 621." He mouthed *mute*, Deb did. "Trouble. A squad car is tracking a Nissan Cube observed at a drug drop. The Cube is registered to Lionel Fowler."

"Your Lionel?"

"A Black man in a wanted vehicle pursued by police." He jumped out of her car and ran to his. She unmuted the phone.

"Detective Deb?" came a squeak.

"It'll be fine," Deb assured her with no confidence.

CHAPTER 40

"**Y**OU SHOULDA CALLED ME FROM THE GET-GO," Bent Nail insisted as Gordy drove from one of the body shops he considered suspicious toward the *Celebrate!* where Dan had been discovered. He was checking possible tow routes for the van that had disappeared that night, and on a Sunday, no one would notice him poking around. Only it was hard not to notice Leif's friend, Bent Nail. Nail wore a sleeveless tee with a camouflage fringe vest over it, and an Aussie-adventure hat with a brim wide enough to shade an extra-large snozzle. As he jabbered away with his mouth and hands, the muscles in his noodly arms bobbled. Gordy wanted to pass on his ideas to the detectives and be done with it. Dorothy dozed in the back where he'd put a pad on the open floor. Summer days, the AC wasn't enough, and she heated up in the crate. Afterwards they were visiting a veteran suffering PTSD, and Nail wanted to observe "the canine therapy experience to the max." A dog as hefty as Newfie Dorothy ought to be the max.

He pulled up to a pump at the *Celebrate!* station. He didn't want to see the dumpster, but a plan's a plan. Nail hopped out while Gordy unscrewed the gas cap. "If that last shop looks dicey, Gordy, I can make the call. I know these detectives. The Deb one—I'm, like, her hawk partner." Did he mean ad hoc? "If you're paying inside, could you get me an ice cream sandwich? Anyway, me and Deb, I'm her all-round wise guy."

Gordy could see that. What he couldn't see was why a Mustang drove close to his van instead of pulling up tight to the pump on the left.

Nail had his eyes on the store. "You already swiped? You shouldn't trust those readers. I'll run in quick for the ice cream. Want one or two?"

Gordy held up two fingers. Dorothy had to keep her strength up. Nail gangled to the store, and Gordy picked up a windshield swabber. He was scrubbing away bugs when hands grabbed him and shoved him into Nail's seat while somebody else hopped in the driver's spot. That man spun off, the safety doohickey on the gas nozzle breaking away. Behind them Nail windmilled his arms and shouted, but nobody slowed down. Out of habit, Gordy clicked his seat belt and goggled at his captor. *No, no, no.* Upside-down-head man, the meanest son of a bitch he could imagine.

CHAPTER 41

Erik's Highlander took the corner wide and sped around a double-parked UPS truck. He drove up on the curve near the eastside Paddy Wagon Bar, where two St. Paul officers had pulled over the Cube. When he'd called ahead to say *nonviolent driver*, they'd cut him off. Erik jumped out. The officers, two white men, were ordering the Cube driver to get *out* hands *up*. The door opened but the boy fell, and the closest officer clamped his hand to his service weapon.

"*He's with undercover Squeegee G-Met Jansson*," Erik shouted in one breath and in the next, "*Lionel, show your hands—it's safe.*" The boy, in a heap on the pavement, extended his hands and the patrol officers hauled him up. The boy's chest heaved beneath his shirt, a bold daisy print fit for a party. Erik ran to the group.

"G-Met," the stockier officer said like it was Erik's name. "What-the-f and who's Jansson?"

"Yeah, G-Met, what-the-f?" echoed the boy. "We didn't talk about meeting like *this*. Hey!" The skinny officer had taken Lionel's wallet from a pocket. "You need permission."

"I'm Detective Erik Jansson, Officers, with Greater-Metro. Lionel Fowler here has information I need."

The stocky one took charge. "Jansson, huh. You know Hangnail and Sleepy?"

"Hairpin and Squeegee."

"So you say. Tuesday night, seven forty-five p.m., the drug unit had an undercover involved in a sting operation at one of the Lake Phalen parks. A dealer told the undercover that he'd have to chill and come back in twenty when fresh oxy supplies arrive. Then things start happening. A customer, we'll call him Kev because that's his name, pulls up in a Lexus. Now get this, he recognizes the undercover because they have kids in the same soccer league. He calls out, 'Hi Mick, Kev here.' The dealer panics and asks, 'Who's Mick?' Kev realizes what's going down. He squeals off in his Lexus just as a Cube pulls into the parking lot, normal-like. The Cube driver sees it's gone south, and *he* peels off. It starts raining, and the camera only caught a partial plate. That partial matches up with this vehicle." He pointed to the Cube. "Which is registered to Lionel Fowler, North Minneapolis address near last week's gang shooting. Registration claims your undercover Lionel is seventeen." He muscled into Lionel's face. "You an emancipated minor?"

Lionel sputtered. "Hey, people're taking pictures of us! I have *aspirations*. Now I'll be on Facebook as a criminal, you pi—you *porcines*."

"What's that mean?" the skinny, slightly dim cop asked.

"It means," Erik weaseled between the officers and Lionel, "that we need to act like Officer Friendly for the crowd." On cue they all relaxed and fell apart. "And we need to move on. Lionel, you can ride with me if you can stand the smell of puke." The lingering aura of Luna's trauma.

"I'm good with them." Lionel shook the dimwit officer's hand and gave the crowd a smile that would make a politician proud.

THE ST. PAUL DISTRICT STATION had the typical blah décor. Erik entered an interrogation room and set down a digital tablet. Lionel had slumped into a suspicious mood and sat with his arms folded across his chest and his hands tucked under his armpits. Erik's experience largely entailed white-on-white crime. Erik knew there was much he didn't know, a chasm between his privilege and the boy's experience. This conversation could go wrong in so many directions.

Lionel masked fear with belligerence. "Hauling me here to the Land of the Un-Woke, huh."

"I apologize for that, Lionel. By the way, your hair looks *leonine*. I heard you call the officers *porcine*."

"They were pigs until you showed up. And what's this about me being an emancipated minor? What kind of reference is *that*?"

"Emancipated Minor is a legal term for a person under eighteen who has certain adult rights. Like the right to own a car and have independent finances. People in that category usually come out of the foster system. Or there are parents who have to be kept out of the picture. Say a seventeen-year-old emancipated minor starts college. He'd be in charge of the bill, the financial aid, and no one else can access those funds. I learned this from my father, who works in campus security in Iowa. He's escorted unwanted adults off campus."

Lionel tilted his chin up. "Is your dad a good guy?"

"If I'm half as good as he is, my life will be well lived." Erik hadn't meant to say that.

"I felt that way about Grandpa Fowler. He died and left me a college fund. My white uncle died of cancer and left me money. My aunt—she practically lives in Edina—signed it over to me. That's how I paid for the Cube. Didn't want my mom's name on anything on account of her cash cravings. My father didn't even hang around long enough to get his name on the birth certificate. I'm emancipated all right. Why should I trust you? You make shit up, that undercover crap."

"Why have imagination if you can't use it for good?"

"Huh." Lionel's arms remained crossed.

Erik wanted to know if Lionel stayed with the mother or the 'practically Edina' aunt. "Where's home for you?"

"Home is the place where, when you go there, they don't turn you in."

An awkward lull. There are no cozy lulls in a police interrogation room. The dimwit officer interrupted to bring in cans of Coke, which he dropped so they rolled across the floor. He sheepishly retrieved them. As he left, Lionel huffed, "*Ovine.*"

Erik held a can at arm's length and waited for ten seconds. "What a treat— all the sugar, all the caffeine, double the fizz." He popped it and cola sizzled over his hand. He set the can down and shook off his hand. Opening the calmer second can, he passed it to Lionel, who was rocking his uneven chair. "There's an issue with the Nissan registered to you. This is an informational discussion, but you can have a lawyer anytime."

"They drop through the ceiling?"

Erik almost admitted his ex was a lawyer. "Sometimes I wish lawyers would drop through the floor."

"Ain't that so." Lionel balanced his chair on the back legs. "Have you ever shot a man?"

"I have never killed a man and my daily prayer is that it will never come to that."

"So shooting people who look like me, what's your quadratic equation for that? Your answer, G-Met?"

Erik sipped his drink and considered. "Love is the answer. But you have to show your work."

"*Pah*, I am so going to use that."

"Here's the situation, Lionel. As the officers said, on Tuesday evening a traffic cam caught a Cube in the area of a drug bust."

"Yeah, like, total alibi for me, babysitting my cousin Gabe."

"Did you loan your car to anyone?"

Lionel banged his chair down. "I would never let my Cube—she's Sheila— be involved in anything skanky. Like, how is sweet Sheila involved in *your* case? That ex-cop you talked about at the Kafka Café?"

"Coming to that. I saw your cousin the pianist at the Hirsch Fest. She mentioned a drug counselor. That counselor drowned Wednesday near Lock and Dam 1. He was fleeing an attacker. We believe his attacker may be a henchman for the escaped drug-lord Vernon Grimes."

"Boy, you guys got caught with your pants down on that one. That dude got clean away. From the *courthouse*."

"Not our finest hour." Erik had to come up with an angle, any angle. "Back at the café, another person had been with you, left behind a bad vibe. A man?"

Lionel angled his chair away and glowered at a corner. "Ra-*moan*."

"Ramon. He's Italian, Hispanic?"

"White like inedible paste. I call him 'Ray.' "

Erik stiffened. "Ray. Do you know his full name?"

"Why?" Lionel's eyes shot back to Erik.

"We're looking for a Ray in regard to the Routh murder."

"*Holy shit*." Lionel swiveled his whole body back. "This dude, Ra-*moan* Kinny or Kenney, has a bad-ass dad. He about killed Ramon. That's what made him leave the café. I sorta joked that his dad had something to do with killing the ex-cop, and he got pissed."

Erik tapped the tablet he'd brought in. "I'd like to show you some sketches." He pulled up six images and slid the pad toward Lionel.

"*WTF*. Number 5 looks like that vampire movie star. And Ra-*moan*. So am I right about his dad or what?"

Erik ignored the dad part. "Ray or Ramon may be involved in activities that exploit young women. Romances them before asserting his 'needs.' It could be he's been forced into a situation."

"Ramon, he's needy. He goes with Retta. He also likes my cousin, Jaylyn."

"The pianist."

"Yeah. Jaylyn thought Ramon and Retta were getting straightened out, only lately Jaylynnie worries Retta's drinking again."

"Retta?"

"Retta Mazzi."

Erik checked his tablet. Emergency updates showed that a Retta Mazzi had been found unconscious at a St. Paul address an hour ago, administered Naloxone, and taken to the hospital.

"What's up, G-Met? You, like, froze? I was worried out there on the street with the porcines, but now you got me really worried. I'm sweatin' out the daisies in my new shirt!"

"Did Ramon ever come to you for help?"

"He sticks me with the bill. Except he left me a twenty that day at the café. I was thinking of framing it as a joke, the Ra-*moan* Miracle." Lionel pulled a twenty from his wallet and tossed it on the table. "Ketchup stained." Erik didn't touch it. "Wait, you think it's blood? Cocaine? Freaking Fatal Fentanyl?"

"Acne bacteria is the most common contaminant."

Lionel was out of his chair. "I'm getting *acne* out of all this? People are dying and I'm getting *acne*?"

"Would Ramon go to anyone else?"

"No, oh no. No." Lionel plopped back and rubbed his face. "Jaylyn. I knew she was too nice, except to me. I knew it. Uhh, she borrowed my Cube to go to a music jam at McMillan on Tuesday, burned up gas. Maybe she let him take it."

"She needs to be notified. Her details?"

Lionel said "Dudek" and gave the girl's cell number. Erik tried it. No response. "Could you call? If it goes to voice mail, say it's an emergency."

Lionel left a message, his voice breaking so it was barely audible.

"Do you know where she is?"

"She was taking Gabe, her brother, to the Apple Valley Zoo because he's into tigers and bears."

"I'm calling zoo security. Does Jaylyn have a family pass, a credit card, anything that would be scanned at the gate?"

Lionel was numb.

"That's all right. There may be absolutely nothing to worry about, but she's Priority One."

"Are you going to the zoo, G-Met? Do I come with you? Where's my Cube? Do I call her mom?"

"I'll connect you with another G-Met officer, James Bond Smalls—yes, the Black James Bond—and he'll attend to matters."

Erik couldn't move fast enough.

CHAPTER 42

THE CHASE HAPPENED OVER AND OVER. Red-faced snow monkeys shrieked and tailed each other over rocks and dead tree limbs within the zoo enclosure. A little one braked on a thick limb and flopped down on the branch in instant relaxation. The larger one behind settled in to pick at the little one's back.

Jaylyn's brother Gabe wouldn't hold her hand. "Look, that baby's sticking his butt in his mom's face."

White kids next to them jumped up and down, hoo-hooing to excite the monkeys.

"Don't do that," Jaylyn warned Gabe. "You know why."

"I ain't no scary flying monkey. Aren't you going to criticize me for saying 'ain't'? Gran says 'ain't' and nobody says nothin'. How come the monkeys have so many nits? Isn't there a monkey keeper?"

"*I'm* your monkey keeper, and I'm picking your nits." Jaylyn tickled Gabe, and he giggled and threw a fake punch at her. She was forcing herself to have fun to keep doom from bearing down on her. Back in Golden Valley, she waited for Gabe in the quiet of Nana's garage, called Ramon, and reached a recording, "Delivery in progress." She left a message, "Got help for Retta, taking bro to zoo." After parking Nana's Buick in the zoo lot, Jaylyn checked her phone for news on Retta, and her gasp frightened Gabe. She had been terrified there would be an announcement of a woman overdosing. Nothing like that, but the name of the man who drowned at the bridge had been released. It was Josh Miller. She started crying. Gabe asked why, and she half lied that a school friend of hers died. "Do you wanna go home?" he asked, his eyes on the zoo entrance. Yes, no. If she went home, she'd fall apart, have to explain everything. She couldn't bear it. "Better I'm away." She honked her nose into a tissue. *Think about something else, anything else.*

Keeping everybody straight—Retta, Ramon, Gran, Aunt Lyndsay, Gabe—had become Jaylyn's full-time job. Needy Lazar might as well be in the mix. He had an inner hedgehog. When she flubbed a phrase and apologized, he scolded: don't burden people with explanations to make yourself feel better. Excuses are poor horses to ride. Yet Lazar had those pills. Did he want cash to pay for pills? She didn't know if she trusted him. Well, she did with music because what he said worked, and his eyes glowed when she played a phrase with new acuity. But the pills—she hadn't had time to do anything with Retta's bottle. If Jaylyn stayed busy, stayed with people, there would be no temptation. Gabe nagged her to catch up. To cover a sob, she chanted, "Duh-uh, it's so fine to have fun in the funky June sun."

"You can't rap. Stick to Beethoven and opera." Gabe sang in an exaggerated boy soprano, *"Time to behold the mighty bears of old."* He dashed ahead to the Russian bear trail, jumped about to face her, and blurted, "Oh, hey."

A squeeze of Jaylyn's shoulder—Ramon, eyes filled with heartbreak.

"Ramon? Whatya doing here?" Jaylyn's hand went to her throat and she flushed. Behind them, the snow monkeys cackled, Gabe yelled *come'on* and she walked ahead, Ramon falling in beside her.

"You said we couldn't hang out because of your brother. I thought, why not hang out here?" Ramon had a quirky smile with one tooth snaggling out to be adorable. "Retta, hell, I don't know what the f—"

"Ramon, this is my brother, Gabe."

"Hey, dude." Ramon stared as if determining that Gabe was real. "First my dad, then Retta. Here I am, working my jobs, then Retta." He choked back emotion. Gabe did what any sensible ten-year-old would do and skipped ahead to distance himself from the embarrassing adults.

"Everything will be all right," Jaylyn snapped. She would turn into White Gran.

"Is that a song?"

"Several songs," Jaylyn softened. "Bob Marley, Sean Lennon, The Killers, *Jesus Christ Superstar*."

"Were you practicing today?" It sounded like an accusation.

"Yesss." Sort of, the Beethoven. She should've played Liszt and *Sinnerman*. That rhythm stuck in her head, *Sinnerman, where you going to run to, where you gonna hide.*

Ahead of them, Gabe pinched his nose by the pasture of a hoofed creature, a funky mutant with plenty of stink. Ramon reached for Jaylyn's hand, but she was rooting through her bag for sunglasses. He sighed, "Retta, she's wipes me out."

This time Jaylyn channeled Nana's consoling hum. "Mmm uhmm."

Addicts, alcoholics, they did that, wiped out the people around them. To her left was a display with no animal in sight, unless one was hiding behind a large rock. *Run to the rock.*

"Wiped me out." Ramon compressed his lips. "Took my money, or her mom did and that naked-ass boyfriend did."

"It'll be okay." The pit in Jaylyn's stomach argued otherwise. Ramon had been damaged, loss after loss, pain and more pain. *Don't you see I need you, rock?*

Ramon jerked at a squeal from the intercom: zoo closing in thirty minutes.

Gabe charged ahead through mock caves. Jaylyn ran after and Ramon caught up and took her arm. "Who can you trust when it's a fucking hellhole? Sorry." Ramon said into her ear, "You're the only one, Jaylyn."

She tingled. There was a strange sizzling in the cave, like the rock cried out.

Ramon pulled her closer. "People can always turn to you and—*hey*, that's my foot!"

Gabe had tramped on it. "Whoops. I backed up to let the little kids see the bear. This one's Cossack. He's like a thousand pounds and goes nose to nose against the plexiglass. See, his side tooth's like a pirate's hook. He's posing."

"Somebody must be paying him." Ramon's tone soured.

Gabe ran ahead. "Maybe the tiger's out."

As they passed the Amur leopard enclosure, Ramon tried to take Jaylyn's hand, but she rubbed her nose. She was shaky. She should feel loyalty to Retta. Ramon put his arm around her shoulder and his lips brushed the hair over her ear. "So you found Retta?"

"I called 911. I didn't go there."

Ramon dropped his arm in shock: "You didn't go? You didn't check on her?"

"Come *on*," Gabe shouted.

"We'll figure out what's up with Retta," she pleaded and rushed ahead. Ramon followed with his hands in his pockets.

Gabe pantomimed a hip-hop routine on the bridge over the tiger enclosure, a half-acre bowl wooded along the rim. "I can't see the tiger. They separated him from the female tiger when she had the cub, so he wouldn't, like, eat his own baby. Maybe Dad's out for dental work, har, har."

A mother and crying toddler rushed from the other direction across the bridge. The woman, disfigured with worry, dragged the toddler along and sniveled into a cell phone, "I can't, I can't." *I can't hide you*, the rock cried out, *I can't hide you.* Then no one but Gabe was in sight.

"Your brother needs to take a piss." Ramon jerked his head back toward the exit. "See how's he's grabbing the barrier?"

"He's dancing." Her brother's jitterbugging made Jaylyn's legs shake uncontrollably. They shook like that before a recital when she was to play

Beethoven's *Moonlight Sonata*. Her teacher Mrs. Norman made her repeat a mantra, *Beethoven requires courage, Beethoven gives courage*. Gabe, pushing the limits, kicked his heels high as he held the bridge fence. Extending down from the fence were curved wire bars.

"That's not safe. He should go back."

Jaylyn didn't speak. *Nina, Ella, Liszt, Beyoncé give you courage*.

"It's hard on me." Ramon's breath was ragged. "I had a brother."

Jaylyn stopped. "You never told me."

"Hard to talk about. My brother, he was real little. My parents used him like a human shield when they fought. My mother took him when she disappeared."

"I thought you didn't remember your mother."

Ramon fiddled with items that *click, click, clicked* in his pocket. "Are you going to that weird teacher who wants cash? Your brother needs to pee. Gabe! You should go back."

Run to the rock tripped through Jaylyn's head. *Run to the rock, Josh, Run to the Rock, Retta, Run to the . . ..* "Stay here." She put a hand up to Ramon then ran to her brother, waving her arms wildly like a joke alarm. She pivoted him in a dance before whispering in his ear, "Go back, call Uncle Ed, call twice. Use your brain."

"Don't joke." Gabe didn't believe her.

She pinched him and felt his surge of terror. "Run. Look happy about it."

Gabe ran past Ramon and picked up speed. "Uncle Ed" was a code. Ed was the Black policeman the family knew. Call twice, call 911 too. You don't forget a brother. You don't act shocked about calling 911 in an emergency. It was Retta whose parents used her as a human shield. And Uncle Ed let slip once a cynical saying, "When seconds count, the police are minutes away." *The rock can't hide you.*

Jaylyn saw no one but Ramon and herself. The closing announcement covered the tremor in her voice. "We have to go back." *I run to the river, it was bleedin'.*

Ramon crushed her upper arm in his grip. "Jaylyn, I need money. I know you care. It's not just Retta. My boss has gone crazy saying I owe—"

Jaylyn should've played along—*I run to the rock*. Instead she lost it. "You're *lying*."

Ray's left hand flipped open a knife as he moved between her and the barrier.

"*Police!*" she screamed, though no one was there, and pushed hard, the hardest she'd ever pushed against muscle and bone. Ray grabbed for her, and she heard the gasping roar of the tiger.

CHAPTER 43

WHEN JAYLYN SCREAMED "POLICE" to scare Ramon, that conjured them. A tall man, the detective from the café, and a zoo security woman buzzed up on a cart, and from the other direction came people with walkie-talkies and rifles. Badges flashed at her and she overhead them strategizing on how to avoid shooting. With shock, she realized it was not Ramon but the tiger they didn't want to shoot. More shocking, she felt the same way.

The detective had a protective vest over his summer shirt. He had muscles. "Detective Jansson. We met at the music fest, earlier at the café."

Her voice was kitten-thin. "You were hurt."

"Hurt? No, your brother Gabe is fine, so's Lionel. Are you hurt? No? Good. Ms. Dudek, is Ray—you know him as Ramon Kenny—is he armed?"

Jaylyn whispered, "A knife."

"Did you see a gun, Jaylyn? Any lumps in his pockets, his waistband?"

"No."

"Did he threaten you?"

Jaylyn almost collapsed, the detective steadied her, and she repeated, "Knife."

"Can you show me where he went over?"

She pointed to the barrier, mid-section. Going over wasn't hard, but iron claws made climbing back impossible.

The zoo woman scanned the enclosure with binoculars. "I see him, 'Ray.' West side at bottom of incline, seven o'clock by my position. See the white t-shirt, beneath the trees and by the rock." *Hide me rock.* The woman scanned the enclosure. "Opposite bank, four o'clock, behind bush, Leo. Leo's crouching and considering his options."

"You named a tiger Leo?" the detective asked.

"He was born under the zodiac sign," she replied testily and then said into the walkie-talkie, "Leo's backing toward the gate. Commence Operation Dead Meat."

The detective focused on Jaylyn. "Is there anything else you can tell us? Take your time." He was so earnest that she teared up. "Ms. Dudek, we're moving you to safety," he said before she could make herself speak. "Oh, Dahlberg, good thing you're here."

That last was to a blonde woman in a sundress. She and the detective exchanged smiles, and then she said to her, "Off-duty St. Paul," and directed her away. Another woman—her sister, the woman said—fell in beside them, and with that protection Jaylyn's throat relaxed. She called over her shoulder to the detective, "*He lies.*"

THE WHITE SHIRT WAS A LIE.

Armed backup had run crouching to the shape, weapons drawn, shouting "*Police! Don't move.*" Erik held back inside the animal enclosure, under a tree. The tiger had been tempted into secure maintenance by a goat hindquarter. At the slight rustle of leaves, Erik rolled away as Ray dropped from the tree, knife in hand. He landed hard on a bloody leg and grunted. Erik was up and facing shirtless Ray from twelve feet away. Too close, a thrown knife could take out an eye. "*Freeze,*" Erik panted and held up a badge. Ray stumbled and stood again, knife gripped tight. They could see each other sweat.

"Detective Jansson. Don't move. Your safety is our priority, Ray, Ramon." *A lie.* Erik was more concerned with the safety of everyone else. The man in ripped jeans didn't *appear* to have a gun, though his eyes were feral enough that he might charge. Erik didn't want to excite him by drawing his service weapon. Ray wasn't cornered but he had nowhere to go. If Leo weighing six hundred pounds and able to leap thirty feet couldn't escape the enclosure, Ray didn't have a chance. "Let's think about this, Ray. We can get you out of here, away from the tiger."

What Erik didn't have was hard evidence of Ray's crimes. He could take him in for threatening Jaylyn Dudek. He could arrest him, on the basis of a sketch, for abducting Luna. The backup officers crept in from the sides, and Erik talked to hold Ray's focus. "Ray, let's walk out. I need to see both hands up." Ray put his empty hand behind his back.

"Drop the knife. Both hands up, Ray." Erik didn't want to fall back on "resisting a police officer," which sounded like crock to the public. "Ray, we can walk out and get you medical attention. We can talk in a cool room with water to drink." If the other option was being gunned down, quenching your thirst while hearing your Miranda rights wasn't so bad.

"Ray, you can help us. Vernon Grimes is at large. He's not going to protect

you. Grimes is the reason you need help, and we could use information."
Erik caught the eye of the officer to his right with a taut nod and took two
steps forward.

Ray stank of fear and blood. What must the tiger smell? Was the tiger truly
secure? A slight shift in Ray's eyes—he was beginning to think, his hand about
to move.

"Now, up in the air!"

Cak cak cak. Ray charged and Erik dodged and heard a Taser's zap. Another
zap, and Ray crashed down. The uniforms grabbed him and the knives.

"Ray Kenny, I'm arresting you for the attempted assault of Jaylyn Dudek."
The officers had Ray sitting up, but he didn't register anything. Erik would
have to wait on saying, "You have the right to remain silent."

It wasn't silent. A low gurgling intake grew into a throaty roar. The tiger
roared again, eager to prowl his territory. First, they had to remove stunned
Ray. There was another stunned form. Ten feet away lay a crow-sized bird,
stark black and white with a red crown. A pileated woodpecker. The second
officer had Tased in the direction of the *cak* jungle cry. Either the zoo people
could revive the woodpecker, or Leo would enjoy a colorful dessert.

Erik, the musky smell of beasts in his nostrils, sensed his phone
vibrating. Deb had been diverted from Luna to chase Grimes, who had
seized Gordy Omdahl.

CHAPTER 44

D EB SHOUTED INSTRUCTIONS to the station attendant about more officers arriving and activated the siren to the G-Met SUV roof. Before Bent Nail's call came, she had swapped out her car for one from the fleet to track down Luna. She hopped in the SUV and hit door-lock. Too late. Nail, in shotgun position, issued commands. She talked over him. "You're a civilian, Nail. I can't take you."

"Deputize me and move it. Right there, your screen, they're feeding you a live map of the area. They'll find the van."

Where's the ejector seat when you need it? Deb maneuvered onto the street. "I am not a sheriff. I do not deputize. This is not Shootout at the O.K. Corral."

"You get those last-known coordinates, Doc?"

"I'd be Wyatt Earp, you'd be Doc Holliday. State Patrol will beat us to the action, Nail. I'll drop you off before."

"You'll need a dog handler. Hup, they sighted the van."

"What? Gordy's dogs are with him?" Deb wove through traffic that didn't understand the whole siren deal.

"Just Dorothy. Hey, that guy cut you off."

"*No giving the finger from a cop car*. That's an order, Nail."

"Gordy and Dorothy, they're hostages. You can get 'em to surrender hostages, can't you?"

It dawned on her. "You want to say, 'Surrender Dorothy.' "

"With a megaphone?"

"Nail, the witch writes that in the sky."

"A cool line no matter how. *Surrender Dorothy*. Oh, heck, they lost 'em again."

Deb's strength was going for the obvious. "Nail, do you have a phone? Is it synced with Gordy's?"

"Hell yes it is. Why you need me. I'm the tracker."

GORDY WAS GRATEFUL HE HADN'T PEED HIS PANTS, but the guy driving meant bad business. He took Wheelock Parkway fast, but not so fast as to catch attention.

"I need to know," Upside-down-head man said, turning Gordy's guts cold, "why you're fucking interested in my places of work?"

Gordy couldn't speak with the loop running through his head, *Save Dorothy, save Dorothy*.

Grimes waved the gun in his right hand. "Give me a fucking break."

Gordy croaked, "You can have the van."

"This fucking bucket? Who talked to you? Can't trust my fucking team." Grimes gunned the van onto an I-35E entrance, slamming Gordy against the door. He was clueless and had lost count of the *fucks*. Dorothy stirred in the back. *Please, please, please save her*. Grimes took a violent swerve to the left, Gordy gasped, and the van squealed with the speed as if terrified. Upside-down-head man's determination was like nothing Gordy had experienced. It sucked the air right out of him. His eyes saw blank, he was blacking out.

"*You dumb shit!*" jerked him conscious. "Those fucking kids ratted to you. That rat college-kid addict? Dead addict now. He talk to you? That kid Ray, he's scamming me? Thinks he has a big brain in his skull. I could crack it like a fucking walnut."

You can't talk about kids that way. "You stop right now, Mr. Grimes."

Grimes barked a loud, sick laugh. Like that Dorothy was on her feet and woofed in his ear. He whapped his gun hand back and hit her wet maw— "What the *fuck*"—and that massive jaw clamped down on the hand.

Grimes screamed and the gun fell. The van spun across the highway, horns blaring at them, sirens coming. They skidded and tipped over on the median, airbags slamming the men against the seats. Dorothy howled.

HANDS WERE ON HIM and Gordy lay on a stretcher. A light shone in his eyes. A voice asked, "Can you hear me, Mr. Omdahl?"

"Dorothy," he wheezed.

"We're getting her. How are you feeling?" It was an EMT guy.

"Like I got the stuffing kicked out of me."

"Then we'll stuff it back in. We're moving you on three."

Gordy was aware of being lifted, of Bent Nail at his side, that Wonder Woman detective, and of a paw pointing at him from a stretcher. *Dorothy, save Dorothy*.

DEB RANG ERIK FROM THE HOSPITAL to report that Grimes had busted his arm, ankle, and noggin, not to mention a dog bite. She couldn't formally charge him until that upside-down head was conscious. She would wait until Gordy was stabilized. Dorothy had been taken to a vet, where she wasn't allowed to eat until she had been observed for twelve hours. Not a happy puppy. Deb had insisted that a St. Paul officer debrief Bent Nail because he wouldn't stop asking her if she wanted to join him and his girl for a double date.

That left Erik alone with Ray on a Sunday night at the deserted G-Met station. The two of them almost knee to knee at a round table, Erik let Ray talk himself into corners. He let Ray blame the "real" drug dealers who "planted" evidence like a handgun in his van, and then blame Jaylyn Dudek. "She's so nervous about performing she'll do anything for drugs," Ray sneered. Erik deliberately misunderstood and repeated, "Luna's nervous and wants pills, you're saying." To straighten Erik out, Ray revealed more than he initially claimed to know, mentioning Retta and dropping Luna's name again. Erik ended the interview at that, frustrated from toes to eyeballs that he didn't yet have the ammunition to throw Dan Routh in Ray's face. He saw that Ray was locked away and went home to the mundane, to his stack of dirty laundry.

Laundry . . .. Young men often screw up laundry. That was something to think on.

CHAPTER 45

IT WAS THE THURSDAY NOON after the Sunday capture of Ray Kenny, and Deb had to hustle back to G-Met to join Erik in the interrogation. Why had Nancy LeClerc insisted on seeing her at her tower? At least Deb would pass the dress code. She'd dressed to the nines in a skirt suit. After meeting Nancy, she'd slip out of flats and into high heels to confront Ray, because she was never more terrifying than when she was glammed-up and 6'4". She could borrow an imperious expression from Nancy LeClerc. Meanwhile, this meeting with Nancy had to be about as pleasant as chatting with an executioner after a hanging. Deb exited 494 to park by the office tower. Drug enforcement officers had arrested Geoffrey LeClerc yesterday, while he was meeting a "patient" at a Hilton, for falsifying opioid prescriptions and facilitating drug dealing. Geoff had been smart enough to say nothing and call his lawyer.

However, when Deb had interrogated him first thing this morning, Geoff lost it at the sight of her and spit out that he'd been blackmailed. "Blackmailed by the Grimes organization or your own greed?" she asked. Before his lawyer could stop him, Geoff ranted about people biting the hand that feeds them. An anonymous source had sent G-Met digital evidence that indicated Geoff abused the LeClerc loyalty system for his dealer associates. He defended himself: he pushed back at the parking lot vermin, as Deb should remember, because he was adamantly against people trafficking. "Not enough against trafficking," Deb fired back, "to let it stop your drug dealing. You could have told your 'Aunt Nan,' who would have stopped it."

Geoff's reply, "You haven't stopped it either. That market's not closed."

Prior to that nastiness, Cyber Paul had explained to Deb how the digital trail on the loyalty system traced back to Nancy's computer during the time of her cancer treatments. Deb guessed that the Sibs Sutton and Blair had hacked into their grandmother's system to ferret out Geoff. That family betrayal of the favorite could result in the Sibs being banned from decorating the house for the holidays. Deb also guessed that Geoff summoned a Grimes operative to cause a disruption at Betty Danger's before she could learn anything. Deb and the Sibs, however, had been early and the crash too late.

Nancy's business office was on the floor below CEO Luis Peña's. The receptionist led Deb to an inner room where Jude stood up from a desk. She wore a gray-and-white sheath dress with a fuchsia scarf setting off her dark bob and canny eyes. "Greetings, Detective. You look fantastic, and I hear you're a hero for arresting Vernon Grimes."

"During one of his mean awake moments. It will be a while before the trial because he has to recover. At least he gets to recover, unlike all those people dying from his drugs."

"It touches everyone." As Jude messed with papers on her desk, her voice quavered. "Ask my mother." She lifted her head, back to alluring. "I could ask how your day is going so far, but I suspect it's not going improve."

"As incentive, I promised myself a few hours of golf Saturday morning."

Jude cocked an eyebrow. "You know, none of us knew about the hotel incidents involving Geoff until you mentioned them on the Wunderlyn Golf Course. I thought he was concerned about Nancy, but he was trying to pry what I knew out of me. Well, I could tell something was wrong when the sight of you turned his graciousness to slime. Anyway, Nancy's expecting you."

Deb opened the door. No Frenchy stuff in the private office of sleek gray metal, grained wood, and neutral tones. Primitive artwork stood out. Nancy, in ecru slacks and a dull blue top, had angled her chair toward a picture window. Without standing, she straightened her spine. Her face, however, had lost the fight against gravity, and the wrinkles seemed etched by red ink. "Detective Metzger, please sit."

Deb sat. A side table held a computer setup. Nancy's desk was barren except for a lamp, a purple orchid, and framed photos Deb couldn't see. The artwork turned out to be children's paintings. The largest depicted a lopsided goat and a stick-figure goatherder on a Swiss Alp.

Nancy did not look at Deb. "I understand you are seeking a warrant for Geoff's emails sent through the company system. That seems unnecessary. You already have information."

"It's better to have thorough documentation every step of the way." Deb wanted to know if Geoff manipulated managers, but she didn't want to voice her worst assumptions. "It's procedure."

"You don't seem the type to tolerate tedious procedure. You barely keep your composure in an office chair."

"That's, um, true. Procedure's not the dream part of my job."

"What is the dream part of your job?" Nancy's tone could clear drains.

"Knowing I've done what I can to protect women and children."

Nancy appeared to expect more.

"Also, the adrenaline rushes."

Nancy turned fully toward her. "Yes, I can see that. Notifications to cooperate will be sent to LeClerc technical and legal departments. If there are difficulties, contact me. No, Luis. Contact Luis."

"Yes, Nan—Ms. LeClerc."

No move on Nancy's part. Deb was about to stand when another answer to the Dream Job question came to her. "The closure with a case. It's rarely complete, but I like closure."

Nancy picked up a framed photo from her desk. Deb couldn't see the subject. "I'm told I'm hard on women."

"Corporate competition must warp everything."

"Nothing warped my life so much as my father murdering my mother. I'm hard on women because, unlike men, they can't simply be average to survive. They need nerve to rise above being a pretty pawn, though I doubt you were ever a pretty pawn."

"More of an overgrown heifer in a china shop."

Nancy's eyes glinted like the room's gunmetal gray. "Men, with a few exceptions like my husband, Luis Peña, and Sutton, I expect to be merely capable. Geoff made it through offshore medical school, but he was a lazy doctor. I tried him at executive work. He could lighten the day, not the workload. He was a good rainmaker, bringing LeClercs to people's attention, the wrong people as it turns out. Is that withholding love, to expect less?"

"I'm not a philosopher, or a football player. My dad would have liked it if I could have been a football hero."

"Then enough of this. Good day, Detective Metzger."

At the door, Deb gave a final nod. Side lighting picked up wet streaks on Nancy's cheek, and she caught Deb's gaze. "I raised Geoff like a son. I loved him as best I could. You can't imagine how terrible it was to go through with it. At least he had the decency to be arrested on a Hilton property. You should leave."

Deb closed the door behind her, saw that Jude had left the room, and the truth hit her. Nancy had taken charge. Nancy had leaked the information.

THE BCA HAD FINALLY DONE THEIR JOB and captured Charles Monteiro. Surveillance videos led to the conclusion that Charles had attacked Josh Miller and chased him into the river and, days later, attacked Retta Mazzi. Charles gave up Ray/Ramon in half a heartbeat as the facilitator who phoned in those orders.

Erik presented that information to Ray during the opening moments of the interrogation to hear "No comment." Then Ray, believing he had a story better than one any lawyer could concoct, wove tales of woe and betrayal going back to childhood. A degree of truth woven in with more degrees of falsehood, Erik assumed. Tragic that a boy's soul had been squandered. However, adult Ray showed no desire to be a better man, only to be a better con. Ray shifted his attention to Deb, who had armored herself in a suit fit for a Wall Street interview—lethal heels, a loud silence, and an expression unfit for print. Erik, who knew Ray's father had been in a Michigan prison for three years, shifted to Luna's escape. Ray interjected, who would believe Luna? I believe Luna, Erik said, and Deb seconded his remark with a predatory grin. Then Erik moved on to Dan Routh.

"It appears, Mr. Kenny, that Dan Routh followed you. This happened after Luna told you in the Simple parking lot that Routh was an ex-policeman who wanted to help her, and he could help you too with your abusive dad. But you realized how a man with Routh's experience would read the situation of men providing drugs to vulnerable girls before a 'party.' You push Luna into a van and peel off. Only, Routh follows. Luna escapes, which maybe you didn't see and Dan does not see. Your van barely makes it to the store. You panic and hide in the dumpster. You scream for help because it's scary in a pit of garbage, or you're deliberately luring in Routh, witness to Luna's abduction. Maybe the scream sounds girlish, and Routh, running on adrenaline, thinks it's Luna. Routh was the kind of guy who would leap to help anybody."

"You're making this up." Ray's leer displayed a tooth like a vampire fang. "Even if something like that happened, and you have no proof, it'd be self-defense. You're not so sharp."

Deb grated her chair back, which set everyone's teeth on edge, and broke her silence. "If someone's hanging by their toenails from the Washington Avenue Bridge near the University, how much of a drop is that?"

"Seventy feet," Erik answered, "a killer. That's near the place, Ray, where you lived with your boogeyman father, Ray, then Retta Mazzi, only you told her it was a new place and not the one you'd always had. That's where we found your belongings. We understand that you had a favorite moto jacket. It's disappeared."

He twitched. "Jackets get lost."

"They're lost more often when covered with another man's blood. Also, you threatened Jaylyn Dudek with a knife. That knife had previously been cleaned with bleach." Before this interview, Erik had asked Jaylyn for any details she recalled about Ramon, no matter how inconsequential they seemed. She said he liked sharp clothes.

"It went through the laundry in my jeans pocket."

"None of your jeans show traces of bleach. They're an expensive label. You probably wouldn't dump chlorine on them. Sprays reduce a blood stain as it goes through the wash. Now I've made this mistake: putting jeans right in the dryer. The dryer sets the stain, a stain that might not be visible to the eye."

Pale Ray paled further as Erik continued, "Oh, I just remembered something about self-defense. People who defend themselves call the police. They don't take the time to arrange a tow for a van that isn't theirs. They don't take the deceased's personal items. That watch you claimed your father gave you—we know who bought it and we know Dan Routh wore it. His hair is caught in the band. Your hair is caught in the band. The lab also checked a twenty-dollar bill. Cash generally fails as evidence. But this bill has recent stains from two blood types. Take a guess."

That's when Ray asked for a lawyer. He looked like he'd been slammed into a wall and had dribbled down into a puddle. All Erik needed was a Shop-Vac to clean him up.

CHAPTER 46

It was the end of the rainy June, and Gordy's grass remained green as Ireland. He did fret over the weeds among his marigolds. He'd paid the ten-year-old neighbor minimum wage for the weeding. He could have shelled out an intern's rate since Gordy had to identify each pigweed sprig. But if you're going to have principles, you should stick with them. Next week he'd have loosened up from the rollover accident and could do it himself. His yard had been nominated in the neighborhood garden competition for Best Use of Color—he wasn't too sure which colors—and the judging was this Friday afternoon. To avoid local favoritism, the judges had been recruited from the Northeast Minneapolis Garden Club. He sat down in a folding chair by the drive and waited. Tamra, who had doted on him in the hospital, couldn't come for moral support now, but she was definitely coming for dinner.

It was the detectives who pulled up. The dogs barked themselves to their feet from their shaded sleeping spots and Gordy pushed himself up—tricky with a flimsy chair.

"Good afternoon, Gordy," Big Deb said. "I see Dorothy is healing." Dorothy, like Gordy, had a wrap around her middle to stabilize her ribs. "What's wrong with Rainbow?" Rainbow bumped the detective's shin with the cone that encircled her border collie head.

"Nothing. She's too helpful. Otherwise she'd pull off Dorothy's bandages. Here's what's bothering me and why I called."

The detectives waited.

"It's great you got Grimes in jail. He made me so mad I coulda kicked my socks off. Are you going to charge somebody with Dan's murder?"

"We're building a case," that nice Erik said. "Your van has not been recovered."

"Probably been sold on. Here's the thing. Remember how my garage door stuck? I forgot how Dan stuffed a box of his files high up on my shelf—the outside's dated eight years back. Anyway, the box tipped over on the tracks." Gordy was anxious. There could be bad stuff in that box about things Dan did when he wasn't sober. He wished he hadn't found it, and he practically sobbed, "I thought you might need it. I asked innocent-project type folks. They're overloaded and said Dan was a big help in freeing somebody."

Those two looked at each other. She said, "Personal items belong with Dan's estate. Contact his daughter and stepdaughter."

"They say shred it."

Big Deb opened her mouth, but that nice Erik beat her to it. "I'll take it off your hands."

Gordy collapsed into the chair in relief. "Another thing, you know how helpful Bent Nail is?"

Erik leaned over to scratch Rainbow and Deb did the same for Dorothy. Since they didn't seem to catch what he'd said, he put it differently. "Nail's thinking is that he and I should go into business as consultants for investigators. There's so much bad out there. We got to do something." The pair exchanged glances. "You think it's foolhardy."

"Being that kind of fool requires training," Deb said.

Erik picked up Ellie. "Your therapy work with the dogs . . . involve Nail in that. Catching people isn't enough—it's what happens after, as you know already. Recovery, reparation, the hard parts. Two rescued women, Luna and a friend of hers, would love sessions with the dogs."

Deb agreed. "I heard that the Resource received an anonymous donation to start a scholarship fund in honor of Dan Routh. Was that your doing?"

"Gosh. That's the whole cake and icing too." Gordy teared up. Someone else saw Dan did good, real good. "Guess I could toss in my reward dough."

"I have an idea about that," Erik said. "There wasn't a single phone call that said, 'Here's your perp,' but a young man and woman, cousins, led directly to the capture. My understanding is that they could use new safe vehicles."

"Take good care of yourself, Gordy," Deb tossed in. "And the dogs, of course."

"They take care of *me*. Whoa, it's the garden judges driving up. Mrs. Dudek, she's a hard nut." Gordy teared up when that nice Erik took his hand warmly and touched his arm. He almost hugged the woman but stuck with a handshake. The detectives said goodbye and walked away. Then it came to Gordy, and he called after them, "You know, people tell me that in languages like French, *dog* isn't *god* backwards. But there's got to be a connection. Dorothy, she just has to *be* and everything's better."

At that, Dorothy went to him, leaned against his leg, and slid down to sleep with her enormous head on his foot. The judges would have to walk around them.

CHAPTER 47

S HE KNEW WHEN HE SQUEEZED HER HAND. That's what Jaylyn told Detective Metzger and Sharon Nordin days after Ramon's capture. The way he squeezed her hand, she sensed Ray was not what he seemed.

Jaylyn's hand held steady as she applied lipstick in the cramped green room of downtown St. Paul's *Nouvelle Musique*. On a humid Friday night, the air conditioner didn't rid the basement of its dank. Teddi, swooping on cat eyes, elbowed Jaylyn. Upstairs in the swanky bistro, Mom and Nana were wining and dining. They'd drop in on "Teddi and the Tough Graces" for the second set. Aunt Lyndsay had finally come to the Twin Cities, and she and Gran Dudek were at each other in the Tudor-trimmed house over a dinner of mac 'n' cheese. The big question: would senior living allow orange Snippet, who wouldn't leave Gran, to move in as well?

Jaylyn endured multiple interviews after the capture of Ray "Ramon" Kenny. Twenty-seven-year-old Ray, not twenty-three, had several fake IDs, and what settled it all was the GED exam. Ray had put in the correct information to qualify for the high school equivalency, and days before his capture, he passed the test, honestly. When his father was jailed in Michigan for a prescription drug scam, Ray moved to the Twin Cities and became a facilitator in a drug-and-sex-trafficking ring, the cover being his part-time delivery job. His double life split apart when the girl Luna escaped and he killed a man.

Jaylyn had the sickening idea as the interviews about Ray started that her opioid use would surface. Hard to believe that the two different spells added up to nine weeks of the past, so few and so terribly significant. She feared that she'd be held responsible. Not at all the case. The detectives said she saved Retta, her brother, and herself. The list grew of women Ray had manipulated.

To start, Luna and her friend Pammie. After losing Luna, he'd given Pammie's contact to another operative, and she had to be rescued from a hotel room with the help of a 911 dispatcher. Then Jaylyn, Sheila the Cube (Lionel's addition), and Retta. While Retta survived a thug pushing pills down her throat, her system was in addiction mode, her insurance grossly inadequate, and her will beaten down. The Resource placed her in residential rehab to improve her chances at healthy independence. When Jaylyn visited Retta there Thursday, it was a depressing half hour. Ray had damaged something between them.

Detective Jansson—he had such searching eyes—wanted Jaylyn to discuss with his partner Detective Metzger and the Resource Director Sharon Nordin how Ray operated. The director said the first thing, "You may be tempted to take the blame." She was right. If Jaylyn hadn't been to Rehab, if she hadn't met Ramon, hadn't introduced him to recovering Retta . . .. "But you're guiltless. This man's job was to make women feel responsible for his wellbeing. The women create their own narrative about his 'irregularities' to affirm their sympathies."

Detective Metzger added, "He's completely to blame. Though that type doesn't understand blame. He may have felt panic over knifing a man, but no guilt. He is *not* your responsibility."

That's when Jaylyn explained. The night of the jam at McMillan, after Ramon attempted a drug drop using Lionel's Cube, two things happened. Josh showed up to break her focus on Ramon. Later, Ramon walked her to the Cube and he squeezed her hand, her pianist's hand. "It was like he was feeling for a bone to break," she told the women. A sign that he'd ruin anyone's life on a whim. No, Jaylyn did not feel guilty.

THE *MUSIQUE* CROWD WAITED NOISILY. "Is our set list set?" Teddi asked. Wolfman read it down from his smart watch. "Tiger Rag"—hold that ti*ger*, hold that ti*ger*—would be the opening, and "Hit the Road Jack" the finale of the first set. Jaylyn had gotten by with a little help from her friends: her school ones nagging her to finish her paper on African American composer Florence Price and take the math final, and the music ones to play gigs. She was ready to pack her bags for dorm life. Jaylyn's performance nerves pushed grief aside for the moment. Josh was dead. There were holes in his story, as with most addicts. Josh had been emulating Dan Routh, who pulled him to sobriety once. He would relapse and search out drugs, only to see kids using, and he'd call in tips on the dealers. He had apparently seen Ray (Ra-*moan*, what a jerk) delivering drugs, and suspected he was hanging around Jaylyn for his own benefit. Josh had gone to a drug "dispensary" in the morning to check Ray's identity. Ray saw him and called a Grimes henchman who attacked Josh with a heroin-loaded hypodermic. When Josh made it to his truck, the man chased him into the river. Josh had tried to warn her—was that it? It cost him everything. The grief would come unbidden.

Jaylyn spiraled her freed hair upward—be that ti*ger*, be that ti*ger*. Teddi danced onto the platform, and Jaylyn sashayed with fringe swinging from her breasts and hips. She had used up her nervousness at her university audition this morning. After spending fifteen hours with him (and paying by check), she took Lazar's advice to pursue not a music-ed major, but a performance degree. Mrs. Norman had made her a musician. Lazar goaded her into being a performer.

The guys were doing their noisy macho amp tests when Teddi called Jaylyn away from adjusting a microphone. "Your groupie's here."

Must be Lionel with his new girlfriend. When this girl he crushed on ranted about *everything* being screwed up, he wowed her by proclaiming, "Love's the answer, but you got to show your work." Lionel, the answer to everything.

It wasn't Lionel. Flying fingered Franklin, with his light Afro, the musical wonder, fidgeted by the stage edge. "You're Jaylyn, right?"

"So who wants to know?" she flirted.

"I heard you'll be in the U's performance program. My prof says you're his new student. We'll have classes together."

Jaylyn's fingers flew to her lips, "Oh."

"I heard your cousin Lionel is like a police consultant now. Not long and he'll be governor of the state."

"He wishes!"

"Well . . .." Franklin was at a loss for words.

"Well," Jaylyn echoed coyly, "see you at break." She danced back to the piano, her dress shimmering.

She was too hyped to recall details from the audition except that when she sat at the piano her hands wouldn't stop shaking—that's why you start with Bach, a steady rhythm to settle body and soul. She closed her eyes and heard a voice. It seemed like the voice of Bach—Bach loved a god—or the voice of Beethoven, the raw voice of Nina Simone. No, not theirs, but she swore she heard a voice, and it pronounced with certainty, *You're the real thing*.

It had to be her own.

CHAPTER 48

I T'S A WISE MAN WHO KNOWS HIS OWN HEART. Erik didn't feel particularly wise before coffee on a Saturday morning. Ben slept in an innocent sprawl as Erik gathered from the bedroom items needed for the camping trip. The past week he'd been praised for his cleverness, even by Drees, in constructing a case against Ray "Ramon" Kenny for the killing of Dan Routh. Drees then tried to trap Erik. Did Erik know that the "mentor" had broken his ex-wife's heart—was he going to rescue her? Erik wanted to ask in return, is she down a well or swept away by a tornado? If not, she can rescue herself. He said out loud that he knew (having been told during a Ben transfer) and she was fine. Cleverness fell short in knowing what to do about broken hearts. He couldn't fully diagnose his own.

The young conman, Ray, had played with hearts. Luna was a sexy pawn with access to prescription drugs. Ray may have considered himself sincere in his attraction to Retta Mazzi, until she needed his financial support after she lost her job. He seduced her into drinking to control her and her phone. He ordered Charles Monteiro to take care of her after she suspected his behavior; then Ray texted Jaylyn Dudek with his phone *and* Retta's to cover himself. Jaylyn reminded Erik of his poet sister. When attentive, both were brilliantly perceptive; when caught up in their imaginations, supremely oblivious. Jaylyn told Erik and Deb that "Ramon" would look her in the eye while retelling his traumas. But she had come to think that ordinary people drop their gaze when overwhelmed by the weight of intimacy. Ray's blankness wasn't pain, simply blankness, and she said he'd trained his eyes to lie.

Erik went to the kitchen to steep French press coffee. He'd been trained on how to save people in bodily danger. As for danger to the soul, you had to realize you were in trouble and you had to desire salvation. Josh Miller had, and unwittingly sacrificed himself. Ray Kenny intended to perpetually sacrifice others.

Criminals like Ray and Geoff LeClerc were selfish: they weren't the only ones. On the way to divorce, Erik and Kristine had been spiteful before her cheating—stunning to realize their selfishness in regard to Ben. When Erik agonized over the split—more accurately, the preceding fissures in their marriage—he approached the subject like a case. A case with two suspects whom he wouldn't, couldn't, question fairly. He wanted the case expunged, or a door slammed shut on it and all attendant passions. Erik believed he had loved Kristine. But had he always acted lovingly? Had he done that man thing where you don't see, pretend not to see, the woman and her situation, and then you climb into bed at night with your own demands? Had she done the woman thing and assumed he could intuit her feelings and alter his behavior without a word? If only every man came with an on/off switch and every woman with a complete set of directions.

He pushed down the French press plunger, and the brew gave off a rich aroma. He had to move forward with an imperfect understanding of why the marriage had imploded and a clear awareness that it was over.

There were other women, that St. Paul officer . . ..

But it was time for Erik's heart to take a vacation. He felt no urgency, no duty, to pursue anyone or anything today but outdoor thrills with his boy. Erik rinsed local strawberries, stirred up corncakes, heated the griddle, and warmed syrup. He would wake Ben after flipping the first cake. You save yourself not to be the sole winner, but to buoy up others. Not everyone makes it. There were no shortcuts to wisdom; however, Erik was accustomed to taking the challenging trail at top speed with twists, deviations—at times a necessary duplicity. Not always necessary, but otherwise, where's the fun? *Be yourself, everyone else is taken.*

DEB LOADED HER GOLF CLUBS into the car. It was a god-awful early tee-time for Saturday morning. Originally, a G-Met empathy retreat had been scheduled for this weekend, but it had been postponed because of valid disagreements. Several recommended having input from LGBTQ groups and Black Lives Matter. Some wanted to re-enact past confrontations—shootings of people of color, tussles with mentally ill individuals—that resulted in the fatality of a civilian or an officer, confrontations that went wrong in the worst ways. Others argued that re-enacting bad behavior would not move officers beyond prejudices but stir up fear, resentment, and defensiveness—better to use mock cases. The disagreement led to the formation of a committee to find outside consultants on de-escalation and overcoming bias. Deb was on it (assigned, not volunteered), along with Cyber Paul, Jimmy Bond Smalls, and two officers she didn't know well. Ibeling was back and not on his back. A yoga mat was stashed in his office.

After Erik left the office yesterday, the chief emailed her. He had an item for her to take to Jansson. She hurried to Ibeling's suite, deserted, saw a tackle box with SVEN'S taped to the lid and took it. She saw another item to grab. Drees caught her coming out, and she hid the second item behind her back as he came at her. He feigned empathy by asking, "Is Jansson chasing after a new woman? It's too soon." She summoned her most devastating look—"None of our beeswax." Drees, that tool, disappeared, and she examined the item she'd seized: G-Met's long-lost plaque that read AGGRESSIVE on one side and PASSIVE on the other. Now, how to spirit it onto Drees's desk?

She had returned to her office for car keys, and, spirited on her desk, was the Bambi family. Papa, mama, and baby deer. THE BUCK STOPS HERE sign had been replaced by one that read, THERE'S NO PLACE LIKE HOME.

Saturday morning wouldn't last forever. Deb loaded her clubs and Sven's box into her car. Fun times ahead. Find a new place and be on a committee. Bothering her was that she was supposed to remind her partner of something— what was it? She drove four miles over speed to Erik's Linden Hills apartment. He was in camping duds loading his Highlander. His Highlander was clean. Clean because—*holy cow*—he'd gotten a new hybrid. Ben, on the sidewalk, gave commands to an old Labrador retriever.

"I'm to deliver this." Deb walked up with the box, and for a second Erik flinched—still recovering from injuries? He relaxed when he saw the box. She'd never seen him so relaxed. A tension in her shoulders melted away, and she remembered that 'Sven' had tasked her to deliver advice. "I, um, I'm supposed to remind you that you don't have to be a martyr."

He smiled slightly. "I'm not taking the Internal Affairs job, if that's what you mean." The smile quirked into a grin. "I recommended Drees."

"Knew that," Deb said. *No, she didn't.* "A St. Paul officer forwarded places where Grimes met with facilitators and added he'd be out of touch in a pain management program. What's that the one you contacted?"

"All I said was that I had heard rumors about his area, and I asked if he received adequate care for his injuries. Very limited conversation."

Ben, bored with adult blather, pulled Deb's hand while the dog licked her other. "Grandpa's Molly is riding with us. Grandpa and Grandma are already on the road."

"That's great. I'm off to the links."

"Thanks. Score however you're supposed to score in golf." The trunk on Erik's new model shut itself.

Deb jogged to her Prius. She looked back to see Erik pick up Ben and give him a bear hug, the boy protesting, "I'm too big!" His father swung him in big circles and laughed and Ben laughed too, making Molly bark and jump up and down, happy as a dog can be. Deb did not have to save her partner from anything today.

On the course, she took a cart and buzzed over a hillock to the first tee. She had told Nancy she liked closure. Sure, she liked the bad guy caught and the victim no longer a victim but a survivor. But "closed" also meant an end of options. Deb could use openings. The public course felt private; the only motion was outlawed dandelions bobbing their fringed heads along the perimeter. The blue sky fed energy everywhere. With no one around, Deb had amazing luck. She teed up to make a drive on the fairway for the 13th hole. She swung. Beautiful. The ball dropped, and beyond the ball stood Jude, pristine in a white shirt and blue gingham skirt, waving.

PRISCILLA GREW UP on a dairy farm in Maine, a state of woods, lakes, and rivers. She now lives in Minnesota, another state of woods, lakes, and rivers, not far from urban Minneapolis and St. Paul. She received a B.A. from Bowdoin College, a Ph.D. in English Literature from Boston College, and was a college professor. She has previously published a children's book, *Howard and the Sitter Surprise*, and a book on Robert Frost and Andrew Wyeth, *Abandoned New England*. She participates in community advocacy and literacy programs, takes photos of birds, and contemplates (fictional) murder.

The first in the Twin Cities Mystery series, *Where Privacy Dies*, was a finalist for a 2018 Foreword Indies Book Award. You can follow Priscilla on her website "Priscilla Paton" (priscillapaton.com), Goodreads (priscillapaton), Facebook (priscillapatonmystery), and Twitter (@priscilla_paton).

www.ingramcontent.com/pod-product-compliance
Lightning Source LLC
Chambersburg PA
CBHW011117100726
47898CB00011B/3128